KEEPER OF THE REALMS

CROW'S REVENGE

MARCUS ALEXANDER

PUFFIN

PUFFIN BOOKS

Published by the Penguin Group
Penguin Books Ltd, 80 Strand, London WC2R ORL, England
Penguin Group (USA) Inc., 375 Hudson Street, New York, New York 10014, USA
Penguin Group (Canada), 90 Eglinton Avenue East, Suite 700, Toronto, Ontario, Canada M4P 2Y3
(a division of Pearson Penguin Canada Inc.)
Penguin Ireland, 25 St Stephen's Green, Dublin 2, Ireland (a division of Penguin Books Ltd)
Penguin Group (Australia), 250 Camberwell Road, Camberwell, Victoria 3124, Australia
(a division of Pearson Australia Group Pty Ltd)
Penguin Books India Pvt Ltd, 11 Community Centre, Panchsheel Park,
New Delhi – 110 017, India
Penguin Group (NZ), 67 Apollo Drive, Rosedale, Auckland 0632, New Zealand
(a division of Pearson New Zealand Ltd)
Penguin Books (South Africa) (Pty) Ltd, 24 Sturdee Avenue, Rosebank,
Johannesburg 2196, South Africa

Penguin Books Ltd, Registered Offices: 80 Strand, London WC2R ORL, England

puffinbooks.com

Original edition published as *Who Is Charlie Keeper?* by Troubador Publishing Ltd 2008
First published in this revised edition 2012

007

Text and character illustrations copyright © Marcus Alexander, 2008, 2012
Illustrations by Lobak Oren
Map by David Atkinson
All rights reserved

The moral right of the author and illustrator has been asserted

Typeset in Sabon by Palimpsest Book Production Ltd, Falkirk, Stirlingshire
Printed and bound in Great Britain by Clays Ltd, Elcograf S.p.A.

British Library Cataloguing in Publication Data
A CIP catalogue record for this book is available from the British Library

ISBN: 978-0141-33977-1

www.greenpenguin.co.uk

For my parents and the naughty Moll,
for their burning love,
their devotion . . .
and for always picking me up when I stumbled,
tripped
or plummeted screaming
over the cunning tripwires and sneakily hidden booby
traps of life.
You're the best.

xx

BELLANIA

Charlie's Waterfall

DEEPFOREST

Sylvaris

Alacorn

THE
WINGED
MOUNT

Southern Cities

Contents

1

Mr Crow

The house sat at the end of the small London street and it looked wrong.

Not wrong in itself, although it was a peculiar-looking house, but wrong for the neighbourhood. Big, cranky and ancient, it squatted between its smaller neighbours and glared down the narrow backstreet as though daring anyone to say anything about its battered appearance.

Yet beneath the grime and bird droppings were small scraps of evidence that pointed to grander times. Worn silver lining could be glimpsed on the window frames, bronze gilt hung in shreds from the oak front door and carvings of dragons peered out from beneath the creeping ivy. The building had been old even when London was young, but was now in dire need of renovation. Or demolition.

Charlie Keeper was well aware of how it looked. As she gazed out of her small bedroom window, she knew that her house was a source of discomfort for the wealthy locals, and that her neighbours complained about its scruffy appearance. But she didn't care. The place felt like home, felt like a part of her and, more importantly, reminded her of her missing parents.

Trying to put thoughts of her grumpy neighbours aside, she rubbed the sleep from her eyes and did her best to pat her messy blonde hair into something that resembled a ponytail. Stuffing her feet into a pair of scuffed sneakers, she stomped her way to the bathroom to clean her teeth. She slapped some toothpaste on to her brush and began to scrub furiously.

Charlie wasn't happy.

In fact, she wasn't happy most days. It wasn't that her neighbours were always rude to her – thirteen-year-olds knew how to put up with adult foolishness. It wasn't even that she got bullied at school, returning home with new bruises every day. And it wasn't that life appeared to be stacked so unpleasantly against her.

After all, there were good things going on too. She got to live with her grandma, and although her elderly relative suffered from amnesia she was, in Charlie's mind, a wonderful woman with a kind heart. Her best friend, Tina, even lived down the street. And Charlie was, of course, a Londoner. She loved the grimy city. Her favourite afternoons involved sneaking off to watch the b-boys and freerunners practising along the south bank of the River Thames, and she got a secret thrill out of deciphering the twisted graffiti and loudly coloured street murals that decorated the capital.

Life would have been bearable. Really it would have . . . apart from one thing. One *person*. Mr Crow. Since her parents had gone missing, he was (according to her family's estate, will and testament) her lawyer, her custodian and the house steward. He held all the purse strings, had control over her grandmother's health care and sent Charlie to the strictest of schools. And, although Charlie couldn't prove it, she had a niggling feeling that Mr Crow had been selling antiques and furnishings from the house for his own financial gain.

Charlie, without a doubt, hated him. And to make matters worse he was due at the house any moment now. She rinsed out her mouth and stomped back to her seat at the bedroom window.

As her forehead creased up and her mouth twitched at the mere thought of the man, she saw him turn into the street with his customary black cape flapping behind him. Charlie's neighbours hurriedly ducked out of sight. While they could ignore the house, it was altogether another matter ignoring the lawyer.

Mr Crow homed in on the house like a venomous snake striking its prey, his long, skinny legs carrying him down the road. He used his rolled umbrella to prod an unfortunate passer-by who was too slow in making way.

'Get out of my way, you clumsy fool!' snapped the miserable lawyer. 'Can't you see I'm on important business? Make way!'

Crow stalked up to the house and slammed through the front door, pausing to let his eyes grow accustomed to the dim light inside. He took a deep breath, cracked his knuckles and called out as he made his way to his study, 'Charlie, my filly, my pretty filly. Come to Uncle Crow. There's work to be done and papers to be signed. Come, come.'

'You're not my uncle,' Charlie growled under her breath. But she knew better than to keep him waiting. Hurrying to the lawyer's study, she walked straight up to the large leather-bound desk, lifted the pen that rested on its surface and, without needing to be asked again, signed the papers that Crow held out to her. As usual Charlie had a sinking feeling that she was signing away more of her inheritance, but what could she do?

The fiercer part of her soul wanted to scream out in protest or at least question him about what she was signing. But the other part of her soul – perhaps the wiser part – kept her mouth shut. She remembered the first time she'd dared to ask, how his face had changed and how he had beaten her back and forth across the study until her skin was black and blue. Now she always signed. Quick and easy was better than battered and bruised.

She had told her grandmother, who was only too willing to help, but halfway through confronting Mr Crow her amnesia would kick in, she'd lose track of the conversation and end up asking him for tea and biscuits. Charlie had tried to tell the teachers at her school, but because the lawyer paid them so handsomely they simply wouldn't hear a bad word said against the 'charming Mr Crow'. All in all, Charlie honestly had no idea what to do. And apart from sticking her tongue out at his back and the few occasions she had gathered up the nerve to put ink in his tea (Crow would walk home with blue lips and an odd feeling that people were laughing at him) she didn't feel as though this was a situation she could fix.

The lawyer's words pulled her back to the present.

'Thank you, dear Charlie,' he purred, with a look of ill-disguised greed. 'That was easy, wasn't it? Never let it be said that work should be hard! And now, my little filly, I must ask you to leave me in peace, as I have much to do. Oh yes! Crow's work is never done!' And, so saying, he ushered Charlie out through the study door.

As soon as the door was shut, she promptly screwed up her face and stamped her foot. She hated him! He took her money but wouldn't arrange to fix things and he certainly didn't pay for the heating in the winter – Charlie always froze. But, worst of all, he wouldn't get the right medical treatment for her gran.

Furious, she turned her back on the study and headed into the depths of the house.

She had known from a young age that her home was different from most buildings. Since her parents had disappeared, it was the only place that she ever felt safe, but it didn't obey the rules that all other houses were inclined to follow. Charlie was pretty sure that it was bigger on the inside than it was on the outside. Much bigger. She had been running riot around the house all her life, yet she was still discovering doors that led into new unexplored parts. Fortunately her grandmother stayed to the front of the house and never strayed, which meant that Charlie could wander to her heart's content.

Now she found herself striding through dusty corridors and along deserted hallways that echoed with the sound of her footfalls. She stumbled down stone staircases carved with strange and ornate mythical animals, and passed marble archways and cavernous rooms full of ancient and eroded statues. Emblems and old signs of chivalry and heraldry stood proud on the walls and doors. Lions, unicorns, griffins and even stranger-looking creatures were depicted with such skill that they appeared to wriggle and writhe as she walked past. But

Charlie, used to these everyday wonders, ignored the intriguing surroundings and stomped deeper and deeper into the house. Every once in a while, unable to contain her rage, she would shout, 'It's not fair!' and kick the wall. Midway through yet another shout of, 'It's not fair!' and halfway through a wall-kicking a voice rudely interrupted her rampage.

'Child, wotcha think yer doing? Don't go kickin' the wall. It's bad for the house, bad for business and also, methinks, bad for yer feet!'

Losing all composure and kicking grace, Charlie squawked and spun round.

Standing there was a man quite unlike any she had ever seen before. His rich brown hair was tied into a topknot that danced merrily above his head. He wore a green sleeveless shirt, olive shorts that reached just below his knees and a pair of wooden sandals. His big beak of a nose was pierced with a shell and a large plumed feather was stuck through his topknot. But strangest of all was his skin. It was a glorious dark green and polished with oil so that it glinted in the light. Charlie, who wasn't tall by any means, was only a little smaller than the man and she couldn't help noticing that he smelt of vanilla and unusual spices. And as odd as it was to find such a stranger in her house, strangely Charlie didn't feel alarmed. His friendly appearance calmed her more immediate concerns, and for some unknown reason she couldn't shake the feeling that she knew his face from somewhere. It was as though an old, old memory was trying to float to the surface of her consciousness.

Being a reasonably polite girl, she did her best not to comment on the man's strange appearance. 'I, uh, I was letting off steam,' she replied with an embarrassed look. 'I didn't mean to cause any damage, honest.'

'And why were ya letting off steam?' the stranger enquired. Wooden bracelets clattered when he moved and his large ears were pierced with sandalwood hoops. 'Ya don't look like a steam engine or a new-fangled locomotive. So tell me, wot's got ya so angry that ya've gotta go stompin' around like an angry Hippotomi?'

Charlie had never heard of a Hippotomi, but she was getting more and more inquisitive. Regaining her composure, she began to reassert some of her natural curiosity.

'If you don't mind me asking, why are you in my house? Did my gran let you in?'

'No, no, lass. I let meself in,' the stranger replied.

'Say what?' choked Charlie in disbelief. 'You can't go around sneaking into people's houses – that's crazy!' She was about to demand that he leave, but once again her curiosity got the better of her. 'Where are you from anyway? And why's your skin that colour? And while I'm at it, why are you wearing those funny clothes? Don't you get cold?'

'Oh, jeez, ya ask a lotta questions, don't ya?'

'Well, you're the stranger in my house, so I think the least you owe me is some answers.'

'Ah, good point.' The stranger grinned sheepishly. 'Well, me skin is dis colour cos I was born with it. And I wear these clothes because I look good in them and also cos it's real warm in Bellania at the moment.'

'Bellania?' muttered Charlie to herself. She mulled the word over a bit in her head, like a new sweet on her tongue, one she didn't know whether she did or did not like the taste of. 'Bellania,' she said again. 'That sounds really familiar. Where is it?'

'Wot? Ya mean ta tell me ya've never been ta Bellania?'

'Hmm . . . well, I went to Paris once when I was younger, with my parents, but I don't think I've ever been to Bellania. Is that in Europe?'

'Europe? Oh, bless me Glade and cripple me Sapling!' shouted the stranger, slapping his hand to forehead. 'Hippotomi, we clearly gotta have a little chat. Yer very, very far behind in yer upbringing. Yer education is sorely lacking.'

Charlie didn't know whether to be amused or angry. Just what was the proper procedure for addressing a greenskinned stranger who sneaked into your house and then insulted your schooling?

'My education is fine, thank you very much.' She crossed her arms and started tapping her foot. 'You know you're almost as bad as Mr Crow, telling me I'm not good enough. Seriously, though, why is your skin that colour? And don't just tell me you were born with it. I want a proper explanation.'

'Yer an insistent little lass, aren't ya?' chuckled the man. 'Do ya always cross yer arms and do that thing with yer feet when ya want questions answered?'

'My house,' reminded Charlie. But she did stop tapping her foot, although her arms remained firmly folded.

'Oops, how could I have forgotten so soon?' The stranger straightened his lips in an attempt to stop smirking at Charlie's scowl. 'Well, lass, me skin is green because I'm a Treman.'

'Huh? A what?'

'A Treman,' repeated the stranger. 'Do ya honestly mean ta tell me that ya've never heard of a Treman?'

'A Treman? What's a Treman?' asked Charlie.

'*I'm* a Treman, lass. Who's yer teacher? Whoever he is, he ain't doing a proper job. Tell me, little Hippotomi – and don't stomp yer feet at me – do ya know wot a Stoman is, or a Human?'

'Well, of course I know what a Human is! I'm one. But I've never heard of a Treman or a Stopman.'

'Stoman,' corrected the stranger. 'She knows nothing! Nothing!' he mumbled to himself. 'So, were ya gonna tell me wot had ya so upset in the first place?'

'Well, it's . . . it's Mr Crow. He's so horrible, he always makes me sign things I know I shouldn't sign, he doesn't help my grandma, he steals and if I don't do what he tells me to do he beats me. It's not fair!' She stopped suddenly, worried she'd said too much. If this stranger was in the house, then maybe he was friends with the lawyer.

The man grimaced in sympathy. 'Well, if he's the one in charge of yer purse strings, then it comes as no surprise yer education has holes in it. That man is a nasty piece of work. But tell me now, would ya be Charlie?'

'Uh, yes,' said Charlie, surprised to hear the stranger use her name and also relieved that he shared her views on Mr Crow. 'How did you know?'

'Ha! We been hearing lotsa things and we been hearing of ya for a long time. I'm surprised I haven't bumped inta ya before now. Nice pendant by the way. Is it an egg or an acorn?'

'I'm not sure,' Charlie replied. Her fingers subconsciously rubbed the beautiful pendant that hung from her neck. 'It was a gift from my parents.'

'Well, look after it, lass. A stompin' Hippotomi like yerself could lose something precious if she wasn't careful. Now,' he said, looking around, 'I gotta run, cos I'm late. But not ta worry – now that I know ya I'll be sure to make time to see ya.' And, so saying, the stranger promptly walked off down the hallway.

'Wait!' cried Charlie. 'You didn't answer all my questions. What's your business? What are Treman and . . . and . . . and Stoman, what are they?' stuttered Charlie.

But the figure continued to walk briskly away, topknot and feather bouncing along in time with his footsteps. 'I'll tell ya next time!' he shouted back at her.

'When's that?' asked Charlie, hurrying after him as he disappeared down the corridor.

'Probably the next time the house complains about yer kickin' and stompin'!' laughed the stranger. 'And look after that pendant!' he called as he stopped by a small door. He paused to wave at Charlie, then dashed on through.

'Wait, please wait!' called Charlie. 'I don't even know your name!'

But it was too late. The door had shut and Charlie was sure the stranger couldn't have heard. Raising her foot to deal out some serious stomping and stamping to the floor-boards, she was interrupted by the door reopening.

Out popped the stranger's head and with a twinkle in his eyes he sang out to Charlie, 'Jensen the Willow is me name!' Then his head ducked out of sight and the door began to swing shut. Before it could close it banged back open and Jensen's head re-emerged. 'And no more stompin'!'

The door crashed shut.

Charlie, who was still standing on one foot, mid-stomp, nearly toppled over.

Rushing down the hallway, she yanked open the door and dashed through. She came to a shocked standstill. She had never been in this room before.

It was huge.

A domed ceiling was hidden in shadows and the curved walls on the far side were a good stone's throw away. On brackets evenly spaced across the walls were blazing torches that flickered and cast dancing silhouettes over the floor. Carved on the stone walls were huge snarling dragons that seemed to flail and thrash. Massive circular doors punctured the walls at regular intervals. Charlie stood there and gaped, mouth wide open. Turning round, she discovered that she was alone; she couldn't see Jensen anywhere. The cavernous room was empty.

How could this room possibly exist in my house? Charlie thought to herself. She was used to the idea that there were far more doors and corridors than should really be within its four walls, but this room was something else.

Realizing she probably looked pretty stupid with her tonsils showing, Charlie snapped her mouth shut and went to investigate the nearest door. It was gigantic. Standing next to it, she had to crane her neck right back to see the top.

The door was constructed from a huge slab of stone. Wonderful carvings of roses, vines and thorns criss-crossed its surface in complex patterns. An oversized handle of black rock jutted outward. Grasping this with both hands, Charlie tugged, pulled and pushed with all her might. But the door refused to budge.

Frowning, she moved on to the next door. It had been made from timber and was so cleverly constructed that no joints could be seen. Carvings of trees and birds swept across its surface. Trying the handle of the door, Charlie was annoyed to find that it too wouldn't open.

With her mouth set in a determined line, she went from door to door, trying the handles and getting more and more frustrated as each successive door failed to open. Finally she found herself back at the smaller door that had led into the room.

'Fine then, don't open! See if I care!' she grumped aloud.

Taking a last look at the strange room with all of its bewitching carvings, she sneaked back through the little door and hurried to check on her grandmother.

2

Cookies, Croissant
and a Dark Visitor

Mr Crow sat alone at his desk. He was cracking his knuckles and using his long, ink-stained fingers to pick his nose. On sudden impulse the lawyer stood up and walked over to the enormous steel safe that loomed in one corner of the room. Entering the safe's combination, he opened the door and stared at all the money stacked high inside.

'Lovely, lovely,' he crooned. His dark eyes blinked slowly as he ran his knobbly fingers gently up and down each bundled tower of notes. With the smell of money still lingering in his nostrils he locked the safe and returned to his paperwork and nose-picking. But his concentration was broken a few moments later when the safe gave a little tremor. Looking up, Crow stared at the steel casket with puzzled concern.

His safe certainly shouldn't tremor.

Giving it a sharp look, the lawyer returned his attention to Charlie's latest bank statements.

Out of the corner of his eye, he could see the safe shake and quiver for a second time.

Knitting his brow in puzzlement, Mr Crow stood up to investigate. Reaching for the door, he yelped and then fell over on his backside in alarm as the safe began to clamour and boom as though caught in an earthquake.

As the noise coming from the safe reached a crescendo, the study lights began to flicker and dim. Suddenly it fell silent, although not for long.

'Open the door,' commanded a voice that issued forth like rumbling thunder.

Crow stared at the safe. It sounded like the voice was coming from inside, but that was impossible.

'Open the door, you bumbling Human, or face my wrath!'

The blood drained from Crow's face. 'Who's that speaking? Who's there?' squeaked the lawyer.

'You chittering, chattering fool! Open this Portal or I shall suck the marrow from your spindly bones and squish your brain!' threatened the dark, growling voice.

The lawyer's hands shook as he reached for the safe's lock and entered the combination. With a violently trembling arm, Mr Crow pulled back the door.

The money had disappeared. In its place a dark shadowy figure emerged . . . and kept on emerging and emerging.

It was a man, or at least it looked like one. But Crow had never seen anyone as large as this before. The figure almost filled the room, towering over the desk and making the lanky lawyer look tiny in comparison. For the first time in his life Crow felt fear. Fear that snatched at his bladder, fear that sent cold waves screaming up his spine and locked all his muscles into a spasm. This . . . thing that now stood in his study could not be Human.

'You will do as I warrant, you little wretch,' spoke the hulking figure. 'Fail to please me and I shall tear your skin into lengths, rip your hair into twine and use your finger- nails as buttons. I will make you into a garment to be worn. Do I have your atten- tion, you little squashy maggot?'

'Yes, yes, yes!' stammered Mr Crow. 'All my attention, all of it, you've got it, yes, yes.'

'Stop your babbling.'

Mr Crow's jaw clamped shut. He stared at the menacing figure. It was almost as wide as it was tall, wrapped head to toe in black bandages, its head covered by a heavy cowl. Crow quailed as he stared into the dark depths of the hood's shadow.

'There is something that I desire and you, little maggot, shall be of use in my hunt for it.'

The figure continued to talk. Mr Crow, dwarfed by the hulking figure, grovelled and nodded his head in quick agreement as the newcomer laid out his demands. At one point Crow interrupted, 'But how will I recognize this if I've never seen one before?'

'I will send one of my Shades with a sketch of its likeness. You may bide your time until then, but bear this in mind, little worm: I will suffer no failure on your part. Fail to please me and your life will be forfeit.'

Mr Crow gulped.

'Understood?'

'Y-yes!'

'Yes, what?' growled the figure.

'Yes, er, lord?'

'Good.' The giant nodded his head. Turning, he strode towards the safe and, placing one oversized foot inside, he paused. 'Something to remember me by, little worm.' He upended his fist and a scattering of rubies tinkled across the wooden floor. 'But a word of caution, greedy Human. My generosity is great, both in reward and in pain.'

Turning once more, the giant climbed back into the safe. One of his bulging arms reached out and pulled the safe door shut with a quiet click.

Mr Crow wiped cold sweat from his brow. He took an unsteady step forward, then hastily sat down in a heap before his shaking legs gave out. Surrounded by glinting rubies, his heart still hammering in his chest, he let out a long, long sigh.

The weekend arrived and Charlie had seen nothing more of the mysterious green Jensen from Bellania. Also, despite endless searching, she hadn't been able to find the strange domed room where he had disappeared.

She stumbled into the kitchen for breakfast. As usual, her hair was a mess.

'Good morning, Charlie, my scruffy little angel. Now then, who's got a kiss for her gran?'

Charlie gave her grandmother a hug and a big kiss.

'Ooh, what a sweetie you are! And what have you got planned for today, poppet?'

Charlie sat on a stool as her gran took out a big wooden comb and began to pull the knots from Charlie's bedraggled hair. Even though she did this every day, it was still a mess.

'I'm going over to Tina's. Her mum's going to drive us to gymnastics, so we're going to hang there for a bit, then spend the afternoon chilling back at her house.'

'That's nice, poppet. Be sure to be home before dark, OK?'

'Of course, Gran,' said Charlie. 'Ouch! Have you finished with my hair, or were you planning on pulling all of it out by its roots?'

'Oh, Charlie!' laughed her gran. 'Don't be such a baby. I'm just making you presentable. It's important, you know.'

'Hhmpf.'

'Your mother always complained as well.' Gran's laughter tinkled across the kitchen. 'All right, there you go, my pet. Now then, off you run.'

Charlie, with her hair combed into two crazy-looking pigtails, gave her gran another hug. Sliding off the stool, she grabbed a croissant from the table and scampered for the door. Turning to say goodbye, she saw a familiar slackness shudder across her gran's face.

'Charlie! Good morning, my little angel. And where are you off to this beautiful day?'

Charlie struggled not to let her despair show. Running back to her gran, she gave her another big hug.

'Nowhere special, Gran, nowhere special.'

Running out of the kitchen, she almost bumped into Mr Crow, who casually slapped her round the back of the head in passing.

'Clumsy girl, watch where you step,' he snarled.

Charlie's turquoise eyes narrowed. 'Sorry,' she forced herself to say.

'Sorry what?'

'Sorry, sir,' she grumbled.

Her reluctance did not go unnoticed by the lawyer. 'Just remember, my little filly,' he hissed, too low for her grandmother to hear, 'if you don't play ball with me I'll have social services take you away. Then you really will be an orphan and your dear grandmother will have to look after herself. Now get out of my way.'

Charlie hurried down the corridor, feeling sick to the stomach and full of unvoiced anger. She hated confrontations with Mr Crow and despised his constant barbs about her missing parents. She still couldn't believe that they had been in her life one day and then gone the next without even the smallest clue as to what had happened to them.

Part of the reason she hated Crow so much was that she was sure he knew more than he was telling her about their disappearance. He said he had organized an investigation – and she had certainly signed a form to pay for one – but not one policeman or detective had ever spoken to Charlie.

Stepping out of the house, she let loose a sigh as the front door shut quietly behind her. She began to feel better as she headed further away. By the time she reached Tina's a smile had appeared on her face. She always enjoyed gymnastics and loved working on new acrobatic moves.

Tina answered the door to Charlie's knock. 'So, are you ready, then?' she asked, hopping from one foot to the next. 'I'm super excited!'

'Of course! Anything that gets me out of the house and Crow's way sounds good.'

'Is that skinny old idiot still being a pain?' asked Tina with a grimace as they went into her bedroom. 'My neighbour had a run-in with him yesterday. Crow clobbered the poor man around the head with his umbrella when he didn't move out of the way fast enough.'

'Yeah, that sounds like the miserable fool,' sighed Charlie. 'I wish I was big enough to tie his skinny legs together.'

'Ha! That's at least a couple more years away, unless you're planning on having a huge growth spurt,' laughed Tina. 'Come on now. I've got to go tell my mum we're ready.'

Charlie always enjoyed being around Tina, who had a knack of making her forget about her home and all the problems it contained. They walked into the kitchen, where Tina's mum was sitting at the table with her laptop.

'Hiya, Mrs Bagley. How are you?'

'Charlie, how wonderful to see you. I'm well, thank you. I'm guessing this means you're ready to go, so why don't you both grab a cookie for the car journey and we'll be on our way?'

They filed out of the house, with Tina talking excitedly about gymnastics.

As she sat in the back of the car, Charlie thought back to her odd meeting with Jensen the previous weekend.

'Mrs Bagley, have you ever heard of a place called Bellania?' she asked.

'Bellania? No, I don't think I have. Transylvania sure, but never Bellania. Why, is it in Russia somewhere?' she asked.

'I'm not sure myself, Mrs Bagley. I heard it mentioned recently, on the telly, and I just wondered where it was.'

'Maybe it was a movie or something,' said Tina. 'It doesn't sound like a real place. Bit like you still believing in dragons, isn't it?'

'But dragons are real!' protested Charlie.

'Sure they are,' chuckled Tina. Reaching over, she gave Charlie a playful punch on the shoulder.

3

An Angry Giant

Mr Crow was quietly sitting in his office. He couldn't stop
fidgeting. Every once in a while he would turn round and
stare with nervous eyes at the safe. Going up to it, he would
reach out to unlock the door, but each time his hand would
start shaking so violently that he would have to return to
his desk, sit down and wait for his nerves to calm down.
Crow was fiercely annoyed. Fear of huge bulking giant had
finally conquered his love for money and now he dared not
open the safe, not even to play with his money.

Sitting there with his head held in his hands, the lawyer
didn't see the Shade as it slid under the door. However, the
sudden drop in the study's temperature caused Mr Crow to
look up.

Yelping in terror, he tipped backwards in his chair and
fell in an untidy heap. Hunched on top of his desk, a shape-
less, inky-black monstrosity pulsed and writhed. Extending
what could have been either an arm or a paw, it offered a
parchment, rolled and bound in black ribbon.

'Take it,' the Shade's voice whispered like a chill winter
wind. 'Take it, miserable Human.'

'Hhmpf, I assume you're the Shade my new benefactor

was referring to.' Crow snatched the parchment. Unravelling the ribbon and breaking the seal, he stared in disbelief at the sketch.

'Ahhh! It's been under my nose all this time – I don't believe it! I'll skin that little filly alive! Quick, you! Go and tell your master it's here, that I know where it is!'

The Shade didn't budge.

'Well, hurry, you piece of bile. Do what you're told! Go on, shoo! Go and tell your master!'

The Shade jumped off the desk and thrust its shadowy head into Crow's face. Cold, fish-like breath washed over the lawyer.

'Your master too, Human, yours too. Don't forget.'

With a snarl the Shade shook itself. Turning, it slid from the room.

Charlie had had a really enjoyable day. Breaking a sweat at gymnastics and hanging out with Tina had helped ease her worries and concerns. She finally felt strong enough to return home. But stepping through the front door Charlie groaned. Mr Crow was waiting for her.

'Well, well, my filly. Had a good day, did you? Been out cavorting and playing with your friends while poor Crow has been working his fingers to the bone?'

Charlie's anger levels suddenly soared. She would never be free of him, she realized. Losing all sense of caution, she stepped forward to speak her mind.

'You've never done a real day's work in your life, you

lazy sack of bones. You're just a bully. You pick on me because I'm small, and you can get away with things because my gran can't help. Well, you'd better watch out – cos when I get bigger I'll make you pay!'

Crow's eyes bulged, his fingers twitched and his face went red, then purple. Charlie shrank back. She knew she'd get punished, but she didn't care; some things had to be said. Suddenly Mr Crow laughed. His mouth twisted into a sneer. Cracking his knuckles, he leaned forward.

'When you get bigger? *If* you get bigger, my filly. IF!'

Striding forward on his long legs, Mr Crow grabbed Charlie by the hair and dragged her down the hall.

'You're in luck, my pretty. It's not me you have to worry about. Someone else has expressed an interest in you. Oh yes, your precious little neck has more value than you think and it's time for you to meet the new master of the house!'

Crow shouldered open the study door and, hauling Charlie kicking and screaming into the room, threw her to the floor by the safe. Stepping back, Crow called out, 'My lord, she's here! And she has what you want.'

Charlie looked up at Crow in bewilderment. Had the skinny lawyer lost his mind? Who was he talking to? She knew Crow talked to money, much like one talked to a pet, but surely calling it 'master' was a step too far?

BOOM!

Charlie stared as the safe door shook like a leaf in a gale.

BOOM!

The door began to buckle and bend.

KRA-KKOOM!

The safe door flew across the room and landed on the

floor with a loud clang. Charlie sat up. What had just happened? All of a sudden she felt sick and butterflies tore around the inside of her stomach. She couldn't believe it. A huge foot was sticking out of the safe. Charlie began to whimper as the foot stepped out and a leg the size of a tree trunk followed.

Standing up and filling the study with his bulk, the creature radiated such a sense of menace that Charlie began to shake uncontrollably.

'This is the one? She holds the key?' asked the hulking giant in his deep voice. Stooping, he lifted Charlie up easily with one mammoth hand. Turning her head from side to side, he scrutinized his find. 'Yes, I can see the family resemblance.' Then, tilting Charlie's head backwards, he examined her pendant. 'You have done well, worm. She does indeed carry the key.' Casually dumping Charlie back on the floor, the giant turned to Crow. 'Remove the pendant and bind her. I will take them both.'

'My pendant?' said Charlie, instinctively grabbing it.

Mr Crow scurried over to Charlie. Kneeling down, he slapped her hand away and removed the necklace with his spider-like fingers. Unclipping his braces from his trousers, he leaned over to tie up Charlie with them. But, recovering her senses, Charlie grabbed the lawyer's hand and bit him with all her might.

Crow screamed, grabbing his bleeding hand as he leaped back. Charlie snatched up her pendant and made for the door, but before she could reach it enormous python-like fingers grabbed her leg and hauled her into the air.

'Going somewhere, little maggot?' chuckled the giant.

Charlie yelled in terror and instinctively lashed out with her hands. The pendant whipped round and hit the giant's arm. Immediately, thick bubbling smoke erupted where the necklace had made contact. The giant roared and Charlie found herself airborne as she was flung across the room. She quickly struggled to her feet and turned round to see the giant bellowing in pain and Mr Crow still holding his mangled hand. She bolted for the door.

'Fool! Grab her!' roared the giant. Crow made a lunge for Charlie but tripped over his braces. 'Idiot!' the deep voice boomed. 'Shades, come to me. Come now – your master commands it!'

Opening the study door, Charlie glanced back. Mr Crow was on his hands and knees on the floor; the giant stood arms outstretched and silhouetted in the centre of the room. But what made Charlie go cold were the shadows tumbling and oozing out of the safe. Mewling and snuffling, they crowded around the giant's feet. Turning, she fled.

Racing through the house, Charlie sped away as an unnatural howling and barking followed her. Bolting through doorways, scrambling up and down stairs, she ran from the pursuing Shades. While she paused for breath at the top of a flight of stairs, Charlie tried to take stock of the situation.

'Oh no – Gran!' she cried.

Turning to head back and warn her grandmother, Charlie was confronted by a Shade rippling up the stairs. She yelped, quickly changed direction and bounded through the nearest door. Snatching a look over her shoulder, she glimpsed more Shades tumbling after her.

Putting her head down, Charlie pumped her legs even

faster. She jumped through a door, almost tearing it off its hinges, and quickly turned the key in the lock. Looking round, she was surprised to find herself in the corridor where she had so recently met Jensen. Lungs heaving and with a stitch beginning to burn in her side, she raced down the hall.

BAA-BOOM!

The door in front of her burst apart and, as the dust began to clear, Charlie saw the black-robed giant brushing past the shattered doorframe. His huge bulk completely blocked her exit. Looking back, she saw a Shade oozing under the locked door behind her.

'Yes, little maggot, what are you going to do now? Give me the pendant, squishy Human girl, and I might not feed your fleshy carcass to my Shades.'

The Shade behind her hissed in anticipation. But spying the small door Jensen had used earlier Charlie scrambled through into the huge vaulted chamber. It may have been her fevered imagination, but the dragons carved on the walls seemed to move and writhe even more than earlier. There was no sign of Jensen.

Hurrying over to the nearest door, she tried the handle, but as before it was firmly locked. Remembering her previous lack of success with opening the doors, Charlie began to panic. She hurried over to the next one, but it too was locked.

A deep, rumbling chuckle filled the room. Knowing what to expect, Charlie slowly turned towards the sound. The giant stood there with his arms crossed as Shades boiled and twisted around his feet.

'Oh no! Oh no! Not good!' Charlie raced to the next door – the one made from wood – and began to scream and shout as she pounded on it. 'Help! Help me! Jensen, where are you? Gran, help me! Someone, anyone! Please!'

Turning, she saw the giant stalking towards her. The Shades had spread out across the room, foiling any possibility of escape.

She scrabbled at the handle and pounded on the door again. 'Let me in! Let me in! Jensen, please let me in. Please open!'

An icy wind suddenly filled the chamber. Snapping at Charlie's ponytails, it howled across the room and blew at the bracketed torches, causing the flames to flare. On the walls, the dragons snarled and lashed their tails, definitely moving this time. The giant bellowed as his robes flapped around him and the Shades screamed. Charlie fell over and stared in disbelief as the door swung open.

She could see nothing through the doorway, just a throbbing deep blackness. But the giant's angry bellow of rage brought Charlie sharply to her senses. Gathering all her courage, she took a deep breath and jumped into the darkness.

4

A High Dive

Charlie hit the ground hard and fell in a heap. Rolling on to her knees, she stared back at the approaching Shades. They came bounding and leaping towards her, screaming and spitting venomously, their rage and terrible anger causing Charlie to flinch in horror. The giant was also nearing the door, his black, bandaged hands reaching out. She could hear him repeating a fevered chant as his legs stumbled their way across the floor.

'Squeeze her, crush her! Suck her marrow! Squeeze her, crush her! Suck her marrow!'

Charlie recoiled in fear. Springing for the door, she tried to force it shut. Pushing all her weight against it, she attempted to close it, but the door wouldn't move. Steadfast and stubborn, it stayed ajar.

'Oh no, oh no, oh no! Shut, shut, shut, SHUT!' cried Charlie. She stamped her foot in frustration. 'Shut, shut! Oh, please, please shut!'

Incredibly, the door began to move. The giant, seeing his prey about to escape, put on a sudden burst of speed. Jumping towards Charlie, he lashed out with clawed fingers, but the door was faster. With a thunderous bang, it slammed

shut, cutting off the terrible cries of her pursuers and leaving
her alone in the dark. Reaching out, Charlie placed her
trembling hands on the wooden surface. She could feel faint
tremors from their frenzied efforts, nothing more. The door
stood firm. It didn't budge, not even an inch.

Charlie released a shuddering breath, then turned round
in an effort to get her bearings. As her eyes became accustomed to the darkness, she began to make out faint details.
She was in what she guessed to be a large tunnel, and spaced
at regular intervals along the walls were what looked like
statues, but in the gloom she couldn't be sure. Following the
walls, she began to edge her way along and soon she became
aware of the sound of rushing water.

Turning a corner, Charlie's path joined a much larger
tunnel lit by smoky torches that spat and popped in the
moist air. A river cascaded down a causeway and graceful
bridges spanned it at regular intervals. In the distance, Charlie could see a circle of daylight.

A terrible and sudden thought brought her to a halt. Her
house was enormous and she had, of course, seen many
unusual sights and wonders within its walls, but nothing as
strange as a whole river. Charlie had a sneaking suspicion
she wasn't in her house any more. The thought almost made
her stop, turn round and head back. However, the idea of
returning to confront the giant wasn't exactly appealing.
Besides, she had a curious nature. She had never tired of
discovering new territory inside her house, so why should
this be any different? Setting her mouth in a determined
pout, Charlie hurried towards the light, eager to see where
it led.

The bright end of the tunnel opened out on to a cliff face. Standing at the edge of the path, Charlie gaped in delight as she took in the view. Spread far below her lay an immense forest. Huge trees thrust their foliage skyward to form an extraordinary ocean of green that stretched as far as her eyes could see. Many of the trees were in bloom and the scents that filled the air and tickled at her nose – lavender, vanilla, aniseed and others – were unlike any she had experienced before. Gazing in wonder, Charlie saw huge pink birds that reminded her of flamingos gliding above the forest canopy.

Beside her the river emerged into the sunlight and fell to form a vast, roaring waterfall before continuing on its winding, snaking way into the distance. Near the base of the waterfall was a large clearing. Through the spray Charlie could just make out a small group of figures sitting around a blazing bonfire, with more people fishing nearby on the riverbank.

A sudden menacing growl coming from behind Charlie made her jump. Had the giant made it through the door? Spinning, she grabbed her pendant and prepared to put up a fight. But to her shock – and immediate fear – she found she was facing the largest dog she had ever seen. Hunching forward, the beast was nearly the size of a pony. Powerful muscles bunched and rippled beneath a gleaming black coat and a strip of white fur ran down its spine. Peeling back its lips to reveal enormous teeth, it growled. Clearly it wasn't happy.

Charlie groaned. 'Can my day get any worse?' she muttered to herself. Bending down, she picked up a nearby stick and threw it down the path. 'Er . . . fetch?'

The dog wasn't amused. Snarling, it slowly padded towards Charlie, who just as slowly backed away.

'I guess you're not the sort of dog that pet shops hope to sell to urban, fun-loving girls, are you? Er . . . no? I didn't think so. So why am I getting the really, really, really bad impression that you're maybe the sort of dog that likes to EAT urban, fun-loving girls instead?'

Looking over her shoulder, Charlie realized with sudden alarm that the dog had backed her into a corner. On one side was a sheer drop down the cliff face and on the other was the river. Lying on the floor a short distance away was a tree limb, worn smooth from its passage through the water. Charlie started to inch her way towards it. If she could just get her hands on it, she could use it to keep the dog at bay, maybe even scare it off.

The dog, with canny foresight, moved between Charlie and her goal.

'Oh, for crying out –'

The dog suddenly leaped at her. Teeth snapping, it shot

through the air. Charlie fell backwards in an attempt to get out of its way, but abruptly found herself submerged in icy-cold water. The realization that she was in the water and nearing a plummeting waterfall sent adrenalin pumping through her body. Kicking out in a frenzied front crawl, she tried to reach the riverbank, but it was too late. The rushing water dragged her under. Spinning and tumbling, Charlie lost all sense of direction as she dropped over the cliff face.

The twisting free-fall seemed to go on forever. Charlie, dizzy beyond belief, saw the foaming surface of the river rushing up to meet her.

'Aaaaaaaaaaaahhhhhhhhhhhhhhhhhh–'

She slammed into the water, which cut off her scream. Battling against the rushing water, she struggled back up to the surface. Gasping, she managed to drag in a lungful of air before the pounding waters pushed her under again. Struggling harder, Charlie swam with all her might against the powerful undercurrent, but with no success. The waters dragged her down and spun her along the stony riverbed.

Charlie could feel herself beginning to tire. The thought of drowning in the murky waters made her thrash about, but a sudden collision caused white flashes and an explosion of pain along the side of her head. A trail of blood slowly disappeared into the murky water as she blacked out.

The giant stood there, staring with a focused rage at the carved wooden door. His anger and fury was so intense that it could be seen pulsing around him like a dark halo.

For a long, long time his only movement was the slow opening and shutting of clenched fists. The Shades cowered in silence to either side, forming a rustling and whispering carpet of shadow.

With a shudder, the giant awoke from his bitter trance. Turning, he strode across the chamber towards the stone door and firmly grasped the criss-crossed carvings on its surface. Then he began to chant. His voice was a deep, rumbling baritone, a combination of whale song and distant thunder. The stone door began to glow a deep red until the giant's powerful voice filled the chamber, rippling back and forth as it rose to a crescendo. As the chant built in power, the colour brightened from red to orange and finally to a luminous white. The eerie singing continued for a few moments, then suddenly stopped. The giant released his grip and stepped back.

'Open,' he said.

Smoothly and silently, the huge door swung open. The giant strode forward with his shadowy servants following at his heels. Stopping halfway through, he turned to one of the Shades. 'Fetch me a garment that belongs to that squishy little girl. Ensure it is rich with her disgusting and vile scent. Bring it to me in the Western Mountains.'

He watched the Shade slink away. Slipping under the small door on the far side of the chamber, it disappeared back into the house. The giant grunted his approval before striding through the door with the remaining Shades, leaving the chamber empty and silent.

5

New Companions

Charlie groaned as she came to. Sitting up, she stared around her and found that she was resting on the riverbank. She didn't remember getting there; in fact, the last thing she remembered was the horror of drowning.

'Hello, lass. Nice swim?' said a voice.

Charlie looked up and saw a figure looming over her.

'Uh, hi,' she said. Immediately she noticed that the man looked a lot like Jensen and she relaxed slightly. 'Um, are you by any chance a Treman?'

'Ha! Of course I'm a Treman. Wot else would I be? Look! Big nose, big earlobes and let's not forget me green skin! D'ya meet many Humans that look like dis? I can see yer mind must have been turned ta mush after swallowing all that water!'

'Uh, sure . . . Well, thanks anyways for saving me. I really appreciate it.'

'Don't thank me, blossom, thank Sic Boy. He was the one that pulled ya outta the water.'

'Is that him?' asked Charlie, pointing to a very fat Treman who was walking along the bank, whistling a jaunty tune as he came. His big green stomach, too large to be contained by his leather shirt, bulged over his belt. Charlie couldn't help noticing that his belly button was pierced.

'Ha! Ya must be kidding. Kelko the Fat Oak swimming? The only thing he's good for is floating!'

'So who's Sic Boy, then?' asked Charlie.

'Sic Boy?' said Kelko, who had just arrived and was now sitting down on the bank next to Charlie. 'I just saw him off chasing squirrels. He'll be back in a minute.'

Charlie raised her eyebrow. *Chasing squirrels? Riiiiight.*

'Nice dive, by the way,' said Kelko. 'I especially enjoyed all the arm waving and screaming. Very stylish, wouldn't ya say, Stotch?'

'Oh, sure. Real stylish,' answered the Treman who had first spoken to Charlie. 'Of course, ya've gotta be the only girl stupid enough not ta take the stairs,' he added, pointing towards the cliff face.

'Stairs? What stairs?' asked Charlie.

'Those really, really big stairs cut inta the cliff face,' said Kelko. 'Ya know, the ones that are really hard ta miss.'

Charlie looked back at the cliff face. Kelko was right: there was indeed a huge staircase carved into the rock.

'Well, it's not as if I didn't intend to use them, but I never got the chance.'

'And why's that, then, lass?' asked Stotch.

'Because I got pushed into the water by a blooming big, black-furred monster, that's why!'

'Monster? Around here?' said Stotch, surprised. 'Hey, Kelko, ya haven't seen any monsters around here, have ya?'

'No, not since yer sister stopped coming around!' said Kelko.

'Shut it, ya big green lump o' blubber!'

'Hey, I'm serious!' Charlie interrupted. 'It jumped at me and . . . Oh, my days! There it is! Quick, run!' she shouted.

Stotch and Kelko stared around in puzzlement.

'Wotcha going on about, lass?' asked Stotch.

'See, I always said Humans were a few acorns short in the head,' added Kelko.

'What are you two? Blind? There, right there!' screamed Charlie.

The huge dog was sitting calmly on top of the bank. Opening its huge mouth, it yawned and scratched its flanks.

'Ha! Lass, don't be stupid now, that's Sic Boy,' laughed Stotch.

'Sic Boy?' said Charlie. 'No, it's not. It's the monster that chased me into the river.'

'Sic Boy chased ya inta the river?' said Kelko. 'He wouldn't have done that on purpose. Although I've gotta admit he does have a rather wicked sense of humour.'

'Wicked sense of humour? He tried to bite me in half!'

'Nah, he probably just wanted ta play a bit. He's a bit feisty sometimes. Anyway, don't forget he's the one that pulled ya outta the water,' said Stotch.

'Hhmpf,' grumbled Charlie. She still wasn't convinced that the huge dog wasn't going to pounce down the bank and try to gobble her up.

'How's yer head?' asked Stotch.

'Really sore, but I've had worse beatings from Mr Crow.'

'Who's Mr Crow?' asked Kelko.

'A skinny, deceiving, miserable . . . um . . . Never mind, he's not important.'

'Well, then, lass, if ya can walk, let's go see the others, get ya some grub and something dry for ya to wear,' suggested Stotch.

Bending down, he scooped up his fishing gear, his catch (which consisted of some brightly coloured fish) and his fishing rod before clambering back up the riverbank with Kelko wobbling by his side. Making sure that the two Tremen were between her and Sic Boy, Charlie followed slowly after.

'Hey, um, Kelko, is this Bellania?' she asked.

Kelko stopped and turned to her. 'Of course, lass. Where else would ya see a forest like dis?' he said, gesturing around him.

Reaching the top of the bank, Charlie saw that they were in a clearing about half the size of a football pitch. The trees lining the clearing were gigantic, bigger than any she had seen in London. The trunks were wider than buses and the trees themselves towered high enough to look like small skyscrapers. A couple of the pink birds she had seen earlier were walking about, plucking at seeds and insects in the grass. Every once in a while one would lift its head and trill out a whistling song.

In the centre of the clearing a group of maybe ten or twelve Tremen were sitting around a roaring bonfire. They all seemed very merry, passing a leather gourd to one another and eating freshly barbecued fish. A couple of the Tremen were pounding out complex rhythms on leather-bound drums. Some were singing along and several others were dancing and cavorting about. They all cheered when the four of them came in sight. Charlie did a double take when she saw a familiar face.

'Jensen!' she cried.

'Charlie! Wotcha doing here?' he asked, clearly pleased to see her. His eyes took in her wet and dishevelled clothing and the big bump on her head. 'I see ya've been in the wars. Everything all right, me little Hippotomi?'

Before Charlie could reply the other Tremen began to badger Jensen.

'Who's she, then?'

'Who's the lass, Jensen?'

'Yeah, who's she?'

Jensen waved his hands for silence. 'All right, lads, dis is the little lady I was telling ya all about. Say hello ta the stompin', stampin' girl, me little Hippotomi, Charlie!'

A large chorus of 'hello's and 'hi's greeted Charlie, who couldn't help but grin. The Tremen were very welcoming and their good cheer and big smiles were infectious. Many of them tried to come up and ask her questions.

'Stand back! Stand back, ya useless lotta weasels!' shouted Jensen. 'Let's give her some grub and a chance ta dry out before ya all start bothering her!'

Jensen led Charlie over to an empty seat, sat her down and got one of his companions to fetch a towel. The smell of the freshly cooked fish set Charlie's stomach rumbling; it had been hours since she had eaten. Accepting a plate of the Tremen's dinner, she tucked into it straight away, washing it down with a drink that tasted like fragrant vanilla, lime and raspberries.

'Charlie, me lass, are ya all right?' asked Jensen, obviously concerned. 'That's quite a big bump on yer noggin.'

'My head's OK,' said Charlie. 'I think it just looks worse

than it is.' Seeing the worry in Jensen's eyes, she added, 'Really, though, I'm fine.'

'Well, if ya be sure, but if ya don't mind I'll have Lentol look at it later,' suggested Jensen.

Charlie nodded, wondering vaguely who Lentol was.

'So, tell me, lass, wot brings ya ta Bellania?'

'Urm, I didn't really have a say in the matter. I kind of got chased here,' said Charlie.

'Chased?' said Jensen. 'By who?'

'By a really, really big giant with poor anger management and a whole load of black, hissing shadows!' explained Charlie.

'Big giant, black shadows?' muttered Jensen. His face suddenly looked very grave. 'Dis giant, did he keep his face covered?'

'Yes, that's right. And everything else was covered in black bandages.'

'Bane!' hissed Jensen.

One of the Tremen sitting close by promptly fell off his seat upon hearing the name. Silence fell across the campsite and all the Tremen turned to stare at Charlie.

'Bane? Who's Bane?' asked Charlie.

'Bane, the Western Menace, is bad, bad news,' said Jensen. He spat into the fire to prove his distaste. 'He's an evil thug with a thirst for power. And he's been a right pain in the neck. He's been closing down a lotta the trade routes, forbidding travel through the Stoman lands and amassing a huge army. He's a bringer of war.'

'Oh, he's worse than that,' cursed Kelko. 'He's an eater of flesh! Children from all three races have been sold ta him in slavery and then never seen again. It's said he has an unquenchable hunger and appetite, with a particular fondness for bone and marrow.'

'Stomen,' asked Charlie. 'What are they?'

'Stomen are one of the three races in Bellania,' explained Jensen. 'They live mainly in the mountains. Big fellas too. Trust me, ya won't mistake one for a Treman or a Human when ya sees them. Bellania used to be a pretty peaceful place . . . Sure, ya would get an occasional rumble or bicker between peoples, but just over little things. Now things are different and Bane has got a lot ta do with that.'

'Um, any idea why he's chasing me?' asked Charlie.

'I've got a couple of good ideas,' said Jensen. 'But I've taken a vow of secrecy ta the Jade Circle and certain matters take precedence. Although I must admit I wasn't expecting ta see ya here in Bellania. But, never fear, yer safe here. We'll get ya to Sylvaris and there the Jade Circle will take ya under their wing and sort matters out.'

'But if you know something surely you can tell me? For heaven's sake, I've had a giant tearing around my house, threatening to feed me to his sidekicks, and now I'm in a strange place that I know nothing about. I've got no idea what's going on! Jensen, come on, you've got to tell me something!' implored Charlie.

'Blossom, he would if he could, but a vow ta the Jade Circle is unbreakable,' said Kelko, coming over and placing a calming hand on Charlie's shoulder. 'If he were ta speak he would be banished from Sylvaris and he'd spend his life as an outcast. Listen, we'll take ya ta Sylvaris and there all yer questions will be answered.'

'But my gran – is she safe back at home on her own? How can I leave and not know for sure if she's OK?' asked Charlie.

'Me little Hippotomi, matters have been taken outta our hands.' Jensen shrugged apologetically. 'Bane is too dangerous ta face – ya can't go back ta yer house. Even if ya had us by yer side it wouldn't be enough ta ensure yer safety, not from Bane. But I'm sure yer gran will be fine. I can't see an old lady having a part in Bane's plans. For now the only way forward lies with the Jade Circle. They know wot the deal is with ya and yer family. They'll help ya for sure.'

'What's the Jade Circle?' asked Charlie. 'Hang on a sec. How come they know about me? I've never been here before and I only met you for the first time last week!'

Jensen rubbed at his forehead and sighed. 'Charlie, there's something I gotta tell ya.' He cleared his throat.

'The thing is . . . I know yer parents. The Jade Circle know yer parents –'

'You know my parents?' squawked Charlie, jumping to her feet. 'Where are they?' she half demanded, half pleaded.

Jensen looked uncomfortable. 'I can't tell ya where they are, Hippotomi. In truth, yer parents have worked hand in hand with the Circle like, well . . . like all yer family have done for generations.' He smiled at Charlie, trying to reassure her. 'Little lass, yer family are the Keepers. *Gate*keepers, that is. They protect one of the few paths between Bellania and Earth.'

But Charlie wasn't concerned with being a Keeper, whatever that meant. 'But you know where they are, right? Where are they, Jensen?'

'Charlie, I took an oath ta the Jade Circle not ta talk about the whereabouts of yer parents.'

'But they're *my parents*. You've got to tell me. At least tell me why they haven't got in touch with me. Why haven't I heard from them? They've been gone for almost seven years! YOU'VE GOT TO TELL ME!'

Charlie wanted to kick something, hard. To actually find someone who might know where her parents were but refused to tell her was enough to have her spitting with rage.

'Charlie, I can't tell ya, I'm sorry. I know the vow don't mean much ta ya right now, but I promise ya it's important. Please, for now, just trust me like yer parents have always trusted me.'

Charlie had a sudden urge to kick Jensen in the shin. Fortunately he turned away before she could act. 'How long will it take us to get to the Jade Circle?' she asked, a little more calmly.

'If we push it, we can make six leagues by nightfall,' said Jensen. 'And if we can keep the pace up we'll make it ta Sylvaris and the Jade Circle in five days.'

'Five days!' protested Charlie. 'There's no way I can leave my gran alone for that long. No way, no how. I'm sorry, but I thought we could get this sorted a lot quicker, but if we're talking five days or more then I've got to go home.'

Jensen shook his head in sorrow. 'Charlie, lass, if ya go home now, Bane is gonna get ya. Yer of no use ta anyone if ya get eaten, and that's wot'll happen if ya return. Please trust me: the Jade Circle is the only way to help yer family.'

While Charlie was thinking about his words, Jensen turned back to the group. 'Lentol, come over here and take a look at the bump on Charlie's noggin. The rest of ya, pack yer bags – we're going back to Sylvaris.'

Jensen supervised the packing as everyone sprang into action. Water was flung on the fire, food hastily wrapped and fresh water taken from the river. In a very short space of time the Tremen were ready. Bags slung across backs and over shoulders, they began to trudge towards the forest. The pink birds scattered, breaking into flight at their approach.

Stodel, a young, enthusiastic-looking Treman, held a hurried conversation with Jensen by the edge of the clearing. Giving up his heavy backpack, he accepted a lighter bag and several flasks of water in its place. Shouting out his good-byes, he then jogged down the path, his topknot bouncing from side to side.

Charlie turned to Kelko. 'Where's he off to?'

'We're sending Stodel ahead to give the Jade Circle the heads up.'

She nodded, then peered behind for a final view of the waterfall. The path leading up the cliff face was her only way back home. Racked with sudden indecision, she turned to Kelko.

'What's Sylvaris?'

'It's our city, lass. The home of the Tremen. "The Flower of Deepforest".'

'And that's where I'll find the Jade Circle? They'll answer all that I need to know about my parents . . . and about Bane?'

'Yes, lass.'

Charlie sighed. *I'll be home as soon as I can, Gran,* she promised. With Sic Boy striding by her side, she then turned her back on the cliff and marched boldly into the forest.

6

An Education

Bane watched as the door that led to the other realm swung shut behind him. Flexing his shoulders, he marched down the stone-flagged corridor. The Shades, no longer needed by their master, disappeared through the low archways on either side. Approaching the end of the corridor, Bane clapped his hands together and the two mighty red-panelled doors in front of him opened. Cowled servants, dressed in magnificent blood-red livery, bowed in unison as Bane strode into the lushly carpeted hall. Several approached him bearing fruits, spiced cakes and liquors to refresh him after his journey. Bane dismissively waved them aside.

'Just bring me my robes of office,' he growled. 'I have no time to dawdle.'

Two of the footmen removed Bane's travel cloak and replaced it with a magnificent black hooded robe that was decorated with gold embroidery. A third footman approached and placed a heavy gold chain round his neck. Its dark red stones flickered and glowed with a soft light.

Checking his image in a polished brass mirror, Bane grunted his approval, then marched from the hall, his giant stride carrying him quickly along the passages. Opulent furnishings lined the way: great paintings depicting ancient battles, jade vases, marble statues, jewel-encrusted weapons and more hung from the walls. Bane thumped past with uncaring eyes. Opening a portcullis, he entered a large, dank room with a circular pit in the middle. Mildew covered the sandstone walls and fires had been lit in braziers in an attempt to keep the oppressive cold at bay. A heavy, rusting metal grate covered the pit's mouth, while in the ceiling a shaft led to an overcast and turbulent sky far above. Silent guards, shadowy and helmeted, stood about, shuffling in obvious discomfort, although whether that was caused by the cold or by Bane's presence, it was hard to tell.

'Guard, how have they been?' asked Bane.

'Restless, my lord. It has been some time since they tasted fresh meat,' replied one of the heavily muscled guards.

'Well, that is about to change,' said Bane, walking over to the pit. He looked into the darkness below, then pulled out something from his pocket, brought it near his face and sniffed at its scent. It was one of Charlie's T-shirts. Bane addressed the pit's occupants. 'Bring me back that squirming, squishy little Human girl. Bring her to me, kicking and screaming, writhing and wriggling. Bring her to me and I will feed you fresh, succulent meat. Little Treman children shall be your feast, yours to suck upon and gnaw, yours to chew and gnash upon. Bring me the disgusting little maggot and I shall show you my delight and endless gratitude.'

Bane stepped up to the lip of the pit and dropped the T-shirt into the darkness below. A loud hissing and clicking noise boiled up from the hidden depths.

The walls of the pit shook as they were struck and beaten from within.

'Open it,' said Bane.

Two of the guards began to turn a huge winch. Chains hanging from the ceiling pulled taut as the grate slowly lifted upwards in an arc, then fell to the floor with a thunderous clang. The guards edged back from the gaping hole and pressed themselves against the walls.

The things in the pit, smelling their fear, began to simmer in the darkness. Faster and faster they moved, repeatedly striking the walls of the pit until the whole room started to shake. Soon the hissing was so loud that the guards were forced to press their hands to their ears in an effort to dim the blistering noise.

'GO!' roared Bane, flinging his hands towards the shaft above. 'Go and do not return until you have the girl! GO!'

The pit erupted as a tide of taut muscles and serrated teeth flashed in the air. The sinuous predators were long in body, grey and worm-like. Slime-covered scales festered along the length of their bodies and ragged dragonfly wings hummed as they beat powerfully against the air. Bane's robes were swept up around him and flapped in the wind. The creatures spun and coiled around the room, the sound of their scales brushing and rubbing against one another with a deafening screech. Spinning once more around the room, they brushed against Bane's outstretched hand, then they were gone, flinging themselves up through the shaft and out into the darkening twilight sky.

Bane stared up through the shaft at the dwindling silhouettes.

'Maggot, I do not think your luck will last much longer . . .'

'Bless me Leaf, Charlie, but ya never seem ta shut up!' moaned Jensen. 'All right, I can see it might be a little hard ta understand if ya've never been ta Bellania, but listen for a bit before ya start having another tantrum.'

Charlie stopped walking and crossed her arms. 'Tantrum?' she squawked. 'I don't have tantrums! I . . . uh . . . merely like to be vocal when I express my displeasure.' Her foot was impatiently tip-tapping on the leaf-littered forest floor and a terrible frown was plastered across her face.

Kelko laughed loudly. The whole party of Tremen had ground to a halt and now they stood around waiting to see how Jensen would react.

'OK, OK! Look, if I start answering yer questions, will ya please stop all that stompin' and carry on walking?' pleaded Jensen.

Charlie pulled a face, but continued along the path.

'As I was saying,' continued Jensen, 'once upon a time, Bellania and Earth were the same place. However, many thousands of years ago, earthquakes, floods, volcanic erup-tions and all sorts of terrible things happened. We called dis time the Great Cataclysm and that was when the two worlds got separated. The Tremen, Stomen and a few of ya Humans decided ta move ta dis side, but the bulk of ya Humans decided to stay put where they was. There are still protected paths between the two sides, but travel and interaction has slowed over the years. Now it's just us merchants and a few adventurers who cross over. Me and me boys are one of the more successful merchant groups out there. In fact, we was just about ta cross over again when we stumbled inta ya.'

'You keep telling me you're a merchant, but what do you trade?' asked Charlie. 'I don't see you guys carrying anything to sell.'

'Ha! Ya got good eyes, me stompin' Hippotomi, but not that good! Here, take a look at dis,' said Jensen. Reaching for his backpack, he pulled out a plain-looking leather pouch.

Opening it, Charlie peered inside. It contained a light-blue powder that sparkled in the sunlight and had the most unusual smell. It reminded Charlie of all the great food that she had ever eaten, all the wonderful home-made pastries that Gran had baked her and all the most refreshing drinks that she had ever had.

'What is it?' she asked.

'That, me dear, is me little something-something and it's guaranteed ta make anything, absolutely anything in the whole world – Bellania or Earth – taste yummy.'

'Your little "something-something"?' said Charlie, looking doubtful.

'It's Moreish powder,' explained Jensen, with a wicked twinkle in his eyes. 'Made from Lindis flowers. It's an ancient Willow family recipe, made by me great-great-grandma and passed down from generation ta generation . . . ta yers truly, Jensen the Willow.'

'Moreish powder?' said Charlie.

'Sure Moreish powder. Once ya've had a little, yer gonna want more. More . . . more-ish . . . Moreish! It makes for a top-seller and all yer big manufacturers pay serious money for it. Ya Humans can't produce good grub without it!'

'Are you trying to tell me that you supply all the biggest food corporations in the world with this? Do you honestly expect me to believe that?' said Charlie.

'Sure, and why not?' asked Jensen, the grin on his face getting even bigger. 'Ever wonder why ya always feel like having another ice cream straight after yer first, or why one chocolate is never as good as two? Do ya really think it's just down ta good baking and cooking skills? Of course not! It's because me Lindis plants produce the best Moreish powder and, wot's more, I'm the only one who knows the secret ta producing it!'

'You're lying!' said Charlie, convinced that Jensen was pulling her leg.

'Ah-ha! But I bet ya didn't believe in Tremen, or doors that led ta Bellania, or Bane until ya saw them, right?' said Kelko, coming to Jensen's aid.

Charlie, who was just about to answer back, snapped her mouth shut with an audible click. 'Er . . . Well, how come I've never heard of, let alone seen a Treman before now?' she said, changing the subject.

'That's one of the laws that all Bellanians follow,' Jensen explained. 'Bellania and Earth were separated a long, long time ago and they're supposed ta stay separate. If Humans ever found out about Bellania, how long d'ya think it would take them ta mess things up? They ain't got no respect; they just ruin and waste everything. Besides, if the two sides were whole again, the risk of another cataclysm would be too big.'

'But what about the people you trade with? Surely the corporations know who they deal with?' said Charlie.

'Well, of course they do! But it's only a handful of people, the very big bosses and the top executives, that know the truth, and they certainly aren't gonna spill the beans on their products, are they? Can ya really see them admitting that they get their secret ingredients from little green men?' chuckled Jensen.

'Hmm . . . well I guess that kind of makes sense. Although I think it's weird no one has ever caught sight of you guys, or that after all that time of trading you haven't slipped up once,' said Charlie.

'Well, ta be honest, it does happen every once in a while, but who's gonna believe the occasional poor idiot who does see us? Who's gonna believe some poor fool screaming and hollering about green-skinned men with big ears? Sure, ya get yer wild stories in the newspapers about elves and pixies and gremlins and aliens, but no one takes them seriously. That's wot's so great about yer side – ya Humans have got closed minds and a really skewed sense of perspective. It makes trading so much easier.'

Charlie walked quietly besides Jensen. It took a little while for her mind to grasp these new facts. She sighed to herself. None of those soft drinks and sweets would ever seem the same again.

'OK, so tell me about this Western Menace character, Bane,' she said after a while.

'Well, lass, rumours coming outta the Western Mountains say that Bane went hunting for some ancient and powerful relic that was lost in the Great Cataclysm. Apparently the evil fool found it and used it ta win over the Stomen and he's got 'em all fired up. They think they can take over Bellania now he's the Stoman Lord. Don't get me wrong, not all Stomen have followed Bane down his path. There's still some tribes that stand apart from the war and some that still live among us. I'm sure ya'll meet some of them in Sylvaris,' said Jensen. 'But now, me little Hippotomi, if ya will excuse me for a minute I gotta go talk with Kelko. He still owes me from our dice game last night and if I don't nag him I probably won't be seeing me silver!'

And with that Jensen hurried off, leaving Charlie alone with her thoughts.

7

Tree Song

As she passed through the forest, marvelling at all the gigantic trees, strange flowers and bizarre wildlife, Charlie couldn't quite get over what she'd heard. To think that *her house* protected the entrance to a whole new land. But, more importantly, Bellania seemed to hold the answer to her parents' disappearance. Her palms itched at the thought of unlocking the secrets that the Jade Circle was keeping. They had to tell her where her parents were!

Walking along surrounded by her new Treman friends, Charlie realized that for the first time in ages she felt . . . safe. Safe from Mr Crow anyway. She wasn't too sure about Bane, though. It was typical that having escaped from one bad thing in her life, another had followed her here.

She felt for her pendant. It was special to her as a reminder of her parents, but she knew now that she wasn't the only person who thought it was important. Well, this Bane wasn't going to get it from her, she decided, her resolve hardening.

'Gran,' she suddenly whispered, as an image of her grandmother home alone at the mercy of Crow came into her mind. She gritted her teeth and hoped that Tina and Mrs

Bagley would be good enough to check up on her, and that Crow hadn't done anything to her in the meantime.

So busy was Charlie with her thoughts that she ignored the sudden spurts of wind whistling through the trees, the spatter of heavy raindrops and the silent flash of a nearby lightning strike. It was only when the Tremen started panicking and shouting at her that she snapped back to attention.

'Get outta the way!' screamed Jensen. 'Watch out, Charlie! Move!'

'What?' she asked, twisting round to see what they were shouting about, but all the Tremen were pointing behind her. She turned back.

'Move!' shouted Stotch.

Charlie wished that she could move, but her whole body had frozen in shock at the awesome sight unfolding in front of her. In a corner of her mind she registered the sound of everyone hollering and screaming at her, but her attention was firmly focused on the immense tree, split by the lightning and falling in slow motion towards her. She could almost feel its weight as it plummeted near her. She wanted nothing more than to move out of the way, but shock and disbelief had frozen her body to the spot. Creaking and groaning, cracking and splitting, the tree came down.

A blurring shadow shot towards Charlie and a sudden blow to her stomach winded her as she felt herself propelled backwards. Coming to a halt in the mud, she lay flat on her back, staring up at the thunderous clouds tumbling overhead in the stormy sky. The ground trembled and shook as the mammoth tree struck the forest floor beside her.

Slowly Charlie sat up. Sic Boy was standing next to her,

calmly shaking leaves and mud from his fur. Charlie felt a shiver run up and down her spine and goosebumps prickled her skin. That had been close.

Too close.

With stiff fingers, Charlie reached over and gently rubbed Sic Boy's muzzle in a 'thank you' gesture. The large dog stared back at her with his huge eyes before casually yawning as though to say it was no big deal.

'Blight me Leaf, Charlie, but ya sure know how ta have a close shave!' yelped Jensen. Relief was clearly stamped across his face. 'Now tell me, lass, why didn't ya move?'

'Move?' asked Charlie.

'Yeah, ya know, get outta the way of big falling objects? Y'know . . . move?'

'Oh yeah, move. I'll have to remember to do that next time,' said Charlie, who couldn't stop staring at the fallen tree. Its sheer size and immensity was overwhelming. She wouldn't admit it to Jensen, but it had been fear that had seized her muscles.

'Well, make sure ya do next time, lass. I don't think ya would make a good pancake, and I'm betting that's not the last storm we sees before Sylvaris.' Jensen gave her a helping hand up and plucked a couple of leaves from her hair. 'Right, then, let's go and inspect the damage.'

'Damage?'

'To the tree,' said Kelko, coming over. 'Gotta see if we can save it.'

Charlie stared up as sunlight broke through the cloud layer. It seemed as though the storm would clear almost as fast as it had started. Looking around, she could see the forest return to life. The wildlife slowly emerged from hiding and the cries and whistles of birds resumed.

'Save it?' she asked.

Kelko was busy organizing the Tremen. They were clambering over the broken tree trunk, running their hands along the cracks and tears, and gently patting the ruptured bark. 'We're checking ta see wot parts of the tree can still be repaired,' he explained.

'But it's fallen over,' said Charlie. 'How're you going to fix that?'

'Wait and see, blossom,' said Kelko with a faint smile across his lips. 'All right, boys, let's do it!'

The Tremen placed their hands on the broken tree stump and in silence bowed their heads. Charlie stood there, looking around, wondering what was going to happen. Suddenly she could feel it: an unseen presence, a change in pressure as the temperature seemed to rapidly rise and fall. A heavy silence descended on the forest as the birds stopped singing and the smaller animals stopped rustling in the bushes. The monkeys that had been hooting, chittering and chattering in the distance quietened and stopped.

Then the air began to shimmer around the stump. One by one the Tremen raised their heads and, still holding on to the tree, broke into song. Their warm voices rose and fell, echoing around the greenery of the forest. As the song grew in volume and in strength, Charlie could smell the faint aroma of freshly cut grass intermingled with cherry blossom and lavender. To her astonishment she could see the stump begin to bulge and writhe beneath the Tremen's fingers. Green shoots and leaves erupted from the torn bark, twisting and turning as they grew. The new growth quickly gained height, thickening all the while. The Tremen's melody slowly quietened until, one by one, their voices fell silent.

Kelko was the last to stop, and Charlie noticed that his voice was surprisingly warm and tender. Releasing his hold on the newly healed tree, the Treman stepped back and smiled cheekily at Charlie. 'Well, blossom, wotcha think of that?'

Charlie stared in disbelief at the tree stump. Where before it had been broken and blackened from the lightning strike, it now sprouted fresh growth. The cracks had healed and growing from the stump was a young sapling. It was nothing like as tall as the original, yet it still stood higher than a three-storey house.

'Wow!' said Charlie.

'Yup, ya could say that!' said Kelko. He enthusiastically patted the new tree. 'Give it another couple of years and it'll be big enough ta throw a party on.'

'How'd you do that?' asked Charlie.

'Invite all the neighbours round for a nice brew and get some funky music going! Oh yeah and party clothes. A party ain't a party without slick outfits, fine food, good drink and an outrageous helping of naughtiness!'

'No, no!' Charlie rolled her eyes. She pointed at the flourishing sapling. 'How did you do *that*?'

'Oh! We just encourage it ta grow a wee bit. Ya know, give it a little push, a little helping hand. It's one of the Treman rules: ya gotta look out for the trees. We provide for them and they provide for us.'

'Was it the singing?'

'Well, yeah, the singing is how we tell the trees what ta

do.' Kelko could see Charlie didn't quite understand. 'Blossom, it's wot's done in Bellania. The Tremen treesing and harvest the forest, and the Stomen sing to the stones and manage the rock fields. I can't explain it any more. It's like eating and breathing; it's wot comes naturally ta us.'

'Right . . .' said Charlie.

Jensen had been admiring the new tree growth. Now, noticing that the clouds were clearing and the sun had started to shine again, he rallied the Tremen together.

'Good job, boys! Now then, let's get moving or we won't be reaching Sylvaris any time soon!'

The young Stoman had been tending his family's rock fields, harvesting crystals and storing them in the large leather sack slung over his shoulder. As the sun began to dip beneath the horizon, he prepared to finish his day's work.

A shrill keening howl that echoed across the distance made him pause in his tracks. In all his thirteen years of tending the rock fields he'd never heard anything like it. The cry sounded again, sending shivers down his spine. Climbing a nearby finger of rock, he stood and shielded his eyes from the setting sun's glare. Gazing around, he tried to locate the source of the sound.

His thick, gnarled skin rippled nervously as he heard the howling yet again, and this time it was joined by other similar voices that hissed, chittered and chattered. The shrieking drew nearer and the sounds echoed back and forth, bouncing from the towering rocks and causing small stones to tumble and shatter on the rocky floor below.

Close to panic, the young Stoman peered out from the ledge, desperate to locate whatever was making the noise. The screeching increased in volume, the sound tearing at his eardrums.

Suddenly a thick sinuous shape spat overhead, the wind from its passage almost knocking the boy from where he stood. Others soon followed, their scaled bodies glinting horribly in the setting sun. Huge talons and wicked teeth shone and twinkled in the light. Calling and hissing to each other, the creatures sped through the air, lashing at the rock spires with their barbed tails as they swept past. The whir of their dragonfly wings reverberated around the stone surroundings. The young Stoman clung to the outcrop with white knuckles, shivering and sweating.

With a final rush of wind and a flashing glimpse of scales, they were gone, their cries dwindling into the distance.

'Legends, they're only supposed to be legends,' the boy whispered to himself. 'They can't be real, they can't.'

Sliding from his perch, he fled home to tell his rock-siblings that Wyrms once more flew in Bellanian skies.

8

An Introduction to K'Changa

'We'll set up camp here for the night,' said Jensen.

After yet another hard day of marching with the Tremen, Charlie was ready for a rest. All the amazing sights she'd seen over the past three days, the strange creatures and the entertaining company, had kept a smile firmly plastered on her face, but her feet were aching.

The Tremen busied themselves making a fire and preparing food.

'Can I help?' Charlie asked Jensen, who was clearing a space for sleeping.

'Ya just rest, lass. We've set a good pace. I reckon another day and a half will see us in Sylvaris,' he said, the constant twinkle in his eyes brighter than ever.

'Will I like it?' asked Charlie.

'Like it? Why, of course ya will! It's not called the Flower of Deepforest for nothing. But we'll be there ta look after ya, me little Hippotomi, and it'll be a pleasure ta show ya around and introduce ya ta the Jade Circle.'

'Promise?'

'Of course, so long as ya promise not ta start stompin' those feet!' snorted Jensen.

'Hhmpf!'

'Hey, boys, we got a grumpy lass in our midst!' shouted Jensen. 'Wot say we give her a little K'Changa demonstration?'

Charlie grabbed Jensen by his ear. Pulling him down to her head height, she whispered quite sternly, 'I'm not grumpy!'

'I know, sweetheart, but dis gives me an excuse ta beat Kelko and some of the boys at K'Changa. It's been a while and if I don't stay on top of them, they'll say I've lost me edge!' whispered Jensen.

'OK, but what's K'Changa – a board game?' asked Charlie.

'Ya'll see!' he said, and threw her a cheeky wink. As he walked off, Charlie could hear him talking and chuckling to himself. 'K'Changa a board game? Ha! A board game!'

Before Charlie could ask what he was talking about, Jensen, Kelko and five of the other Tremen stripped off their shoes and shirts. Walking to the centre of the clearing in just their trousers, they began to stretch and warm up. Stotch, with a blazing torch in his hand, burned a wide circle into the grass.

'Hey, Stotch, what's K'Changa?' asked Charlie.

'It's a sport, blossom. It's like dis: the boys are gonna fight over a shuttlecock, which we call a Zephyr. The one who can hold on ta it for a slow count of ten wins. Wot makes it difficult is ya can't actually *hold* the Zephyr, nor can ya drop it ta the floor. Ya have ta keep possession through striking it – knees, feet, hands, chest and head are allowed, but absolutely no holding. Anyone who grabs it gets an instant disqualification. Nor can ya leave the circle with the Zephyr – that'll get ya disqualified too.' Noticing that Charlie looked thoroughly confused, he pulled her over to the edge of the circle and they sat down. 'Here, watch and see.'

The Tremen who weren't playing also sat down. They brought out their drums and soon a wild and fiery rhythm was flying around the clearing. Stotch threw extra timber on the fire and when the flames were roaring and the drums beating, the players prepared to start the game.

'All right, then!' called out Jensen. 'Cos ya lazy lumps can't hope ta match me grace and sheer talent, I'll let whoever first wins the Zephyr keep it for a count of five before I join the game!'

Stotch, who was sitting next to Charlie, began to whisper commentary. 'Jensen's one of the best – trouble is he knows it. The boys will really hope ta take him down a peg or two!'

'A count of five?' roared Kelko. 'That's crazy talk! If ya give me a head start like that, y'know I'm gonna kick yer skinny green backside!'

'Ha! Let's see, then!' cried Jensen. 'Stotch, throw in the Zephyr!'

Stotch pulled a shuttlecock from his bag. It had been made with startlingly blue feathers and bound with golden thread. With a casual flick of his wrist, he threw it into the centre of the circle.

The Tremen burst into motion. Spinning and somersaulting, they kicked and struck at the Zephyr, keeping it aloft. Green bodies gleaming, they flashed and spun through the air. With jewellery clattering and feet stomping, they timed each movement to coincide with the rolling drumbeat.

Charlie's jaw dropped open. She didn't know what to make of it. It was like nothing she'd ever seen before. The closest thing she could compare it to was martial arts mixed with dancing and gymnastics, but all ferociously blended together by a tornado. She loved it.

Kelko, amazingly graceful considering his huge bulk, hooked the Zephyr out of the air and, with rapid taps, weaved the shuttlecock past all the other Tremen. Flipping on to his hands, he kicked it skyward, then flipped back to his feet to regain control of it with a toss of his head. Tapping the Zephyr with his knees, he spun away from the circle's edge and back into the fray.

Stotch began to count and Charlie joined in: 'One . . . Two . . . Three . . .!' Jensen was calmly standing by the side of the grassy circle. 'Four . . . Five . . .!'

With a shout, Jensen burst into the circle. Kelko saw him coming and flipped out of the way. Spinning and weaving, he anxiously tried to keep the other Tremen between himself and Jensen. It didn't slow Jensen down at all. Ducking and gliding and with the beating of the drums pushing him on, Jensen drew closer to Kelko and the shuttlecock.

Charlie was still counting: '. . . Seven . . . Eight . . . Nine . . .!'

Whipping his leg around, Jensen hooked the Zephyr from Kelko. Laughing and catcalling, Jensen cartwheeled away, the shuttlecock seeming to blur and weave around his body. Kelko howled in annoyance and leaped after the jeering Treman.

'One . . . Two . . . Three,' shouted Charlie, starting the count anew.

Inside the circle, all the Tremen were desperately chasing Jensen. The pace intensified and, as the drums began to pound even faster, the booming base of the percussion filled the firelit clearing.

Charlie could feel her blood boil as she was caught up in the excitement. Inside the circle the Tremen were frantically flinging out all their best moves and combinations. Jensen continued to taunt them and laugh at their efforts.

'Four . . . Five . . . Six . . .!'

Bellowing, Kelko clambered up an unfortunate Treman. Using the Treman's shoulders like a springboard, he flung himself across the circle, right at Jensen's back.

'Seven . . . Eight . . .!'

Kelko, stomach wobbling, arms flailing, flew through the air. Stretching out his hands, he reached for the Zephyr.

'Nine . . .!'

'Jensen's gonna lose it!' shouted Stotch.

'It's mine!' cried Kelko, his wrist flicking out to snatch at the Zephyr. 'It's mine!'

'Get 'im!' shouted another Treman.

The rest of the players launched themselves at Jensen's legs.

Laughing wickedly, Jensen flicked the shuttlecock upward and, somersaulting after it, leaped above Kelko's astonished face. The remaining Tremen slammed together in a heap and fell to the ground, groaning and cursing. Kelko flew out of the circle and landed, backside first, in the fire. Screaming and hollering, he leaped up and raced around the glade, beating at his flaming trousers.

Jensen landed cat-like with a huge grin, the Zephyr balancing on his head.

'Ten!' called out Charlie.

'Shazam!' shouted Jensen, flinging the Zephyr overhead. 'Who's the daddy?' He started to dance and jig around. 'Who's the man? Who's the best? Who's got game? Ye-hah! Ride them, pappy, ride them!' He galloped around the clearing on an imaginary horse and waved a pretend cowboy hat in the air. He cackled in delight as he passed Kelko, who was busy pouring water over his burnt backside.

'Wow, that was incredible!' said Charlie, eyes wide with excitement. 'Stotch, you've got to teach me how to do that!'

'Not me, blossom,' he said, joining in with the Tremen's applause. 'K'Changa's not me style at all! But if ya were ta ask Kelko or Jensen I'm sure they'll be glad ta teach ya.'

'Do you think they would?'

'Sure, Charlie, of course they would. Tell ya wot, why don't ya go and ask Kelko? I'm sure he would give ya a couple of lessons.'

Charlie flashed Stotch a big grin. Jumping up from her seat, she ran over to Kelko. 'Kelko, I had no idea you could move like that!'

'Ahh!' groaned Kelko in relief as he poured more water over his blackened trousers. 'Oh, me poor backside! One of these days I'm gonna beat that cheeky Treman! Boss or no boss, he's still a cheating, good for nothing . . .'

'Uh, Kelko, there's something I'd like to ask.'

'. . . smug, mischievous, low-down . . .'

'Hello, Kelko!'

'. . . squinty-eyed, tricky, bamboozling . . .'

'Kelko, please, it's important!'

'. . . shifty, nasty piece of work . . .'

'KELKO!' snapped Charlie, finally losing her patience and stamping her foot.

'Uh, oh, sorry, Charlie,' said Kelko. Sighing, he gave his backside one final rub. 'Wot can I do for ya?'

'Can you teach me K'Changa?'

Kelko blinked and, forgetting his burnt backside, eyed Charlie as though weighing her worth. 'Ya want ta learn K'Changa, eh, blossom? Hmm, let me see.'

Reaching over, he undid her messy ponytails. He then pulled out a wooden comb and gave her hair a couple of quick strokes before, with nimble hands, retying her hair into a topknot. Taking one of his wooden bracelets from his wrist, he fastened it round her newly shaped hair. He stepped back and gave her a steady appraisal.

'Teach ya K'Changa?' he said with a bright smile. 'That, me little lass, is something I can do!'

9

Troubled Thoughts

'C'mon, lass, wake up!'

'Uh?'

'Wake up, sleepy head, it's time ta do some work,' said Kelko, giving Charlie's shoulder another shake.

Charlie looked around and groaned. The sky was still dark; it was before dawn. Rubbing the sleep from her eyes and trying to pat her hair into some kind of shape, she staggered after Kelko.

'All right, then, lass, just follow me and copy me movements. Nothing too difficult ta start with, OK?'

And so Charlie's lesson began. Kelko worked her hard, showing her the basics and getting her to repeat each movement time and time again until he was satisfied. As dawn began to filter light into the forest, Charlie was exhausted, her muscles were stiff and cramping, her ligaments protesting and her back was aching beyond belief.

'Ow! Kelko, I can hardly move. Is it always going to be this hard?' moaned Charlie. Although she was good at gymnastics, she found all of this K'Changa training really difficult.

'Well, blossom, do ya wanna be good at K'Changa?'

'Of course!'

'Well, then, always remember dis: "The first step is always the hardest." Starting something new is always difficult, but with time hardships become easy. Once yer body has become accustomed ta wot K'Changa demands and once yer mind can flow, things will become easier. But till then, yup, it'll be hard!'

'But do I have to keep repeating every movement over and over?' asked Charlie. 'It's so boring!'

'Maybe, but it's the best way ta learn. Ya'll remember each movement perfectly and if ya learn it right now ya won't be making bigger mistakes later. Or, as me father used ta say ta me when I was learning, "He that corrects not small faults, will not control great ones." In other words, blossom, there's two ways ta learn K'Changa: the fast way, which is sloppy, and me way, which'll make ya great.'

Charlie looked around the forest clearing to where the other Tremen were beginning to wake, doing their early-morning chores and preparing for the coming day. She then looked down at her blistered hands. She could feel bruises running up and down her back from where Kelko had repeatedly made her tumble along the ground. Taking a large breath of forest air, which smelt of moss, pine and lily, she let out a big sigh. Kelko was right: if she wanted to be any good she would have to work hard, perhaps harder than she had ever done before.

She staggered after Kelko as he went to check on the breakfast pot. 'I really appreciate you teaching me K'Changa,' she told him, remembering her manners. 'I hope that one day I can repay your kindness.'

Kelko blinked, shocked but pleased by her respectful tone. 'Well, blossom, it was a pleasure teaching ya. Yer a good student, maybe something of a natural. Who knows, keep dis up and ya might go somewhere with it. Anyway, enough compliments . . . we've got a lot more walking ta do. I've got a sneaky feeling yer muscles are gonna be a whole lot stiffer by the end of the day! Now, let's have some of dis breakfast. All that hard work has given me a crazy appetite!'

After a good meal, they packed up camp and started walking. Kelko was right. Within a few hours Charlie's body was stiffening up again. She wished more than anything to be back home and in her own bed, preferably with a hot chocolate and a plate of cookies. But thinking of home only caused her grief. She wished she knew how her gran was. The more she thought about it, the more agitated she became. Was there any way she could have warned her gran about the Shades and Bane? Would Bane and Mr Crow really leave her alone? Would she be safe? So many questions meant so many doubts crossing through Charlie's mind. She began to falter in her step. Was she doing the right thing? Maybe the Jade Circle wouldn't tell her anything about her parents and this would all be a waste of time.

'C'mon, Charlie,' she half snarled to herself. 'Keep it together. It's too late to turn back now.'

Tidying her hair and straightening her back, she marched forward, a determined frown on her face. She would go to Sylvaris, she would speak to the Jade Circle and she would sort out her gran's welfare and her parents' whereabouts, because it was the right thing to do.

'Well, lass,' said Jensen, wandering up beside her, 'we should be at Sylvaris by noon tomorrow.'

'And the Jade Circle, will I see them tomorrow?' Charlie asked.

'I'm sure ya will, me little Hippotomi, I'm sure ya will.'

Charlie couldn't wait. As they walked along, she over-heard some of the Tremen joking and laughing about all the good times they were going to have once they returned to Sylvaris and their families. But she noticed that Jensen wasn't as relaxed.

'Jensen,' said Charlie, 'why the frown?'

'Nothing bad, me little Hippotomi. It's just that I'm wondering where our escort is. Do ya remember when I sent Stodel on ahead?'

'Yes.'

'Well, I sent him ahead as a fast runner specifically ta inform the Jade Circle that we was coming and ta send an escort. But they're still not here,' said Jensen with a scowl. 'I'd have expected them by now.'

'Escort?' asked Charlie. 'Why would we need an escort?'

'Well, mainly just as a precaution. But Bane knows yer here with yer pendant, and I wouldn't put it past him ta try something sneaky. Still, he couldn't have come through the Treman door at yer house and it would take him weeks ta get here from the Western Mountains. But ya never know – it pays ta be prepared.'

'Ha! Don't worry, blossom!' said Stotch. 'We're a long way from Stoman lands and just a day and a half's walk from Sylvaris. Bane is no threat ta us here. Don't take any heed of Jensen. He might be a worrier, but he's a cunning fox and that's wot makes him a good boss. And ta be honest I'd rather have his precautions than none. His foresight has often led our party outta trouble and right ta the profit!'

As the Tremen set up camp again a few hours later, Kelko persuaded Charlie to practise her K'Changa. Although her muscles protested to begin with, after a while they warmed up and she started to enjoy it again. She could already do basic tumbles, and soon the spinning kicks and sweeps, while still not graceful, were something that she could at least perform on demand. Kelko had been right, she was something of a natural.

Charlie smiled to herself as Kelko went off to help with the fire. Things were beginning to look up and, besides, who of her friends and schoolmates back home could claim to have seen or done half of what she was now doing? None of them would ever experience all these strange sights and smells. She wondered if Tina would ever believe a word she said again if she tried to explain Bellania to her.

'Hey, Charlie!' hollered Stotch, breaking into her thoughts. 'Can ya gimme a hand with dis food!'

'What's the matter?' teased Charlie. 'Have you run out of Moreish powder?'

'Oh no, cooking is the easy part! But it takes two ta cook dinner when Sic Boy's about. One ta cook and the other ta keep dis dog and his overgrown appetite outta the cooking pot!'

10

Uninvited Guests and
a New Arrival

With the night sky overhead, the cry of owls echoing through the trees and a stomach full of delicious food, Charlie felt at peace. Even Jensen seemed more relaxed now that they were just half a day's walk from Sylvaris.

'How about ya show me and Kelko some of yer new skills with a game of K'Changa?' he suggested, the constant twinkle in his eyes sparkling brighter than ever.

'What?' snorted Charlie. 'You've got to be joking! I can't keep up with you, at least not yet.'

'Ha! Don't worry. We'll take handicaps,' said Kelko. 'We'll each tie a hand behind our back – that should even things out.'

'A hand behind your back?' mused Charlie, rising to the challenge. 'Er . . . OK, it's a deal. You're on!'

'Stotch, the Zephyr, please, and, if ya would be so good, how's about sorting out some musical accompaniment?' asked Jensen, as both he and Kelko used their belts to tie their right arms firmly behind their backs.

The Tremen formed a loose circle round the three competitors and, with the drums beating out a pounding, rhythmic bass, Stotch threw in the Zephyr.

Even with one arm out of action, both Kelko and Jensen were impossibly nimble. Spinning and twisting, leaping and jumping, they rapidly took control of the shuttlecock. Charlie had to struggle, using all of her newfound skills, just to keep up with the other two. Soon the match came down to a fight between Jensen and Kelko, but with both players handicapped the game was more evenly matched than before.

Even though she hadn't once managed to snag the Zephyr from either of them, Charlie was nevertheless loving every second of the game. The longer they played the easier it became, and with the bass from the drums washing through her she soon began to find a rhythm of her own.

Jensen was concentrating on showing Kelko that he was still the boss and still the better player. Slapping the Zephyr high into the air, he somersaulted backwards. Landing lightly, he began to spin and weave, ducking from side to side, doing his very best to maintain possession of the shuttlecock. When a small foot lashed inches away from his nose and stole the Zephyr, he almost fell over in shock. Charlie, cackling in delight, jumped backwards, slipped between Kelko's legs, then swiftly rolled to her feet with the shuttlecock still firmly under her control. Stotch and all the non-playing Tremen roared their approval. Laughing, clapping and shouting out encouragement, they cheered on Charlie's success.

Suddenly a piercing, whistling scream echoed out from the darkness of the night. Seconds later another haunting howl whipped into the clearing. The terrible sound disorientated Charlie. Losing her rhythm, she stumbled to a halt and the Zephyr fell by her feet as the drums suddenly stopped.

'Burn me Roots, wot the jabber was that?' swore Kelko.

All the Tremen fell silent, and even the cacophony of the owls and tree frogs was suddenly missing. The whole forest was eerily quiet, except for the wind whistling through the canopy.

'C'mon, boys, wot was that?' repeated Kelko. 'I've never heard anything like it before.'

'That makes two of us,' said Stotch. 'Forty-three years in dis forest and I've never heard anything like it either. Jensen, wot d'ya think it is?'

The screaming and howling came again. Closer. Much closer. From the far side of the clearing, another guttural and bestial cry echoed them.

'I've got no idea,' said Jensen, 'and I know these woods like the back of me hand.' Reaching for his pack, he strung his hunting bow and notched an arrow.

Taking his lead, the other Tremen followed suit, and soon all those with bows had them strung and ready. Kelko, Stotch and a few of the others found lumps of firewood to use as makeshift cudgels.

Charlie licked her lips and nervously rubbed at her pendant. Something about the blood-curdling sounds cut her to the very bone. She jumped and only just managed to prevent herself from screaming when something hairy and taut with muscle rubbed along her back. Sic Boy snorted at her jittery nerves and with his massive snout gently nuzzled her shoulder. Wrapping her fingers through his black fur, Charlie took comfort in the huge dog's presence.

Again and again the shrieks ripped through the trees, draw-ing closer and closer. The chilling barks and the deep, rasping clicking noises circling the glade awoke a gut-clenching fear deep within Charlie's soul. The hairs on the back of her neck stood up and goosebumps swept down her arms.

'By me Leaf and Sap, but they don't sound friendly!' shouted Kelko over the muttered fear of the Tremen.

A cracking and rustling of tree limbs above set them all staring up anxiously at the forest canopy. Tree branches and leaves began to drop as things unseen, yet obviously gigan-tic, began to worm and twist their way through the foliage. Hooting and shrieking, squealing and howling, the terrible noises spat downward. Something reptilian briefly swept into view, flashing across the clearing, leaving twigs and leaves to fall in its wake.

'Wot was that?'

'Did ya see it?'

Again and again half-glimpsed shapes spun overhead. The buzz of wings and the occasional flash of scales were the only things to be seen in the campfire's glow.

With a thunderous shriek, a wriggling nightmare burst into the light. Rows of glinting teeth shone, both mesmer-izing and menacing. Shooting forward, the scaled beast hurtled through the group of Tremen, snapping and snarling, squirming and writhing. Its worm-like body hovered above the roaring flames of the campsite fire, then made its way towards Charlie.

'Wyrm!' cried Stotch. 'It's a Wyrm! Leaf protect us!'

Overcome with terror, Charlie stared in disbelief at the onrushing monstrosity. It truly was a nightmare vision. A horrifying cross between dragonfly and maggot, it was all teeth and hooked claws. She didn't doubt for one second what its intention was. To kill her.

The Tremen belatedly burst into motion. Roaring out their defiance, they loosed arrow after arrow at the Wyrm. Kelko, Stotch and the other Tremen armed with cudgels danced in and out of striking range, ferociously bludgeoning at its flesh.

Screaming in pain, the Wyrm hastily backed away. With a frantic buzz of its wings, it disappeared into the darkness.

'A Wyrm!' cried one of the Tremen. 'They're supposed ta be extinct!'

'I guess someone forgot ta tell Bane that!' shouted Jensen. 'Lentol, help Stotch with the wounded –'

Slamming back into the glade the Wyrm returned, shrieking out its fury. A second and a third shape burst snarling into the clearing, then a fourth and a fifth Wyrm, quickly followed by a sixth and seventh.

'Oh, Leaf save us now!' muttered Kelko.

Circling and spinning around the campsite, the Wyrms drove themselves towards a feeding frenzy. The wind from their wings sent debris, leaves and twigs spinning through the air and caused the flames from the campfire to flare up.

'Kelko!' cried Jensen. 'Get Charlie outta here! Ya gotta keep her and the pendant safe!'

'On it!' shouted Kelko, and, bundling Charlie into his arms, sprinted into the forest.

'Sic Boy!' cried Stotch. 'Go with them. Look after Charlie! Go, boy!'

The dog, muscles bunching beneath his fur, followed

Kelko and Charlie into the dark woods. The three of them covered a lot of ground, but they weren't alone for long. Wyrm cry and vicious shrieks soon followed.

'Burn me Sap, they're a determined bunch o' critters!' Kelko dropped Charlie and, with Sic Boy by his side, prepared to face the onslaught. 'Blossom,' he called out, his eyes focused on the darkness, 'looks like yer going ta have ta make dis bit on yer own. Hurry up, lass, get running!'

'Run? I'm not going to leave you!'

'Charlie, ya have ta. Ya have ta get that pendant ta the Jade Circle!'

'I don't care. I'm still not leaving you!'

Shrieks and howls echoed down from the trees above.

'Charlie, now's not the best time ta be arguing. Get going!'

'No!'

'Charlie, ye have ta! Just like yer parents, yer a Keeper and it's yer responsibility ta safeguard that pendant!'

One of the Wyrms burst down from above. Growling, Sic Boy leaped on to the creature's scaly back. Biting and clawing, he dragged the Wyrm to the ground.

'Blight me Leaf! I can't spend all day arguing, now GO! Keep heading south and ya'll bump inta Sylvaris soon enough. Good luck!'

Kelko flashed Charlie a grin, then hurried to Sic Boy's aid.

'Why me?' whispered Charlie.

Turning, she ran.

Stumbling over roots and dead branches, scrambling over half-seen obstacles and with thorns and brambles tearing at her skin, she fled deeper into the forest. Fear and dread for the Tremen's well-being hung heavy in her heart as she stumbled on.

In the distance she could hear the sound of the battle as the Wyrms renewed their attack. Tripping over a root, she fell. Rolling and tumbling down a slope, she dropped off a small cliff and with a thud landed in a moonlit clearing.

Staggering upright, a triumphant scream from behind set her running again. Glancing backwards, she saw two Wyrms wriggling out of the woods and into the clearing. Lungs burning and heart pounding, Charlie ran for her life.

All of a sudden a hulking figure, with muscular ivory skin that glowed in the pale moonlight, stepped out from the trees ahead. He raised a huge bow, nocked an arrow and aimed straight at her.

'Hello, Charlie,' he said, his voice like granite. 'I've been looking for you.'

Charlie stumbled to a halt. The arrow was pointing right at her heart.

11

The Delightful Brothers

'So tell me, were you planning on standing there all night, blocking my view,' said the ivory giant, 'or are you going to get out of my way and let me kill some Wyrms?'

'What?' asked Charlie. She wasn't sure what she'd been expecting when the giant had stepped from the shadows, but it certainly hadn't been this.

'Silly girl!' shouted a scornful new voice, its owner still hidden in the darkness among the trees. 'He means GET OUT OF THE WAY!'

The shriek of the Wyrms and the warm, disgusting odour of their foul breath on her shoulder were all the encouragement Charlie needed. Tucking herself into a ball, she rolled sideways. As she came to her feet, she saw the muscular figure draw and release his barbaric-looking bow, calmly dispatching the leading Wyrm.

'Nice shot,' said the voice in the trees. 'But what are you going to do about the other one?'

'The other one?' asked the ivory-skinned figure. 'Well, I thought I would leave it for you.'

'Oh, very generous.'

From the shadows stepped a much smaller figure. At first Charlie thought he was a Treman, but in the darkness she couldn't be sure. He reached behind his head and drew forth two swords that glinted and shone in the moonlight.

Charlie gasped in astonishment as the small figure ran forward to meet the growling, gnashing teeth of the second Wyrm. Rolling and diving, he easily eluded the beast's frenzied attack. Grabbing hold of its barbed tail, he vaulted on to its bucking and rearing back. Moving with tiger-like grace, the shadowy figure ran along the length of the Wyrm and slammed both swords into its head. He leaped clear as the huge creature crashed to the ground.

Charlie continued to stare as he retrieved his blades, wiped them clean and nonchalantly strolled into the moonlight to stand beside the ivory giant.

'Well, girlie, we didn't expect to find you here, but it certainly makes our job easier,' said the slight figure.

'Er,' said Charlie, 'who are you guys?'

'Who are we?' growled the ivory giant. 'I'm Stones and my brother here is Stix.'

'Sticks and Stones?' said Charlie. She wasn't sure if she was meant to laugh, but looking at the two characters she got the impression that they were serious.

'Yes, that's right. Also known as the Delightful Brothers,' said Stones. His voice was so deep Charlie could feel it rumble right through her stomach.

She stared at the odd couple. Stones, the first Stoman she'd ever seen, was huge. Tall, wide and muscular, his ivory skin was thick and gnarled, almost bark-like. Not a shred of hair grew on his body. His skull looked polished, like a pebble rubbed smooth by the sea. He wore nothing but a loincloth and thick sandals. A large quiver full of evil-looking barbed arrows hung from his back and a string of heavy beads rattled round his neck whenever he moved.

Stix was indeed a Treman, but he looked so unfriendly and pale, not at all like the other Tremen she was familiar with. A huge menacing scar ran across his face. Combined with all the black leather he was wearing and the twin swords strapped to his back, he was the last person you'd want to bump into in a dark alley. Or a dark forest, for that matter.

But perhaps the oddest thing about the brothers (and Charlie could see this quite clearly now that the two had stepped into the moonlight) was that they both had bright yellow eyes.

Cat's eyes.

They flashed and shone, reflecting the light so that they

seemed to twinkle and glow whenever the brothers moved. A shiver ran down Charlie's spine. She might have got out of the frying pan, but she wasn't sure she was out of the fire yet. Especially when she noticed that the Delightful Brothers were giving her a funny look, like a cat would give a mouse.

'Er, hi, guys. Pleased to make your acquaintance,' said Charlie politely. She made extra sure to give them a really big smile. 'Um, if you don't mind me asking, why were you looking for me?'

'Mother sent us to accompany you safely back to Sylvaris,' said Stix.

'And your mother is . . .?' asked Charlie.

'Lady Narcissa, honoured member of the Jade Circle,' said Stones.

'You're from the Jade Circle? Great! Oh, and, er, thanks for saving me,' said Charlie, remembering her manners. 'I really appreciate it.'

'Not a problem. All in a day's work,' said Stix. 'Now then, girlie, if you're not damaged from your little adventure, it's time to get going.'

'Oh, right, of course!' said Charlie, turning back the way she'd come.

'Not that way, girlie,' said Stix.

'Sylvaris is this way,' added Stones, pointing in the other direction with a finger the size of a rolling pin.

'Yes, but my friends are back that way,' said Charlie. 'We have to check they're OK.'

'We?' said Stix with a menacing snarl. '*We* don't have to do anything. The only thing that we have to do is get you to Sylvaris safe and sound.'

'But we can't just leave. We have to find my friends!'

'Mother said to bring you straight back and to stop for nothing,' rumbled Stones. 'And we always make a point of keeping her happy.'

'Yes, but surely she would have made allowances if she'd known that people were hurt?'

'Don't count on it,' growled Stix. 'When she wants something done, there are no allowances. Now then, you either come with us willingly or we tie you up like a little rabbit and carry you. So . . . what's it going to be?'

Charlie wasn't sure what to make of the situation. First they save her from flying predators, then they threaten her. She turned to Stix. 'Don't you care that other Tremen could be hurt and dying?' she asked in disbelief.

'Ha! We hurt and kill people for a living!' he laughed. 'So no, of course we don't care. Now stop your whingeing before we gag you.'

'I will not!' snapped Charlie, fury replacing her shock. 'Tell me, did your "mother" bother to mention to you two cold fish anything about a pendant?'

Stix and Stones looked at each other. A silent and unspoken agreement appeared to be reached between them.

'Maybe she did,' said Stix. 'What of it?'

'Well, I don't have it. When the Wyrms attacked, I left it with Jensen for safekeeping. Now, if it's as important as I think it is, I suggest we go back and check on the others.'

'You left it with someone else?' grumbled Stones, narrowing his eyes in disbelief. 'It's not like a Keeper to burden another with their responsibility.'

'Yeah, well, let's just say I'm new at this Keeper business. In fact, I'm new to all of this. I've only been in Bellania for five days, so *your* ways aren't exactly *my* ways,' said Charlie with the weight of the pendant pressing heavily around her neck. She crossed her fingers and hoped that the shape of it didn't show through her T-shirt. 'So?'

'So what, girlie?'

'So are we going to go back there or not? Or were you planning on taking all night on the off chance that another Wyrm might come along, attack the others and take the pendant while you stand around making up your mind?'

Stix and Stones shot each other a long look. Finally Stones nodded in agreement.

'Very well, then, girlie,' rasped Stix, giving Charlie an evil stare. 'It looks like we'll be having the pleasure of a midnight stroll through the famous Deepforest. But a word of advice: watch that tongue of yours. I've a strong feeling it's going to land you in a lot of trouble one of these days.'

As they walked across the glade, Stones paused by one of the fallen Wyrms. Reaching inside its mouth, he tore out one of its jagged teeth. Seeing Charlie stare at him, he bounced the glinting tooth in the palm of his hand and threw her a humourless grin.

'For my necklace. It carries all the stories of my travels and accomplishments.'

Looking more closely at the necklace, Charlie realized that what she had assumed to be beads were in fact hundreds of teeth. Grimacing, she quickly looked away.

As the three of them stepped back into the shadows of the forest, Charlie carefully and discreetly pushed the pendant even deeper into her top.

The Throne Room was cavernous. Hewn from black stone and decorated with fearsome statues, it was a forbidding and intimidating place. A dry mist that moved independently of any breeze swept across the floor, gently undulating and licking at the statues and stone columns. Whispers and hisses came from dark corners as unseen and invisible things moved and scraped about in the shadows.

Dressed in heavy black robes, Bane sat brooding on his Devouring Throne, the flickering candlelight that illuminated the room never quite managing to penetrate the hidden depths of his hood. Immaculate footmen stood quietly in rank. Men-at-arms dressed in polished red leather and armed with huge axes guarded the towering doors. Yet for all the people present, no one spoke, for none dared break Bane's moody and silent thoughts.

Presently soft footfalls could be heard, muffled by the thick crimson carpet that covered the floor. Passing the guards, a gilded and hooded messenger approached. Bowing, he advanced towards the throne.

'My lord, the warders have informed me that the Wyrms have returned to their pen.'

Stirring, Bane raised his head to stare about him. All the footmen silently bowed.

'Good,' he said in a rolling baritone that rumbled across the room like distant thunder. Standing, he strode from the room and headed towards the Wyrm pen.

12

The Passing of Friends

Charlie could hear her name being called out. The voice sounded frantic with worry.

'I'm here,' cried Charlie. 'Over here!'

'Charlie! Oh, thank me Beloved Oak, yer OK!' Kelko's voice rang out.

Striding through the undergrowth, he ran towards Charlie. As he picked her up, he gave her a big hug and the relief on his face warmed Charlie's heart.

'Are you OK?' she asked.

'We're fine. Nothing a quick drink of brew won't cure. Just a couple of scratches and scrapes. And, as for those Wyrms, Sic Boy lived up ta his name and caught one of them and the other one just flew off.' Kelko stopped abruptly as Stix and Stones swaggered into sight. 'Ah, the Delightful Brothers. I sees our escort has turned up,' he snorted. 'Late!'

'Better late than never, Fat Oak,' snarled Stix.

'I wish it was never, ya sorry excuse for a Treman!' retorted Kelko.

Stix's eyes flashed dangerously, but before anything could

happen Charlie stepped between the two of them. 'Boys, this is no time to be arguing. Let's check on the others.'

The five of them hurried back to the campsite. Charlie was relieved when Kelko and Sic Boy strode protectively on either side of her, creating a screen between her and the Delightful Brothers. She hated to admit it, but she found them very intimidating.

They heard the cries of grief long before they saw the campsite.

The glade was a shambles. Two Wyrms lay coiled, stinking and obviously dead in pools of congealing blood. Large branches and uprooted bushes lay haphazardly across the grass. Torn clothing, backpacks and trampled instruments were scattered all over the place, some still smoking and burning from where they had been knocked through the fire. Dark, horrible stains discoloured the grass. But, worst of all, the Tremen had formed a small crowd around five small figures who lay lifeless on the ground.

'Stotch!' shouted Kelko. Running over, he picked up his friend's hand and wept like a child, his cries filled with anguish and grief.

Sic Boy padded over, snuffling at his master and gently tugging at his clothes. He too began to howl and whine when Stotch failed to respond.

Charlie felt her hands tighten into fists as silent tears trickled down her face. Walking over, she crouched down and picked up Stotch's other hand and held it silently. He looked small and haggard in death; worry lines had set across his forehead and his eyes stared silently up at the forest canopy. Death had robbed him of his good cheer and sense of humour. Charlie felt a terrible wave of sadness sweep across her soul.

'Who else died?' she asked quietly, nodding to the other bodies.

'Toddit, Leold, Jipit and Bandol,' said Jensen in a tight voice. Coming over, he placed a hand on her shoulder.

Charlie bowed her head. Grief and shock was beginning to set in. 'And Bane sent these Wyrms?'

Jensen nodded, his whole body sagging with sorrow. 'Yeah, who else?' he said.

Charlie lowered her face so the others wouldn't see the tears coursing down her face. The blame for these deaths lay with her. If she hadn't been so quick to accept help from Jensen and the Tremen, they wouldn't have become involved. Clenching her fists against her side, she had to restrain the urge to lash out and hit something. Twin feelings of rage and sorrow flooded through her veins, leaving her exhausted and nauseous.

'This is my fault,' she whispered.

'Blossom, ain't no one ta blame for dis but Bane,' said Kelko.

'He's right,' added Jensen. 'Bane's the blight that has sickened our land . . . and, Sweet Sap willing, someone better do something ta heal Bellania soon.' He helped Charlie to her feet. 'Now come on, it's urgent we get get ta Sylvaris as soon as possible. The Jade Circle needs ta be warned.'

Charlie helped Kelko to bury Stotch beneath his tree-sake, a huge gold and bronze-leaved elm. The others, too, were silently buried beneath their individual family trees. Standing back, the Tremen began to sing, their voices mournfully carrying off into the dark. As Charlie watched, small saplings burst from the ground, growing from the fresh graves. When all was done and the Tremen were silent, young trees stood where their deceased friends lay, their soft leaves rustling gently in the wind.

'Leaf bless ya, me friend,' said Kelko as he and Sic Boy bade a final farewell to Stotch.

Gathering their few remaining and undamaged possessions, the Tremen made ready to leave. Jensen, however, was furious when he realized that all his Moreish powder had been ruined in the melee. It lay scattered across the clearing.

'Curse ya, Bane!' shouted Jensen, shaking his fist up at the night sky. 'Ya messed with me friends and me livelihood. If I ever get the chance, be sure I'll get even with ya!'

'Big words for a little man,' sneered Stones. 'I wonder if you'd have the guts to carry out that threat if you got the chance.'

'Little I might be, brick-head,' said Jensen, eyes suddenly flashing, 'but don't ever doubt the strength of me resolve!'

'Your resolve and strength of character *for gold*, you mean,' laughed Stones.

'Why, ya thick-skinned, walking abattoir –'

'Enough, Jensen,' growled Stix. 'Hand over the pendant and we'll be off. Mother doesn't like ta be kept waiting.'

'Pendant?' said Jensen, puzzled. 'I don't have the pendant, ya dopey idiot. Charlie has it!'

Stix turned to Charlie. 'Is this true?' he hissed, his eyes glinting dangerously. 'Have you led us on a wild-goose chase?'

'That was no wild-goose chase! I came back to check on

my friends, which you should have done anyway!' she snapped, stamping her foot to emphasize her point. 'Did you really expect me to leave them behind? If you had half a heart, you'd know what friendship means!'

'Why, you . . .' snarled Stix. The scar on his pale-green face turned a livid red.

Suddenly he found himself face to face with seven irate Tremen and an oversized dog. Kelko raised an eyebrow at the Delightful Brothers as though daring them to step closer. Somehow all the Tremen had cudgels or bows in their hands.

Stix eyed them all up. 'Hurry up and pack your bags,' he spat, taking a step back. 'Time to get back to Sylvaris and Mother.'

With a final furious look at Charlie, Stix and Stones turned and strode off down the path. Grabbing their bags, the Tremen trailed behind with Charlie in their midst.

The portcullis clanged open. Bane marched into the damp and clammy Wyrm pen. A nervous warden, fat and greasy, with food stains splattered across his uniform, waddled up to Bane's side.

'Well,' growled Bane. 'Where is she?'

'Your Highness, she isn't here,' squeaked the warden.

'What, you scuttling cockroach! What do you mean she isn't here?' said Bane, his deep and threatening voice resounding across the dank and dripping room.

The guardsmen did their best not to draw attention to themselves. Hunching their shoulders and shuffling backwards, they looked everywhere except at Bane and the terrified warden.

'Bah! Open the grate!' snapped Bane.

Stepping up to the pit, Bane stared into the depths below. The Wyrms, half hidden in the darkness, coiled and slithered uneasily beneath his gaze.

'I asked a question: where is she?'

'I-I-I don't know, my lord,' stammered the snivelling warden. 'Only two Wyrms came back.'

'ONLY TWO WYRMS CAME BACK?' roared Bane.

The huge guardsmen, thick-skinned and war-bitten soldiers that they were, flinched at Bane's ferocious shout. One of the more nervous guards dropped his sword, which landed with a sharp clang.

Bane's voice sank to a whisper. 'You mean to tell me only two of Bellania's most feared predators returned from a confrontation with a squishy little Human girl? Are you telling me a clueless, squirming brat got the better of four-teen tons of flesh and teeth?'

'Er, she is a Keeper, my lord. Maybe she had the Keeper's luck,' whined the warden.

'Well, luck is the one thing that you do not have!' roared Bane. Picking up the warden by one of his legs, he shook him like a rag doll. 'How dare you allow this to happen? You insolent piece of offal, you wriggling little toad! You prom-ised me the Wyrms were ready for any task. ANY TASK!'

With a thunderous shout, Bane threw the squealing warden into the pit. The shrieks and screams shattering out of the pit did little to lessen Bane's fury. Raising his arms to the stone ceiling, he began to sing. With his glowing hands and his terrible rage pulsating around him like a black shadow, the guards quickly lost what little nerve they had left and sprinted for the exit.

Cracks and fissures began to appear across the ceiling. Bane's furious voice carried his song spitting and snapping around the circular room. Waves of black energy rolled back and forth along the shaft, through the pit and up into the stone ceiling. With a beast-like roar, Bane pulled the roof down around him. The shaft imploded to fall rumbling and booming into the dark pit, crushing the Wyrms and burying the torn and lifeless body of the warden.

As the cloud of dust settled, Bane, the giant and furious Stoman Lord, was the only thing left standing.

13

Sylvaris and the Jade Circle

'Not much further now, blossom,' puffed Kelko. 'Sylvaris is on the other side of dis hill. Hey, Jensen, is it me or does dis hill get bigger every time we climb it?'

'Nope, it's just yer fat legs keep getting bigger, ya lazy Treman,' said Jensen. 'C'mon now, hurry up. I wanna get ta the Jade Circle before we run inta any more mischief.'

Charlie kept quiet and carried on climbing the forested hillside. The loss of Stotch still preyed on her mind. She was tired, hungry and didn't feel safe with Stix and Stones nearby. All she wanted to do was reach the Jade Circle, find her parents and get back to check on her gran. She was so intent on watching her feet and thinking about home that she walked straight over the crest of the hill and started down the other side without looking up.

'Whoa! Whoa there, lass!' hollered Jensen. 'Charlie, rest up a minute. Yer missing the sight of a lifetime!'

'What?' said Charlie. Glancing up from her weary feet, she looked back up the hill to where Jensen, Kelko and the others were quietly standing. 'Where?'

'Ha! Behind ya, lass!' snorted Jensen.

Turning, Charlie let out a gasp as she took in the view that lay spread beneath her.

Sylvaris.

The forest rolled across the contours of the land, still lush and vibrant, its colours mesmerizing and bewitching. Thrusting its way from the foliage was the Treman city. Tall spires and minarets reared above the forest canopy. Graceful bridges spanned the gaps between buildings and joined together to form floating highways that stretched high across the rustling green sea of leaves. Flowers flourished everywhere, on the bridges, down the sides of the buildings and even across the rooftops. Huge flocks of exotic birds soared on the thermals that eddied between the bridges and flying buttresses. And floating across the wind was the rhythmic sound of Treman song, rising and falling in lilting melodies. Sylvaris called to Charlie and strangely she felt like she was returning home.

'Now ya know why Sylvaris is known as the Flower of Deepforest,' said Kelko with a gentle smile. 'C'mon, lass, not much further now. The Jade Circle waits on us.'

Walking down the hill they stepped on to a pathway that weaved its way between the great trees and buildings that lined the outskirts of the city. Sic Boy bounded ahead, regaining some of the enthusiasm that he'd lost since Stotch's death.

'That's odd,' said Charlie, wrinkling her forehead in puzzlement. 'If Sylvaris is a city, where are all the people? There's hardly anyone about.'

'That's because no one lives at ground level,' said Jensen. 'The city proper is up above.'

'But how do we get up there? None of the buildings have doors in them!'

'Over here, blossom!' laughed Kelko.

The Treman led her to one of the huge tree trunks. Placing his hand against the bark, he sang softly and to Charlie's astonishment a doorway creaked open. Inside was a spiral staircase that rose through the centre of the tree. Kelko chuckled quietly at the look on Charlie's face.

'Hurry up, fatty,' growled Stix. 'We ain't got all day.'

Kelko hunched his shoulders, but didn't reply. Quick to support her friend, Charlie threw Stix a withering look but for once managed to keep her mouth shut. Stepping on to the smooth wooden steps, she followed Kelko up. The comforting smell of sap and pine accompanied them all the way to the top.

Charlie got her first view of the city proper from an intricately carved walkway that ran between the trees and the buildings. Sylvaris seemed to be a bustling metropolis.

Tremen were everywhere, singing and tending to the trees and flowers, passing this way and that, going about their daily business. Charlie was surprised to see a few Humans engaged in conversation with Stomen or walking past. The Stomen seemed comfortable wearing as little as possible, leaving their gnarled ivory-coloured skin open to the elements. Precious stones and heavy jewellery seemed to be in fashion among the giant race, jangling against their rippling muscles as they walked among the smaller Humans and much smaller Tremen. And, unlike Stones, all the Stomen that Charlie could see appeared to be capable of smiling.

As Jensen and Kelko led the way deeper into Sylvaris, saying

hello to friends and acquaintances as they went, Charlie
continued to marvel at the city and its inhabitants. Everywhere she looked bright colours and strange sights filled her
vision: Treman children running and playing games, shop-
keepers selling exotic wares, minarets and spires soaring
into the clear skies, brightly plumed birds and giant butterflies fluttering about. They even passed a crowd of wildly
cheering spectators watching a game of K'Changa that was
taking place on a cramped and narrow walkway.

'Hey, Charlie, stop daydreaming. We're here,' said Jensen,
nudging her shoulder. He pointed up to an enormous tower
sporting green flags and pennants that snapped and shook
in the brisk afternoon wind.

Walking across the lowered drawbridge, they approached
a huge doorway. Treman guards waved them through, smiling and chatting to Jensen and Kelko as they passed into
the tower. Charlie noted that the guards pointedly ignored
Stix and Stones.

She and the others were made to wait in a corridor hung
with garlands of flowers and fresh herbs, while Jensen went
in to speak to the Jade Circle. Soon they were shown into a
vast circular chamber – all except Sic Boy, who was made
to wait outside.

A large, round table of the most amazing greeny-blue
colour almost filled the room. Seated around it were a variety of Tremen, Stomen and Humans, all dressed in green
robes of state. Many wore jade jewellery woven through
their hair or draped around their necks.

All the solemn faces turned at the sound of their entrance.
Charlie felt like a bug under a microscope, as everyone

seemed to be staring solely at her. She had to struggle not to fidget beneath the weight of their combined gaze.

An old Treman lady, wrinkled and with grey hair, stood up, opening her arms in greeting. 'Charlie Keeper, Sylvaris and the Jade Circle bid ya welcome.'

Aware that all eyes were on her, Charlie stood a little straighter and did her best to be polite, but her nerves were beginning to fray. 'Er, thank you, ma'am. It's a . . . erm, pleasure to be here.' She immediately felt stupid. That wasn't the best response in the world and now everyone would think of her as a stuttering little girl. Her cheeks began to blush a deep crimson.

'This is the Keeper?' asked a scowling Human with bushy eyebrows. His thick grey beard seemed to bristle with bad temper. 'She holds the pendant? This little girl holds our lives in the balance? Pah! I say turn over the pendant immediately and let the Tower Treasury hold it for safekeeping!'

Other members of the Jade Circle nodded in agreement. Charlie was shocked when several of those seated turned and gave her a hard look. Her hand darted to her necklace. Taking a deep breath to steady her nerves, she tucked it deeper into her T-shirt and glared back.

'Nazareth, where are yer manners?' said the old lady. 'Charlie Keeper has only just arrived. We must show her all due respect. Her family has done great things for the Jade Circle and it does no harm ta be polite. We will discuss the pendant presently, but for now, Nazareth, keep a grip on yer tongue.'

'This matter is too important to wait for the others, Dridif,' grumbled Nazareth.

'That is not for ya ta decide. No matter of importance has ever been decided without a full vote,' snapped the old lady. 'Now be silent.'

Nazareth, thick eyebrows quivering in tune with his bad mood, harrumphed loudly but managed to do as he was told.

'Who's she?' asked Charlie as she leaned over to whisper in Jensen's ear. 'She's really impressive.'

'Lady Dridif, the Royal Oak and First Speaker of the Jade Circle,' whispered Jensen. 'Famous for her iron will and quick tongue!'

'Charlie Keeper,' said a soft, lilting voice.

Charlie gasped as she turned to the new speaker. She was Human, with snow-white hair and lily-coloured skin, and was the most beautiful woman Charlie had ever seen.

'Welcome to Sylvaris. Please forgive our outbursts, for now is a time of strife and hardship across our lands. Nazareth meant no harm and merely expressed concern for our safety and continued peace across Bellania. It is a feeling that many of us within the Jade Circle share, for you do indeed hold the key to our success – or perhaps our downfall.'

'Lady Narcissa . . .' said Dridif with a raised eyebrow, as if in warning.

'But as the First Speaker has so kindly informed us,' continued Lady Narcissa, as though Dridif had never spoken, 'now is not the time to raise the subject of the pendant. You must be weary after your journey, and from what I can gather your journey was not uneventful, so please accept our hospitality and for now relax. Perhaps we could reconvene tomorrow, giving you adequate time to rest? No decisions shall be made until then.'

'Lady Narcissa, it is not for ya ta be making such decisions without consultation,' said Dridif, 'but I agree. Charlie, we shall allow ya a day's rest before we decide wot ta do with yer pendant. Kelko, take Charlie ta see the First Maid. Instruct her ta lodge and take care of our guest.' Standing up, the elderly First Speaker indicated that the audience was at an end.

'Wait!' said Charlie. 'I have questions. Jensen promised me you would answer them. I want to know what happened to my parents!'

'Now is not the time,' said Dridif, an odd look crossing her face.

'Not the time?' snapped Charlie. 'Everyone keeps saying that! *Not now, Charlie. I'll tell you later, Charlie. I can't tell you, Charlie!* Well, I'm not leaving until you tell me, and you can certainly forget about the pendant! No one touches it until I know what happened to my parents.'

'Blossom –' began Kelko, but he was cut off by Lady Narcissa.

'Charlie is a Keeper and deserves to know the truth.'

'The child is weary from her travels. Perhaps now is not the time,' insisted Dridif.

'She is a Keeper,' said Nazareth, his beady eyes glaring out from beneath his thick eyebrows. 'I second Lady Narcissa on this matter. Any Keeper deserves the truth.'

'Yes, but we all know you second Lady Narcissa on most matters,' said a softly spoken Stoman. His voice sounded like a whale song, melodic and warming. Charlie thought his muscular body was at odds with his gentle and wise face.

'Nevertheless, the motion has been seconded,' Nazareth pointed out. 'Will a third finalize the matter?'

'I will!' said Jensen.

'Be quiet, Jensen!' snapped Dridif. 'Yer not a member of the Circle and ya should know better!'

'But I promised her she would know the truth!'

'Now is not the time. Be quiet or be removed from the chamber.'

'I will third the motion,' said a deep, powerful voice whose owner was hidden beneath a cowled hood and sat in the shadows. 'I understand you are trying to shield the girl, Dridif, and I applaud you for your nobility, but delaying the matter will only add to her discomfort. Please tell her.'

'Very well,' said Dridif, obviously displeased. 'The Circle has decided, Charlie. I will tell ya wot happened ta yer parents.'

14

The Truth

Bane's footsteps thundered across the room. Still furious, he stamped up on to the blood-red dais and seated himself on the Devouring Throne. His silent anger and irritation flickered around him like a pale, ghostly mist.

'Shade, come here.'

At his lord's bidding, a Shade materialized from the shadows. Flowing across the floor, it crouched by Bane's feet.

'The young Keeper is obviously headed for Sylvaris. You and your brethren will go there. Seek her out. Bring her and the pendant back to me. I do not care what condition you bring her back in, remove her limbs if you wish, just ensure she can still talk! Do. Not. Fail. Me.'

Hissing its agreement, the Shade slunk off.

'Very well, then, Charlie Keeper: the truth,' said Dridif. The chamber fell silent as everyone waited to hear what she would say. 'Seven years ago yer parents, Mya and Elias Keeper, went ta the Winged Ones ta seek their advice and ta ask for their help against Bane, the Stoman Lord. The

Winged Ones in their wisdom hastened ta provide wot aid they could. Although time prevented them from mustering all their might and force against Bane, they were able ta give yer parents a key of great power ta be used in their absence. A key that now hangs round yer neck, Charlie Keeper.'

'Wait a minute,' interrupted Charlie. 'You're going too fast for me. Who are the Winged Ones?'

'The Winged Ones,' explained Dridif, 'have governed and kept the peace within Bellania throughout the ages. They are, so ta speak, Bellania's watchguards, neutral in all aspects other than keeping the balance between the three races.'

'So why did they give my parents a key to their power? Why couldn't they act themselves?'

'Keeper!' snorted Nazareth in indignation. 'Your education is sorely lacking!'

'Yeah, so everyone keeps telling me,' muttered Charlie under her breath.

'Nazareth, please! Allow me ta finish – dis is not a matter ta be treated lightly,' scolded Dridif, her gentle face breaking into a scowl. 'I'm sure anything Charlie's parents chose not ta tell her was for her own good.' She turned back to Charlie. 'The Winged Ones have managed ta survive through the millennia, their formidable strength and intelligence leaving them unaffected by Time's passing. But, as with everything, there is a price ta pay. Every twenty-one years the Winged Ones must withdraw from the face of Bellania ta renew and regenerate themselves. They must endure a seven-year hibernation, wherein they shed their old skin and hatch anew. Dis they call the Chrysalis Period. Dis is the key ta their immense strength, but it is also their one weakness. Bane has surely timed his rise ta power for dis reason. If his plans succeed, he will have conquered all of Bellania during their absence, but, worst of all, with Bellania at his feet, Bane could quite feasibly bar the Winged Ones from ever return-ing. Without the presence of the Winged Ones and their wisdom, Bellania is doomed ta live in darkness.'

'And the key, what does it do?'

Dridif glanced at Jensen. She cleared her throat. 'No one knows,' she admitted.

'What?'

'Yer parents were the only ones ta be told its purpose.'

'So where are they, then?' demanded Charlie. 'If you know where they are, you've got to tell me!'

As an uncomfortable silence settled across the chamber, even the sour-faced Nazareth managed momentarily to stop fussing.

'Charlie, I'm truly sorry,' said Dridif. 'Bane took yer parents.'

'What do you mean he *took* my parents?'

'We aren't a hundred per cent sure of the details, but according ta our sources they were abducted on their way here – ta the Jade Circle ta help us in our hour of need. The Shades took them ta the Western Mountains.'

Dridif fell silent. A pensive expression crept across her face.

'And?' prompted Charlie.

'They became part of Bane's Tapestry.' Again, Dridif fell silent, unable to meet Charlie's questioning eyes.

'Come on! Stop doing this to me!' implored Charlie. 'I'm obviously not from around here – I didn't know about the

Winged Ones – so I'm certainly not going to know about Bane's Tapestry, am I?' She stared around the Jade Circle, as some of the councillors squirmed uncomfortably on their seats. Many refused to even look at Charlie, yet for some inexplicable reason Nazareth appeared to be quietly smiling to himself.

That was it. Charlie lost her temper. Slamming her hand down on the table, she shouted out, 'Have none of you got the guts to tell me what happened to my parents?'

There was a shocked silence, as if no one present could believe that a young girl would dare address the Jade Circle like that.

Again, it was the hooded council member who had spoken out earlier in Charlie's defence who broke the silence. His calm and collected voice resounded across the chamber. 'Young Keeper, what the First Speaker fears to tell you is that Bane, in his sick and twisted way, has created a living art form that he saves for only his most valuable enemies and his most prized conquests. He sets his captives in an embryonic amber liquid, then freezes them in postures of his pleasing. Over the years he has accumulated quite a collection of fallen foes that he displays in his Throne Room for all to see and to know just how great and terrible his power is. Neither dead nor alive, the people that form his tapestry live in a state of, how should I say . . . suspended animation I think is the correct description.'

Charlie flinched as the words sank in. The blood drained from her face, and pins and needles crept up and down her legs. With an effort she focused and did her best to compose herself.

'How long have they been there?'

Now that the worst had been said, Dridif found the strength to answer her. 'Since the start of the Chrysalis Period. So nearly seven years.'

'All that time? They've been stuck there for all that time . . . I can't believe it,' muttered Charlie. Then louder to the Jade Circle, 'What have you done to save them?'

'All that we could, Charlie, all that we could. Many have died trying ta save them, but now with Bane's forces set against all of Bellania we no longer have the power ta try. I'm truly sorry, young Keeper, but if it is of any consolation, know that they still live and there remains a chance that they may yet be freed.'

All that time, thought Charlie. After all the years of worry and loneliness, of sorrow and loss, now she knew what had become of her parents. Her mouth grew dry and her palms began to itch as slowly her sight dimmed and the room began to spin.

Her parents . . .

As Charlie slowly toppled over, Kelko and Jensen sprang forward, only just managing to catch her before she hit the floor.

15

The Willow Tower

'C'mon, lass, wake up,' said a voice that seemed far, far away. It was insistent and, to Charlie's great annoyance, just wouldn't go away. 'C'mon now, me Hippotomi, just open yer eyes for me.'

'Uuhh?' groaned Charlie. She wasn't ready to open her eyes, although she didn't know why. She just knew that if she did then she would surely remember something that she would rather not, something that hurt.

'Here, wave this beneath her nose,' said a feminine voice. 'I guarantee it'll wake her up!'

Charlie didn't understand – why couldn't everyone just leave her alone?

All of a sudden she inhaled the most offensive smell she'd ever encountered.

'Yuck!' she yelped, sitting up with a start. 'What is *that*? And . . . where am I?'

'Ha! That seems ta have done the trick!' said Dridif. Leaning over Jensen, she took the small bottle from his hands and tucked it back into her skirts. 'Hello, young Keeper. I'm Lady Dridif and yer in the Council Chamber of the Jade Circle. In Sylvaris. Do ya remember?'

As Charlie looked around, everything came rushing back to her. Her parents had been imprisoned by Bane! She wanted to scream and shout, to cry her eyes out, but she couldn't – not here. Not in front of all these strangers. Wrestling with herself, Charlie pushed back her grief, pushed it back into the dark hole within her heart. She would deal with it later.

'Are ya OK, blossom?' asked Kelko.

'Of course she's OK,' said Dridif. 'She's a Keeper. It might be hard, but I'm sure she can cope with any news, good or bad. C'mon, young lady, up on yer feet.' Dridif held out her hand.

Charlie grabbed hold and stood up. She couldn't help but blush after fainting like that. *I must look like a real wimp*, she thought, and blushed even harder.

'First Speaker,' said Jensen, 'I'm not sure the First Maid should be looking after Charlie in some cheesy guest room. It would be no problem for her ta stay the night in the Willow Tower with me and me sister. That way she'll be with friends.'

'Agreed,' said Dridif after some thought. 'But bring the young Keeper back ta the Jade Tower tomorrow by ten o'clock sharp. We must decide wot ta do about the pendant.'

'What?' snarled Nazareth in disbelief. 'You're going to let this girl out of our sight with the pendant? Are you mad? I thought it was supposed to be the one thing that could definitely defeat the Western Menace. How can you possibly let it go unsecured?'

'Nazareth, I warn ya ta treat me more courteously. Do not make me lose me temper,' said Dridif. 'I'd hate ta have

ta give ya a lesson in manners!' Something hard and dangerous flashed in her eyes. 'She'll be safe enough within Sylvaris.
Bane ain't so strong that he can send his Wyrms here without us knowing of it. The pendant can wait one more day.
Charlie Keeper, ya will return ta us tomorrow, when we will
discuss wot ta do with ya. Until then, I bid ya farewell.'

As Kelko and Jensen led Charlie from the Jade Circle,
she felt all the councillors' eyes on her back. She stood a
little straighter and resisted the urge to run from the room.
She relaxed only when the large doors swung silently shut,
sealing the Council Chamber behind her. Suddenly the pressure dropped from her shoulders. She no longer felt as
though she had to impress anyone. But, even so, now wasn't
the time to cry for her parents. Especially while there was
still a chance they could be saved. Sic Boy, sensing her inter-
nal dilemma, nuzzled up against her side and licked her
fingers.

'Thanks, boy,' she said under her breath, scratching him
behind the ears.

Jensen and Kelko turned to Charlie. Both of them gave
her encouraging smiles.

'Ya did very well in there, me little Hippotomi,' said
Jensen. 'Very well indeed.'

'We're proud of ya, blossom.' Kelko grinned, his teeth
flashing in the afternoon sun. 'Not many who meet the Jade
Circle fare as well as ya did today. More than a few strong
men and women have trembled and stuttered in their presence.'

'Methinks it's time we took ya home,' said Jensen. 'It's
been a long day and I've still got ta sort out me business

details. So, little lass, wotcha say . . . wanna come and see the Willow Tower?'

'Willow Tower?' asked Charlie.

'It's me family home. Well, ta be honest, me and me sister, Salixia, are the only ones who stay there now, but it's where the Willow family have always lived.' Turning to Kelko, he added, 'And ya, ya fat wobbly lardball, are ya coming too?'

'Watch who yer calling lardball, ya skinny bag o' bones! I'm a perfect example of Treman manliness,' smirked Kelko as he rubbed his portly stomach. 'Nah, I won't be coming with ya.' His cheerful face grew serious as more sober thoughts came to his mind. 'If yer looking after Charlie, then methinks it's best that I go and break the terrible news ta Stotch's family, then to Toddit's, Leold's, Jipit's and Bandol's,' he offered, and Jensen nodded in appreciation. 'And someone's gonna have ta look after Sic Boy now,' he added, patting the giant dog on the head. 'Methinks that person is gonna be me. Let's face it, we both think with our stomachs! So, Charlie, come here and give me a big fat hug. I'll see ya tomorrow!'

The chubby Treman walked off, trying to appear cheerful despite the weight on his shoulders of the bad news he had to deliver. Sic Boy, dangerous as ever, kept pace beside him, leaving Charlie and Jensen alone.

'All right, lass. I know ya've had a rough day, but I hope me home'll cheer ya up. C'mon, it's dis way.'

The two of them walked along the sweeping bridges of Sylvaris, past suspended fields of flowers and hanging gardens, between the great soaring minarets and spires of the city. The floating sounds of Treman song followed their footsteps.

'Here we are,' said Jensen with a note of pride in his voice. 'Me home, the Willow Tower. Wotcha think?'

Charlie blinked in astonishment. The Jade Tower had been impressive, overpowering even, but this was something else.

Jensen's tower soared into the turquoise sky, twice as high as any other she had seen. Graceful and elegant, it twisted and turned, like a piece of coral she remembered seeing from one of her few trips to the beach. Delicate stained-glass windows dotted its sides and blankets of flowers hung off curved balconies.

'Awesome!' she breathed.

'Ha! Yeah, well, I guess ya could say that. Me great-great-great-great-great-great-grandmother grew it and it's been in the Willow family ever since.'

'She grew it?'

'Yup. Word has it she was one of the great Tree Singers. It takes a real voice ta sing a tower like dis.'

'You mean she sang it into . . . Hang on, let me get this right. She built this tower by singing?'

'Yup.'

Charlie craned her neck right back to see where the tower's summit flowed outward like the petals of some huge flower. 'Wow, now that's got to be magic!'

Jensen rolled his eyes. 'Wot is it with ya Humans? Blight me Leaf! No matter how many times I try ta tell ya! It's not magic, it's tree song – it's wot we do! Tremen sing ta the trees and Stomen sing ta the stones! That's wot we do and blah, blah, blah, it's still not magic!'

'It *is* magic!' insisted Charlie.

'Hhmpf!' muttered Jensen, and crossed his arms. 'I'm telling ya, it's not magic. Besides, treesinging ain't always perfect. Look over there, just behind me tower. Ya see that? They call that the Torn Bridge.'

Charlie looked to where Jensen was pointing. She could see it straight away: it was one of the many bridges that formed part of Sylvaris's highways. Graceful and beautiful, but it was unfinished, stopping abruptly before it reached the other side of the gap it was supposed to span. A good quarter of it was clearly missing.

'What happened there?'

'Well, again that was down to me great-great-great-great-great-great-grandmother. She put so much of her song inta making dis tower that she neglected ta do a proper job on the bridge. Because all her time and energy went inta building a great home for her family, she ran outta juice when it came ta the bridge. And look wot happened! The worst thing is, no one's been able ta finish it since, so hence the name Torn Bridge.'

'What can Humans do?' asked Charlie.

'Apart from picking yer noses?'

'Ha-ha!' muttered Charlie sarcastically. 'But seriously – can Humans do anything like that?'

'Most Humans? No,' said Jensen. 'But Keepers? Maybe. But I can't tell ya wot exactly.' He raised his hand in protest. 'Now, before ya start stompin' yer foot –' Charlie's foot was just in the process of being raised for some serious stamping – 'ya should know that ya can only be told by another Keeper.'

Charlie slowly lowered her foot, but couldn't quite stop herself from scowling.

'Just like a Willow can only be taught about Moreish powder by another Willow, ya Keepers have special knowledge held within yer families. So how about I show ya around me Willow Tower!' And before Charlie could object Jensen swept her inside to show her the wonders of his family home.

Bumping into his sister, he made swift introductions. Salixia, with a soft spot for Keepers, offered to make up a bed for Charlie while Jensen gave her a tour. 'Hey, honey, there's food in the kitchen for whenever ya want it. Make yerself at home,' she said as she left them to look around.

Starting the tour, Jensen explained how generations of Willows had added their own personal touches to the building. Ancient trophies, keepsakes, fine pieces of art and exotic wonders from across Bellania lay scattered throughout the interior. There were elaborate suits of Treman armour made from polished bark that glistened and shone, Stoman stone spires that whispered when stroked and ancient tapestries woven from caterpillar silk by gifted Humans. To Charlie's delight and astonishment, a whole wall was covered with shelves containing decades' worth of glass Coke bottles. Jensen embarrassedly muttered that they were something of a family addiction and were smuggled from Earth to Bellania on a regular basis.

Charlie loved the fact that each member of the family had left their mark, making the tower a homely hotchpotch of styles. Seeing all the wonders inside, Charlie could appreciate how years of trading Moreish powder had made the Willow family rich.

The tour went on, but the unspeakable horror of her

parents' fate kept coming back to worry Charlie. Jensen finally noticed how tired his young guest was and guided her up a spiral staircase to a softly lit passageway. Pushing open an ornately carved door, he ushered her into a bedroom.

'Dis, little Hippotomi, is yers. Make yerself at home. If ya need anything while I'm out, just give Salixia a call. I shall see ya in the morning, but for now I got some important business details ta attend ta.' Jensen ruffled Charlie's messy hair and gave her a cheeky grin before heading off. 'I hope ya sleep well, Charlie Keeper. And, please, if ya've got any love for me . . . no stompin' or stampin' in me tower!'

Charlie listened to his jolly laughter float down the stairway before shutting the door. Sighing, she leaned with her back against the doorframe and put her head down.

Her parents . . .

Charlie did her best to fight the wave of bleakness that threatened to overwhelm her but it was no use. The horrendous truth of the matter was simply too powerful to deny. She and her family were in dire trouble. How was she ever going to free her parents from Bane's nightmare? And her grandma, was she really safe back home? Could Mr Crow be trusted? She felt viciously torn between responsibilities. Should she try to make her way home to look after her gran or should she stay strong and push forward to . . . well, to do whatever could possibly be done for her parents?

She could feel tears pooling beneath her eyelids. Crossing the room, she threw herself on to the welcoming plumpness of her mattress and pulled the covers over her head. Finally she allowed the tears to fall free and trickle across her cheeks.

With no one watching, she could afford to show her true feelings. Yet buried beneath the turbulent waves of emotion a slow rage and anger began to smoulder as she considered the damage that Bane and Mr Crow had done to her family.

They had a lot to answer for.

But before she could mull things over any further fatigue took over and she tumbled into a deep, deep sleep.

16

A Moonlit Chase

Night-time brought darkness to Sylvaris and Deepforest. Far beneath the city in the matted and leaf-littered undergrowth of Deepforest the soil began to tremble and gently ripple. The tremors grew in strength and ferocity. A great creaking and cracking noise thundered through the forest, frightening nocturnal creatures and scaring sleeping birds into flight. The ground began to tear and rupture. With a final groan, the surface split asunder to form a crevasse that led into the bowels of the earth.

Slowly and cautiously, the blackness within the fissure began to pulse and move as a shadow detached itself and slunk over the crevasse's rim to sniff at the air. It was soon followed by another shadow, then another . . . and another. Eventually eleven of the colourless entities crawled and slunk around, pawing at the air and scratching at the soil.

As one, the eleven Shades turned to stare up at Sylvaris far, far above them. The largest of the pack turned and addressed the others. 'She is somewhere up there. Come, we must do the master's bidding.'

The largest Shade took point and led the way as they darted between the tree trunks towards the broad base of one of Sylvaris's many towers. Gripping on to the sides with clawed talons, they swiftly climbed upward and into the city. Jumping noiselessly on to one of the sweeping bridges, the Shades paused to sniff and lick at the air, testing and tasting for the scent of the Human girl.

There it was, the scent that they wanted. Snuffling and snarling, they crept deeper into the sleeping city until at last they had the Willow Tower in their sights. Jumping the gap from bridge to tower, they slunk through an open window and silently entered the building.

The girl was so close they could almost taste her blood, almost sense the beating of her Human heart. Lashing themselves in eager anticipation, they burst up the final flight of stairs. As the bloodlust took over, they began to hiss and cackle with excitement. The girl would be theirs . . .

With a start Charlie awoke from a terrible dream. Her brow was slick with sweat and her stomach churned from the memory of it. Even now faint flashes of her grandmother trapped at home with Mr Crow, Bane and a pack of Shades fizzled across her sleep-befuddled mind.

A shadow moved beneath the door.

'Jensen, is that you? Salixia?' Then she realized that she could still hear the hiss and spine-chilling scream of the Shades from her dream. She pinched herself to make sure she wasn't still asleep. 'Ow!'

She rubbed furiously at the blotchy mark on her skin. *Well, if it hurts*, thought Charlie with a puzzled frown, *then*

I can't be dreaming. But if she could hear Shades while she was awake, then that meant . . .

The door began to rattle and bang. Shadowy black tendrils eased under the door as it started to buckle and bend, losing its shape. Finally it exploded from its hinges as fierce guttural cries filled the room. With shark-like grace, the Shades streamed into Charlie's bedroom. Howling and hissing, they swept across the floor and poured on to her bed, eager for blood.

She wasn't there.

Screaming their fury and frustration, they scrambled around the room, searching for any sign of her. They sniffed and scratched at the carpets, tore at the panelled walls and overturned wardrobes, tables, chairs and closets.

It was the flutter of curtains in the breeze that gave away the girl's escape route. Snarling, they scampered out on to the balcony, screaming in triumph when they saw their prey.

Charlie took one look at the shadowy, hungry mass that streamed towards her and, swallowing her fear, jumped. Arms outstretched, she barely reached the woodwork of the neighbouring balcony. Her fingers scrabbled for purchase and her hips slammed heavily against the railing. She gasped in relief as she secured a handhold. Ignoring the pain and the tears that leaked from her eyes, she pulled herself up and over to drop breathlessly on the other side. She then scrambled to her feet, her eyes wide in sheer horror when she saw the Shades scuttling across the wall in a lizard-like fashion.

Quickly she tried the door that led into the neighbouring tower but it was bolted from the inside. Spinning around, she hurriedly took stock of her options.

There weren't many.

'Blast, blast, blast, BLAST!' she spat.

The fetid, cold, corpse-like breath of a Shade on her shoulders told her that she had run out of time. Gulping in a huge lungful of cold night air, she took aim, bent her legs and jumped.

'Oof!'

The smooth wooden plumbing that ran down the side of the tower knocked the wind out of her, but she held tight and began to slide down the drain like a fireman on a pole. Faster and faster she descended, the windows of the tower blurring past. As she got to the bottom she closed her eyes tight and, sucking up all her courage, she kicked off and leaped away from the building.

'Ouch!'

Dusting herself off, she scrambled to her feet. In her opinion, her rough landing on to the bridge should have been a lot more graceful. She'd be sure to talk to Kelko about her K'Changa training. Maybe it had something in it that would help with falling and hopefully include some advice to prevent her from landing on her bottom.

The screech and shrieks of the pursuing Shades soon had her focused and running down the bridge.

'Help! Help me!' she hollered as loud as she could. 'Help!'

But no one appeared to hear and Charlie soon shut up. *Screaming seems to work well for people in the movies*, she thought as she raced along the roads of Sylvaris, *but not so well in real life*. Putting her head down, she concentrated on pushing her legs as fast as she could. It seemed a wiser option than just screaming like a little girl.

Unsure where to go, she headed towards the tower of the

Jade Circle. Surely there would be someone there who could help. She'd even put up with the obnoxious Delightful Brothers if it meant she was safe.

Glancing back, she caught sight of the Shades leaping from Jensen's tower and on to the bridge. They quickly gave chase and, to Charlie's horror, soon began to narrow the distance between them and her.

She really began to panic. Looking from side to side, she hunted for any means of escape.

Any. Means. Of. Escape.

Running close to the bridge's edge, she looked over the side. Nothing. Veering over to the other side, she again peered over. There! Another bridge, graceful and sleek in the pale moonlight and not too far away. Could she make the jump?

She'd have to.

Backing up a couple of paces, she dug her nails deep into her palm, then sprinted as hard as she could and leaped . . .

To her astonishment, she made it! She cleared the gap easily! Laughing with unexpected pleasure, she turned to see the Shades gathering at the other bridge's edge. They weren't able to make the jump. Hissing, spitting and snarling their fury, they hurried off to find another way over.

Charlie grinned, her teeth shining in the pale moonlight. She didn't know how she'd made such a mammoth jump, but she had! And with the head start she'd just given herself, she'd be able to make it to the tower of the Jade Circle ahead of the Shades easily.

Smirking, Charlie trotted off down the bridge, but as she crested the peak and stared down the other side of the curved bridge she almost choked.

The bridge she was standing on wasn't finished!

It came to a halt and ended a good stone's throw before it reached the streets on the other side of the gap. The Torn Bridge! She should have realized!

Gaping foolishly, Charlie turned to sprint back the other way. Maybe she could make it before the Shades caught up. Maybe! Arms pumping and legs pistoning, she practically flew back the way she'd come, but as she reached the bridge's crescent she stumbled to a halt.

She could see the Shades starting up the other end of the bridge. She was trapped! Her earlier bravado disappeared in a puff of fear. Frantically she stared around for any way out, but there was nothing.

Maybe, thought Charlie, *now would be a good time to start screaming again.*

'Help! Help! Helppppppppppp!' she cried, as loud as she could. Surely someone would hear her, surely someone would wake up. 'Help! Help! Oh! Please! Help! Someone, anyone, HELP!'

The pendant hanging around her neck suddenly began to vibrate. It grew warm, then hot, as a thick beam of light abruptly shot out from where it hung beneath her shirt and speared out into the night sky. Charlie was so shocked that she just stood there, foolishly staring at her pendant, the threat of immediate danger temporarily forgotten.

'It's never done that before . . .' she muttered in wonder.

Shrill screams and echoing shrieks snapped her attention back to the present and she sprinted for the torn and broken end of the bridge. It was her only choice.

The Shades were so very, very near.

But when she reached the end of the bridge, what then? She felt goosebumps running up and down her back – she really, really didn't want to die.

'Blast, blast, blast!' she swore through clenched teeth. The pendant had stopped its strange glow and now hung about her neck as though nothing had happened.

'Young Keeper!' cried a strong, lion-like voice from above. 'Hold on, I'm coming!'

Charlie slid to a halt and gasped as she saw a figure leap from a nearby tower to float softly towards her.

She couldn't believe her eyes. The distances were huge . . . surely no one could make such a jump. The approaching figure was covered in a dark robe that flapped behind him in the night air and for a brief second, backlit by the crescent moon, he looked like a great bird flying through the air towards her.

Lightly and almost soundlessly, the mysterious figure landed beside her. A soft hood covered his head and it crossed Charlie's mind that she had been whisked back in time to another place so that now she stood next to a medieval monk. Stranger things had happened to her recently, she had to admit.

'Stand behind me,' commanded the stranger as he turned to face back down the bridge.

The Shades came bubbling over the bridge's crescent like a black wave, their eager, bloodthirsty cries turning the air thick and sour as they shot venomously forward.

'BACK!' cried the hooded stranger, punching his hands forward in a clawing motion. A thick rippling wave of golden light gushed from his fingers to push at the Shades. 'Get you back!'

The Shades screamed and tore at the beam but it held them fast. To Charlie's unbelieving eyes, it appeared as though they were fighting a gluey, impenetrable torrent of light that simply could not be broken. Her mouth hinged open and all she could utter was a little 'Oh!'

'You foul creatures, how dare you enter Sylvaris with your rotten stink?' growled the stranger with his booming voice. 'Get you gone from here! I will not abide it! Be gone!'

Arms outstretched, he braced himself as the light trapped the Shades, holding them fast. Straining, he began to walk forward, step by step, pushing the writhing and furiously spitting creatures backwards. 'Be gone, I said!' And with a last thunderous push, he heaved them off the side of the bridge.

Charlie rushed to the edge just in time to glimpse the still-screaming Shades as they plummeted towards the Deep-forest canopy far below. She breathed a deep sigh of relief before turning to stare at the monk-like figure that stood next to her.

'Oh, my days!' she said, grabbing his arm as amazement overcame her fright. 'That was awesome! Totally and completely awesome!'

The stranger peered over the edge of the bridge, the light from his hands completely gone.

'Hey, don't I know you?' continued Charlie, now she was looking at him properly. 'Aren't you from the Jade Circle?'

'That is correct, young Keeper,' said the stranger, pushing back his hood to reveal an old, wise-looking face. 'I am indeed from the Jade Circle and I heard, or rather I *felt*, your cry for help.'

Charlie studied his Human features. His head was completely bald and his bronzed skin shone softly in the moonlight. Long, thick eyebrows hung low to merge with his huge grey beard, which swept majestically to his chest. Wooden beads had been threaded through his beard and they softly clicked and clacked together as the night wind blew across the bridge.

For all his obvious age, he looked incredibly powerful and strong. Charlie couldn't help but think of paintings she had seen in the National Gallery back home in London. The ones that showed powerful Roman generals and Greek gods, greying, aged, but still mighty and very much in control of their elements.

'You were the one who told me about my parents and Bane's Tapestry, weren't you?' Charlie said. 'In fact, you were the third to support the motion that the Jade Circle tell me the truth about my parents.'

'That is correct, young Keeper,' he said with his warm, golden voice.

'Who are you?' asked Charlie.

The stranger smiled warmly. 'My name is Azariah . . . Azariah Keeper.'

17

The Awakening

Graceful, ancient columns that stretched as far as the eye could see reared up to caress the vaulted ceiling. The walls, if there were in fact any, were hidden in the darkness.

The chamber smelt old, musky and faintly of liquorice. A layer of unmarked rock dust lined the floor, free of any footprint or mark. A slight breeze, almost unnoticeable, wafted around the huge space, gently stirring rows and rows of brightly coloured silken cocoons that hung from the ceiling.

Excluding the rhythmic swaying of the pods, all was silent and still and had remained so for a long, long time.

Until now.

A thick beam of white light burst into the columned room, invading the darkness and washing the ceiling with a warm glow. The chamber soaked up the light, taking on a golden radiance that pulsed and throbbed rhythmically, like a living heart. After a short period, the light slowly faded and, once again, the room returned to its former darkness.

One of the cocoons began to bulge. Flexing and stretching, it shook as its occupant, after almost seven years of silent sleep, awoke. A sharp talon poked its way through and began to saw at the thick membrane of the pod. Bit by bit, a tear was made, and, withdrawing its talon, the pod's inhabitant slowly began to force its way through. After a brief struggle a dark, mysterious shadow wriggled free and fell, quite clumsily, to the hard floor, where it landed with a thud and a billow of dust.

It lay there for a while, in the shadows, collecting its breath and allowing its eyes to adjust to the gloom. Then it eased itself to its feet and stretched. Really stretched. Muscles that had never before been used cracked and groaned. Shaking its lithe, powerful body, it padded across the chamber, sniffing at the air and looking up longingly at the other cocoons that lined the ceiling. All were silent and still.

Slowly it collected its thoughts.

Something had awoken it.

It remembered a voice, a needy voice. A voice that had cried out in fear. A voice that it somehow knew. A voice that tasted like the scent of family. Raising its head on its long, sinuous neck, it again stared upward at the other dormant cocoons containing its brethren, its sisters and brothers. Up there was its family.

But oddly enough it was quite sure that the frightened voice also belonged to a member of its family. And that was reason enough for it to have awoken. Family and all matters relating, it took very seriously and to heart.

The creature didn't know why it would have family outside this chamber. Or why they might need its help so urgently. All it knew was that it had to go. A strong urge was pulling it, tugging it northward to an unknown destination. Somewhere that was far, far away.

Powerful muscles bunched and tensed. With long, smooth

bounds, the creature took off. As it ran past the eerily silent columns, it realized with a sinking feeling that it would never reach this mysterious family member in time. The distance was too great. It sensed days of travel lay between the two of them and that whatever danger threatened its relative was already perilously close. But nevertheless it had to try.

For family.

The columns flashed by as it began to sprint faster and faster. Head down, tail outstretched, it streaked into a narrow tunnel. Warm, musky air filled its lungs as it bounded up the tunnel's slope. Twisting and turning, the passageway led upward, always upward.

The tunnel's darkness began to fade and ahead the mysterious creature could see a slash of night sky. With a triumphant growl, it burst out and, increasing its stride, tore along the barren mountainside. Charging forward, it headed at breakneck speed towards a sheer cliff. Ligaments stretching and muscles popping, it approached the drop and, with a last, final effort, it jumped.

The sound of the wind rushing by and the glorious sense of free-fall delighted the creature. As it plummeted, a fierce grin crept across its face. It was enjoying itself. With a sharp, snapping noise, leathery wings unfurled and sprang open, catching at the air, halting its unchecked descent. And with broad sweeps of its wings, the creature began to fly northward.

Searching for Charlie Keeper.

Hissing in pain and making half-hearted attempts to lick its wounds, the Shade dragged its broken body along Deep-forest's hidden paths.

Unlike its comrades, it had been fortunate enough to survive the long fall from Sylvaris. The forest canopy and countless branches had slowed its tumbling descent. Bouncing from tree limb to tree limb, it had miraculously survived.

But it wasn't happy. It had failed and failed miserably in its task. The master would not be happy.

Growling, muttering and gasping, it crept painfully through the undergrowth and slid, worm-like, into the dark recess of the newly created crevasse. It would take the dark paths back to the Western Mountains and there it would inform the master of all that had happened within Sylvaris. Perhaps, with luck, the master would grant it a quick release from its pain.

18

Questions and
Answers

'Oh, my days!' squawked Charlie, as a thousand questions tumbled and flickered across her mind. 'Are you part of my family? Did you know my parents? And how did you do that? That jump was amazing – I can't believe you managed it. And that light, what was that? How did it come out of your hands? Could I learn to do that? Are the Shades dead or have you just stopped them for now? How did you hear –'

'Young Keeper,' broke in Azariah, putting an abrupt end to Charlie's torrent, 'you must learn to control your mind and through that your tongue.'

'But –'

'No buts. Conserve your energy. Observe, listen and you will learn a lot faster,' intoned Azariah. 'Now then, I think that perhaps it would be wise for me to escort you back to Willow Tower. Along the way I will allow you to ask three questions.'

'Three questions!' gasped Charlie, 'Why just three? I've got so many –'

'Because I do not desire to spend the whole night answering

the questions of a young girl who should really be in bed!' interrupted Azariah. 'By asking less and studying what occurs around you, perhaps you could answer some of these questions for yourself. Now then, that was one question answered, so you have two more to ask.'

'What! But that's unfair! That wasn't a real question – at least, not one of the three that I wanted to really, really ask you.'

'Well, young Keeper,' said Azariah, 'this is exactly what I was talking about. If you engaged your mind more you would not make such foolish mistakes!'

Charlie wanted more than anything to just stand there and stamp her foot in indignant rage. Was he mad? Just three questions! And what was worse, she had the distinct impression that her saviour was smirking at her from behind his beard.

What questions to ask? What was most important to her? That light was amazing: how did he do that? And that jump, no Human could have done that. It must have been magic!

Ooh! thought Charlie. *Two questions weren't enough. No way!*

But she realized there was one burning question that had to be asked first. The others could wait.

'You said you were Azariah Keeper,' she ventured. 'Does that make you family?'

As the two of them walked side by side, Azariah stared down at her with something approaching admiration.

'So you did manage to focus your mind. Well done, young Keeper. You do your family name proud.'

He was silent for a while, but Charlie didn't press him.

She could tell he was collecting his thoughts.

Finally he answered her in that strong, strange voice of his. 'No, I am not family, or at least you and I are not tied by blood connections. We are, however, bound to one another in our duties to safe-guard the Ways and Paths of the realms of Earth and Bellania. I am aware that at your young age, and as a direct result of not knowing your parents for these last seven years, you will not have been instructed in your duties and sacraments, but nevertheless as a Keeper of the Realms these are yours to maintain and be true to. In this, our honour-bound obligation, you and I are in a sense family. And as such you can rely on me to protect you as well as I can while you are in Sylvaris. Now then, Charlie, your final question of the night.'

Charlie tried to take in all that he had said before she

asked the final question. Things just seemed to get weirder and to think that her parents had seemed so, well, *normal*. It was hard to believe that any of this was real, but when she pinched her arm it hurt so she knew she wasn't dreaming. Charlie sighed. As desperate as she was to know all the details of tonight's occurrences, there was something more important to be asked.

'Were you and my parents friends?'

'Yes, Charlie, we were. In fact, I owe my life to Mya and Elias Keeper. Without them I would not be here now,' said Azariah. 'And that is all I will say on the matter. Tonight I have answered all the questions that I care to answer.'

The two of them walked on in a bearable and oddly comfortable silence until they reached Willow Tower.

'I assume,' asked Azariah Keeper, 'that Jensen the Willow is not in, correct?'

'I don't think so,' admitted Charlie. 'His sister is home, but Jensen said he was going off earlier to sort out his business, and then I fell asleep.'

'Very well. I shall escort you inside and await his return.'

Jensen had been to visit Stotch's family and share their grief. Not stopping at Stotch's house, he had also visited the homes of the other four fallen Tremen to pay his respects. Bane's war had been hanging over Bellania for longer than he wanted to remember, but it had never come this close to him before. Charlie's arrival was proving a turning point in more ways than one.

Returning home from his weary evening, he entered the Willow Tower. Jensen paused at the foot of the spiral staircase. He would check on Charlie to make sure everything was all right before making his own way to bed. The poor girl had had a lot of shocks the past few days. Jensen grinned ruefully. She was a strong girl – like her parents – and had a good heart.

Jensen frowned as he approached Charlie's bedroom. He could hear voices coming from inside. That certainly wasn't right.

Slowly and silently, he removed one of the unlit torches that were bracketed to the wall. Hefting it above his head as a makeshift cudgel, he burst into Charlie's bedroom.

'Hi-yaaa! Take dis, ya – oh.'

'Jensen, what are you doing?' asked Charlie.

She stared at the shocked Treman, who for some reason held an unlit torch foolishly above his head. He looked like a very poor (and short) imitation of the Statue of Liberty. She turned to Azariah and shrugged her shoulders in an 'I don't know what he's doing' motion.

'I thought ya might be in trouble . . .' mumbled Jensen, looking slightly abashed as he lowered the torch. Snapping out of his embarrassment, he stared at all the things lying scattered about. 'Charlie! Ya cheeky Hippotomi, did ya make dis mess? Or was it ya, Azariah? Ya Jade Councillors don't know when ta stop, do ya? Always making a muddle and a clutter outta everything!'

'What!' squawked Charlie, suddenly realizing how things must appear to Jensen's eyes. She probably could cause such an impressive, chaotic mess if she put her mind to it, but she would never have the poor manners to do it in a friend's house! 'Of course I didn't make this mess, it was the Shades. They came looking for –'

'Shades?' barked Jensen, abruptly interrupting her. 'Shades in Sylvaris? In *me tower*? Blight me Leaf and Burn me Sap!' He turned to Azariah, who merely nodded his head in confirmation. 'Charlie, lass, are ya OK? I should never have left ya. I thought me tower was the safest place in Sylvaris. Ya weren't bitten or scratched, were ya? Tell me yer OK!'

'I'm fine, really. They never touched me.'

'Wot about that scrape on yer knee?' accused Jensen, pointing to a tear in her jeans.

'Oh, I got that when I ran away. Honestly, Jensen, you don't have to worry,' said Charlie, who was secretly quite chuffed that he was so concerned about her.

'Wait – where's Salixia? Is she OK?'

'Yes,' said Azariah. 'She's fine. I've asked her to go and notify the guards at the Jade Tower. I think more patrols will be needed now that Shades have shown themselves in the city.'

'Azariah got rid of the Shades,' said Charlie with wide eyes. 'He threw them off a bridge.'

'Threw them off a bridge, huh? Sounds like Keeper stuff if ever I heard it. Still, I know better than ta question a Keeper about their methods,' said Jensen, wrinkling his nose in unmasked curiosity. 'But, burn me Sap, Sylvaris is supposed ta be one of the last safe places in Bellania. Ta think that Bane can reach so far!'

'Enough of that, Jensen of the Willow. Such remarks can wait till tomorrow. For now I think it would be prudent to get this young Keeper off to bed. After all, she can hardly sleep in this room, at least not in this condition,' said Azariah, raising one eyebrow at the room's chaotic state.

'Of course, of course. Not ta worry. I know just the room ta put Charlie in. In fact, if I'd been thinking straight earlier tonight, I'd have put her there in the first place. Used ta be me great-great-great aunt's bedroom and it'd suit Charlie right for sure.' Jensen grinned before a sudden thought caused his brow to wrinkle. 'Yer quite sure ya got rid of the Shades, Azariah? They won't be coming back some time tonight, will they?'

'No. No, they won't,' assured Azariah. 'In fact, I seriously doubt any of them could have survived such a fall. If one did have the good fortune to survive, it would be in no fit state to threaten us. I will, however, send a squad of Treman guards down to Deepforest tomorrow to search for survivors and to remove any corpses. But for now I strongly recommend that Charlie Keeper be put to bed.'

'But I'm not tired,' insisted Charlie, hiding a huge yawn behind her hand. 'Please let me stay up for just a little longer. There's so much I want to know.'

'I thought we had already had our discussion about unnecessary questions,' said Azariah. 'In your tired state, young Keeper, you are in no fit state to be asking intelligent questions. You need sleep.'

Charlie tried to hide another huge yawn, but her companions weren't fooled. 'OK, OK. I get the message,' she sighed. She really was too tired to argue the point. 'I'll go to bed.'

'Good, I shall show myself out. Charlie Keeper, Jensen of the Willow, I bid you a goodnight.'

'Azariah?'

The councillor paused by the doorway. 'Yes, Charlie Keeper?'

'Thank you for saving me,' she said.

Azariah's beard wrinkled slightly, as though he was smiling beneath its thick embrace. Nodding his head slightly to accept her thanks, he turned and left.

'C'mon, lass, I'll show ya ta ya room,' said Jensen.

Charlie followed the Treman through a series of dark passageways. Eventually she staggered thorough a final doorway that Jensen held open for her and, without looking around or even bothering to take off her shoes, stumbled into bed. Almost immediately she fell into a deep sleep, yet a nagging doubt dragged her back to a state of alertness.

Jensen, who was still standing by the doorway, appeared to read her mind. 'Don't worry, lass. I'll keep the door open and if ya need anything just holler. I'll be sleeping right outside – there's a big comfy chair here with me name on it. Salixia should be back in a wee bit and hopefully she'll have brought some guards from the Jade Tower. And in the morning I'll see about arranging for Sic Boy ta come over and be yer guard dog. So don't worry yerself. Everything's gonna be fine.'

Charlie really did do her best to say thanks but it came out all muffled. For some reason she just couldn't lift her head from the soft, silky pillow. Before she knew it she'd plummeted into a deep, dreamless sleep.

19

Lady Dridif, the Royal Oak

'For crying out loud! You're telling us that this silly little girl has been in Sylvaris for just one day and we nearly lost the pendant to the Western Menace's Shades?' snarled Nazareth, his thick beard trembling as he thumped his fist on the jade table. 'First Speaker, how can you call this acceptable? I demand that stricter measures be taken to prevent such an occurrence from happening again!'

Several other councillors rumbled their agreement, some of them even daring to glare openly at Dridif, the Royal Oak.

'Do not be so presumptuous with ya quick tongue, Nazareth!' she shot back. 'Who here would ever have thought that Bane's hand could stretch so far, or that he would move so fast ta lay claim ta the pendant? Never before have his forces managed ta get dis close ta Sylvaris. Did ya assume or even think that he would have struck so soon? Or perhaps ya are only a mortal like the rest of us poor councillors and cannot see inta the future? Because if by some amazing chance ya do possess the ability ta look inta the future I'm sure all of us here could benefit from yer pearly wisdom!'

'Stop trying to distract us from the point, First Speaker,' sneered Nazareth, easily brushing aside Dridif's pointed sarcasms. 'Your incompetence almost lost us one of our greatest assets. And I doubt that I am the only one here who shares that viewpoint.'

Again there were more rumbles and mutters of agreement among some of the councillors.

Dridif's eyes flashed dangerously, as though daring Nazareth to continue.

Foolishly he did.

'In fact, if I were to go on, which I will, I might dare to say that your guidance and leadership of this council isn't good enough,' spat Nazareth, his beady eyes glinting with malice. 'Perhaps it is time that the Jade Circle voted for a new First Speaker?'

'Not good enough?' roared Dridif. The room suddenly dimmed and her eyes blazed like lightning. Fierce anger sent her robes flapping and writhing, and in the dim light of the Council Chamber she appeared to grow in stature. She slammed down both palms to crack like thunder on the jade table in a fit of fury. 'How dare ya judge me! Never forget ya stand before Dridif, the Royal Oak, First Speaker of the Jade Circle. I stood and fought for Sylvaris and Bellania before ya were even born, Nazareth, ya idle, scheming spider! I was fighting off armies and negotiating treaties ta preserve our way of life when ya were swaddled in nappies. Never raise yer voice at me again, ya poor-mannered excuse for a Human, or I will provide ya with a penance and punishment that will be yer curse for decades ta come!'

Charlie, who had been quietly standing with Jensen and Kelko to one side of the room, stared in awe as Dridif appeared to physically shake with raw power. The petite First Speaker now reared above the table, making all those seated around it look childlike in comparison.

'We will not discuss dis matter any further. None here could have foreseen Bane's agents appearing in Sylvaris, so there is absolutely no point in looking for a scapegoat.' Having had her say, Dridif's anger lessened slightly. 'The reason we are all here today is ta discuss how ta keep Charlie and her pendant safe. Now then, can anyone present offer a suitable solution?'

One of the councillors, a large Stoman who was almost covered from head to toe in heavy jade and turquoise jewellery that rattled and clinked whenever he moved, slowly stood up.

'Yes, Flint,' welcomed Dridif, her temper now cooled somewhat.

'The pendant, even though we do not understand its function, is obviously one of Sylvaris's most precious resources. If the Winged Ones promised us that it could destroy Bane, then it is a treasure beyond compare. Perhaps even our only chance of winning the war,' rumbled Flint. 'Our strong room and safes are famous throughout Bellania for the sole reason that no one has ever been able to rob them. Why, even the Western Menace himself would have to first conquer the city before he could even hope to gain access to the Jade vaults. I say we simply place the pendant in the strong room alongside all our other treasures.'

'But would the young Keeper be willing ta give up the

pendant for such security measures?' asked a wizened old Treman, whose skin was cracked and wrinkled with age.

'No, I would not!' boldly interrupted Charlie as she felt a flickering of rage awaken deep inside herself. Why did adults always feel they could treat children like idiots? They all talked about her like she wasn't even in the same room! 'We had this discussion yesterday – I will not part with it. It's the last and most important gift my parents ever gave to me and I'm not going to take it off, even for a minute or a second and not for all the money in the world! D'you hear me?'

'OK, OK, youngster, I get the message,' cackled the ancient Treman as he tugged at his long white goatee. He appeared to be impressed with Charlie's bravado and keen spirit. 'I was just testing the water!'

'Pah! Enough of this useless banter! How does any of this secure Sylvaris's future?' grumbled Nazareth, almost tearing out parts of his beard in sheer frustration. 'The pendant can be used to defeat Bane, yet we don't know how. If it remains around her neck we will not be able to examine it to study its mechanisms. Nor will we be able to use it. It needs to be placed under Jade Circle control for these rather obvious reasons. Just confiscate it from the brat – she might be a Keeper, but she doesn't know what to do with it. Can't you see she only keeps hold of it for sentimental reasons?'

Charlie narrowed her eyes and stared at the horrible old man. How could he be so loathsome? Her stomach began to squirm as she stared at the awful Nazareth. Clenching her fists tightly by her side, she suddenly realized that she hated the man.

'You cannot remove the pendant from the child,' said a powerful voice from within the shadows. 'It is a gift from the Winged Ones. It cannot be taken without her permission. To attempt to do so would mean breaking the law. Furthermore, it would anger both the Winged Ones and all of the Keeper families. The Jade Circle cannot afford to be so rash.'

Charlie smiled as she recognized the voice of Azariah.

'So is this what the Jade Circle has become? A weak committee of grannies and wet nurses who have to ask a child's permission before they can get their hands on the one item that will save the realm?' snapped Nazareth, thrusting his angry red and bearded face across the table. 'Stop asking for the whining girl's consent and just take the blasted thing!'

'Just you try, you big hairy chump!' hollered Charlie, the rage within her suddenly igniting. 'If I catch you trying to lay one finger on my pendant I'll bite it off!'

Nazareth's face turned an even darker shade of purple-red and the veins along the side of his forehead began to pulse. Furiously he drew up his robes, then, sliding back his chair, he began to stalk around the jade table, his eyes fixed talon-like on Charlie.

Half the councillors looked ready to join him, while some just sat stunned and white-faced. A few, however, quietly and diplomatically hid smiles behind their hands. The old Treman openly chuckled at Charlie's outburst.

'Enough!' roared Dridif, slamming her palms on the table once more. Breathing heavily, she took stock of the situation. 'Nazareth, ya should know better! Stop baiting the young girl and sit back down. And Charlie Keeper, ya better get a grip on that temper of yers or else I will throw ya outta dis room and let ya cool yer heels in a cell with mouldy bread and stale water for company! I will not have dis council turned inta a schoolyard, so all of ya . . . buck up yer ideas!'

Charlie recoiled from Dridif's angry face and took a step backwards, where to her further embarrassment she stood on Kelko's toes.

'Ouch!' he shrieked.

'Sorry!' whispered Charlie. She wished her hair would cover her face. She could feel her skin go bright red in a heady mix of anger and humiliation as every eye turned to watch her. What had she been thinking of, challenging the councillors like that?

'I think yer doing great,' whispered Jensen encouragingly from her side. 'I've never seen anyone stand up ta the Jade Circle before!'

Charlie was so shocked by his words of support that she turned to gape at her two friends. Kelko raised his hands in a thumbs-up gesture . . . Maybe she wasn't making such a fool of herself as she had first thought.

'Now then, for the last time, any useful suggestions?' snapped Dridif.

'I have a solution that I am sure will be found pleasing by all within the council,' said a lady's voice from the far end of the table.

Charlie craned her neck so that she could see who had spoken. It was Lady Narcissa, still breathtakingly beautiful, and lavishly dressed in flowing, white silk robes. The only indication that she had any association with the council was a slender Jade tiara that rested lightly on her snow-white hair. Charlie was in awe.

'Yes, Lady Narcissa,' said Dridif. 'By all means, please speak up.'

'It would be my pleasure if the young lady were to come and live with me in my Ivory Tower. My security is second only to that of the Jade Tower. My home, as you all well know, is guarded day and night by a full regiment of Alavisian Watchmen. Furthermore, my adopted sons, the Delightful Brothers, can guarantee the safety of both the Keeper and the pendant,' said Lady Narcissa as she addressed the Jade Circle with her melodic voice. 'And in regard to Charlie's day-to-day well-being and happiness, I'm sure she would enjoy living with myself and my daughter, Constantina, when she returns from the Alavisian K'Changa Championship later this week. In fact, if I were to act as her mentor and guardian I feel that I could show her a real taste of Bellanian life, which would also benefit her in the long run.'

'Hmm,' mused Dridif. 'Yer proposal does, I must admit, have some advantages over wot has previously been suggested. Does any councillor have any misgivings or opinions about dis suggestion?'

The councillors remained silent. Charlie held her breath to see what the outcome would be. She liked the idea of meeting another girl who was into K'Changa. Maybe this Constantina could teach her a thing or two.

'Who is more suitable than Lady Narcissa to ensure the child's well-being?' rumbled a dark, almost purple-skinned Stoman who sat opposite Flint. 'Lady Narcissa's great sense of charity and kindness is well known throughout Sylvaris and Deepforest. If the young Keeper has the good fortune to live with her, then she should count her blessings.'

Rumbles of agreement echoed this sentiment. It appeared that for once all the councillors could agree on something, although Charlie noticed that Azariah failed to show any enthusiasm for the proposal. But with his large monk's hood covering his face she couldn't really be too sure.

'Very well, then. It is settled,' announced Dridif with a big smile of satisfaction on her face. 'Charlie Keeper, I place ya under Lady Narcissa's guardianship. The council will reconvene in two days' time ta discuss wot is ta be done about the pendant. Until then, young Keeper, I bid ya a good day.' Dridif smiled warmly at Charlie before leaving the Council Chamber, with most of the remaining councillors following her.

Charlie stared after Dridif. She couldn't quite make up her mind about the old Treman lady, who seemed like a wise, grandmotherly woman one moment, then a hard-as-nails leader the next.

'Come, young lady, follow me and I shall show you to my tower,' said Lady Narcissa, interrupting Charlie's thoughts.

'What about Kelko and Jensen?' asked Charlie as she eyed her steadfast friends.

'Go on, lass, don't worry about us,' said Jensen. 'We'll come round and see ya dis afternoon.'

'But I thought I was staying with you!' stammered Charlie. Although she'd been aware that she was moving into Narcissa's tower, it only now dawned on her that this would mean leaving Jensen and Kelko behind.

'Yeah, I know, lass, I know,' sighed Jensen, his large ears slightly drooped. 'But the Jade Circle has decided otherwise and it's not for me ta argue. Don't worry. I'm sure dis will only be for a day or two at the most, so cheer up.'

'He's right, blossom,' muttered Kelko with a glum look. 'Dis is really for the best if it means keeping ya safe from Bane.'

Charlie felt a little crestfallen. Why was life always so unfair?

'Come now, Charlie, this way,' said Lady Narcissa before Charlie could complain.

Striding off briskly, Lady Narcissa gracefully made her way from the Council Chamber and Charlie had no choice but to follow. After a quick farewell to the two Tremen, she hurried after her new guardian.

20

Two-faced

The Shade half slid and half dragged its broken body into the Throne Room. Mewling in agony and fear, it crawled towards the Devouring Throne.

Bane, looking very much like a carved statue, sat impassive and still. Silently he watched the slow approach of his broken and injured servant. Offering no remorse or compassion, he just waited.

The Shade reached the foot of the dais and wearily hauled itself up the carved stone stairs to huddle at Bane's feet.

'Master, only I survived. All the others perished.'

'That is of no concern to me,' growled Bane. 'What of the pendant and the squishy Human maggot?'

'We failed to attain either, lord.'

'Bah!' spat Bane. 'That fleshy girl still runs free! How could you let this happen, you useless cur! Tell me what happened. Tell me all of it and leave nothing out!'

The Shade painfully pulled itself upright and despairingly began to relate to the Western Menace all that had occurred within Sylvaris. Bane sat silent and still on the throne as he listened to the Shade's account. Only when the black shadow fell silent did he say anything.

'You failed me, Shade, when I commanded you to perform a simple task,' he rumbled as he stared down at the wretched shadow lying at his feet. 'You know the penalty.'

'Aye, lord.'

Moving so fast that he practically blurred, Bane reached down and snatched up the Shade with both hands. It wriggled and flopped within his iron grasp.

'How dare you fail me?' hissed Bane, his temper rising to shroud his silhouette with a dark cloud. 'How dare you?'

And with a huge, furious roar he tore the black shadow in two and flung the still-writhing pieces of Shade to the Throne Room floor. Hissing faintly, the wriggling flaps of darkness dissolved into a puddle of black, ash-like powder.

Bane stared briefly at the miserable stains that blemished his floor before snapping his fingers. One of the many silent footmen hurried over.

'Tell me something good,' snarled the Stoman Lord. 'Tell me that the treasonous councillor from the Jade Circle has finally promised to deliver me that squishy Keeper into my hands.'

'My lord, our agent in eastern Sylvaris has just informed us that the traitor has requested the presence of a Shade to finalize details. Hopefully the deal shall be settled by this evening.'

'It had better be. Now get me my generals. I wish to know what new lands my armies have conquered. Go.' Cracking his knuckles, he watched as the footman hastened from the Throne Room.

Lady Narcissa's Ivory Tower glinted and glimmered in the midday sun. Flags and pennants fluttered in the breeze and long garlands of white lilies cascaded down from the many tiers of balconies that graced the slender tower. As they drew closer, Charlie noted that Lady Narcissa's crest, featured on all the white flags, was a black and silver heron with a rose caught firmly in its beak.

They walked across a narrow drawbridge and passed silent yet fierce-looking guards who wore strange, spiked armour. Striding beneath a thick portcullis and passing yet more guards, they entered the tower. Marble hallways and delicately painted corridors led to willowy staircases as the two travelled deeper into the building. Charlie was getting slightly nervous. Her new guardian, she noticed, had not spoken a word since leaving the Jade Tower.

Stealing a look at Lady Narcissa, Charlie was shocked to see that her beautiful pale face was spoiled by a horrible frown. Anger lines wrinkled Lady Narcissa's forehead, causing her stunning green eyes to squint and peer. But even worse, her wide mouth had puckered and shrunk into a thin line, making her seem mean and cruel. She looked like a completely different woman. What had caused such a change?

'Lady Narcissa, is everything OK?' asked Charlie with concern. Maybe her new host was ill.

'Of course everything is all right!' snapped Lady Narcissa. Without slowing her brisk stride, she threw Charlie a scathing look.

Charlie almost stumbled over her feet in shock. What had happened to the beautiful, caring Lady Narcissa? Had she done something to offend her?

'In here,' said Lady Narcissa curtly, and pointed with a perfectly manicured finger to a door near the end of the corridor.

Charlie drew back in alarm as the door they were approaching opened. Inside she could see both Stix and Stones, the Delightful Brothers. Charlie stopped. She didn't like the look of this. Not at all. Something fishy was going on.

'Why are they here?' she asked.

'How dare you question what happens in my house!' snapped Lady Narcissa, her beautiful face twisting into an angry mask. 'Did you not hear me say that my adopted sons were to be a part of your security? Now do what you are told and get in there!'

Stix and Stones came out of the room and stationed themselves on either side of the door.

'I don't care what the Jade Circle said!' shouted Charlie, her fear quickly turning to anger. 'You can't just tell – ow!'

Lady Narcissa, eyes blazing like a crazed woman, slapped Charlie furiously on the cheek.

Charlie saw stars and lost her balance. She frantically tried to regain her senses, but while her head was ringing Lady Narcissa grabbed her by the hair and forcefully dragged her into the room.

Laughing at Charlie Keeper's misfortune, Stix slammed the door shut.

21

The Isiris Bracelets

Charlie still felt woozy, so when Lady Narcissa let go of her hair she was only too happy to slump to the floor.

'Hello, Mother,' rumbled Stone's unforgettable voice, as he and Stix followed Charlie and Lady Narcissa into the room. 'I see you've brought that little minx of a Keeper with you. Do you want us to do anything with her? Perhaps cut off her feet?'

'Or tear out her nails one by one and stick them back in upside down?' suggested Stix.

'No, my beautiful, strong sons. We can do nothing too permanent to her otherwise the council will know. However, if the little brat doesn't do exactly what I instruct her to do, when I tell her to, beat her. Beat her hard but not so that it shows.'

'We can do that. In fact, we might just do that anyway,' leered Stix, and laughed as Charlie tried to regain her feet. 'It would serve the brat right for fooling us back in Deepforest.'

'Enough chatter. Put the mongrel child on that chair,' said Lady Narcissa.

She watched as Stix and Stones dragged Charlie on to the seat.

Bending over the girl, she sneered, 'Now then, young and foolish Keeper, you must learn not to be so trusting. Are you not aware that the whole of Bellania is at war, and that you and your pendant play a very large and important role in this? Well, know this, you brainless little girl: Bane, the Western Menace, is not going to be stopped, not by the Jade Council, not by the armies of Alavis and Alacorn, not by the Winged Ones, not by anyone. And definitely not by you! He's an unstoppable force and I shall use you as a stepping stone to become one of his most trusted allies. With my position on the Jade Council, and my knowledge of Sylvaris and Deepforest, it will be a deal he can't refuse.'

Charlie rubbed at her stinging cheek. It still hurt like crazy. Lady Narcissa certainly packed a mean punch. 'I think you missed your cue just then,' she said. 'Aren't all crazy, psychotic women with ugly children supposed to do an evil laugh after such a long speech?'

'Why, you little –' growled Lady Narcissa, drawing back her hand to slap Charlie's other cheek.

'Wait, Mother,' interrupted Stix. 'You don't want to be doing that.'

'And why not?'

'Because I can do it better,' he said. And so saying, with his yellow eyes glinting, Stix reached over and slapped Charlie on the other side of the face. Then, just for good measure, he viciously kicked her so that both she and the chair flew over backwards to land with a clatter on the marble floor.

Charlie lay there, breathing heavily as she spasmed uncontrollably in pain. How could this be happening? Surely someone had made a mistake along the way?

The room suddenly spun as Stones casually leaned over and righted the chair with Charlie still in it.

'Enough of your smart comebacks, girlie,' Stix growled in Charlie's ear. 'I can torture you all day and, when I do it right, it'll never leave a mark.'

'Yeah, well, glad to hear it, cos I can keep my mouth moving all day too, you mangy, flea-ridden mistake of a person.' Charlie grinned through the pain, unable to help herself. She wouldn't go down without a fight.

'Enough!' spat Lady Narcissa. 'We don't have all day for this. Besides, I have just the thing to handle this meddlesome wretch.' Reaching into a polished oak and brass-hinged chest, she pulled out two dazzling amethyst bracelets. 'Here, put these on her,' she commanded.

'Bracelets?' taunted Charlie. 'Ooh, I'm shaking in my shoes!'

'For your information, young Keeper, these are Isiris Bracelets. In days gone by Stoman bishops would use these to bind uncontrollable and disobedient slaves.'

Charlie tried to wriggle free as Stix fastened the bracelets around her wrists, but Stones, with his incredible strength, held her fast, allowing his brother to finish the job. With a click the bracelets snapped into place.

Charlie froze, waiting for something to happen. A clap of thunder or perhaps a puff of smoke, but there was nothing.

'That's it?' stuttered Charlie.

'Not quite,' smirked Lady Narcissa. Reaching back into the ornate chest, she pulled out a small velvet pouch from which a rather plain and nondescript ring tumbled into her palm. Slowly and lovingly, she pulled it on to her slim forefinger. 'Consider this the last part in the link. This ring is what makes the Isiris Bracelets work. I issue a command and you obey. Now then . . . get down on your knees and lick Stones's sandals.'

To her utter shock and complete horror, Charlie found herself sinking down to her knees. She couldn't stop herself. Her mind remained clear and free, but her body acted as though it had a will of its own.

She had no control.

None whatsoever.

Her head lowered over Stones's scabbed and calloused foot. Slowly her tongue stuck out and, to her disgust, she began to lick. She had never, ever felt so humiliated. Nothing that Mr Crow had done came close to this. The shame was so overwhelming that she would quite happily have died there and then.

'Enough, silly girl. Stand up and face me,' instructed Lady Narcissa.

Charlie's body pulled itself to its feet against her will. Cheeks blushing uncontrollably, she stared into the eyes of the woman who was supposed to be her guardian. The woman who she had admired and then trusted not just with her life, but with protecting the pendant that might one day lead her to her parents. Never had she felt a hate so complete. Never had such an anger awoken within her heart. That very instant Charlie felt something deep inside her move and change. Something in her soul sickened and died and in its place something darker was born. This was a moment that would be etched eternally into her mind. She would never forget. Never forgive.

'Had enough, have you, my little princess?' asked Lady Narcissa. 'Would you like to go home now, or perhaps go and see your good friends Jensen and Kelko? Wouldn't that be nice? Well, you can't! You and your pendant are mine! Now then, back down on your knees! This time you can lick Stix's shoes clean and when you've finished you can do mine!'

'What of the pendant, Mother?' asked Stix, talking to her over Charlie's kneeling form. 'Are you going to remove it for safekeeping?'

'What, and raise suspicion? Just think of the uproar it would cause if a member of the council should see the girl without it around her scrawny neck! Besides, she isn't going to go anywhere, say anything, or remove that pendant without my say-so.'

'How do you know that?' asked Stones.

Lady Narcissa sighed and rolled her eyes. Some days she just couldn't believe how stupid her adopted sons could be. 'Because of the Isiris Bracelets! Watch. Maybe you'll learn something.' She turned to Charlie. 'Charlie Keeper, look at me. You will not leave this tower without my or one of my sons' permission. Neither will you remove the pendant unless I tell you to and you will not remove or attempt to tell anyone about the Isiris Bracelets.'

Charlie didn't feel anything, nor did she feel any different, but she knew that Lady Narcissa had just effectively ended any chance of escape.

'And now, Charlie Keeper, I find myself sickened by the very sight of you. I think that I should find something suitable for you to do while I finalize all those essential, nitty-gritty little details required to commit *treason*.'

'Send her down to the Alavisan Watchmen. I'm sure they could put her to work,' chuckled Stones.

'Hmm, I'm sure they would, but I would like something a bit more . . . degrading for her.'

'The sewers need a decent service. Put her to work mucking the plumbing out,' suggested Stix.

'Better. I like the idea, but I'm sure neither of you wants to volunteer to check she's done the work afterwards. No, I think she should be sent down to the Spinnery. She can work the looms and the threads. It's a gruelling task and I know Aranea takes pleasure in working her staff into the ground,' said Lady Narcissa. 'Charlie, you delightful little girl, many thanks for cleaning my shoes. You've done a wonderful job. Now then, I would like very much for you to go downstairs and introduce yourself to Aranea, Mistress of the Spinnery. You are to work for her and only when the late shift finishes and the last loom falls silent may you return here to sleep. Now smile, thank me and go.'

Charlie's face creased into a beautiful smile, she just couldn't stop it. 'Thank you, Lady Narcissa.' Without being able to help herself, Charlie turned and walked towards the door.

'Oh! And, Charlie, please tell Aranea that I consider you to be a troublemaker and that she should be sure to work you hard. Very hard.'

Charlie gritted her teeth. Her body may have been under the control of the traitorous councillor but her mind was not. As she walked back down the corridor the sound of the Delightful Brothers' laughter fuelled and fanned the hate that grew like a black lump within her heart.

22

The Spinnery

'What do you want?' asked the seamstress.

Charlie stared at the woman. There was no hint of a smile on the woman's face. Indeed, there was no hint that she had ever smiled in her life. Her face was all cold angles and sharp lines. And although her bright red dress was beautifully made, its high collar, tight seams and spiky buttons only added to the unfriendly appearance.

'Well, don't stand there gawking,' said the seamstress. 'I don't have all day.'

'My name's Charlie Keeper and I've been sent to speak to Aranea,' Charlie said, jutting out her chin defiantly.

'The Spinnery is no place for girls,' frowned the woman. 'Be off with you. Shoo! Come back when we're not so busy.'

'But Lady Narcissa sent me.'

The seamstress paused at mention of Narcissa's name. She looked Charlie up and down and her mouth twitched from side to side. 'Come with me,' she said curtly. Pushing open the large door she led the way into the Spinnery.

Charlie blinked in astonishment. The long room was filled with the clack-clack-clack of looms and the snick-snickerty-snicker of spindles, giving it an atmosphere of organized chaos.

'Well, don't just stand there with your mouth open! Come on!' snapped the seamstress.

They walked past great rows of brightly coloured fabrics and long lines of workers sorting through bundles of unrefined cotton until at last they reached a quieter section of the Spinnery. Here there was only one loom, which was larger and more intricate than the others they had passed. An old, severe-looking Human woman sat at its side. Her hands moved over the loom in a series of precise but unusual jerking movements. But the finished cloth that dropped from the loom into the catching basket was startlingly beautiful. It seemed to glimmer and shimmer in the light. This woman was obviously a master of her craft.

'Mistress?' enquired the seamstress by way of announcement.

'What is it?' asked the woman.

'It's this girl, Mistress. Lady Narcissa sent her.'

The old woman stopped working and turned to fix Charlie with cold eyes. 'And who might you be?'

'I'm Charlie Keeper. Are you Aranea?'

'That I am. I'm the Mistress of the Spinnery. Why did the lady of the house send you here?' she demanded.

Charlie tried really hard to clamp her mouth shut, to turn and run from the Spinnery as fast as she could, but the Isiris Bracelets were overpowering. 'Lady Narcissa says that I am to work for you. And could you please work me hard because she considers me to be a troublemaker?'

'A troublemaker, eh? Well, we'll have to see about that!' She pointed a finger at Charlie. 'Just you remember, little girl, that although this might be Lady Narcissa's tower, this is my Spinnery. If there's to be any trouble here I'll be the one to cause it. Anger me just the once and I'll show you what "trouble" really is.' Aranea paused as she took in Charlie's clothes. Torn and as dishevelled as they were, it was obvious that her jeans and T-shirt weren't made locally. 'What fabric is this?'

'Huh? Oh, uh, denim and I think the top is maybe . . . polyester?'

'Denim? Polly-Heather? Where are you from?'

'London.' Seeing their blank faces, Charlie added, 'You know, from the Other Realm?'

She heard the seamstress beside her gasp in surprise.

'The Other Realm, you say?' said Aranea. Leaning forward, she plucked at Charlie's clothing with her scuttling, spider-like hands. Charlie tried not to shiver. 'Your clothes, I want to study their weave. Give them to me.'

'What?' said Charlie, instinctively taking a step backwards. 'No! You can't just take the clothes off my back!'

'Silly girl! I'll give you a set of clothes far finer than these in exchange. Now get undressed.'

Charlie was actually quite tempted by the offer. After her recent adventures in Bellania her clothes were certainly the worse for wear, but something inside her rebelled. She hated being told what to do. Hated that she was here against her will. And she hated the feel of Aranea's greedy fingers on her jeans. But above all she was fed up with everyone in this cruel tower.

'No. I said no and I mean it.'

'Don't be cheeky with me, girl!' snapped Aranea. 'I could have them taken off you and force you to work in a coal sack.'

'You could,' said Charlie, taking a gamble, 'but Narcissa needs me to look presentable for my meetings with the Jade Circle.'

Aranea begrudgingly took her fingers off Charlie's jeans.

'Very well, young girl, if you want to play it like that so be it. Now tell me, what can you do? What do you know of the weave, the warp and the weft?'

'The weave? Warp? Uh, nothing.'

'Nothing? Well, what about shedding, picking and batting?'

'I-I . . . er, well, nothing,' Charlie admitted. 'I've never been inside a Spinnery before today.'

'What? Useless, absolutely useless.' The old woman sighed. 'I've no idea why Lady Narcissa would send such a whelp of a girl down here in the first place, and then one who's never worked the weave before. Well, if you're a troublemaker I know just where to put you. Melita! Melita!' Aranea called out in a sharp voice.

A large but gentle-looking Stoman woman approached. 'Yes, Mistress?'

'You're to take this girl with you to the vats, where she can dye the threads. She's not from our Realm and we're behind schedule as it is, so feel free to work her fingers to the bone.'

Melita curtsied. 'Yes, Mistress.'

Aranea turned to Charlie. 'Working in the vats is grunt work. Something that even a novice can't get wrong. But if you cross me or cause any mischief, then I'll have your hide. Understood?'

Charlie nodded.

'Good. Now be gone.'

Once they turned a corner Melita smiled nervously at Charlie. 'I'm guessing that you must have upset someone upstairs to be sent down here to work in the vats. But don't worry, not everyone is as mean as Aranea.'

Charlie returned Melita's smile, glad to find someone in this tower who was actually nice.

'We're in here,' said Melita. She ducked through a side door into a dimly lit and very, very smelly room.

Charlie looked around in fascination. The room was filled with silk threads and cotton fibres that had been laid to dry on racks that stretched from floor to ceiling. Against the far wall was a row of bubbling vats filled with brightly coloured dyes.

'This is the dyeing and drying room,' explained Melita. 'It's our job to take the plain threads, dye them the right colours and then hang them to dry on these racks. It's a simple job but tough. You'll feel it in your lower back and shoulders by the end of the day.'

'But what's that awful smell?' asked Charlie.

'That's the dyes. The blues and oranges are the worst.'

'Really? What goes into them to make them stink so bad?'

'Oh, it depends on the colour. Look.' Melita pointed to a series of shelves that were filled with glass containers and wooden caskets. 'All the ingredients for the dyes are here. The sea snails and Tygris weed are used for the purple. It's the Tygris weed that really stinks. And these Hyron stones are crushed and the dust is used in the scarlet dye. They don't smell now but when you crush them up the stink is outrageous.'

'What's this?' asked Charlie. She pointed at a sealed glass jar that contained a murky brown liquid. The jar had warning signs on it.

'Oh, that's the Firehaven Sourlax. We use it in the orange and yellow dyes, but it doesn't smell bad. In fact, it smells kind of good, like citrus and strawberries.'

'So why does it have warning signs on it?'

'Well, it's not poisonous, but it's from the Firehaven plant.'

Charlie looked blank. Clearly she was supposed to know what that meant.

Melita suddenly remembered. 'Oh, sorry, I forgot you're not from Bellania. It's a strong sedative,' she explained. 'Get it on your skin or breathe in its fumes and you'll be asleep for two days.'

'What?' exclaimed Charlie, taking a step back. 'Well, I'm not touching the orange or yellow dyes, then!'

Melita laughed. 'Don't worry. When it mixes with the other ingredients the toxin is neutralized.' She rolled up her sleeves and headed towards the stinking, bubbling vats of dye. 'Come on, enough of the grand tour. I think it's time we got to work before Aranea finds something else to moan about.'

Charlie nodded and, shaking the Isiris Bracelets in frustration, followed after her.

23

An Agreement

The evening light was fading and Sylvaris was beginning to slow as the night drew in. The markets were packing up after a busy day's trading and the bridges and walkways, so full of people earlier, were beginning to become quieter. The shadows lengthened and stars twinkled overhead.

One of the shadows detached itself and began to sneak from wall to wall and corner to corner. The Shade easily evaded the inefficient city guards and, slinking over a final bridge, headed towards Narcissa's tower. But the Alavisian Watchmen that stood on the drawbridge were a far cry from the lazy city guards. They were always alert, always ready to confront trespassers and always ready for a fight.

Yet they did nothing as the Shade approached. They had firm orders to let it pass, so they looked away as it slithered between their ranks. The Shade headed into the tower and squeezed beneath a closed door into a dimly lit room.

'Welcome,' said Lady Narcissa. She was seated in a chair with Stix and Stones standing by her side. 'Are you ready to talk business?'

'Of course.' The Shade paused as it looked around the room. 'Where is the Keeper child?'

'The girl . . . is somewhere safe, as is the pendant. You need not worry about that. What should concern you is the price that the Western Menace is prepared to pay for her hide. So come, just how greatly does Bane desire what I have to offer?'

The Shade hissed. 'You are speaking bluntly. Very well, so shall I. My master has instructed me to offer you a thousand bars of gold, a hundred baskets of rubies, the deeds to the Eron Diamond Mines and the pick of a hundred of the freshest slaves from his cattle pens. Finally he offers to make you one of his land barons and grants you a third of all Deepforest once he has conquered Sylvaris. Is this suitable?'

Lady Narcissa could barely hide her grin. Greed glinted in her eyes and she couldn't quite prevent her hands from gleefully rubbing together. 'Oh yes, I think that is a most satisfactory offer.'

'Excellent. Now, hand over the child.'

'What? Do you think I'm stupid? First your master must show me some sort of gesture of good faith. I will not simply hand over Charlie Keeper and her pendant without something to show for it!'

'Yes, I was told you would say something like this. Would the rubies and the gold suffice?'

'Hmmm. Yes, I believe that would do nicely. But tell me, Shade, how do you plan to bring me all of that into Sylvaris without being detected?'

'That is not your concern but ours. Have the girl and the pendant ready by midnight tomorrow and I will arrange for the gold and jewels to be delivered,' hissed the Shade.

Lady Narcissa nodded her agreement and silently the shadowy messenger slunk back the way it came.

Charlie groaned and knuckled her back. The work was as gruelling as Melita has warned. Stirring great tubs of stinky dye and being forced to carry large loads of thread were not Charlie's idea of a good time. And to make matters worse Aranea would stick her head in every so often to harass and threaten her. If it hadn't have been for Melita's kind words and the drinks and snacks that she had thoughtfully sneaked past Aranea's back, Charlie wasn't sure how she would have coped.

But Charlie hadn't just been toiling away. She'd also been thinking of ways to get out of her unfortunate predicament. At one point she had tried to tell Melita about the Isiris Bracelets, but her tongue wouldn't budge, and when she had attempted to be cunning and write it down, her hand had refused to hold a pen. She had even tried to sneak out of the Spinnery while Aranea disappeared for a tea break, but when she reached the door her feet had seized up and she could only move when she inched her way back towards the vats. She was furious, but still determined to find a way to beat the bracelets.

Sighing, she wiped the worst of the indigo dye off her forearms before it could stain her skin. She wrinkled her nose in disgust. Not only was it slimy to the touch but it stank like dead fish too.

'Stop daydreaming and do some work or you'll feel the

bite of my cane on your backside!' snapped Aranea, who had silently tiptoed in to check on Charlie's progress.

It was more than Charlie could bear. If she couldn't give Lady Narcissa a piece of her mind, then at least she could give this spiteful old woman a good talking-to. She opened her mouth, then shut it in surprise when she saw Stones standing by the door.

'Stones,' said Aranea when she realized she had company. 'What can I do for you?'

'Is she giving you trouble?' he rumbled.

'Nothing a beating cannot fix,' said Aranea, hefting her cane.

'Well, I've no doubt she deserves it but it will have to wait. I have a task for her.'

'As you wish.'

'Good. But she needs to be presentable. Girlie, go scrub your arms clean. Aranea, is there anything you can do to disguise the smell? She stinks.'

'Well, that's vat work for you.' Aranea shrugged. 'A good wash with some lemon juice will remove the worst of it, and if you want we can scent her with some of the fragrance we use on the silks. I don't think there's anything I can do for her hair, though. I've never seen anything so tangled before.'

Stones waved his hand. 'Forget the hair but get her smelling clean. I want her outside the Spinnery in five minutes.'

Aranea pulled her mean lips together at the short deadline but nodded in agreement. Melita stared at Charlie, clearly intrigued by the presence of Stones in the Spinnery. Charlie gave her a weak smile. To her his arrival could mean only one thing: her day was going to go from bad to worse.

24

Betrayal on
the Bridge

The winged creature hastened through the skies, stopping only when it really had to. The strong need to find its sibling hadn't decreased over time or distance. Indeed, if anything the closer the creature got to its destination the greater the urge had become. It could feel that its sibling was still in danger.

Pinning its ears closer to its head for greater speed, it bunched its powerful shoulders forward and, with great sweeps of its broad wings, began to hurtle through the sky.

Dipping its wings it banked sharply and flew into a thermal. Slowly but steadily it rose higher and higher as the warm winds aided its ascent. The thermal, spiralling around and around like a great corkscrew, did its work and lifted the streamlined muscular creature to greater heights. The air slowly thinned and the ground dwindled into the distance. Cattle became specks of dirt, the few houses in sight were reduced to dots and the roaring, tumbling river shrank to become a blue, meandering ribbon.

With an inbuilt awareness the creature realized it was high enough. Tilting its wings and arching its long neck, it left the thermal and began to glide through the air. With slow, steady, thrumming wing-beats, it started the last stage of its journey.

As it began to fly over the beginnings of the golden-green canopy of Deepforest, the creature felt a warm sense of excitement. Sylvaris was close by.

Stones met Charlie outside the Spinnery door.

'Better, much better.' He nodded at the sight of her. 'And at least you no longer smell like something washed up on the beach.' Opening his clenched hand, he showed Charlie what lay in his palm: the ring that went with the Isiris Bracelets. Charlie groaned at the sight.

'Listen up. Both your bumbling friends, Jensen and Kelko, are being difficult. This is the third time today that they have come calling for you. First we told them that you were busy settling in and they left. The second time we said that you were jewellery shopping with Mother's daughter, Constantina, which should provide a suitable explanation if they ask about the Isiris Bracelets. But this time they refuse to leave without speaking to you. They've had the cheek to sit themselves down right in the middle of the drawbridge and they say they won't budge until they see your face. Mother isn't pleased and I can't bear to see her unhappy, so it's time to do something about those two ridiculous idiots.'

Charlie felt a flush of elation. Loyal Jensen and Kelko had come to check on her! Maybe this was her way out. Maybe . . .

'Forget it, girlie,' smirked Stones, as he read the emotions on her face. 'You won't be going free, not today, or at least not while I hold this ring. Now come with me and do as I tell you.'

At his command, Charlie's unwilling feet walked up the long flight of stairs, matching Stones's massive stride. The two of them marched towards the tower's entrance and out on to the drawbridge. As they approached, Charlie was delighted to see that Kelko and Jensen had brought along Sic Boy, presumably as insurance against any heavy-handed action from the Alavisian Watchmen. The enormous dog sat at their side lazily licking his chops and gazing with mild interest at the moths that fluttered in the night sky. Next to him, the two Tremen were engrossed in what sounded like a heated card game.

'Oi! Ya big blubbering ball of lard, stop cheating!' shouted Jensen. 'Don't think I didn't sees ya try and slip that ace inta the pack.'

'Wot? Wot ace?' said Kelko, feigning innocence. 'Wot are ya going on about?'

'Wot ace?' cried Jensen, mimicking Kelko. 'Dis ace! And here, hang on a minute, wot's dis, then?' Jensen leaned over and swiped at Kelko's lap. A spare, sneakily hidden pack of cards tumbled across the drawbridge. 'Call yerself a legitimate card player, do ya?'

Charlie almost burst out laughing when Sic Boy, bored with watching Kelko and Jensen, eased himself over to the side of the bridge and relieved himself right on the leg of one of the uptight Watchmen.

Stones's thick hand cuffed her around the back of the head.

'Pay attention! I didn't bring you here for your entertainment. I need to get rid of those fools,' he snarled. He taunted her again by waving the ring in front of her face. 'Go over there and tell your friends that you no longer want to see them and that they are wasting everyone's time by being here. If they protest too much, you are to tell them that they are beneath your new social standing. As a Keeper and a new friend of my mother, you feel that you should associate with a better class of people. And do not under any circumstances tell them that we are keeping you here against your will, or even hint at what the Isiris Bracelets are.'

Charlie felt like she'd been smacked in the face. Any thoughts of escape or plans for alerting her two friends to her predicament withered and died. She was being forced to effectively destroy her relationship with the two Tremen, and not just that, she was being instructed to spitefully insult them too!

Stones leaned down so that his grinning face was mere inches away from hers and his yellow eyes shone with nasty mirth. He was enjoying this. 'Now go and do as you are told and make it convincing!'

Already feeling guilty, Charlie walked across the drawbridge. Kelko and Jensen looked up from their cards with bright smiles on their faces.

'Ho, ho, it's me little Hippotomi!' said Jensen, jumping up to greet her.

'Finally!' exclaimed Kelko. 'Blossom, how ya doing?'

Charlie's heart began to beat faster. She didn't want to do this. Little beads of sweat began to form down the back of her neck as she did her best to fight the influence of the Isiris Bracelets.

'Lass, are ya OK?' asked Jensen. 'Ya look like ya've seen a ghost.'

Charlie wanted to scream, to cry aloud, to shout up at the very heavens, anything but this. But the cruel jewellery around her wrists forced her to open her mouth.

'Kelko . . . Jensen . . . I think the time has come for me to be honest. I don't want to see you guys any more, as I find it a waste of my time having to listen to your loathsome, dribbling conversation. In fact, it's not just my time you're wasting by being here but Lady Narcissa's and her wonderful family's. Why, even these poor Watchmen have to take extra guard duty just to make sure you don't do anything foolish in your attempts to see me. I think it would be best if you were to go.'

'Wot?' said Kelko, a look of vivid disbelief shooting across his face. 'How can ya say that, blossom? We're yer mates. We've just come ta make sure yer OK.'

'He's right, Charlie. We're just here ta make sure everything's OK and that ya've settled in fine,' said Jensen, who was giving her a funny look, as though he thought this was all just some kind of practical joke.

Charlie, to her horror, felt her face creasing into a thick sneer and her voice sounded cruel even to her ears. 'Just who do you think you guys are? Here I am staying with Lady Narcissa, learning new things about Sylvaris, and you want to come and spoil it. As a Keeper I need to start associating with a better class of people than riff-raff like you two.'

Kelko and Jensen froze with shocked looks of betrayal

etched on their faces. Even one of the Alavisian Watchmen broke attention for a brief second to turn and stare at her.

'Ha! Charlie, lass, ya certainly know how ta tell a good joke! Ya almost got me believing ya mean it!' chuckled Kelko, but Charlie could see the uncertainty and fear in his eyes. He stared anxiously back at her and licked his lips nervously.

Charlie had never felt so heartbroken, but the Isiris Bracelets hadn't finished with her yet.

'I mean it, you fat fool! Leave me be! You're embarrassing to be seen with. How on earth can you think anyone would want to be seen in your company?'

'But, but . . . ya can't mean that!' stuttered Kelko. His lips quivered and he looked as though he might cry. 'Charlie, I thought we were friends!'

'I can't believe ya would say such a thing!' cried Jensen. 'Ya can't just turn yer back on us, not after all we've been through. Tell me ya don't mean it!'

'Bah! I knew you guys were stupid but I would've thought that you'd have got the message by now! I don't want to see you two again, I don't want to hear from you and I certainly don't want to associate with you! Right, I think I've already wasted enough time talking to you two. Now scab off home before I set the Watchmen on you!' snapped Charlie, then, turning her back on her friends, she strode into the ivory tower.

25

A Night to Forget

Devastation swept across Charlie's soul. She couldn't believe what she'd just done. She'd never felt so guilty or so repulsed by herself in all her thirteen years of life. Now that she had done the job and seeing that her back was to her friends, the Isiris Bracelets allowed her true emotions to show. Glistening tears began to slowly trickle down her cheeks.

'Ha, that wasn't so hard now, was it?' chuckled Stones obscenely. He leaned against the wall and casually flicked the ring from hand to hand.

Charlie wanted to hit the muscled giant. She wanted nothing more than to wipe the smile off his smug, smirking face. A sudden thought popped into her mind: Lady Narcissa had foolishly forgotten to forbid her one essential thing when she'd issued the commands with the Isiris Bracelets. She'd never mentioned anything about retaliation.

Grinning through her tears, Charlie slowly yet firmly folded her small hand into a fist. Stepping smartly forward, she punched Stones as hard as she could in the stomach. He staggered backwards, more from shock than anything else. Charlie's knuckles felt like they'd just hit a brick wall, but she didn't care about the pain. It felt good to strike back at one of her tormentors.

'Why, you . . .' snarled Stones disbelievingly. His meaty hand shot out and grabbed her by the scruff of her neck. He yanked her off her feet and held her aloft. Charlie's legs dangled helplessly beneath her, but she was too angry to notice.

'Look who's laughing now!' crowed Charlie. She rubbed cheerfully at her knuckles and carelessly thrust her face closer to Stones. 'Want another?'

Stones growled so low and menacingly that Charlie felt her teeth vibrate in her gums. Raising a massive, bludgeoning fist, he drew it back.

'Stones!' snapped Lady Narcissa as she walked briskly down the long corridor towards them.

Charlie noticed that she had changed into yet another magnificent silver-white dress that shone softly in the light. 'Put her down. I've already discussed the matter of harming the girl. Don't make me repeat myself!'

'Yes, Mother,' said Stones meekly.

He released Charlie, who dropped awkwardly to the floor. On shaky legs, she dusted herself down and rose to her feet.

'Causing more trouble, are you?' sneered Narcissa. 'Well, not to worry, Charlie Keeper. You will only have the pleasure of staying with us for one more day. Tomorrow, I promise you, I will release you from our company.'

'Oh yeah? And why would you do that?'

'Because I have just sold your carcass to Bane, the Stoman Lord.'

Charlie's face paled and her stomach tied itself into knots. 'Wh-what did you just say?' she stammered.

Lady Narcissa smirked evilly as she bent down to stare into Charlie's eyes. 'Hmmmm, let me assure you, you heard me right, little brat. I've just negotiated the sale of your skinny behind for a most pleasurable fortune. So enjoy your last twenty-four hours with us, because shortly after Bane will, I'm quite sure, be snacking on your flesh.'

Charlie had been wondering why Narcissa had taken her in. It had made no sense for the woman to offer her services to the Jade Circle and then turn cold and hard the minute she and Charlie were alone. But this explained it. Lady Narcissa had offered to house her purely for financial gain.

'I congratulate you on getting rid of those tiresome Tremen as well. But now I grow weary. It is late and I need my beauty sleep, so without further ado I shall bid you goodnight. Stones, I think that we should put our young guest in suitable lodgings. Take her to the old cattle pens.'

'As you wish, Mother.'

Lady Narcissa turned smartly and disappeared up the nearby stairwell of her tower.

Stones grabbed Charlie painfully by her hair and pulled her along, through twisting and winding corridors, until he came to a heavily bolted door. Pulling back the bolts, he carelessly tossed Charlie inside.

'Until tomorrow, little rabbit,' he growled. Slamming shut the door, he pulled the bolts back into place and stomped off.

Charlie groaned. Her knees were scraped and bloody and she was sure her shins would be horribly bruised. In her opinion hard stone floors weren't the most comfortable thing to be thrown on. Picking herself up, she plucked the worst of the splinters from her hands and looked around.

Thin moonlight trickled into the dank room through narrow, barred windows that were shrouded by the forest canopy. Damp straw lay scattered across the floor and empty, rundown cattle stalls lined one of the walls. Charlie wrinkled her nose in disgust; it stank of unwashed animals, rot and mildew. Rats, large millipedes, cockroaches and long-legged spiders scuttled, scurried and squeaked in dark corners.

'Nice, real nice,' she muttered to herself. She really wasn't looking forward to spending the night here. How on earth was she going to sleep without creepy-crawlies trying to use her as a new home? The floor was out of the question – it practically heaved with insects. Climbing on to the fencing of one of the stalls, she perched herself up high and by wedging her back against an upright post managed to get reasonably comfortable.

How did she keep getting into these situations? Her adventures in Bellania seemed to lurch from tragedy to tragedy. Every time she overcame one obstacle another two cropped up in its place. She was no nearer her goals. Her parents were still far, far away, while her grandma had been left behind and was now in who-knew-what kind of sticky situation at the mercy of Mr Crow.

Charlie sat there and brooded. Her brain was whirring and ticking over far too fast with memories and fanciful thoughts of escape for sleep to come easily. Hours passed.

After a while a noise that was different from the background chitter of insects roused her from her troublesome daydreams. Pulling a disgusted face and trying not to scream, she plucked an over-inquisitive spider from her hair, sat up and strained to listen. Arguing voices, muffled behind the bolted door, grew closer. With a thick rattle and scrape, the bolts were drawn back and torchlight flooded into the room.

26

Where There's a Will
There's a Way

'You must be mad! Mother would have a shouting fit if she knew we were even thinking about doing this!' grumbled the familiar voice of Stones.

'Well, if you were that worried you shouldn't have allowed me to talk you into coming down here!' rasped Stix with his sandpaper voice. 'Come on, don't worry about it. What's the worst that can happen? Not much when you think about it. By tomorrow night that little brat of a Keeper will be digesting inside Bane's stomach. No one will ever know the truth apart from you and me.'

Stones didn't bother to reply, he merely grunted his consent.

'Ha! That's my brother!' Stix laughed. 'Come on, let's have some fun!'

'What do you two chumps want?' asked Charlie. She had to shield her eyes from the blazing torch that Stix held in his hand. After the gloom of the cattle pens, her eyes weren't ready for the intrusive glare.

'Well, little brat, it's not every day we have a Keeper at our mercy, even a little wisp of a one like you. Me and my brother intend to take full advantage!' smirked Stix, his sharp teeth and feral yellow eyes glinting in the darkness.

'Hang on, Stix,' rumbled Stones. 'Do you really want to do it in here? How about back in our quarters?'

'Definitely not! That's far too close to Mother's room. We can't risk waking her.'

'OK, how about the Great Dining Hall?'

'Make it the Lower Dining Hall and it's a deal,' said Stix.

'Done.'

The Delightful Brothers fixed Charlie with their squinting, cat-like eyes.

Stix held up the Isiris Ring and slowly put it on to his finger. 'Follow us.'

Charlie, her will bound by the bracelets, did as she was instructed.

The three of them trekked back along the corridors and through a rather plain-looking door into a large dining room. Long tables and benches formed two lines down the length of the room and large white banners showing Lady Narcissa's heron and rose lined the walls. Stix stopped Charlie right in front of a huge polished mirror that hung from floor to ceiling.

'Right, then, girlie, open a door to . . . to New York.'

'Hold on,' said Stones. 'I thought we agreed that if we were crossing over to Earth we would go to Paris.'

'Paris, Paris, Paris!' snapped Stix. 'What is it with you and Paris? Everyone that's ever crossed over said Paris was the place to go and see . . . two centuries ago! New York is supposed to be the place with the flavour these days.'

'Paris or nothing,' growled Stones.

'New York!'

'Paris!'

'New Yor– OK, look, this is getting stupid,' reasoned Stix. 'Let's pick another city. We both want excitement, a chance to terrorize and the opportunity to steal something spectacular, so how about –'

'London!' exclaimed Stones.

Stix grinned in agreement. 'London, then. It's a deal.' He snapped his fingers at Charlie. 'Girlie, open the Portal.'

The Delightful Brothers looked at Charlie expectantly. The torch held in Stix's hand cast a sickening glow over both their faces. Already hard and unpleasant, they now appeared more brutish than normal.

'Portal? What Portal?'

'Use the mirror, you silly girl!' hissed Stix.

'You're joking, right?'

'Don't play dumb with us,' growled Stones. 'You are a Keeper. Everyone knows that Keepers can open doors and paths, so don't try and be coy with us. If you muck around, I'll break all your fingers . . . Just open the blasted doorway!'

'How on earth am I supposed to do that?' asked Charlie in disbelief.

Stix kicked her painfully on her already bruised shin. 'Stop stalling. We aren't known for our patience. Now hurry up and open it before we do something unforgivable.'

Charlie looked from one brother to another. They weren't joking. They seriously expected her to snap her fingers and magically open some sort of 'doorway' back to London. She knew she couldn't do it, just as she knew she couldn't jump over a skyscraper or walk on water . . . yet for some reason they thought she could.

Strange.

Charlie could sense the threat that now hung in the air. Stones opened and closed his fists with a murderous look in his eyes and Stix stroked his sword hilts in a most unnatural manner. They obviously expected a result . . . and soon.

'Um . . . if this is something a Keeper is supposed to be able to do, you're going to have to remember I haven't grown up with my parents or anyone else who might have taught me how to open a "Portal". So please, please, please believe me when I say I can't do it.' She eyed the brothers some more, then added, 'And please, please don't hurt me. I honestly don't know how to do whatever it is that you want me to do. And believe me, I would do it if I could. C'mon, don't you guys think I want to see London as much as you?' Charlie, realizing she was gabbling, shut her mouth. Standing with her shoulders hunched protectively forward, she waited to see what would happen.

'Hhmpf . . . maybe she's telling the truth,' said Stones. 'Remember we heard the Jade Circle discussing her parents' fate.' He rubbed his chin speculatively and stared at Charlie.

'Hhmm, she could be,' agreed Stix. 'But that doesn't matter, does it? If she's never been shown how to open a Portal she should still be able to do it, right? She's a Keeper – the ability is inbuilt. So all we've got to do is teach her how to do it.'

'What?' exclaimed Stones in his massive, rumbling voice. 'Are you joking? Show a Keeper how to open a Portal? How are we going to do that? Killing is one thing, torturing another . . . Those are all areas that we have expertise in. Doorways and Portals . . . that's another ball game altogether. Let's just forget it, get some food and throw the girlie back into the pens.'

'Pah, where's your sense of adventure, brother? We've got the Isiris Bracelets and she's got the ability. All we have to do is put them together and BLAM! Come on, where's the harm in trying?'

Stones cocked his head to one side. After some thought he said, 'OK, let's do it.'

'Great!' Stix fixed Charlie beneath his gaze. 'All right, girlie. I am going to teach you, to the best of my abilities, about the theory of opening Portals, so make sure you listen up and listen up good. I'm not the sort of Treman who likes to repeat himself.'

Charlie didn't need telling twice. And even though she would have preferred to learn such knowledge from her parents or perhaps from Jensen or Azariah this was still going to benefit her. She was going to learn something new, something about herself and her heritage.

'I'm sure even you must have learned by now, girlie, that Earth and Bellania were many thousands of years ago the same place, but since the events of the Great Cataclysm they now exist on almost two separate and different plains of existence, right?'

'Er . . . right,' muttered Charlie.

'Wrong,' grinned Stix nastily. 'They both exist in the same place, but one on top of the other. Like a coin – it has two different sides, heads and tails, but together they make the whole. Right?'

'Er . . . right?'

'Correct, little girlie. Now then, because Earth and Bellania are seen as different sides of the same coin it should therefore be impossible for the two sides to meet. After all, with a coin you cannot bend the head side round to touch the tail side, can you?'

'Er . . . no?' said Charlie, and although she was slightly confused she thought that she did have a basic grasp of what Stix was telling her. Perhaps she would have found it easier if he didn't glare at her every five seconds like he wanted to skin, bone and slowly cook her.

'Right again . . . but this is where things get confusing. Now we head into the more bizarre world of Keepers. All Bellanian children, be they Stoman, Human or Treman, are taught what I have just told you. However, what I am about to explain to you is something that I and Stones can only guess at, as this is a field normally taught exclusively to the Keepers.'

Charlie felt herself buzzing with excitement. As much as she loathed Stix and Stones, this was one of the most fascinating things she had learned since her fateful escape from home.

'Somehow the two realms, Earth and Bellania, do connect. The Cataclysm was so powerful, so mighty, that it tore the very fabric and laws of the universe. One of the results of this is that the two opposite sides of the coin do, against all rules of logic, touch. These points where Earth and Bellania touch are special and quite rare. It is in these locations, girlie, that the two realities collide and overlap. And it is in these strange places that you will find the homes of Keepers. It is their job, their duty and their obligation, to guard these sites and keep them hidden, particularly from the uneducated Human idiots back on your side. Also, they must ensure that foolhardy or ignorant people do not unwillingly or mistakenly cross over. In fact, none may cross over unless they have the Winged Ones' permission. Your house, I believe, is one of these points.'

'Oh!' uttered Charlie.

So that explains . . .

'Don't interrupt me, brat!' snarled Stix. Gathering his thoughts, he continued, 'Where was I? Right, so your house sits on a point where paths between Bellania and Earth merge. The name for the exact opening point of a path is a "doorway". These doorways are stationary and cannot be moved. However – and this is what makes your family so annoyingly powerful – Keepers can also forge their own pathways between the sides. These pathways, unlike doorways, can be opened anywhere on Earth or Bellania. These movable paths are known as "Portals". Do you follow me, girlie?'

'Yes . . . well, at least I think so,' said Charlie, ticking off the points on her fingers. 'A doorway cannot be moved, is quite rare and occurs naturally and can be used by anyone, so long as they have permission from the Winged Ones. But a Portal is an artificial doorway that can be opened only by a Keeper, right?'

'And can be opened anywhere, unlike a doorway, which occurs only at points where the Cataclysm tore reality apart . . . Are you still following me, brat?'

'Er . . . I think so,' said Charlie.

Stix nodded. 'You'd better understand, because if you mess this up Stones and I are going to . . .'

'Yeah, I know.' Charlie sighed. 'Hurt me like I've never been hurt before and blah, blah, blah. I get the message. I'm really not as dumb as you like to think.'

'Yeah, well, if you were so bright perhaps you wouldn't be in this situation, would you, you cheeky little brat?' rumbled Stones.

Charlie grimaced. He had a point. 'OK, I'm sorry I opened my mouth. Please continue.'

'What I *want* you to open is a Portal from here to London,' snarled Stix, who was getting fed up with all the interruptions.

'And how am I going to do that?' asked Charlie.

'By using your Will.'

'My "Will"?'

'Yes, your Will!' snapped Stix. 'This is what makes Keepers stand out from the rest of you foolish Humans. Your Will! Stomen can stonesing. Tremen, treesing. Keepers can manifest powers through concentrating their Will.'

'Wow . . . magic!' breathed Charlie, a huge smile erupting across her face. She couldn't help it. Here she was stuck in a strange land, in a strange city, in some horrible witch's tower with two terrible brothers who enjoyed inflicting pain. And tomorrow she was to be traded like meat to an evil, flesh-eating giant, but she didn't care. She had just been told she could do magic!

'What is it with you Humans? Why do you always insist on calling simple, day-to-day things magic?' hissed Stix. 'Are you all dumb animals living in the Dark Ages? It is not – and

I'll say it again, because I can see how stupid you are – it is not magic! This is a skill, a focusing of Will, nothing more, nothing less!'

'Magic!' smirked Charlie, who wasn't listening to a word that Stix was saying. She was too busy off daydreaming in a world of her own.

'Bah!' snarled Stix in disgust as he stared at the young girl.

27

A Glimpse of Trafalgar Square

'OK, brat, snap out of it,' commanded Stix. 'I want you to focus your Will on this mirror. Look at it, feel it, try to do whatever comes naturally to you as a Keeper. Now then, be aware of where we are, in Mother's tower, in Sylvaris, in Bellania. Good, now focus on where we want to be, which is London. I want you to think of . . . Trafalgar Square. Picture it in your mind: Nelson's Column, the lions, the National Gallery, the fountains, the pesky pigeons and the sheep-like milling tourists. Good . . . you're doing well . . . Now then, Will us to be there,' he said.

His face was wrinkled in concentration as he stared from Charlie to the mirror. The Isiris Ring on his finger glinted in the torchlight.

'Focus your Will. You must want more than anything to be in London.'

Charlie didn't need the Isiris Bracelets to force her to do this. She would have been more than willing to try it at any time. Grimacing, squinting her eyes and frowning hard, she concentrated like never before. She squeezed her fists into tight balls, her tummy muscles cramped up and she began to shake.

She ignored it all. She forgot who she was with, disregarded her sticky predicament. All her attention was focused on the mirror in front of her. Her reflection stared back at her and she could see Stix and Stones standing behind her, with the dining room disappearing into the darkness behind them. Then something began to change. The image wavered and grew hazy, as if she was seeing it beneath a fast-moving river, or in a desert through a wall of shimmering heat.

She focused even harder. London, Trafalgar Square, Nelson's Column, the lions, the National Gallery. Thick golden light, similar to what had come from Azariah's hands, lit the room. With a giddy sense of wonder, Charlie realized that the light was coming from her. *Focus*, she thought, *I must focus*.

And suddenly it was there. The reflection and the mirror had disappeared, leaving behind just the wooden frame, and through this, a short distance in front of her, was Trafalgar Square. Rich afternoon sunlight streamed into the dining room. The hustle and bustle of London traffic could be heard: the roar of large trucks, the grating noise of double-decker buses, the horn of some annoyed cab driver. She could see tourists, lots of them, with their brightly coloured backpacks and cameras. Some of them turned and pointed right at Charlie in amazement. Just as she could see them, they could see her!

A thick jet of water shot through the mirror and splashed both her and the Delightful Brothers. She had opened the Portal right in the middle of one of the fountains! Water, unleashed by the complete opening of the Portal, was now rushing into the dining room. It gushed everywhere, bringing Coke cans, mangy pigeon feathers and old plastic shopping bags with it. The sheer rush and power of the small wave knocked Charlie off her feet.

With a loud cracking noise and a powerful boom, the Portal snapped shut. The force of Charlie's Will, now unfocused, sent her ricocheting across the room. With a thud, she crashed against the far wall, then rebounded into a tangled heap on the floor.

'You idiot!' screamed Stix.

Beside him Stones was raging. The Delightful Brothers weren't happy.

'You incompetent fool! Look what you've done! I can't believe you opened a Portal right in a fountain! What were you thinking?'

With murder in his eye, Stix stalked forward.

'Well, what did you expect, you chumps?' screamed back Charlie. She was fed up with being bullied, fed up with being pushed and prodded around and, what's more, she felt exhausted after opening the Portal. 'It's the first time I've ever done that! How was I to know that that was going to happen? Besides, did you not say to Stones: "What's the worst that can happen?" So surely some of this blame lies with you. Perhaps you should have taught me better! So stop bullying me and leave me alone! I'm wet, tired and hungry! I've worked all day long with my arms stuck in hot stinking vats and I've had to sleep in a room full of creepy-crawlies, so if you think you could do better under the circumstances go ahead!'

Such was the anger and rage coming from Charlie that

Stix actually stopped in his tracks to stare at her. With a sudden start, Charlie realized he wasn't exactly looking at her, rather he was staring at her hands. Looking down, she was stunned to see they were still giving off a soft golden glow. Stix nervously licked his lips as though he was threatened by what he saw. As the Delightful Brothers gazed at Charlie, it took her a few slow seconds to realize that, in their odd sort of way, they were giving her a touch more respect. As though she could one day, given time and training, become someone to fear.

'Oh, my sweet chops!' wailed a voice in the distance. 'Where did all this water come from? What in Bellania is going on here?'

Charlie sat upright. The glow in her hands extinguished as she looked up at the Delightful Brothers and around at the soggy, partly flooded room.

'That sounds like one of the Alavisian Watchmen,' growled Stones. 'We'd better get out of here. I'd hate to have to explain to Mother how we managed to ruin one of her halls.'

'You're right, let's go,' agreed Stix. Beckoning Charlie over, he headed for the nearest doorway.

As Charlie hurried after the two brothers, she gazed at the mirror in passing. Had she really done that? Had she really just opened a Portal to London?

'Hurry up, brat!'

Hastening from the room, Charlie had to duck as two lost and wayward pigeons nearly knocked her on the head as they frantically flapped across the dining room in the near-darkness.

28

The Morning After

Eager to avoid getting caught, the Delightful Brothers ran back down the winding passageways with Charlie held between them. Tearing open the bolted doorway to the cattle pens, they threw her inside and scampered off. No doubt, thought Charlie, to make themselves look as innocent as possible.

Lying there in the dark, she raged at her predicament. How had she ended up in this situation? How was she going to escape from this cursed tower? Picking herself up, she stomped her way up and down the room – squishing hundreds of bugs at the same time – cursing her bad luck.

A sudden idea wormed its way past her angry thoughts of escape and stopped her dead in her tracks. What did fate matter when she'd just opened some sort of a Gateway to London? What did they call it . . . a Portal! She'd opened a Portal. She could do magic!

A thick grin slowly blossomed across her face.

Magic!

Ignoring the rustles and scamperings, scuttlings and scurryings of the many long-legged creepy-crawlies that infested the cattle pens, Charlie immediately began to practise.

'So tell me, what news?'

'My lord, the Lady consented to your offer,' said the Shade, rubbing itself cat-like against Bane's massive leg.

'Of course she did.'

'But, my lord, she has requested the gold and rubies as a down payment. She will not part with the child until then.'

'Bah! Gold and jewels are nothing to me. I have no use for such trinkets. Power is what truly matters. Power and might are the only things worth caring about. Financial seductions are only for the spineless, weak and worthless,' growled Bane.

With a sweeping wave of his hand he sent a trickle of sapphires, rubies, emeralds and diamonds tumbling to the floor.

'Give the money-hungry woman what she desires. I care not. Just bring me the squirming maggot of a girl. This matter is dragging on far too long for my liking. Take a full pack of your siblings, make sure the deal proceeds and ensure that nothing goes wrong. I wish to have that writhing, scurrying wisp of a girl and the pendant under my control by tomorrow's last bell. Now go, for I must discuss weighty matters with my God.'

Bane watched as the Shade silently and sinuously writhed off to do his bidding. No doubt the matter would be finished and finished soon. With luck he would be sucking on squishy young Keeper bone marrow and gnawing on stringy ligament and cartilage in no time at all.

Rising from his seat on the Devouring Throne, Bane made his way to the rear of the Throne Room. Passing into a concealed shadowy tunnel, he went to greet his source of power. His Dark God.

'No, Mother, we don't know how the Lower Dining Room came to be in such a mess,' said Stones for perhaps the ninth time that afternoon. 'It was probably the chef, drunk out of his mind and just causing trouble. You know how he favours the cooking sherry.'

Lady Narcissa eyed her two wayward sons. She didn't really believe a word they were saying, but without proof it all amounted to nothing. Oh, she trusted them all right, trusted them with her very life, but it was the little things that she had to look out for. Some days she still thought they hadn't managed to grow up at all. Big kids was what they were. But dangerous, lethal kids.

'So if you knew nothing about it why weren't the two of you in your quarters when I came looking?'

'Because we'd already heard the alarm. We had gone to investigate,' said Stix. 'That's our job, isn't it, to protect your safety at all times?'

'Hhmpf!' sniffed Lady Narcissa. She still wasn't buying their excuse, but neither was she all that annoyed. She loved her sons. As ugly and as mean-spirited as they were, they were completely loyal and for that she could forgive them almost anything. 'Oh well, I'll guess we'll just have to find a scapegoat or two . . . Go and grab a couple of servants and behead them. That should set a good example to everyone else. After all, we can't have people thinking I've gone soft, can we?'

'No, Mother,' murmured the Delightful Brothers in unison. They were only too glad to be off the hook.

'Good. Right, then, what time is it?'

'Three o'clock,' replied Stones.

'Hmm, the Shade is due at midnight. Just think, nine more hours until we're rich. Rich beyond our wildest dreams! Stix, I want you to put the Keeper brat back to work in the Spinnery, and Stones, I want you to concentrate on security. Between now and tonight nothing must go wrong. Now, enough with the talking. Get to it!'

29

The Breakout

Charlie was in a foul mood.

She hadn't been able to sleep last night, not even a wink. She had tried for hours to open another Portal but got almost nowhere. The best she had been able to do was make her hands glow, giving off that strange golden light. Which was, she admitted to herself, kind of cool. But the downside was that when she did it for too long she got a pounding headache, the kind that throbbed and pulsed painfully behind her eyelids. Exhausted, she had tried to sleep, but guilty thoughts of Kelko and Jensen had kept her awake. After yesterday's confrontation on the draw-bridge she doubted they would ever want to see her again. It hurt her to think that she had treated her friends so shamefully.

Eventually, she had abandoned all thoughts of sleep and decided to practise her K'Changa instead. And that was how Stix found her, slipping from K'Changa pose to pose, flipping and tumbling and leaving a trail of squashed insects in her wake.

And now, once again, she was back at the vats, working her arms until they were stiff and her lower back cried out in protest. But unlike yesterday she had no friendly companion. When Aranea found Charlie and Melita laughing together she banished Melita to work with the cotton bales, leaving Charlie to heave great armloads of silks and threads into the slippery, stinking dye all by herself.

Pulling a face, Charlie spread another pile of threads over the drying racks. 'Stinking tower,' she grumbled. She stomped her way back over to the vats. 'Stupid bracelets.' She slapped in another load. 'The Delightful Brothers are chumps, Narcissa's a witch and Aranea is nothing more than a greedy idiot!' She stamped her foot as her fury grew to an almost uncontrollable level. 'Got to get out of here,' she muttered to herself. 'Got to get out. Got to –'

Her cursing tumbled to a halt as her gaze fell upon the shelves with all the ingredients necessary to mix the dyes. An idea slowly began to swirl and take shape in her head.

She knew what the Isiris Bracelets were capable of and she knew how they stopped her escaping from the tower. But she knew that they didn't stop her fighting back. Maybe that was a weakness she could exploit.

Charlie grinned as she looked first at the jar with the Firehaven Sourlax, then the Hyron stones and then at the threads drying on the racks. She was no longer just a girl trapped in a tower. She was more than that.

She was a girl with a plan.

The Delightful Brothers approached Lady Narcissa.

'Mother, it's nearly time,' rumbled Stones.

'Good.' The thought of Bane's down payment arriving shortly caused her eyes to glitter. 'Good indeed. Stix, go and grab the brat. I want her presentable for the Shades, so get her washed and put her in some new clothes. I don't want any trouble from her, so take the ring with you too. Stones, I want you and the Alavisian Watchmen to go and greet the Shade, but don't allow it entrance to the tower until you're certain it has brought all of the payment. OK?'

'Yes, Mother,' chorused the brothers.

'Excellent.' She eyed her two sons with pride. 'Now go and get it done.'

First checking the heft of his bow, Stones turned and trudged up the spiralling stairs to muster the Watchmen. Stix flexed his shoulders and, with the ring on his finger, descended into the lower levels to deal with Charlie Keeper.

Using a thick but scruffy pair of gloves that she had found next to the vats, Charlie dipped thread after thread into the Firehaven Sourlax. Standing on a stool, she began to hang them from the top of the doorframe, using the Hyron stones as weights to keep them fixed in place. Careful not to allow the soggy fibres to touch her, Charlie leaned back to admire her work.

The latch on the door lifted and Charlie, caught off guard, lost her balance and fell backwards. Fortunately a pile of unprocessed silks and cotton broke her fall. A round of vicious laughter caused her to look up. It was Stix and behind him stood Aranea.

'What have we here?' he chuckled. 'Still up to your tricks and tomfoolery, Charlie Keeper?'

'You know, Stix,' said Charlie as she picked herself back up, 'one of these days someone's going to give you the lesson you deserve.'

'Is that so? Well, that's not going to be today and it's not going to be you doing the teaching.' Still grinning, he held up his finger to show off the ring. He walked towards Charlie, and Aranea followed him. Neither of them saw the Firehaven Sourlax threads that hung from the doorframe, although they both felt them brush against their faces as they walked forward.

'What was that? Cobwebs?' asked Stix, wiping his face.

'Cobwebs?' echoed Aranea, looking around in puzzlement. 'There shouldn't be any cobwebs here. I'll put this brat to cleaning after you're done with her.'

You'll have to get someone else to do the cleaning in here. This is the last time you'll be seeing our famous guest.'

'Very well, I'll have Melita . . . I . . . er –' Aranea swayed and had to hold on to a drying rack to stop herself falling over.

'What's the matter?' asked Stix.

'Must be the heat . . . I think . . .'

'Uh,' grunted Stix. Slowly he put his hand to his head. 'Get me some water. I-I –' He staggered and almost fell as his face turned a sickly shade of green. He turned accusingly to Charlie. 'What have you done to us? Quick, tell me, you little imp. Tell me before I gut you with my swords!'

'Ha! Does this jar seem familiar?' smirked Charlie triumphantly, looking at Aranea. She pointed at the glass jar and then to the toxic threads dangling from the doorframe.

'Firehaven . . . Sourlax! You piece of scum . . . you flotsam! I knew . . . you were . . . trouble,' murmured Aranea. She could hardly speak and her words came out as a faint whisper. 'She's drugged us!' Her eyes rolled up and she collapsed in a heap.

'You . . . you . . .' said Stix, his gravelly, rasping voice fading. With slow, heavy movements he erratically stalked towards Charlie, at the same time drawing one of his swords.

Charlie, quite unafraid, boldly stepped forward and, with a firm hand, shoved him in the chest as hard as she could. 'Oh, be quiet, you chump!'

Stix staggered backwards, tripped over Aranea and fell, stiff and immobile, to the floor. Drugged and motionless he might have been, but he still glared furiously at Charlie through his half-open eyes. One of his hands pulsed and twitched spasmodically near his sword. Speaking through the side of his mouth, he whispered with a numb tongue, 'You'd . . . better . . . run . . . far . . . away . . . girlie . . . Next . . . time . . . I . . . see . . . you . . . I . . . will . . . kill . . . you . . .'

Holding on to her courage, Charlie applied some of the slimy dye to Stix's finger and, avoiding his mad, staring eyes, she tugged the ring free. Removing the Isiris Bracelets from her wrists, she stuffed them in her trouser pockets and sighed in relief. At last! At last she had a chance to escape!

'We . . . shall . . . see . . . who . . . has . . . the . . . last . . . laugh . . . brat!' snarled Stix breathlessly from the floor, a long line of dribble leaking from his leaden mouth to puddle on the tiled floor. Beside him, Aranea began to snore.

Charlie raised her eyebrows in disbelief. She couldn't

believe he was still threatening her! All the pent-up frustration from the last two days suddenly erupted. The tight knot of darkness that coiled and boiled within her heart roared to life.

'What is it with everyone in this stupid place?' she asked sarcastically. 'I've had enough! Enough, do you hear me? Stop chasing me, stop hounding me and leave me alone! If you mess with me again, I'll show you I'm no pushover!'

'You're . . . dead!'

'Oh yeah?' Charlie grinned with a fierce look in her eye. Leaning over, she picked up one of Stix's swords from his nerveless fingers and with quick movements – SWISH! SWISH! – she lopped his beloved topknot from his head. Holding it jubilantly in her hands, she stared down at the evil Treman. 'That's for locking me in the cattle pens full of creepy-crawlies.'

Grabbing a handful of brushes, she dipped them into various coloured dyes, then scampered back to Stix. Doing her best to ignore his continued threats, she proceeded to paint his face. With a liberal amount of red, white and green, she transformed his frozen scowl into the grin of a clown. 'And that's for being a nasty piece of work with no sense of humour!'

Chuckling in delight and with a final cheeky wave, Charlie raced off.

30

A Midnight Trade

The Shades slid noiselessly through the twilight of Sylvaris. Writhing and creeping from graceful bridge to cobbled boulevard, the Shades slunk towards Narcissa's tower. Crossing the drawbridge, they drew up short. Stones and the Alavisian Watchmen blocked the entrance.

'Have you brought the agreed advance payment?'

'Of course,' hissed a Shade. 'Do you doubt my word, or that of my master?'

The pulsating Shadow extended a dark tendril that was neither hand nor paw. Balanced on the end was a small woven, wicker basket. Nestled inside were fat and very plump rubies that glistened and twinkled hypnotically in the starlight.

A second shadowy tendril upended a small stack of gold bars that clunked heavily as they struck the mighty drawbridge.

'That is just one basket and a mere ten bars. You promised us a hundred baskets and a thousand gold bars,' snorted Stones. 'This is but a hundredth of the down payment, I trust that you have the rest with you.'

'But of course,' said the Shade. Letting out an eerie, shrill whistle that echoed across the drawbridge, it motioned its brethren forward.

There was a faint rustling, as though a hundred silk curtains were being slowly drawn. The pack of Shades drew closer. Each held a basket and stack of gold aloft.

Together, Stones and the Watchmen gasped as a twinkling sea of red and gold stars unfolded in front of them. After a brief display the Shades withdrew their bounty back into their shadowy folds.

'Satisfied?' asked the Shade.

'More than satisfied,' admitted Stones. 'This way.'

The large Stoman guided the long line of Shades beneath the portcullis and into the tower. Once inside the pack of shadows followed Stones as he led the way down splendid gilded hallways and up a grand spiral staircase. Pushing open an elaborately carved set of wooden doors, he ushered the Shades into the Great Dining Hall.

The Great Dining Hall was the complete opposite of the Lower Dining Hall, the sole purpose of which was dining. This room conveyed an overwhelming sense of opulence and wealth. It was obviously meant to impress . . . and it did. Luscious gold and silver panels lined the walls and splendid bouquets of wild orchids cascaded from magnificent blue-tinged vases. Elegant chandeliers lit with hundreds of candles hung from the painted ceiling, and ornate tables and chairs dotted the marble floor. Carved into the far wall was Narcissa's emblem and beneath it stood Lady Narcissa herself.

'Welcome, welcome!' she greeted. 'Please come in. Can I get you anything? Perhaps something to eat or to drink?'

'We do not care for mortal food or drink. It does not suit our tastes,' hissed the Shade. 'We are here to trade, not socialize. Bring us the girl and the pendant.'

'Certainly,' replied Narcissa smartly. 'However, I would prefer to have the payment first. Only then will I supply the girl.'

The Shade nodded its consent and motioned its pack forward. Shuffling and mewling, the thick carpet of shadows slunk forward like an immense wave of black velvet. The Shades briefly lapped and puddled around Narcissa's white-clad feet. There they writhed and wriggled for a short moment. Then, like some great black tide, they retreated and in their place was Charlie's ransom. Rubies and gold had been piled together to form a carpet of wealth.

Lady Narcissa grinned. Clapping her hands sharply, she ushered in a line of butlers and housemaids. At her command and under Stones's watchful eye, they collected the treasure and staggered out to the tower's vault. Lady Narcissa could barely hide the greed in her eyes.

'Our thanks to Lord Bane,' she smirked.

'And the girl?' questioned the Shade.

'I've sent for her. In fact, she should be here by now,' said Narcissa.

'Should be?'

'Well, yes. My son Stix is making her somewhat more . . . presentable. But not to worry. I assure you, Stix is most trustworthy and he shall, I'm sure, be here soon.'

'Presentable does not concern us. Simply give us the girl and the deal shall be done.'

'Please just wait a few minutes more.'

'Wait? We do not wait. Take us to the girl now,' snarled the Shade. 'We have shown our good faith and now you must show yours.'

'If you do not trust me, fine,' snapped Narcissa somewhat angrily. 'Stones, please escort our suspicious guests down to collect Charlie Keeper. I believe she and Stix can be found in the servants' quarters.'

'Yes, Mother.' He turned to the pack of shadows. 'Follow me.'

Stones stalked from the Great Dining Room and made his way down the wide spiral staircase with the Shades swarming behind him. Opening one of the narrow entrances to the servants' quarters, he hunted up and down the corridors searching for his brother.

'Stix, where are you?' Receiving no answer, he grabbed a nearby servant by the collar. 'Where is my brother?' he demanded.

'I-I-I don't know!' stuttered the man, petrified by the Shades.

'Gah!' growled the irate Stoman. 'You! You there, my brother? Where. Is. He?'

'Aaahh!' screamed a young maid as she too saw the mass of shadows. She turned to run, but Stones's thick hand snatched her up by the hair. Kicking and screaming, she writhed in his grip.

'Tell me where my brother is or I'll feed you to them!'

'I don't know! I honestly don't know! He's not here! I've been here all evening and I haven't seen him at all. Please, please don't feed me to them!'

'Bah! What is this foolishness?' Irritated, Stones flicked

the housemaid aside. He puffed up his chest and roared down the corridor. 'Open your doors and pay attention, all of you! Show me your heads or I'll cut them off and play K'Changa with them!'

Within seconds four dozen doors opened and shy, timid heads slowly appeared.

'I will ask this once and only once: has anyone here seen my brother or the Keeper girl?'

Most of the heads shook from side to side. One hand, however, went up.

'You there, speak!'

It was one of the seamstresses. 'Er, yes, my lord. I've seen your brother. The last I saw of him was in the Spinnery, with Mistress Aranea. That was almost an hour ago now. Sir.'

'Almost an hour ago?' Furiously Stones turned around and waded back through the tide of Shades to head for the Spinnery.

'Stix! Stix! Where are you?' he shouted as he burst into the large sewing room.

'Er . . . he's over here,' squeaked a small voice.

It was one of the cotton pickers. At his side were Melita and several of the seamstresses and labourers, all of them staring down at something at their feet. They were doing their very best to hide wide grins behind their hands.

Striding over, Stones caught sight of what attracted their attention.

It was Stix and Aranea.

Unconscious.

There was no sign of the girl. Or the pendant.

'What is going on here? What's wrong with them? My

brother, is he OK? And will someone please tell me why he's painted like a clown?'

'Brother . . .' grunted Stix from the corner of his mouth.

'Stix, what's wrong? Tell me who did this to you and I'll break their bones!'

'Keeper . . . the . . . girl . . . drugged . . . us . . . escaped . . .'

'Charlie? The brat did this to you? That little rabbit?' exclaimed Stones, his mouth hanging open in shock. He'd expected some cunning fiend to have been responsible for this, not some poxy little Human girl. 'Where did she go?'

'Not . . . sure . . . she . . . left . . . about . . . half . . . an . . . hour . . . ago . . .'

'Bah, never mind, she can't have gone far. The Isiris Bracelets will keep her imprisoned within these walls. It is just a matter of time until we catch her. You there,' he instructed a labourer, 'go fetch my mother, Lady Narcissa. She will deal with this.'

'No . . . Bracelets . . .'

'What was that?' Stones frowned. Cupping a hand around his ear, he leaned closer to his brother.

'She . . . stole . . . ring . . .'

'What?' roared Stones. Raising a huge hand, he pointed at one of the seamstresses. 'Quick, go and raise the alarm. Tell the Alavisian Watchmen to shut the tower down. No one is to come in or go out without my consent. And you! Yes, you, go and tell the sergeant he is to bring up the tracker hounds. We must search for –'

'Forget all of that!' interrupted the prime Shade scathingly. 'We can locate her. Her scent is still fresh.'

'Kill . . . her . . . for . . . me . . . revenge . . .'

'My pleasure,' sneered Stones, and reached for his bow.

'You may not! The deal is done and the girl is ours. You may not harm her,' hissed the Shade. 'Wait here and attend to your brother, while we hunt down the Keeper.'

The Shades, sniffing and licking at the dyeing and drying room floor, picked up Charlie's scent and gave chase. Rustling and growling, they swarmed out of the Spinnery.

Stones stared at his stricken brother lying on the floor, then at the retreating pack of Shades. 'I will not stand by and allow our family honour to be stained and left unavenged. Stix, I will have the girl's skin hanging from my belt when I return. No one touches one of the Delightful Brothers without paying for it!' He unstrapped his great bow and, scowling like black thunder, stamped from the Spinnery.

Melita silently wished Charlie good luck as she watched the furious Delightful Brother leave. *If anyone deserves a break*, she thought, *it's Charlie Keeper.*

31

Nowhere to Run

Charlie snorted in disgust. Three times she'd managed to take the wrong direction. Three times! Narcissa's tower was like a maze with its winding corridors, spiralling stairs and corridors that seemed to go in circles. It was only by heading in what Charlie was certain was the wrong direction that she was at last able to find herself in the vicinity of the tower's entrance.

Sneaking down the hallway, Charlie peered around the corner. 'I can't believe it!' she whispered furiously to herself. 'Will my luck never change?'

Not only was the drawbridge heavily guarded by the Alavisian Watchmen but the brutal-looking portcullis was down as well. Her exit was well and truly blocked. She would have to find another way out . . . but how?

Charlie was mulling over her possible options when she became aware of an eerie hissing and shrieking that echoed down the hallway. After her past adventures she recognized the noise immediately.

Shades!

They tumbled around the corner like a black fog. Catching sight of her, their screams rose to a fevered crescendo.

Bounding and leaping, they tore towards her. The Watchmen, hearing all the commotion, joined the chase. Charlie immediately turned and ran.

She pumped her arms like crazy and sprinted for all she was worth. Practically flying from the hallway, she scurried up the nearest flight of stairs, through a door and onward. The terrible shrieks of the hunting Shades spurred her on, up more and more stairs and along narrow corridors.

Sliding around a corner, Charlie felt the hot whizz of something flash past her face. It was an arrow! Stones stood facing her at the far end of the hall. Feet planted widely apart, he plucked another cruel arrow from his quiver, drew back the string and took aim. Smiling evilly, he released the bowstring.

With a thick twang, the arrow spat towards her. Charlie threw herself out of the way, feeling the hot swish of its feathering as it narrowly missed her. Unchecked, the arrow hummed onward, slicing into an unfortunate Shade that had slipped around the corner. Both Shade and arrow slammed into the far wall with a thud and a wretched scream.

Stones cursed and, bellowing his frustration, plucked another arrow from his quiver. Charlie didn't hang around. Pulling open the nearest doorway, she ducked through as yet more Shades gave chase. Huffing and puffing, she sprinted from room to room until she found she could run no more. She had reached the summit of the tower. The staircase that she was on petered out and opened up on to a wide, sweeping roof. There was no other obvious way down.

Charlie spun around to race back the way she had come,

but a hissing and spitting Shade blocked her path. More of the foul Shadows joined it, as too did a group of Watchmen who looked enraged that they had had to chase her so far. She slowly backed away until her feet rested right on the cornerstones of the rooftop. Behind her lay a fearsome drop. Wild winds tugged at her hair and blew against her clothing. Spreading her arms wide, Charlie fought for balance as she wobbled unsteadily on the edge.

'Make way! Make way, I said!' Stones forced his way to the front of the baying crowd. He grinned in delight as he saw Charlie, cornered and helpless. 'Well, well, little girlie. I see you can't run any further. How sad.' Slowly, with loving devotion, he pulled another arrow from his quiver. Unravelling a long length of wire from his pocket, he knotted one end to the arrow's shaft and the other he tied around his waist.

'Wait! What are you doing? You must not harm her!' snarled the lead Shade.

'You want her alive, don't you?'

'Of course!'

'Then think things through. Look at where she's standing. If you rush her, she might fall, and if she falls from this height you might never recover her body, or the pendant. But if we do things my way, which is to harpoon her like a wayward fish, she might fall but she'll just dangle from my line. All we will have to do is reel her in! At the worst she might lose a limb or two, but at least she'll live to reach the Western Mountains. I get my revenge, you get your pound of Human flesh and your precious pendant, my mother has her deal and everybody goes home happy.'

'Apart from me, you useless idiot!' interjected Charlie. Terrified that she might fall and equally petrified that Stones would actually harpoon her, she did the only thing she could. Removing the necklace, she held it over the roof's edge. 'Back off or I drop the pendant! I mean it, you chumps, just you believe it! I've had a rotten day and I'm really, really stressed, so don't push me!'

'I don't care, girlie,' growled Stones, his yellow eyes flashing dangerously. 'Drop your trinket for all I care. It, unlike you, can survive the fall. All we have to do is send the Watchmen out to find it – job done, end of story. So pucker up and say hello to my arrow!'

Stones released his bowstring.

Time seemed to slow. Moonlight glinted off the Watchmen's armour, small clouds of dust hung suspended around Stones's feet and the sound of the Shades' screams sounded long and drawn out.

Charlie blinked at the phenomenon. The rooftop had taken on the quality of a film in slow motion. Everyone appeared to be moving ever so slowly through thick jelly. She could feel the soft pendulum beating of her heart, the brush of the cool night air on her flushed skin and the gentle drip of sweat down her neck. And beneath it all the volcanic pulse of her anger, drumming slowly within the confines of her chest.

She blinked and everything speeded up.

The shrieks and cries from the Shades spat across the rooftop. Stones roared triumphantly and the arrow hurtled towards her.

Roaring and crackling loudly, a jet of white flame erupted

from out of the dark night sky to shoot across the rooftop. It burned the arrow to a cinder in mid-flight. So intense was the heat that the wood instantly turned to ash and was blown across the roof and out into the night.

Everything and everyone on the tower's roof froze.

From above something growled menacingly. Looks of complete terror and small grunts of dread rippled through the Watchmen as they pointed with trembling fingers to the thing that flew above. The Shades hissed loudly and compressed themselves into tight coils as they too withdrew in fright. Even Stones, powerful and cruel, seemed momentarily taken aback by what he saw.

Again a deep menacing growl erupted from out of the dark sky to cascade across everyone's heads. Charlie slowly, so very, very slowly, turned to look.

32

A New Companion

Charlie inhaled sharply, partly in shock, partly in wonder.

She had always dreamed about seeing one of these creatures, always known within her heart that they were real no matter how many people had laughed and sneered at her at school. And to see one right in front of her, right here, right now, was like a wish come true. Awed and delighted, Charlie forgot all about the Shades, the Watchmen and Stones. Her eyes were fixed like glue on the magnificent beast that flew just in front of her.

A dragon!

Nothing could have spoilt this moment for her. Well, perhaps nothing apart from the small, niggling thought that blundered its way across her mind . . . Surely dragons were supposed to be bigger than this? The creature before her spanned a mere two metres from head to tail, and most of that was its long neck and longer tail. But in Charlie's opinion this was only a minor hitch and couldn't spoil the sheer delight of the image.

The beast was without doubt the most majestic thing she had ever seen. It was covered from head to toe in spectacular emerald-green scales that glinted in the soft moonlight.

Its long, muscled neck supported a powerful and handsome head and its sinuous tail writhed and lashed behind it, allowing it to maintain perfect balance in the rough winds. Its beautifully proportioned wings stretched proudly outward, flapping and beating at the air. But to Charlie's mind the most amazing aspect of the whole creature had to be its fiercely glowing blue eyes, which blazed in awesome fury as it glared at the Shades.

'Wow!' Charlie whispered to herself. And without being able to explain how she knew – she just did – she was very much aware that the dragon was here for her. No matter how fierce it appeared or how dangerous it was to Stones and the others on the rooftop, she knew it meant her no harm.

A ferocious shout from Stones snapped Charlie's attention back to the present. She was still in trouble. Dangerous, perilous trouble. She quickly slipped her pendant back round her neck and tucked it out of sight.

'You idiots, stop standing there gawking!' roared Stones. 'Grab her, quick!'

The Alavisian Watchmen inched forward beneath the baleful eye of the flying dragon. Arms out, they reached for the young Keeper. The dragon snarled. Opening its fanged mouth, it spat out another wave of flame that scorched and stung the guards. Crying in pain and beating at their burning armour, they leaped back.

'Blast you all!' cursed Stones. He slapped and kicked the Watchmen out of the way. 'Same as it ever was: if a job needs doing, do it yourself!'

Growling to himself and casting furious looks at the

Watchmen, he swiftly began to thread another length of wire on to one of his wickedly sharp arrows. He was determined to let neither the dragon nor the young Keeper get the better of him.

Again the dragon snarled. Banking its wings sharply and whipping its tail from side to side, it dived towards the rooftop. Immediately all the Alavisians and the Shades cowered backwards, fearful of its fiery breath, but they weren't its target. Talons outstretched, the dragon snatched Charlie by the shoulders and pulled her off the roof.

Stones gasped in astonishment, the arrow dangling uselessly from his hand, as he stared at the empty space that Charlie had previously filled.

'The pendant!' hissed the lead Shade, shocked and angered.

Stones and the Shade rushed to the edge of the rooftop and anxiously peered over. All they could see before the darkness swallowed them up was a brief flapping of wings and a quick flash of Charlie's ridiculously messy hair rapidly dwindling into the distance. Her taunting whoop of laughter echoed up towards them.

Charlie wasn't the least bit scared. In fact, quite the opposite – she was loving every moment of her descent. While the dragon wasn't big enough to lift her any higher, it was strong enough and had large enough wings to act as a huge parachute. Together, the two of them slowly wafted down through Sylvaris's sleeping landscape. Graceful towers waltzed past them, beautifully arched bridges, boulevards and streets swept by and the trees of Deepforest, still far below, swayed slowly beneath her feet. The sensation of flight mixed with the odd feeling of falling was a heady mix and Charlie soon felt giddy with excitement.

The two of them floated further and further away from Narcissa's tower. Gliding gently downward, they sank lower and lower until at last they landed lightly on a narrow walkway. The dragon released its firm grip from her shoulders and with a final beat of its wings hopped down to stand on all four legs by Charlie's feet.

33

Nibbler

Charlie was astonished to realize that, with its wings folded by its side and its tail coiled around its body, the dragon was no bigger than a German Shepherd or a large Mastiff.

'Gosh, you're tiny, aren't you?' she exclaimed.

'Well, of course I'm tiny, I'm only seven!' stated the dragon in an indignant tone. 'I've got a lot more growing to do yet.'

'Uh . . . you can talk?' stuttered Charlie.

'Of course I can talk!' said the creature.

Its voice was young and quite childish, but it had commanding qualities to it that suggested hidden strengths. Charlie got the firm impression that it was a boy.

'Have you ever come across a Winged One that couldn't speak?' it asked.

Charlie's eyes widened. 'You're a Winged One?'

'Duh!' it said, and fluttered its wings to prove its point.

Charlie didn't quite know how to take this. To see a dragon was one thing; for him to turn around and talk to her was quite another. She decided that honesty and politeness were the best way forward. 'Er . . . I'm sorry, you'll have to forgive my ignorance in these matters. I'm not from

Bellania, you see, I'm from Earth, so my knowledge is – how can I say this? – er ... lacking in certain fields,' she stammered, still not quite sure if she was dreaming. 'So if I do say something that sounds a little silly I apologize in advance. Um ... my name is Charlie Keeper, what's yours?'

'Name? I don't have one yet.'

'You're seven and you don't have a name?' she exclaimed.

'Well, I shouldn't have left my chrysalis so early. I wasn't due to hatch for another month, but I had to, didn't I?' said the dragon defensively. 'But of course if I had stayed in I would have been named by the adults on my first awakening.'

'Chrysalis?' mused Charlie. 'I think Lady Dridif mentioned something about that. But wait just a minute, I still don't get it. Why did you have to leave early and what's an awakening? Aren't you awake now?'

'Well, you're right, I am awake, but I shouldn't be. I'm still supposed to be growing and learning back with the others.'

'So how come you're not?'

'Because you called me, that's why!'

'I did?' said Charlie. She was finding this all very surreal.

'Sure, with your pendant. It told me you were in danger. None of the adults woke up, so it was up to me, wasn't it? Can't leave family in danger, it's not right.'

'My pendant?' asked Charlie. She stared down at her necklace for perhaps the thousandth time since arriving in Bellania. Was it honestly responsible for everything that had happened? Her head felt a little dizzy. This was all so strange. 'Family? I'm family, with you?'

'Yes, that's right. You're a Keeper, which means we're family. We share the same blood.'

'So I'm part dragon, you mean?' asked Charlie, getting slightly excited by the idea of that.

'Yes. Well, no . . . sort of. I can't really explain it. You'll have to ask an adult, but they're all still in the Chrysalis Period.'

Charlie looked dumbly at the dragon.

The dragon sighed and shook his head from side to side in a rather sorrowful manner. 'The Chrysalis Period is seven years long. It's what happens when the adults need to shed their old skins and grow new ones so that they can carry on living in this world. They leave Bellania through the Flawed Gate and don't come back until the full seven years are up.'

'So how come you're here, then? If you can come here why can't an adult?'

'Because they just can't, that's why! And I could only come because I'm still a Hatchling, which means that, unlike the adults, I've never left Bellania.'

'Oh . . . OK.'

'So you understand now?'

'No, not really,' admitted Charlie. 'But I'll take your word for it. For now anyway. But I really think we should get going before Stones and that lot come after us.'

'Where do you want to go?'

'To see Jensen and . . . Wait, maybe that's not such a good idea right now.' Charlie sighed as she shamefully remembered their last meeting on Narcissa's drawbridge. 'Azariah! Azariah Keeper will sort things out. I think we should go and see him.'

'OK, then, so where does he live?'

'Er . . . I'm not sure,' said Charlie. 'But if we go to the Jade Tower, which shouldn't be too difficult to find, I'm sure there'll be someone there who can tell us the way. And, er . . . thanks for saving me back there. I, uh . . . really appreciate it.'

The young dragon grinned up at her, his liquid eyes twinkling merrily. 'My pleasure, Charlie.'

'What am I going to call you?' she asked. 'It doesn't feel right, you calling me by my name when I can't return the favour. Are you sure you don't have a name?'

The Winged One rolled his eyes. 'I think I would remember if I'd been given one! It's not the sort of thing I'd be too likely to forget now, is it?'

'OK. Well, in that case, how about I give you a name?'

'You can't.'

'Why not?'

'Because you don't have wings and, besides, I'm not supposed to have one until I'm hatched.'

'But you're "hatched" now, aren't you?'

'Well, yes, but not really. I'm supposed to wait until one of the adult Winged Ones recognizes me as awake. Only then can I be given a name.'

'OK. Well, how about a nickname?'

'A nickname, what's that?'

'It's like an informal name used between friends.'

The young dragon seemed to think for a moment. 'But it's not a real name, though, is it?' he asked dubiously.

'No, it's not a proper name.'

'OK . . . I suppose.'

'Great! How about . . . Green Dragon!' Charlie suggested, throwing her arms out dramatically.

'What's a dragon?'

Charlie stared at the creature. He was joking, wasn't he? '*You're* a dragon!'

'Me? No, I'm not. I'm a Winged One.'

'Sure, you might be a Winged One, but you're a dragon as well. You've got wings, a long tail, lots of scales and you can breathe fire,' said Charlie as she pointed to each in turn. 'So obviously you're a dragon.'

'Nope,' insisted the stubborn young dragon. 'I'm a Winged One.'

Charlie sighed to herself. She got the impression this wasn't going to be easy. Come to think of it, nothing seemed to be that easy in Bellania.

'OK. How about Emerald?'

'Why would you want to call me after a precious stone?'

'Because in a certain light your scales look like emeralds.'

The dragon cocked his head to one side and gave it some thought.

'No, try something else. That sounds too girlie.'

'Talon.'

'No, too sharp.'

'Blaze.'

'Oh, please! How about something with a bit of dignity to it?'

'Um . . . Flame?'

'Nope.'

Charlie folded her arms. 'Well, if you're going to be so difficult why don't you suggest something?'

The dragon screwed his eyes shut and wriggled his claws so that they click-clacked on the ground.

'Nibbler. I'd like to be known as Nibbler.'

'Nibbler? Why Nibbler? That's not very dragony!'

'For the last time, I'm not a dragon! I'm a Winged One!' harrumphed the dragon. 'And I think you should call me Nibbler because whenever I dream it's always about eating and chewing and munching and scrunching. I always have this same dream, see? It's about big fat juicy haunches of meat that just float and dance right in front of my nose, teasing me with their beautiful, yummy smell. My mouth begins to water, my nose goes all quivery and then I pounce! Next thing I know my mouth is full of juicy, runny, gorgeous meat. And for the rest of the dream I'm quite happily nibbling and feasting on prime steak, spare ribs and sirloin fillet.'

Charlie looked at the young creature: he obviously had a big thing for food. 'OK. So Nibbler it is!' she said in relief. 'I'm glad we got that sorted.'

'Well, if it makes you happier.' The small dragon shrugged.

'But could you please settle *my* curiosity? Is it customary for young girls from your realm to dress in such a messy and bedraggled style?'

Charlie looked down at herself. Her jeans were torn and dirty, her sneakers scuffed and her T-shirt was ripped, shredded and cut in about seven different places. Her nails were filthy and a thick line of dirt caked the back of her elbows. She dreaded to think how her face and hair looked.

'Well, what do you expect?' she grumped. 'Since I've come to Bellania I've been chased by Bane and by packs of feral Shades, thrown off a mountain waterfall by an over-enthusiastic mutt of a dog and almost crushed by a giant tree. I've had to flee down the outside of my friend Jensen's tower and, to add to all of that, I've been repeatedly pinched and slapped inside that stinking tower you just saved me from. And to *really* upset me, two chumps threw me into insect-ridden and spider-infested cattle pens! So if I do look a little rough and just the slightest bit scruffy you'll have to forgive me. OK?'

'So this isn't your normal attire?' Nibbler asked flatly.

'If you mean is this the look I spend hours trying to achieve each morning, then the answer is no!'

'OK, just thought I'd ask.'

Nibbler stared nervously at her from the corner of one eye, just in case she decided to jump on him. He got the distinct impression she was the sort of girl who would do such a thing when annoyed. Sensing now was a good time to change the subject, he hurriedly asked, 'So are you going to tell me why the Shades and just about everyone else in that tower were chasing you?'

Charlie sighed, releasing some of the tension that had built up. 'Sure, but it's a long story and I really think we should get going before anyone or any*thing* starts to chase us. Let's go and I'll tell you on the way.'

34

Bad Debts

The Shade was not pleased. It had delivered its side of the bargain yet the pitiful Human woman and her two useless sons had far from completed their part of the deal. Both the young Keeper and the pendant that the Stoman Lord wanted were now out of its reach. And what was more it would appear that a Winged One had now entered into the equation. This would not do. Pulsing with a thick venomous anger, it stalked back into the depths of the tower.

'You! You had a deal to complete and yet you failed miserably! The master will not be pleased. You must come with me to the Western Mountains.'

'Why would I want to do a thing like that?' scorned Lady Narcissa. 'I admit that the exchange didn't go quite as planned, but the girl is still in Sylvaris. I can get her for you.'

'Yes, but that was not in the bargain – the trade was to be tonight! You will come with me to see our lord.'

'What? You must be joking! See the Western Menace? In person? I think not!'

'I do not joke.'

'Well, I don't care if you don't know how to joke – in fact, I couldn't care if you found it impossible to laugh or even squeeze out a chuckle. Because I absolutely, most positively have no intention of stepping foot in the Western Mountains.'

At that moment the Shade *did* find it possible to squeeze out a dry, chuckling cough of a laugh, but it was all at Lady Narcissa's expense. 'You act as though you have a choice in the matter,' he hissed. 'Brethren, take her!'

The rustling pack of Shades rolled forward. Reaching out with dark tendrils and shadowy appendages, they picked up Lady Narcissa.

'Put me down this instant! Put me down!' she shrieked. A shocked look of panic flashed across her face. 'Stix! Stones! Help!'

The Shade's hoarse, dry laugh echoed throughout the room. 'Your precious sons aren't here. Stix has been drugged by the Keeper girl and Stones, so full of brotherly love, has hastened to his side. It would appear that you have been left unattended.'

'Put me down. Please put me down. Please. We can discuss this. We can come to an agreement,' babbled Lady Narcissa. Her beautiful lily-white face became even paler with fear. 'Please don't take me there, not to the Western Mountains!'

'Too late for pleading, Lady Narcissa,' the Shade mocked. 'Far, far too late.'

The Shades gripped Narcissa's arms and legs and gagged her mouth by stuffing their black, cloudy flesh between her teeth. She struggled vainly to free herself, but the Shades were simply too strong. Clutching their prize, the writhing shadows slammed open one of the large stained-glass windows that lined the room and, flowing outward, they scuttled down the tower's side.

Far faster than one would have thought possible, the Shades transported their catch down from the Treman city and into the dark, sour-smelling crevasse that scarred the leaf-strewn soil of Deepforest. From there they transported her far underground to meet her fate in the Western Mountains.

As Charlie and her new companion walked briskly along the walkway and on towards the Jade Tower, she recounted her recent adventures and explained how she had come to be in Bellania. Passing empty squares and quiet roads, the duo travelled through sleeping Sylvaris, the sound of lonely owls and nocturnal bird twitter from the forest below accompanying them along their way. Every once in a while Charlie would turn to stare at Nibbler. She still couldn't get over the fact that he was real. A real dragon! He might call himself a Winged One, but he would always be a dragon to her.

After a short trek they reached the Jade Tower, where several Treman guards stood on watch.

'Hi, guys. I'm Charlie Keeper and I was, er . . . am a guest of Lady Narcissa and I was, er . . .'

'What she means to ask in her roundabout way is how do we find the lodgings of Azariah Keeper?' asked Nibbler, stepping from the shadows to stand by Charlie's side.

'Winged One,' greeted one of the guards. He and the others briefly bowed their heads. 'This is a most unusual occurrence, even for a youth such as yourself. Is everything OK?'

Nibbler nodded serenely. 'I have been woken with

something urgent to attend to. In fact, if you could be discreet about my arrival I would be most grateful.'

Charlie grinned at the dragon's use of such formal language.

'Of course,' answered one of the guards. 'You will find Azariah Keeper's dwelling on the Seventh Avenue in the Merchants' Quarter. Just off to the left down this main walkway here. It's the only building that ain't a shop.'

'Thank you,' said Charlie.

'Please send our fondest regards to Lady Narcissa when you see her next,' added the guard as they turned to leave.

'Oh, I certainly will!' said Charlie through gritted teeth.

The two of them followed the guard's directions and headed back through the city.

'Why is it that everyone thinks Lady Narcissa is such a nice woman when she's nothing more than a horrible witch?'

'I wouldn't know, would I?' said Nibbler. 'But it does sound as though she has been very good at deceiving people, doesn't it? I wonder how she gets away with it. If she's really as bad as you say she is, surely word would have got around by now that she's a nasty piece of work. Maybe she's had help in maintaining a good image.'

'What, like a public relations officer for deceiving witches?' Charlie laughed. 'Well, I don't care. As soon as we see Azariah we can go back to the Jade Circle and warn everyone that she's working with Bane. We'll see who gets the last laugh then! Here, this is the Seventh Avenue. I think this must be the place.'

Azariah's house was made largely from a rich, copper-coloured wood that had been polished and lacquered until it shone. A path wound its way through a beautifully kept garden, up and over a small bridge that spanned an ornamental pond and finally to a wide wooden door that had been carved into the shape of a leaf. Charlie and Nibbler ventured up the path and she knocked on the door.

A light suddenly glowed from one of the first-floor windows, shortly followed by a sharp click-clack from within as many locks were drawn. The door swung inward to reveal Azariah holding a large candle in one hand. He was still dressed in his robe, but here in the comfort of his own home his hood was drawn back to reveal his shaved head. Charlie was fascinated to see peeking out from beneath Azariah's solemn-looking robe a pair of fluffy red slippers. She had to refrain from giggling. Slippers like those really didn't go with his wise-man image.

'Charlie Keeper, this is a surprise, especially at this hour,' he exclaimed in his rich golden voice. His eyes widened slightly as he caught sight of Nibbler standing on all fours by Charlie's side. 'And you have a Winged One with you too, a Hatchling if I'm not mistaken. How strange. But this is not the place for me to start asking questions. Please do come in.'

Azariah swept open the door and invited the two guests into his house. Charlie gazed around with interest as he led them to the large drawing room. It was tidy and simply furnished yet still managed to give off the impression of being very welcoming. A cheerful fire crackled and popped merrily in the centre of the living space and well-worn carpets and rugs muffled the wooden flooring. Across the width of one wall was an immense oil painting of an exotic-looking woman and on the opposite wall hung a large branch of a flowering cherry tree that was in full bloom, giving the room an enticing scent.

'So, young Charlie, before you tell me why you arrive at my doorstep at such a late hour in such a bedraggled state, and with a Winged One that should be fast asleep many leagues from here . . . could I perhaps offer you a hot drink and a sweet pastry?'

Charlie's rumbling stomach supplied her answer.

'I'll take that as a yes.' He smiled. 'And for you, Winged One, can I tempt you with a bowl of Larva-Larva fruit?'

'You've got Larva-Larva fruit?' Nibbler licked his lips with his long golden tongue and rubbed his two front paws together in anticipation. 'Oh, yum! Yes please!'

As they waited, Charlie settled herself into one of the large, cosy armchairs. Nibbler sat on the carpet by her feet and coiled himself into a ball. The two of them gazed in comfortable silence at the flickering flames and, for the first time in days, relaxed.

Azariah returned with a steaming mug of hot chocolate and a fat almond croissant stuffed with vanilla cream for Charlie, and for Nibbler a large selection of glowing red fruits that smelt wonderfully of peanut butter and peach.

He sat down in one of the other comfortable armchairs. 'Now then, Charlie. I suspect you have a story to tell. Please tell me what has happened since we last met, and know that you may safely speak your mind in my house.'

So Charlie did.

35

A New Master

Lady Narcissa was dropped like a sack of potatoes before the dais of the Devouring Throne. Desperate to hide her terror and striving to retain her dignity, she struggled to her feet. Sucking in a deep breath of the cold, clammy air that sluggishly moved around the room, she slowly raised her head.

Bane, the Western Menace, was seated upon the throne. A flickering black halo of anger pulsed and writhed menacingly around him.

'So you failed to deliver on your promise?' he growled.

Lady Narcissa did her best not to tremble, but her fear got the better of her. 'My, m-m-my lord, I am sorry, truly. But, b-b-but –'

'Be quiet, worm. I do not want to hear any of your bumbling, pathetic excuses. I do not need to hear how you failed in your task, all I need to know is that fail you did.'

'My lord –'

'SILENCE!' roared Bane. The thunderous force of his voice sent Narcissa's white robes fluttering as though caught in a gale. 'Be grateful that I have not stripped your flesh from your bones. Rejoice in the fact that I have not torn your skull from your spine and scooped out your innards, you useless wretch!'

Rising to his feet, Bane descended from his throne to stand above his quaking, shivering and terror-stricken victim. Petrified, Lady Narcissa had to tilt her head back to stare up at the giant's cowled face.

'You have failed to fulfil your side of the bargain. The price for this crime is your soul and your liberty! You now belong to me.'

'But, my lord . . .'

Bane grabbed Narcissa by the jaw and squeezed her mouth shut so that nothing more than a gurgled squawk could pass her lips. Casually, he picked her up so that she dangled like a rag doll from his upraised arm.

'Be quiet, maggot. There is no haggling or debate in this matter – my word is law. You are now mine. My puppet. My slave. My toy. And to think otherwise is to face a fate much worse than death.' Bane dropped Lady Narcissa and, striding back up to his throne, he sat down. 'As my slave my first commandment to you is to ensure that you bring me this Charlie Keeper and her pendant.'

Narcissa was clearly stunned at how fate had twisted her luck. How could she have gone from being one of Sylvaris's most powerful councillors to this: someone else's slave? How could things have gone so wrong, so fast? This would teach her to make deals with the devil, she thought regretfully. However, Lady Narcissa was no shrinking violet and she was determined to wring the best from any situation, no matter how bad it was.

'And my reward for doing this? Does the initial deal still stand?'

'What!' bellowed Bane in disbelief. 'You have the cheek to push your luck in such a matter? I should have you thrown to the Shades for such impudence!'

Amazingly Narcissa's greed got the better of her fear. 'Consider it as an incentive, to speed things up, so to speak.'

Bane was silent for a brief moment. 'You may have the opportunity for reward should you succeed in bringing me the girl –'

'Thank you, my lord, thank you! You will not regret this, I promise!'

'But for your blundering, inexcusable mistake,' continued Bane, 'you shall be punished.'

'Wh-what? B-but I thought . . .' stammered Narcissa.

'You thought that I would forgive your error?' growled the Stoman Lord. 'Or did you merely think that I would simply forget? Clearly you do not quite grasp the fact that I am now your master. It is I who shall decide when to reward you and when to punish you. And I shall do so whenever I feel fit. And now, now you are to be punished for failing me. Guards! Take her to the Chambers of Silence and be sure that she receives a most suitable punishment . . . But do not damage her beyond repair, for she has yet to complete her tasks.'

A pair of muscular Stoman guards forced the squirming, screaming and clearly terrified woman to the floor. Swiftly they bound her legs and feet, trussing her up like a turkey ready for the oven.

'B-but . . . please! Please, my lord, don't do this!' squealed

Narcissa. 'I'm sorry, I'm so sorry. I'll never fail you again. Never! I promise. Just please don't do this to me. Please!'

'Silence her,' commanded Bane.

One of the guards forced a length of cloth into Narcissa's mouth until only a faint whimper could be heard.

'Good. When you return from your penance, we will discuss what you are to do to obtain the Keeper girl and her pendant!'

36

Words of Wisdom

'. . . So that's how we got here.'

'It sounds like you've had quite an adventure,' said Azariah, the wooden beads in his beard clacking as he leaned back in his chair. 'I have always had my doubts about Lady Narcissa – something about her perfect image never seemed to ring true. But for her to turn out to be such a twisted piece of work still comes as quite a shock. In fact, I will go so far as to say that I'm sickened to think that this woman has shared a seat in our council and has sat there unsuspected for so long. I hate to think what atrocities she has got away with in the name of the Jade Council over the years! Still at least we now know the truth. If I have my way the Jade Circle will imprison her and her wayward sons for the rest of their lives!'

'Surely that won't be easy,' said Nibbler from where he lay snuggled up on the carpet. 'She sounds like a major player. I'll bet she's got powerful connections that will shield her from Charlie's accusations.'

'You're quite right – it won't be an easy endeavour. But I think that we have more than sufficient proof to put her away. Charlie's word as a Keeper will be considered iron-clad. If she accuses Narcissa of committing evil deeds, at the very least the Jade Circle will have to sit up and take note. Secondly, we have Charlie's dishevelled appearance to consider. If Lady Narcissa was her custodian, how did Charlie manage to wind up in such a bruised and battered state? Thirdly, and most importantly, we have the Isiris Bracelets. By Sylvarisian Law these are forbidden objects. The fact that Narcissa owns and has used a pair should see her sent to the deepest, darkest prison we have for a minimum of twenty years. And finally, Nibbler, we will have your testimony that you saw Shades on the roof of the Ivory Tower. This will indisputably point to Narcissa's dealing with Bane and her betrayal of Sylvaris.'

'Great!' Charlie grinned. 'Payback time!'

'Indeed, young lady, it would appear so. Yet it saddens me greatly to think that Bane has managed to reach so far into our culture and way of life. Everywhere I look I see the threat of war drawing closer. These are truly dark and unsettled times.'

'Azariah?'

'Yes, Charlie?'

'May I ask a question?'

'You may, but our deal still remains in place: you may only ask three questions of importance at any one time.'

Charlie groaned, although she should have expected no less. Wriggling deeper into her armchair, she took a long slurp on her hot chocolate and composed her thoughts.

'OK, my first question is . . . what is so important about my pendant? The Jade Circle wants it and I know Bane definitely wants it, but what does it do?'

'Hhmm, good question, Charlie. What does it do indeed? Well, to be honest with you . . . I'm not too sure.'

'What?' cried Charlie. 'You're not sure! But you're a Keeper. I thought you would know everything.'

'Ha!' Azariah chuckled, his golden-brown eyes beaming with good humour. 'I wish that I did indeed know everything, but unfortunately such a delicious wish is not a possibility.'

'But surely you must know something about my pendant?'

'Well, yes, I do know certain details, but these are all based on mere whispers and rumours that I have heard over the years. You must not take these as proven fact, but I will share what I know.' He made himself comfortable in his chair. 'So, then . . . Bane, with great cunning, timed his rise to power so that it coincided with the Winged Ones' Chrysalis Period, which as you know is the era during which Bellania has no guardians. This has in effect given Bane nearly seven years to wage war, conquer new lands and consolidate his power without the Winged Ones being present to oppose him.'

'What does consolidate mean?' enquired Nibbler with a puzzled frown.

'In this case it means to increase the strength and stability of his armies and to secure his hold over conquered lands. In other words, Bane has used these years to grow more powerful.'

Nibbler nodded and grinned his thanks.

'Good, now . . . You should know that Bane's suspicious behaviour prior to the Chrysalis Period did not go entirely unnoticed. The Winged Ones, fearing that Bane would attempt to consolidate his might and influence while they were away, apparently drew up plans to be used in their absence – plans that would bring about Bane's defeat. The whispered rumours suggest that the Winged Ones created a secret weapon powerful enough to wipe Bane from Bellania's surface. These whispers also go on to hint that your pendant is the key that will lead to this hidden weapon's whereabouts, which is precisely what makes it so desirable. The Jade Circle wants your pendant so that they can find this weapon, stop the war and bring peace back to the land. While Bane must, at all costs, find and destroy it to ensure he stays in power. Your pendant, young Keeper, can tip the balance of power either way. The fate of Bellania rests, quite literally, around your neck.'

'Wow!' breathed Charlie. She pulled the pendant from beneath her T-shirt and gave it a good examination. 'Nibbler, do you know anything about this?' she asked, running her fingers along its bumpy surface.

'Me? No, first I've heard of it. But can I have a look, see if there's anything that looks familiar?'

'Sure,' said Charlie, getting out of her seat and going over to Nibbler. She held up the pendant.

The young dragon sniffed it, licked it, prodded it and made Charlie hold it up to the firelight so he could examine it all the better.

'Well, do you see anything?' she asked.

'Er . . . well . . . not really. But I can tell you that it looks sort of like an egg . . . or maybe it's an acorn?'

'I could have told you that! Isn't there anything else you can tell us? Surely you must know something!'

'Well, it does taste kind of good. Sort of Tarentellaberry

with a touch of hazelnut. I guess if you got hungry you could always suck on it. Does that help?'

'How can you be a Winged One and not know anything?' growled Charlie.

'Children, children!' interrupted Azariah. 'There's really no need to squabble. For every lock there is a key, for every puzzle there is a solution. We will in time be able to solve the pendant's mystery. What any wise man would do now is take it to someone who has knowledge regarding Winged Ones' artefacts.'

'Are you such a person?' asked Nibbler.

'Unfortunately not. But there are many such scholars in the Jade Council. It shouldn't be too hard to get an informed opinion. However, given recent developments with Lady Narcissa, getting a *safe* opinion might be a different matter. We desperately need to have your pendant examined by someone, otherwise we will never understand its mysteries, but we must ensure that we can trust them.'

'And who would you recommend for that?' asked Nibbler.

'Lady Dridif,' said Azariah. 'She out of all the councillors is beyond doubt. Her great strength and passionate stubbornness for Bellania's cause puts her beyond reproach. What is more, her knowledge and wisdom is second to none within this city. If anyone can unlock your pendant's hidden knowledge it is her. Charlie, I hope that has answered your first question, so if you will, your second question.'

Charlie didn't hesitate: 'My parents, how can I free them from Bane's Tapestry?'

'Not easily, would be my simple reply. Bane's Throne Room is perhaps the most heavily defended site in Bellania.

Whole legions of fanatically loyal Stoman soldiers prowl the Western Mountains, venomous packs of Shades haunt the palace and, according to legend, other more twisted creatures stalk the inner sanctums. And as if that were not bad enough, Bane very rarely leaves his citadel and when he does his Dark God guards his Throne Room in his absence. To enter such a fortified location would be folly in the extreme.'

'What about opening a Portal to the Throne Room and quickly snatching Charlie's parents from the Tapestry? If you did it fast enough I'm sure you could be in and out before anyone could react,' suggested Nibbler.

'A good proposal, Nibbler, but sadly an impossibility. Bane is no fool and will have had his palace, if not the whole of the Western Mountains, shielded from unauthorized travelling of the paths. The second point is that Bane's Tapestry is immense, containing hundreds of his vanquished enemies. We could not possibly open a Portal large enough to transport such an object.'

'So what can be done to get Charlie's parents back?'

'Unfortunately the only option is the most difficult,' said Azariah. 'Bane must be defeated. Only when Bellania is free from his cursed reign can we go about curing the land. With Bane removed we will have access to all of his trapped and imprisoned victims, including those in the Tapestry. There would also no longer be a force to block the imminent return of the Winged Ones. With their wise counsel and experience we could safely remove all of those bound to the Tapestry.'

'And is there really no other way?' asked Charlie.

'I have thought long and hard on this subject and I can honestly say that I see no other option.'

'What about if I trade my pendant for their release? Surely Bane would agree to such a deal?'

'Indeed, he probably would, but then you would have traded away Bellania's liberty.'

'But I want my parents back!' snapped Charlie.

'I know, Charlie, I know,' said Azariah. His lion-like face softened as he took in her anguish. 'But if you were to hand over the pendant, what guarantee would you have that Bane would honour his side of the bargain? And even if he did, he might then take over the whole of Bellania, and what would stop him from going to Earth and trying his luck in that realm? Also please do not forget that as much as your parents love you they are Keepers. It is their – and your – duty to maintain peace and balance in Bellania. To hand over the last chance for freedom from Bane would be a betrayal of their beliefs, no matter how well intentioned.'

'But I want them back,' whispered Charlie, her voice cracking. 'It's not fair. It's just not fair at all!'

'Charlie Keeper, I know it's not fair. But you must worry less about life's little disappointments and concentrate your heart and mind on the good things that come your way. Just think of all the obstacles that you have overcome in your journey getting here. You have succeeded where so many would have fallen! You are an astonishing young lady and don't you ever forget it.'

Charlie was genuinely surprised by his words. She thought that perhaps he was teasing her, but one look at his strong, proud face told her otherwise. Azariah Keeper meant every word that he'd just said.

'Now, the hour is very late and I insist that you go to bed soon. So, if you please, your last question.'

What Charlie had really wanted to ask Azariah ever since leaving Lady Narcissa's miserable tower was if he would teach her how to open Portals and Gateways. After Stix and Stones had given her a brief and tantalizing glimpse into what she could achieve, she really, really wanted to learn as much as possible. The idea of being able to open magical Gateways was as though all her wildest dreams had suddenly come true. But for now there was something she urgently needed help with, something that just had to be asked first.

'Will you help me to prove to Jensen and Kelko that I was forced to say those horrible words to them on the draw-bridge? I would never say anything to hurt them, especially something as cruel and as spiteful as that. Will you help me show them I'm still their friend? Please?'

Azariah's face softened. 'Of course, Charlie. It would be a pleasure to help you with such an endeavour. But now it is long past the time for you to be in bed. If you and Nibbler would be so good as to follow me, I will show you to your sleeping quarters.'

37

Penance

Lady Narcissa gasped as she stood swaying painfully from side to side beneath the Devouring Throne. Her beautiful dress was ruined and hung in tatters. Dark circles had formed around her bloodshot eyes and a layer of sweat caked her forehead.

Her punishment had been intense. Very intense.

A large Stoman guard held her arm in a steel-like grip. It was hard to tell if the guard was there to secure Narcissa or simply there to hold her up in case she fell.

'Little squishy Human, the pain that you have tasted tonight was just a fraction of what I will give you should you fail me again,' said Bane in his stony voice. 'Do not make any more mistakes.'

Narcissa's face, if it were possible, went an even paler shade of white.

'Now that we understand one another, listen well to my instructions. This is what I want you to do when you return to Sylvaris . . .'

Lady Narcissa did indeed listen carefully to her new master. She would be very, very sure to do exactly what he wanted. She never again intended to go through the agonizing and degrading punishment that Bane's servants had devised for her. She would follow his instructions to the letter.

'. . . so I expect you to use their feeble Sylvarisian Law to further my goals,' continued Bane. 'Once you have gone ahead with these commands I will send a Shade to deliver my further instructions. Is that understood?'

'Yes, my lord,' whispered Narcissa. 'But my daughter . . . must you include her in your plans?'

'I will use any tool I deem necessary.'

'But, my lord, she's barely sixteen. She –'

'Enough! Six or sixteen, adult or child, I care not. I claim your family and hold them beneath my fist. All that is yours is mine to command. Now, will you do as I instruct or must I send you back to the Halls of Silence for further punishment?'

'No, my lord. I-I will do as you see fit.' She would have curtsied but she doubted her body could manage it. Shivers of pain still shook her from within, so instead she bowed her head in deference. 'It shall be done as you command. If I may . . . I have one request to ask of you, lord.'

'I strongly advise you not to push your luck any further. I doubt your feeble body could withstand any more pain,' growled Bane. 'But if you wish to speak go ahead. Just remember that I will not accept any insolence.'

Narcissa blanched slightly. Bane's constant threats were incredibly unnerving. Taking yet another deep breath, she gathered what little courage she had left and pushed ahead. 'Stoman Lord, this is regarding the young Winged One. It is unquestionably powerful and its entrance came as a surprise. Surprises, especially ones like this, could be a thorn in your side. I will need an ally to aid me in Sylvaris, someone with powers to match those of a Winged One. Someone who is also strong enough to counter any interruption should another Keeper be stupid enough to get in the way.'

'Hhmm. Not such a foolish request after all. Very well, then, I shall arrange for a . . . suitable . . . servant to come and give you such aid as you might need.'

'When will this servant come to me? I might need assistance sooner than we expect.'

'Pale little maggot, do not worry yourself. He will arrive in plenty of time for my plans to succeed.' Bane clapped his hand together. 'Shades, remove this wriggling wretch of a Human, take her back to Sylvaris and make haste, for she must be there by sun-up.'

Sinuous shadows detached themselves from the murky darkness. Snaking their way across the floor, they removed Narcissa from the guard's grasp. Enveloping her in their sinister embrace, they began to make their way from the Throne Room.

Bane stared after Narcissa as she was borne away by the Shades. 'Do not fail me,' he snarled after her.

The room fell into a deep silence as Bane settled back into the cold embrace of his Devouring Throne. Nothing moved apart from the gentle flicker of mist and shadows that hugged the chamber's floor. Guards and footmen stood at attention, almost statue-like, their attention focused solely on their lord.

It was only after the passing of several hours that Bane once again moved.

'Shades, attend me. I wish for you to bring me that filthy, greedy magpie of a Human from Charlie Keeper's home. Bring me that sneaky lawyer, Mr Crow. I think it is time for him to be put to some use. He will make a most perfect and suitable servant to attend to these matters at hand. Go.'

38

The Law Comes Knocking

Charlie awoke with a groan. As ever, bad dreams haunted her sleep. Pushing her messy hair from her face, she struggled into a sitting position. Nibbler still lay coiled and snuggled up at the foot of the bed.

Swinging her feet out from beneath the bedcover, she stood up and shuffled over to the window. The sun was rising and as usual Sylvaris looked gorgeous. The city was a vision she never grew weary of.

There was a soft knock at the door. Azariah popped his head in. 'Ah, I see you're up. Excellent. I have just sent a runner to inform the Jade Circle that they should expect us. So if you please, get dressed and meet me downstairs.' Azariah pulled the door shut, but his voice shouted back a moment later, 'Oh, and there's food for the two of you on the kitchen table. Help yourselves!'

A little later, after a belly-swelling breakfast of Landlion-Bark Brownies and Calice-Goldenberry Cakes, Charlie felt ready to face whatever new challenges the day would bring. Nibbler had feasted on Thrice-Spiced Kangol Rump, but he had been a bit too greedy when drinking his portion of Ferral and Bokonut Iced Tea and had spent the last ten minutes burping so loudly that he sounded like a foghorn. Fortunately, as his stomach finally digested his bountiful breakfast, the burping had diminished and had now thankfully stopped.

'So are the two of you ready?' enquired Azariah. Charlie and Nibbler both nodded. 'Good. But before we go, a quick word of warning. Not everyone will be thrilled to hear our accusations against Lady Narcissa. She is a well-respected and, though I know this is going to sound odd, a well-loved member of the Jade Circle. She has over the years presented such a kind and caring façade that just about everyone on the council has fallen for it, hook, line and sinker. So when we do raise our accusations against Narcissa don't be too shocked if there's a lot of shouting and anger.'

Charlie nodded determinedly. She wasn't going to let Narcissa deceive the council any longer, but would they really believe what she had to say? Maybe it would be like trying to convince her teachers back home about how horrible Mr Crow was. Because he paid them so well and always wore a false smile in their presence, they consistently ignored her claims.

'Do not worry,' said Azariah, seeing her concern. 'With all of the evidence that we have at hand, it shouldn't take long to open the councillors' eyes to the truth. Hopefully by the day's end Narcissa will be behind bars and we can proceed with investigating your pendant.'

A loud banging interrupted their conversation as a heavy hand beat against Azariah's front door. Nibbler and Charlie both looked up in alarm. Just who was that making so much noise?

'Do not worry yourselves,' said Azariah with a gentle smile. 'I thought it would be prudent to arrange for some guards to escort us to the Jade Tower. After all, we cannot allow Narcissa or the Shades another chance to steal the pendant or harm you, Charlie.'

The banging started up again, louder than before. A small frown creased across Azariah's face. 'They might be guards of the Jade Circle, but there is no excuse for such rudeness. Please excuse me.'

Striding towards the entrance with an irate expression on his face, the councillor began to unfasten the many locks on his door. 'OK, OK, I heard you the first time! There is no need to use my beautiful door as a punch bag!'

Azariah pulled the door open and immediately stepped backwards. A whole squad of Treman guards in Jade uniform crowded his ornate garden, ruining his manicured lawn and trampling across his shrubs.

It was obvious to Charlie that something was wrong. Many of the guards had heavy scowls plastered across their faces and a few had drawn their swords from their scabbards.

The squad's captain – an arrogant and rather haughty-looking Treman – lowered his hand. Apparently he had been enjoying slamming it against the door. He was dressed in a plumed helmet and wore a smart green kilt. Sucking in his podgy gut and straining to push out his chest, he attempted to look as official as possible.

'Azariah and Charlie Keeper, I presume?' he asked, peering past Azariah to stare at Charlie standing nearby.

'Yes, that's correct, Captain. May I point out that

attempting to use my door as a snare drum will not speed up your prospects for promotion!' snarled Azariah. 'And you there, yes, you by the pond, you horrible man, get off my Zephyrillis shrubs this instant! Now, what is the meaning of this? I request an escort to maintain my guests' safety and this is how you respond? Explain yourself immediately before I really lose my temper!'

'Explain meself, ta ya?' leered the captain. 'I don't think so. The only explaining that's gonna be done around here is when ya lot are in jail! Ya and Charlie Keeper are under arrest for treason, for consorting with Bane's agents and for assaulting Lady Narcissa!' Lifting his hand high, he waved his guards forward. 'Men, grab them!'

The Treman guards sprang forward. Rushing up the path, they hurtled towards Charlie and Azariah.

Charlie was astounded. Didn't they know they'd got it wrong? They were supposed to be arresting Lady Narcissa for her crimes, not the other way round. Although the guards, like all Tremen, were small, they made up for what they were missing in size with sheer determination. Shouting and hollering, they sprinted up the garden path.

Azariah stepped forward to meet them. A small vein on his forehead began to throb and pulse as his eyes squinted into a terrible stare. His mouth tugged into a fierce grimace and his clothes began to writhe and ripple in an unseen wind.

Charlie froze. She had never seen Azariah looking so angry. In fact, she'd never seen *anyone* looking quite like that.

'HOLD!' he roared in such a loud voice that the captain's plumed helmet flew from his head. 'HOLD, I SAY!'

Hooking his hands into the odd clawing shape that Charlie had previously seen on the Torn Bridge, Azariah swept out a golden, treacle-like tide of rippling light that enveloped and trapped the startled guards. Punching his hands forward, he knocked all the officers off their feet. Scowling murderously, he marched forward, swinging his arms from side to side, pushing and rolling the guards backwards until, with a great splash, they all ended up in the ornamental pond.

'How dare you!' bellowed Azariah, his anger unabated. 'How dare you believe that you can come to my home and try to arrest me? I am AZARIAH KEEPER! Does that mean nothing to you? I have walked the paths through light and dark. I have held fast the Gateways against the rampant tide of darkness and fought daemons from the abyss! I have travelled where none would dare and you believe that you can treat me and my guests like this? I should tear the very heavens down around your heads!'

Azariah stopped shouting and blinked. The guards, waist-deep in water, were petrified. Shaking and shivering with fear, they groaned and begged forgiveness. The captain, covered with pondweed, was weeping and blubbering like a three-year-old, while a frog perched nearby was quite happily croaking away on the captain's floating helmet. The guards had gone from dangerous foes to bundles of whimpering jelly in four seconds flat.

'Gah!' snorted Azariah, his anger quickly mellowing. 'What are you, men or children? Come on. Stand up, all of you. Come on. Up you get. Good . . . Now, if you would . . . Hey, you! Watch out for my lilies! OK, look, just line up on the path and don't touch anything.'

'Y-y-ya won't hurt us?' whimpered the captain. 'Ya won't turn us inta skunks or nothing?'

'No, no,' promised Azariah. He threw Charlie and Nibbler a quick wink. 'I won't do anything like that. Just so long as you behave.'

'We will, we will!' promised the tearful captain, his kilt now heavy and dripping with water. 'I'm sorry ta have been so rude, b-b-but I was just following orders.'

'Yes, I'm sure you were,' agreed Azariah, quite amicably. 'And out of interest, whose orders were they?'

'Lord Nazareth's, yer honourship.'

'Aah,' said Azariah, giving Charlie a knowing look. 'Everything becomes clearer now. And what were his exact orders?'

'Ta place ya under arrest and bring ya back ta the Jade Circle.'

'Oh, how very surprising,' said Azariah in a dry drawl. Charlie got the impression he wasn't at all surprised by this news. 'Hhmm, well, we can't allow you to disappoint Lord Nazareth, can we?'

'Er . . . no, yer . . . lordiness,' gabbled the captain. 'We can't?'

'No of course we can't. Arresting me and my guest is obviously out of the question, but I'm sure that no harm would come from you escorting us to the Jade Tower. What do you say?'

'Uh, wotever yer most excellent excellency requires,' the captain quickly agreed as he clutched at the few straws on offer.

'Glad to hear it, old chap. Very well, then. Nibbler, Charlie, if you would be so good as to join me.'

Charlie grinned, impressed by how quickly Azariah had turned the situation around in their favour. Nibbler smirked as he passed the sodden Treman guards. The captain was on his hands and knees, struggling to reclaim his helmet from the pond and the bemused frog.

Once all the guards had collected their discarded armour from across Azariah's lawn, they fell into place behind the three companions to form a guard of honour, albeit a very soggy and dishevelled one that squelched as it marched across Sylvaris to the Jade Tower.

39

A Courtroom Fiasco

People began to point and stare as the small procession walked past. Much of the attention was reserved for Nibbler, but the city's inhabitants were also curious as to the identity of the scruffy young girl walking at the head of the small parade. Charlie began to blush at all the attention. Nibbler, on the other hand, appeared to love it and soon he was strutting up and down by Charlie's side.

'Stop it!' hissed Charlie. 'Everyone's looking!'

'I know. Great, isn't it?' smirked Nibbler, puffing out his chest and prancing about. 'I could get used to this.'

'It's embarrassing!'

'What? No, it's not – it's great! Hey, look at those guys, they're all waving! Hiya! Hi, guys, how you doing? Hey, look at me! Check these bad boys,' bragged Nibbler, tensing his muscles, pulling some fancy footwork and flapping his powerful wings for everyone's entertainment. 'Wheee, yeah! I'm hot, I'm smoking, I'm on fire!'

Charlie slapped her hand over her eyes as Nibbler started blowing smoke rings, shooting out little jets of flame and generally making an exhibition of himself. Did he have no shame?

Azariah smiled fondly as he watched the antics of his young charges. Turning off the main boulevard, he led the small procession across a sweeping bridge and into the Jade Tower.

Upon their arrival, servants swung open the many doors that led into the Council Chamber. Footmen cried out to announce their arrival as the unusual procession swept in to meet the Jade Circle.

'At last,' spat Nazareth. His beady shark's eyes glared at the trio.

'A Winged One?' exclaimed Dridif, observing Nibbler. 'But the hibernation period is not yet over.'

Nibbler stepped forward as the other councillors expressed their shock at the sight of the sacred creature. They all quietened as he spoke. 'I am a Hatchling,' he explained. 'My Chrysalis Period was interrupted by a call for help from this young Keeper.' He nodded towards Charlie. 'But I'm afraid I don't yet possess the wisdom of my elders.'

Dridif nodded, but looked unsettled. Nazareth was quick to react. With a grand, eloquent gesture he bowed formally to those gathered around the table. Before anyone could say a word he launched his attack.

'As a councillor I would like to formally lay charges of aggravated assault and treason against Azariah and Charlie Keeper.' His words were laced with poisonous intent. 'And seeing that they have finally managed to grace us with their presence, I should like to move briskly forward and proceed with the prosecution.'

Immediately there was uproar as the whole chamber

dissolved into bedlam and chaos. Voices screamed and hollered, fingers were pointed and wild accusations were flung about as Charlie, Azariah and Nibbler stood silently, shocked by the mayhem.

Through the pandemonium Charlie couldn't help but notice that Lady Narcissa, seated on the far side of the Jade Table, was calm and collected, the perfect image of innocence. She gave Charlie a knowing smile. But Charlie wasn't fooled: she could still see the cold, icy look of hatred hidden deep in the councillor's eyes. Stix and Stones were standing nearby with menacing expressions plastered across their faces. Charlie shivered out of reflex before rebelliously glaring back at her opponents.

It was Dridif, the Royal Oak, who returned order to the Council Chamber in her usual manner of slamming her hands on the Jade Table. It was like a thunderclap going off right inside the room.

She then stared pointedly at each and every councillor until they looked away, shamefaced. One by one the blushing and embarrassed councillors took their seats. Finally only she and Nazareth were left standing. Dridif raised one eyebrow.

'Why aren't those two Keepers in irons?' snapped Nazareth, ignoring Dridif's warning look. 'They are supposed to be under arrest. Handcuff them!'

'Nazareth,' said Dridif.

'Well, don't just stand there, Captain. Arrest them!' hissed Nazareth, still pointedly ignoring Dridif.

'Oh, Nazareth . . .' whispered Dridif in a soft, sing-song voice.

'Captain, I won't tell you again,' threatened Nazareth, unaware that the room had gone deathly quiet and that all eyes were upon him. 'Those two are traitors and as such . . .'

'NAZARETH!' howled Dridif.

Charlie flinched. She'd never heard anything like it. It was the roar of a banshee, the shout of an angered goddess, the scream of a hundred thousand voices all hollering in unison.

Nazareth, caught by the full force of Dridif's hurricane, was hurled across the room to slam heavily against the far wall. Slowly he slid to the floor. Dridif made a slight clawing gesture with her finger and Nazareth's unconscious body tottered upright and lurched back to his chair. Releasing her hold upon him, Nazareth slumped forward so that his head rested on the table's surface. He began to drool down the side of his mouth.

'I will not abide any – ANY! – disobedience while I hold dis chair!' snapped Dridif. Her old, wise face creased with anger. 'If there are ta be any accusations levelled here today it will be done in a calm, polite and professional manner.'

Once again Dridif fixed each and every councillor with her steely gaze. When she was sure she'd got her message across, she made another little whirling motion with her finger. Nazareth awoke with a start. Looking wildly around the Council Chamber, he hurriedly straightened his robes, sorted out his beard and wiped the drool from his face. Folding his hands neatly together on the table, he straightened his back and generally tried to sit still like a good little boy.

Charlie couldn't quite stop a smirk from appearing on her face. Curiosity also got the better of her. 'How does Lady

Dridif do that?' she whispered to Azariah. 'It's not tree-singing, is it?'

'No, it is not,' replied Azariah, also whispering out the side of his mouth. 'Dridif's strength comes from the Jade Table. It is a gift from the Winged Ones. As a sign of their support and belief in the Jade Circle, they have embedded the table with some of their power. Whoever leads the Jade Circle controls its powers. In this case it's Dridif and while she's in this room she is very much the boss.'

'So it's magic?'

'What is it with you and magic? It isn't magic, it's a –'

'Stop that whispering!' scolded Dridif. 'Now, if we can all agree ta act like adults we shall begin again. Nazareth, ya wish ta accuse Azariah and Charlie Keeper of assault and treason?'

'Er . . .' Nazareth coughed slightly and did his very best not to shoot a quick tell-tale glance in Narcissa's direction. Still dazed, he shook himself and hurriedly collected his thoughts. It didn't take long for his lofty, self-important expression to settle back on to his face. 'Yes, I do.'

'And why do ya wish ta make these charges?' enquired Dridif.

'Because that little brat,' snarled Nazareth, getting back into the flow of things, 'in association with Azariah Keeper, conspired to sell the secrets of her pendant to Bane, the Western Menace. When she was caught in the act she, with the aid of the rogue Winged One we see before us, assaulted Lady Narcissa, near-poisoned one of the Delightful Brothers and made good her escape by using a forbidden set of Isiris Bracelets on the remaining Delightful Brother.'

At that point Charlie took a step forward to protest, but Azariah held out his hand to stop her.

'I would also like to point out,' Nazareth continued, 'that before she fled the scene of the crime she and the Winged One tried to hide the evidence of her actions by setting fire to the Ivory Tower. Fortunately only the uppermost floor was burned before the brave Alavisian Watchmen managed to extinguish the blaze. That little girl is a clear and present danger to the safety of Sylvaris! I demand that she be jailed!'

Charlie couldn't believe it. They'd changed everything around so that she was the scapegoat! Nazareth was setting her up to take the fall for Narcissa's evil dealings. Charlie's jaw dropped open. She was, for perhaps the very first time in her life, completely and utterly dumbfounded.

'And can ya prove these accusations? Do ya have any witnesses?'

Nazareth smirked. 'Oh yes, I most certainly do. And I have evidence to prove their guilt. In fact, if I could call forward my first witness, Aranea, Mistress of the Spinnery, then I'm quite sure –'

'There will be time for witnesses later,' interrupted Dridif. She stared at Charlie and Azariah as though weighing up their worth. 'And what do ya have ta say about all of dis, Charlie Keeper?'

'It's a great big, dirty, stinking lie!' retorted Charlie. 'You might all think that Lady Narcissa is a nice and kind woman, but she's nothing of the sort! She beat me, slapped me, forced me to do horrible, twisted things, let her two sons bully me, threw me into her stinking cattle pens and tried to sell me and my pendant to Bane! She's the traitor, not me!'

'Oh, come now, you surely can't expect anyone here to believe that?' chuckled Nazareth. 'The word of a scruffy, spoilt teenager against the word of Lady Narcissa, one of our most valued councillors? Oh, please!'

'It's true!' shouted Charlie, stamping her foot in frustration. 'She's in league with Bane and she means to sell you all out!'

'Well, it appears as though we have a contradiction in accusations here,' said Dridif, staring first at Charlie and then at Nazareth, a shrewd look in her wise eyes. 'Nazareth, ya accuse Charlie Keeper of dealing with Bane and ya say that ya have proof. Correct?'

'That is quite right, your Honour, absolutely –'

'A simple "yes" will suffice, Nazareth. Please don't get carried away with grand gestures. It annoys me and I know that ya wouldn't want ta displease me any further.'

'Er, no, First Speaker,' muttered Nazareth.

'And you, Charlie Keeper, you accuse Lady Narcissa of the same crime, do ya not?'

'Yes, I do!' said Charlie, with a fierce glare at Nazareth. 'And the Delightful Brothers, they're in on it too!'

'Well, thank ya for clearing that up.' Dridif smiled, but there was no humour or kindness in her eyes, just cold logic as she added up all the facts. This wasn't Dridif, the nice old Treman who had first welcomed Charlie into Sylvaris; this was Lady Dridif, the Iron Councillor, whose first and foremost duty was to protect her city. Dridif clapped her hands together sharply. 'Guards! Seal dis room. No one is ta get in or go out without me express permission!'

A muttering and rumbling of disbelief erupted from all

the councillors as heavily armed Treman guards took up positions in front of all the doors. As one, they drew their swords.

'Might I enquire why you feel it necessary for such an action?' asked Flint, the large Stoman councillor. 'No blade has been drawn in this Council Chamber for the past one hundred and twenty years!'

'Is it not obvious?' said Dridif. 'Logic dictates that if each is accusing the other of the same crime, then one of them must surely be guilty. Guilty of treason against Sylvaris! With the exits barred, the traitor is trapped, so now all we have ta do is discover who is lying and who is telling the truth.'

40

A Dark God

'Pah! What is the meaning of this?' sputtered Mr Crow, as he was manhandled along by two writing Shades. His large nose quivered with indignation. 'You foul things! Release me at once!'

'Our lord requires your presence and you will obey,' hissed one of the Shades as it pushed and prodded the lawyer.

'Let me go this instant, you miserable dogs! I'll-I'll sue you if you don't release me! And when I've finished with you, you'll be so deep in debt you'll be denied credit forever! Stop prodding me, you loathsome things, I'm a lawyer! Wherever you're taking me to . . . this, this "Bellania" . . . I will make things very difficult for you if you don't listen to me!'

Crow was so furious that he failed to register where he was. After being dragged through doors and whisked along tunnels, it came as a shock when one of the Shades tripped him and he fell, face-first, on to the lush red carpet of Bane's Throne Room. Raising his head to stare around in wonder, Crow fell silent for the first time that day.

'Oh!' he finally breathed as he stared at the fearsome, threatening majesty of the Devouring Throne.

Looking down from his dais, Bane sneered at the cower-ing lawyer. 'So the cringing worm once more plays a part in this great act. Crowman, you are in luck. It would appear that you might be of some use to me after all.' The hooded giant descended the steps from his throne and, reaching down, picked up the whimpering lawyer. 'You, you miser-able, greedy, pulsating piece of flesh, will come with me. It is time to reassess your beliefs, renew your faith and meet Bellania's one true God.'

Striding along with Mr Crow tucked under one arm like a rolled-up newspaper, Bane marched the length of his Throne Room and passed under an arched doorway bearing a sign carved into the likeness of two blazing eyes. The lawyer stared miserably up at the carvings and to his horror the eyes hungrily glared right back. Crow flinched away from the terrifying sight.

Bane stamped his way down a passageway. Deep, deep into the darkness the two of them went, through lightless canyons and along dead riverbeds, past ancient corridors and forgotten paths. Eventually the walkway grew warm, the walls became hot to the touch and the air turned brack-ish and humid, tasting stale and sulphurous. Bane finally slowed to push through a huge door which again bore the strange carving of two blazing eyes. Once inside he uncer-emoniously dropped the skinny lawyer to the floor.

'Ouch!' squawked Crow. Dusting himself down and rubbing at his bruised backside, the lawyer slowly stood and looked around.

The two of them were on a bridge that dwindled into the distance. Crow could see no end to the bridge or to the room itself. It was an unsettling image, and if he looked too long his stomach began to cramp and squirm. Such a sight was unnatural.

Crow sidled to the side of the bridge and peered over. Far below he could see a bubbling, boiling river of molten lava. The incredible heat and sulphurous stench arising from it singed the lawyer's eyebrows and set his eyes watering. Hastily he scurried back from the bridge's edge as his body began to shake and shiver. He couldn't help it – this place was abnormal and alien.

'Come, worm, cease your snivelling,' said Bane. 'Time for you to meet Bellania's true master.'

As Crow was forced down the never-ending bridge, he was surprised to see a red star in the distance. He was sure it hadn't been there before. Desperately trying to calm his nerves, he cracked the knuckles on his long skinny fingers. The lawyer was quite certain that he was in this predicament due to some fault of Charlie's. If he ever got out of this mess that little nuisance of a girl was going to pay, and pay dearly.

The red star grew in size and luminosity until it was like a small sun. Blazing in eerie glory, it almost covered the bridge, stretching from wall to wall of the chamber. As the ball of light approached, Bane dropped down to one knee and bowed his hooded head.

'My God,' said Bane, 'I greet you and pay you worship.'

With a sudden shock, Crow became aware that the sphere that writhed, spat and pulsed before him was alive. This thing was Bane's God! The realization sent his brain reeling. Foul red light swamped everything, casting the surroundings in a bloody but surprisingly cold glow. Against all logic, the blazing flames seemed to suck out heat and life, leaving whatever they touched weaker. Mr Crow felt his legs turn to lead and his heart start to beat erratically, first fast, then slow. Sharp pains and cramps gripped at his flesh, making him shake and twitch as a dreadful terror coursed through him.

Something was beginning to form within the twisting flames. A diamond-shaped head with piercing, glowing eyes slowly appeared, then two impossibly long reptilian hands emerged to grasp and paw at the air. Crow's eyes rolled in his head as the fear became almost unbearable. The thing's skin was carbon black. Crisp and burnt like coal. Mr Crow wanted to flee, to run screaming, to pull at his hair and pluck out his eyes – anything to hide from the fearful sight before him – but his body refused to move. Dread bound him to the spot far tighter than any iron chain or steel manacle ever could.

'My God, I would ask a favour of you,' rumbled the Stoman Lord.

'What would you ask of me?'

The thing had no visible mouth, but nonetheless its voice thundered across the chamber and filled Crow's head almost to the point of bursting.

'My God, Bellania is almost mine for the taking, but still the pendant evades me,' said Bane, ignoring Crow's discomfort. 'I believe this mortal has the will and desire to complete the task of fetching the pendant and crushing the Keeper girl, but while his mind is eager, his body is weak. I would ask that you augment this Human and make him capable of the task. I ask that this fleshy, pulpy Human be made a pawn in our game of power.'

The face within the light stared at Mr Crow. Its hands spasmed and clasped at the air, insect-like. Suddenly the lawyer screamed. He could feel something icy and sibilant picking its way across his mind. Something that plucked and strummed its way through his memories. The God curiously studied details of the lawyer's life. Cold and merciless, it forced its way deeper and deeper into Crow's being with no apology for the pain it was inflicting.

Finally the alien and corpse-like presence withdrew from Crow's mind. His knees sagged in relief. Opening his eyes, he squealed in shock at the sight of Bane's God only inches away. Its blackened face was almost pressed up against his own, eyes shining with some unspeakable hunger. Lunging forward, it snatched at the lawyer and pulled the struggling, skinny figure into his burning, reptilian embrace.

Bane settled down to watch the show. He always enjoyed hearing the screams.

41

A Case for the
Jade Circle

'And how do you plan to do that?' asked Azariah.

'Do what, Azariah Keeper?' said Dridif.

'Sift fact from fiction. How do you plan to reveal the truth of the matter? Lady Narcissa is a well-known and well-liked member of this council. I doubt that any here would ever refute her word. And as for me and Charlie, we are both Keepers. Our word is considered sacred, so surely whatever we say must be considered the truth too. With all three of us being such honoured and respected individuals, prying the truth from the matter is going to be no easy task. So how do you intend to go about solving this case?'

'With logic, of course,' said Lady Dridif. 'I would suspect that all of ya have amassed evidence and witnesses ta prove yer innocence and yer opponents' guilt. By listening ta both sides I will be able ta deduce who is fabricating lies and who is innocent. Do not forget that I am Lady Dridif, the Royal Oak, and that I can sniff out the smallest of lies no matter how well hidden.'

'But surely such a process is prone to error, not to mention being long and time-consuming . . .'

'Azariah Keeper, I can see ya are trying ta lead me somewhere with dis. If ya have a better suggestion please just spit it out.'

Azariah grinned at the First Speaker. 'I'm sorry for beating about the bush, Lady Dridif, but old habits die hard. What I would like to suggest is that we use these . . .' Azariah dug into his robes and pulled out the Isiris Bracelets.

'See!' hollered Nazareth triumphantly. 'I told you Charlie Keeper used the Isiris Bracelets on Stones! Azariah has just proved Charlie's guilt by his own hand. Quick, you there, arrest them!'

'Nazareth, I've told ya once before! I will not tolerate any more outbursts! So sit down and be quiet!' snapped Dridif.

'But that proves my case. It does, I'm telling you it does! Guards! Get –'

Dridif shook her head and sighed. With a distracted gesture she hooked her fingers together before flinging her hand forward. Nazareth squawked mid-sentence like a startled chicken before once again flying through the room to thud against the far wall. This time Dridif just left the councillor where he lay.

'What are ya suggesting?' continued Dridif as though she'd done nothing more strenuous than putting out the garbage.

'Simple. You place the Isiris Bracelets on each of us in turn. All you have to do is hold the ring in your hand and instruct us to tell the truth.'

'Ya know that I do not approve of those . . . pieces of jewellery,' said Dridif with obvious distaste. 'They are forbidden.'

'Of course you don't, because they are instruments that can too easily be used for wicked purposes. However, I'm sure that you would agree that they would be most suitable for solving our predicament.'

'Hold on!' interrupted Lady Narcissa hotly. 'How can you think that I would consent to such an idea? Those bracelets are forbidden for good reason: they are wicked beyond doubt. I will not accept this. Use some other means for solving this argument.'

Several of the councillors rumbled their agreement.

'Come now, Lady Narcissa,' reasoned Azariah. 'Surely you of all people wouldn't use such a poor excuse for sidestepping the one thing that can guarantee us the truth in the matter?'

'Truth? You will get no truth from using such evil tools!' scorned Narcissa.

'That didn't stop you from using them on me, though, did it?' accused Charlie. 'Don't try and act all innocent! Put on those bracelets and see what I had to put up with! We'd find out the truth soon enough then, wouldn't we?'

Lady Narcissa ignored both Azariah and Charlie and turned her attention back to Lady Dridif. 'I shall have nothing to do with this. Why can we not simply use our traditional methods of presenting material evidence and providing trusted witnesses?'

'Because we all know you've just faked everything!' snapped Charlie. 'If you're too scared to use the Isiris Bracelets, I'll wear them first! Come on, then, I dare you! We'll soon see who's telling the truth and who's the liar.'

In all honesty, Charlie couldn't stand the sight of the

bracelets. But right now she was so furious she was willing to go through anything to prove Narcissa's guilt. Even if it meant wearing them one more time.

'A moment of the council's time, if I may,' rumbled Flint, his heavy jewellery rattling as he spoke. 'I for one do not agree that the Isiris Bracelets should be used. We have banned them from Sylvaris and Bellania for good reason. If we are to start using them now, no matter how fitting we believe the circumstances are, we would still be betraying our ideals.'

'Nonsense!' snorted a wrinkled old Treman councillor. 'I believe that dis is the perfect time ta use the Isiris Bracelets. It will solve who is lying and who is not and, more importantly, it will do so in a very short period of time. They are the perfect solution! I say we should boldly stride ahead and use them . . . Besides, I don't know about all of ya lot, but I'm dying ta know who the liar is!'

Once more the Jade Circle erupted into shouted arguments. The councillors were obviously divided in their opinions. Lady Dridif wearily pinched the bridge of her nose as though she were doing her best to hold a large and painful headache at bay. She stared first at Lady Narcissa, then at Azariah Keeper. Slowly she held her hands up for silence.

'We are all getting distracted from the matter at hand. There is without doubt a traitor in dis room. Now put aside all ya foolish passions and pride and let us push ta the heart of dis matter. Azariah proposes that the Isiris Bracelets be used ta uncover the truth. Now, I can see that many of you, perhaps wisely, oppose dis idea, so as the law demands, we shall put the proposal ta the vote.'

Throughout this exchange Lady Narcissa's finger had been tapping on the table. Looking down the table at Azariah, then over to Dridif, she struggled to reach a decision. Her finger began to tap faster. Perhaps now would be the time to implement Bane's instructions.

Her finger stopped. Lady Narcissa stood.

'Sit down, Narcissa,' instructed Dridif. 'We are about ta vote.'

'No,' said Narcissa.

The table fell silent. Dridif frowned. 'Excuse me?'

'I said no.'

'Now ya listen here –' began Dridif, but Narcissa interrupted her.

'I have no confidence in this council! I believe that some of you have been corrupted by Bane. I believe that some of you are traitors. Therefore I cannot allow myself to be hostage to any vote. I lay claim on my rights to be judged by a Winged One.' She looked at Nibbler scathingly. 'A *real* Winged One.'

A mutter of disbelief swept through the council members.

'Narcissa.' Dridif wearily pinched the bridge of her nose again. 'There are no Winged Ones other than dis Hatchling. And although their Chrysalis Period is almost at an end, they are not due to return for another twenty-one days. And that is being optimistic. If worse comes ta worst, Bane could block their return.'

'Nevertheless, it is my right to demand a trial by Winged One.'

'Foolishness!' snapped Dridif.

Lady Narcissa shrugged.

'As bizarre as the request is,' said Flint, 'it is her right.'

'But wot good can that do?' protested Dridif. She turned her scrutiny back to Narcissa. 'There are no Winged Ones ta judge you and if you insist on following dis antiquated law you must realize that if no Winged One appears within seven days the right ta judge you falls back ta the Jade Circle. At best you are only giving yerself some breathing room. At worst you are raising suspicion and doing nothing ta eliminate any possible treachery within the council.'

'I don't care,' hissed Narcissa. 'I feel unsafe. After Charlie Keeper's actions last night, which I can only assume were orchestrated by Azariah Keeper, I have no doubt that some councillors have been seduced by the Western Menace. I cannot and will not place my trust in the Jade Circle. I demand my right to trial by Winged One.'

Dridif gave Narcissa a long, level stare. 'If ya wish ta take dis road, Councillor, so be it.'

'What?' stormed Charlie in disbelief. 'You're going to let her just walk away?'

'It is her right,' explained Flint.

'Right?' Charlie couldn't believe it. 'Look, we all know she's guilty, but you're going to let her get away with it? That's crazy.'

'Charlie Keeper,' snapped Dridif, 'dis is the Jade Circle. We have rules and laws that must be followed. Without law there is chaos. Narcissa has claimed her right ta trial by Winged One. I will stand by the law and allow her dis. And in seven days' time, if no Winged One appears, I will reconvene the meeting and get ta the bottom of dis.' Her stare grew steely and she turned to look at each member of the council. 'But beware, each and every one of ya. I strongly suspect that there is foul work at play. Be it Charlie Keeper, Azariah, Narcissa, Nazareth or any of ya who are guilty of working with Bane, know that I will find the darkness hidden within dis council and I will, believe me, cut it out.'

'You can't –' protested Charlie, but Dridif cut her off.

'Silence! I have spoken.' Dridif looked furious and Narcissa's jubilant smirk quickly disappeared. 'Know that I am not happy with dis. It would appear that Sylvaris is entering dark times and ta safeguard the city I shall triple the guards that patrol the streets. Furthermore, bear in mind that all of ya will be under me scrutiny. If I find one of ya is a traitor, ya will feel me wrath. Now get outta here. Dis meeting is adjourned.'

42

Crow Gets His Wings

As usual the Throne Room was silent. Yet this time there was a sense of expectancy, a feeling of suspense that crept and sneaked throughout the imposing chamber. It showed in the impatient fidgeting of the heavily muscled Stoman guards standing sentinel by the large doorways. It showed in the slight turning of heads as the cowled and liveried footmen stared towards the dark recess at the rear of the Throne Room. Even the Shades were restless, rustling and writhing as they haunted the misty shadows. Their attention was also focused upon the archway that led to their God's lair. Eventually their patience was rewarded.

A sound echoed out from the gloomy tunnel, growing in volume as a tall silhouette strode into the Throne Room. The footsteps drew nearer to the dais, where Bane sat patiently. The guards stopped playing nervously with their swords, the footmen held their breath and the Shades finally grew still as a lanky figure stepped out from the shadows and into the torchlight.

It was Mr Crow, but it was quite obvious that there was something very different about the skinny lawyer, something in the way he held himself and the way he moved. No longer did he cower in Bane's presence, he walked with purpose in his stride. And his eyes, if they were dark before, were now like deep oily pits. Black as the night, unwavering and unblinking. When he stared at anything, he did so with a hungry and carnivorous expression. Truly this was no longer the old Mr Crow. No longer was he a secretive, grubbing and spineless scavenger. He had the look of a predator.

A hungry predator.

He stared briefly at the Shades, footmen and guards before dismissing them as being unworthy of his attention. He focused his gaze upon the throne and its occupant.

'Crowman, come here.'

Mr Crow did as he was told. Moving forward with silky grace, he approached the Devouring Throne's steps.

'You remember Charlie Keeper, do you not?'

The lawyer nodded, his head moving with a quick, jerky motion.

'Excellent. You are to go east, to Sylvaris, the Treman city,' commanded Bane. 'Once there you will aid Lady Narcissa with her task. She has been instructed to deliver to me Charlie Keeper and her pendant. You will ensure that this task goes smoothly and to plan. Do you understand my demands?'

Crow silently nodded.

'Good.' Bane rose to his feet. Stretching out his arms, he opened his mouth and in his deep craggy voice he began to sing. The dais began to shiver, the stone floor quivered in soft waves which rippled, fanning out across the room, rocking the Shades and forcing the footmen and guards to fight, like drunkards, for their balance. Crow, however, remained unaffected and silently rode out the tempest that rocked the chamber. The ripples ran up the walls and into the darkness, disappearing into the shady heights of the vaulted ceiling. Bane's voice grew stronger, deeper. The song intensified and the soft glow in his hands blossomed, then violently burst into fierce flames. With a great cracking and growling, the heavy ceiling tore itself open into a massive chasm that cut through a layer of bedrock, revealing the night sky twinkling far, far overhead.

Bane lowered his flaming arms and sat back on the Devouring Throne.

'There, Crowman, is your exit. Take it and make your way east. Fulfil my commands and, should you succeed, know that I will reward you in ways that you never dreamed possible.'

The lawyer bowed once more to his lord, then with a hop and a bound launched himself into the air. Flapping his lanky arms, he hurled back his head, arched his spine and opened his mouth to reveal newly sharpened teeth before bursting apart into a hundred black and evil screeching birds. The creatures flapped, cawed and clawed their way from the hidden bowels of the earth where Bane kept his kingdom, up the chasm and out into the unsuspecting night sky.

The footmen and guards stared after the swiftly disappearing Mr Crow in morbid fear and sickened astonishment, while Bane, the Western Menace, laughed in delight.

Charlie was fuming as she, Nibbler and Azariah left the Council Chamber and walked the long corridors of the Jade Tower.

'So what, she just gets away with it?' she stormed. 'What

kind of stupid law lets her walk free like that? How can Lady Dridif let that happen?'

'Because Lady Dridif believes in the law,' answered Azariah. 'She upholds it even when it doesn't work smoothly.'

'But why?' insisted Charlie.

'Because she believes that without law there is chaos. Sticking to the law is Dridif's way of fighting against corruption.'

'Well, it obviously doesn't work that well, does it?' said Nibbler. 'I mean, if Narcissa can walk free as easy as that, then something's wrong.'

Azariah sighed. 'Dridif believes in the big picture. Today Narcissa might walk free but in seven days' time Lady Dridif is certain she'll find the truth. It might have cost Dridif in the short term, but she always, always looks at the long term.'

'But that gives Narcissa an extra seven days to cause trouble!' complained Charlie. 'Your laws are seriously messed up.'

'I have been to Earth several times in my life,' admitted Azariah, 'and I do not believe that the laws in your realm are foolproof either. I remember hearing stories of legal battles going on for years. I have seen how the large corporations in your realm bend the law to their gain. Life, young Charlie, as you well know by now, is not always fair.'

Charlie scowled. 'So we just stand around and let her get away with it?'

'No! Of course not. The law is for Lady Dridif and the Jade Circle. You and I are Keepers and young Nibbler here is a Winged One. We do not uphold the law. We uphold what is right.' Azariah flashed Charlie a reassuring smile.

Charlie hesitantly returned it. 'So what are we going to do?' she asked.

'We are going to have a discreet word with Lady Dridif. Come, we shall go and talk to her in her study. This way.'

Charlie and Nibbler obediently followed the old Keeper as he led the way through the maze of corridors and into the grand hallway.

'Look, the war is killing me!' said a familiar voice. 'If I don't get me Moreish powder flowing back along the Spice Route and through ta the markets of Alavis and Alacorn, me business is doomed!'

'Wot about, ya know, popping over ta the Other Realm?' suggested another familiar voice.

'The Other Realm? Oh, sure, no problem apart from the tiny, incy, wincy fact that Bane has got his blooming Shades watching all the Gateways. I've got no choice but ta ask the Jade Circle for help.'

Rounding the corner, Charlie came face to face with Jensen and Kelko.

They stopped and stared, first at the sight of Nibbler, but then at Charlie.

Butterflies began to flutter their wings inside Charlie's stomach and almost immediately her palms grew sweaty. Hot waves of guilt washed her face red with shame.

'Oh, look who we've got here,' snorted Jensen. 'Miss I'm-Too-Good-For-The-Likes-Of-Ya! Surprised ta see people like us in such a posh tower? Well, don't ya worry. We'll soon be outta yer hair and back ta where "riff-raff" like us belong!'

Jensen's snide remarks hit Charlie hard. The guilt in her stomach and the remorse running up and down her spine intensified. Kelko, standing next to Jensen, didn't say anything. He just looked shamefacedly down at his fat stomach before quickly walking off.

Which was worse. A lot worse. Charlie would have preferred the sarcastic remarks from Jensen rather than having to see the awful look of hurt across Kelko's gentle face.

'Look, I didn't mean to say those things! It wasn't really me saying any of that! It was –'

'After all the help we gave ya and that's how ya go and repay us?' interrupted Jensen. 'Charlie, we thought ya were a nice girl. But yer a real piece of work, ya know that?' Not waiting for an answer, he stalked off.

'B-but . . .' stuttered Charlie.

Azariah gazed softly at Charlie. 'Young Keeper, there will be time enough for that later. But right now it is imperative that we see the First Speaker.'

'But –'

'Later,' insisted Azariah. 'I shall, as I promised, help you. But please remember that a Keeper must always face up to his or her responsibility. And at the moment that means having a quiet word with Lady Dridif.' He held out his hand. 'Now, come this way.'

The young Stoman boy paused on his way to the market. On his back was a large pannier of crystals and rock fruit that his father had instructed him to sell. But the pannier was heavy and the road long. Pausing for a break and a sip of water, he eased the pack off his back and sat down to massage his aching legs. But . . . what were those noises?

Caws and raucous shrieks began to tear along the pathway, echoing back and forth, growing louder and louder. The boy stood up fast. His heart jumped and kicked wildly within his chest. Wyrms! It had to be! They were coming back. Coming back for him!

Panic coursed through his veins like a wild electrical fire. He tried to sprint for safety but his tired legs were in no shape. Cramp sent its cruel fingers digging into his calf muscles and with a hoarse cry the boy fell over.

The shrieks grew louder and louder. Closer and closer the strident call came and then it was there. Whipping around the corner a thick black cloud of rushing, streaming, cawing crows cascaded towards him. Hooked yellow beaks and needle-sharp talons flashed in the afternoon sun. Dark feathers fluttered fiercely. The harsh sound of hundreds of beating wings tore at his ears. The endless tide of shadowy birds blocked out the sun, leaving the boy to whimper and scrabble in the gloomy dust.

And then they were gone. Croaking and screaming, the crows sped onwards, hurtling down the path and disappearing into the distance.

It took the young boy a long time to gather his wits together and longer still to fasten the heavy panniers upon his back. First Wyrms and now this.

'What is happening to Bellania?' he said aloud, before hastening to the market.

43

Planning Ahead

'And why, might I ask, do ya want ta see the Isiris Bracelets?' asked Lady Dridif.

'To prove a point,' said Azariah, as though it was the most reasonable request in the world.

'And wot point would that be?'

Azariah sighed. 'Lady Dridif, I have known you for eighty-seven years. I would like to think that perhaps, after all this time, we could finally learn to speak openly with one another. You and I both know the threat that Bellania faces. You and I both know that the shadow of Bane will soon cover the land. We need to make bold decisions and we need to make them now.'

The four of them – Azariah, Charlie, Nibbler and Lady Dridif – were standing in the First Speaker's comfortable study. A large fireplace occupied one wall and along another was a huge map of Bellania. The third wall was covered by bookshelves and the fourth was one enormous window that looked out across the beauty of Deepforest.

'We both know that the Jade Circle has been compromised,' continued Azariah. 'At least one of Bane's agents, if not more, is a councillor. After this morning's accusations you know without a doubt that either Lady Narcissa or Charlie works for the Western Menace. Give me the Isiris Bracelets, right here, right now, to use *privately* in this room and I shall prove to you that Charlie is beyond suspicion.'

Dridif silently turned away. Walking over to the window, she rested her forehead against the cool glass and stared out across her city.

'I have been on dis council for more than two hundred years and of those I have held the position of First Speaker for one hundred and eleven. After all that I have seen and endured, after all that I have had ta fight for ta ensure Bellania retains its freedom, I have grown weary. I'm tired, me bones are old . . .' Lady Dridif took a deep breath before standing up stiff and straight. She stared at Nibbler, who remained solemn and silent.

When Dridif next spoke her voice had grown hard. 'But of course that ain't wot ya want ta hear, is it? And ya shall not, for I'm still Lady Dridif, the Royal Oak, First Speaker ta the Jade Circle, and I still hold the ideal and promise of liberty close ta me heart. So I will fight against Bane in any way that I can, even if it means betraying some of the principles that I hold dear. The bracelets are there. Use them and show me the truth.'

Charlie looked to where Dridif was pointing. Without hesitation she walked over and clamped the cold jewellery over her wrists. Picking up the Isiris Ring, she passed it over to Dridif.

'Ask me,' said Charlie quietly. Then, because that didn't feel quite right, she said it again but this time in a more determined voice. 'Ask me.'

'Charlie Keeper, I bid ya ta tell the truth. Do ya work for or in any way aid or abet Lord Bane, the Western Menace?' asked Dridif.

'No, I don't!' declared Charlie. 'Help that angry idiot? I'd rather have all my hair cut off and have my name changed to "Bob" before I helped that horrible grumping stumping oaf of a giant!'

'Young Keeper, a simple "no" would have sufficed, but thank ya all the same,' said Dridif, fighting to retain a prim and proper expression on her face. 'Very well, then, the truth is revealed. Lady Narcissa is the traitor.'

'My turn,' said Azariah.

'Wot?'

'I insist,' he said. Stepping over to Charlie, he unfastened the bracelets from her wrists and slipped them over his own. He stared expectantly at Dridif.

'Very well, then. Azariah Keeper, I also bid ya ta tell the truth. Do ya work for or in any way aid or abet Lord Bane, the Western Menace?'

'No.'

'Well, then, if you can do it so must I,' grumbled Lady Dridif.

'But you're the one we had to prove our innocence to!' protested Charlie. 'Why would you have to wear the bracelets?'

Dridif held up her hand. 'If Bane has succeeded in reaching with his dark fingers all the way inta the Jade Circle, then no one, absolutely no one, is above suspicion. Trust is a luxury that we can no longer afford,' she said, snapping the bracelets over her green wrists. 'Azariah, would ya be so kind?'

The elder Keeper nodded respectfully and repeated the question.

'No,' replied Dridif. 'I do not.'

'Can I have a go?' asked Nibbler. 'Can I try them on?'

Azariah chuckled. 'The bracelets would not work upon a Winged One, even one as naughty as yourself. But do not worry, young Hatchling, you are above suspicion.'

'Oh,' said Nibbler, looking a bit crestfallen. 'How boring.'

'Who else do ya suspect?' asked Dridif.

'Flint.'

'Flint?' exclaimed Charlie. 'Don't you mean Nazareth?'

Azariah shook his head. 'Nazareth? As pompous as Nazareth is, his heart is for Sylvaris.'

'But how come he's always helping Narcissa?' said Charlie.

Azariah smiled. 'I would have thought that was obvious. The old fool is in love. Completely and utterly smitten. No, the secret mover behind the scenes is Flint.'

'Why do you think Flint is working with Narcissa?' asked Nibbler.

'Simple. Every time we backed Lady Narcissa into a corner, or it appeared that we might wriggle free from beneath her accusations, who would help her out with his well-placed words?'

'Flint would, but it didn't really seem like he was helping her,' said Charlie.

'Well, that's the whole point of being a "secret" accomplice, young Keeper! No, what he did with his well-timed words was sway the way the whole council was thinking. After Lady Narcissa he was second to protest against using the bracelets. He was the first to agree with Narcissa's right to trial by Winged One. And have you forgotten that Flint also tried to aid Narcissa by having you placed in the vaults so he could "study" your pendant? Hhmph, if he had succeeded in having you locked away I doubt it would have taken long for you to have an "accident" and for your pendant to mysteriously disappear.'

Charlie and Nibbler looked wide-eyed at each other.

'I am certain that Flint has sided with Lady Narcissa. As to the others on the council, who can be sure?' said the old Keeper, tugging anxiously on his beard. 'And that is why I would advise against openly declaring Narcissa a traitor.'

'Hhmm, I can see the wisdom in that,' agreed Dridif.

'Well, I don't,' declared Nibbler. 'Why don't you just go right out and tell everyone the truth? Tell everyone that Narcissa and Flint are traitors, then get all the other council-lors to put on the Isiris Bracelets one at a time until you know who's loyal and who isn't! Makes good sense to me.'

'And to me!' agreed Charlie.

Azariah grimaced and rubbed at his bald head. He turned to Dridif. 'You can tell them why that's not such a good idea. I'm getting awfully bored with explaining the obvious.'

'Children!' scorned Lady Dridif and rolled her eyes. 'Oh, all right. The reason why we can't openly accuse Narcissa and Flint of treachery is because we don't know how deep dis betrayal goes. If there are many traitors in the council and we push them too far they might decide ta step outta the shadows and fight. The power struggle which could follow would more than likely destroy Sylvaris and quite possibly Deepforest. I will not tolerate the prospect of a civil war breaking out in me city. It is bad enough that we might have ta fight one war against Bane's armies. Two wars would break Sylvaris.'

It took Nibbler a couple of seconds of quite strenuous lip-chewing to get that idea through his head. Finally he nodded. 'OK, I see your point.'

So too did Charlie. 'But what are we going to do? We can't just let Narcissa get away with it. We've got to do something!'

'And so we shall, little one, and so we shall,' said Azariah.

'Well, what then?'

'Is that still not obvious? Bane is still the ultimate cause of all our troubles. Simply trimming away the decayed leaves on a rotten branch will not fix the problem. The whole branch must be cut off in order to save the tree.'

'Huh?' said Nibbler, with a vacant look in his eyes. 'What d'you mean by that?'

'Wot he means,' explained Dridif, 'is that although Lady Narcissa is of immediate concern, she is not our real enemy. There is not much point in merely clipping at the rotten leaves of Narcissa and whoever else might have fallen inta the ways of treason. We have ta go straight ta the source. If we remove Narcissa, wot is ta stop another two or three councillors being tempted ta turn ta the Darkness? Ta cure the disease that Bane has inflicted upon Bellania he must be defeated. Only then can we truly begin ta heal our land. It is Bane we must now move ta defeat.'

'Oh . . .' uttered Charlie. 'So how do you plan to do that?

'By showing Dridif your pendant,' said Azariah. 'That, young Keeper, is the rather obvious way forward.'

'Um, sure.' Charlie blushed and took off her necklace. 'Here you go . . .'

'Thank ya, Charlie Keeper.' Lady Dridif held the pendant up to the light, then carried it over to her desk.

'The only clue we have,' said Azariah, 'other than that it was given to Mya and Elias Keeper by the Winged Ones, is that Charlie was able to use it to communicate with young Nibbler here. Not in any controlled or sophisticated way,' he admitted. 'But it picked up on her cry for help and called for a Winged One.'

'Interesting,' said Dridif, examining the acorn-shaped necklace. Reaching up to one of her bookshelves, she pulled down a huge slab of a book. Dropping the heavy volume on the table, she leafed through it and then leaned down so that she could squint at the writing. 'Hhmm . . . I thought as much, 'she muttered.

'What is it? What does it say?' asked Charlie, curiosity overcoming her good manners.

'Wot does it say?' said Dridif. 'Not a lot, unfortunately. In fact, ta be perfectly honest it tells me almost nothing.'

'What? But I thought you were an expert with things like this!' moaned Charlie in dismay.

'Oh, and who told ya that?'

'I did,' chuckled Azariah. 'And there I was, thinking you were an expert on Winged Ones. I guess even old men can be wrong.'

'Hhmpf, no one's an expert on Winged Ones except other Winged Ones. But ya are right, I am the closest thing Sylvaris has ta an expert on such matters.'

'So how come you can't decipher its secret, then?' asked Nibbler.

'Because I might be an expert on Winged Ones but I'm

not an expert on Winged One *artefacts*!' snorted Dridif as she returned the necklace to Charlie. 'But I know someone who is.'

Charlie perked up as she returned the pendant safely to her neck. 'Who?'

'His name is Edge. Edge Darkmount. Not a very pleasant person, not by any means. He is a Stoman bishop, one of the old breed. Very religious. And if it wasn't for a sharp disagreement with Bane and his new religion, Edge would still be a powerful bishop residing back in the Western Mountains.'

'Well, where is he now?' asked Charlie.

'He has taken up residence in the University of Dust.'

Nibbler's brow creased. 'The University of Dust?'

'It's a university that specializes in myths, history and legends,' Dridif explained.

'Fine, so let's go there and see this Edge guy!' Charlie grinned enthusiastically.

Dridif threw a meaningful glance at Azariah.

'We can't,' the old Keeper sighed. 'The University of Dust is in Alavis.'

'So?'

'Alavis and Alacorn, the twin Human cities, are currently under siege. Bane's Second Army started their attack on the cities four days ago. Alavis and Alacorn are completely cut off.'

'What? But surely there must be some way to see this man.'

'No, Charlie,' said Dridif. 'The city is surrounded. We can't simply waltz in there, not past all the might of the Second Army. It would be folly ta try.'

'And neither can we risk opening a Portal,' added Azariah. 'The cities and countryside are almost entirely overrun. If we were to open a Portal there is a grave chance that we could open it right on top of a regiment of angry Stoman warriors, which would be a mistake we would never make twice.'

'Why would it be a mistake we'd never make twice?' asked Charlie.

'Because we would be dead. Getting repeatedly stabbed by a horde of bloodthirsty warriors is an experience most people don't get to enjoy more than once!'

'Oh,' said Charlie. She could see his point. 'Well, is there any way we can get a message to him? I don't know . . . maybe smuggle in a note?'

'Child, I am sorry,' said Dridif, 'but when I say the cities are cut off I really mean it.'

'I could do it. I could get a message there.'

They all turned to stare at Nibbler, who was looking at the map of Bellania on the study wall.

'Alavis and Alacorn, right? Looks like it's only three days there and three days back. So if I leave today I could be back here in six days.' Nibbler shrugged his shoulders and threw them a fat smile. 'No biggie.'

Dridif and Azariah eyed one another, an unspoken agreement seeming to pass between them.

'Six days,' mused Dridif. 'He would be back on the day of the Three Winds Festival then, would he not?'

'Aye, he would at that. But is that enough time?' mused Azariah. 'I thought the reports indicated that Alavis and Alacorn wouldn't hold out much longer than a fortnight.'

'That is correct. We have ten days at the most and that is only if we're lucky.'

'But if it would take Nibbler three days to fly there, surely it would take us a lot longer to get there by foot?' stated Charlie. 'Would we make it there in time?'

'Hhmm,' murmured Azariah with the distracted expression of someone deep in thought. 'Oh, not to worry, we would just open a Portal there. We would still get there in time.'

Charlie rolled her eyes in frustration. 'But you just said it wasn't safe to use one!'

'Young Keeper, you must learn to listen carefully. I said it's not safe to use one blindly while there's lots of rampaging soldiers wandering about looking for an excuse to stick their swords into something,' retorted Azariah.

'So how is opening a Portal when Nibbler gets back going to be any different from opening one now?'

'Because Nibbler can ask Edge Darkmount for a safe location. An area that hasn't yet been overrun by Stoman troops. A square, a building, even a room inside the University of Dust. But it has to be somewhere safe. Only someone who is already at the scene will have the appropriate local knowledge.'

'Oh, OK,' muttered Charlie.

'Wot about Charlie's well-being?' asked Dridif. 'Without the Hatchling by her side she will be a lot more vulnerable.'

'Not to worry.' Azariah grinned. 'I know of a couple of minders who can keep her out of trouble.'

'Good,' said Dridif. 'So it is agreed, then, is it not? We pretend everything is normal and that we are waiting for the Winged Ones ta return. Meanwhile the Hatchling delivers our message ta Edge Darkmount. Azariah, ya watch over the young Keeper and I shall do me best ta keep black treachery and treason from growing outta hand in me council.'

All four nodded in agreement. Charlie, filled with hope, gave Azariah a small smile.

'It's a plan, young Keeper,' he said. 'Now let's hope it works.'

44

A Reunion of Sorts

'I don't want ta see her and neither does Kelko!' snapped
Jensen, and slammed the door shut in Azariah's face. Or
at least the door would have shut if the old Keeper's foot
hadn't been in the way.

Azariah turned to smile politely at Nibbler and Charlie.
'If you two would be so kind as to wait for me here, Jensen,
Kelko and I need a little chat. We won't be long, I promise.'
He then tensed his powerful muscles and forced his way
into Jensen's Willow Tower.

'Wot d'ya think ya doing?' squawked a startled voice.
'Hey, wait, wait! Not that, not that –' Jensen's shocked voice
was suddenly cut off as the door swiftly slammed shut. It
rattled briefly, then all was quiet.

Charlie turned to stare at Nibbler. 'What do you think
he's doing to them? All I wanted was the chance to apologize.
You know, sort things out between us.'

'Oh,' said Nibbler. 'Well, I overheard Azariah talking to
Lady Dridif and I think he said something about Jensen and
Kelko being "stubborn, hard-headed, wooden-brained
idiots", so I think what he's doing right now is getting your
point of view across.'

The two of them turned to look as some faint screaming came from the tower. Jensen's face momentarily appeared squashed against a window before rapidly disappearing.

'Is that what he's doing now?'

'Oh yes, I'm sure that's what he's doing. I think he's squaring things up between the three of you.'

'Oh.'

A loud clatter and banging could be heard, a high-pitched scream, then silence.

After a short pause the door opened. Jensen and Kelko – looking quite subdued – staggered out. Azariah Keeper followed behind like a schoolteacher ushering two unruly pupils.

'Er . . . Charlie,' mumbled Jensen. 'I'm sorry for doubting ya. I hadn't realized wot the Isiris Bracelets could do.'

'I guess we didn't know any better . . .' grumbled Kelko. He shyly rubbed his foot from side to side and hung his head so that he wouldn't have to look Charlie in the eye. 'It's just that it sounded so real. We should have known ya were in trouble. If we'd been thinking clearly we would have realized it wasn't like ya ta say such things. And . . . and if we'd been thinking clearer we could have got ya outta there before they did anything else ta ya . . .'

Charlie was horrified to see that Kelko was actually crying. His big shoulders began to shake, his fat stomach wobbled from side to side and he let out big, blubbing sniffs. Jensen too looked decidedly uncomfortable. He began to pick and pull at his collar as though his shirt had suddenly grown several sizes too small for him.

With a start Charlie realized that the two of them felt guilty!

She was quite sure it should have been the other way around. In fact, she *knew* it should have been. So she did the only thing she could think of, which was to go over and throw an arm around both of her friends and give them a big, big hug.

Everything seemed better after that.

Well, almost everything was better, except that Azariah had this really smug look on his face that seemed to suggest that he had just done the right thing.

Whatever that was.

'So you'll be back here in six days?' said Charlie.

'Yup,' said Nibbler.

'Promise?'

Nibbler rolled his eyes.

'Promise!' insisted Charlie, raising an eyebrow.

'Of course I'll be back in six days! Nothing to it. Three days there, drop off a letter, get a reply, then three days back. Not a problem.'

'So you'll be careful?'

'Yes, Mum!'

'Hhmpf.'

Nibbler grinned. Reaching up with his front claws, he checked that the letter was still firmly tied to his back. Then, throwing one last cheeky grin at Charlie, he leaped to the top of the balcony, stretched his neck so that all the bones in it cricked and cracked . . . then he toppled forward.

Charlie gasped and rushed over to the balcony.

Nibbler was a streamlined arrow. His green scales gleamed

as he plummeted straight towards one of Sylvaris's large squares. At the last possible moment he spread his wings wide and shot upward. Soaring over the top of a squat tower, he only just missed slamming into a weathervane, narrowly dodged a trundling cart that was passing over a bridge and almost clipped a startled Tree Singer as he stood working on a walkway. With a delighted laugh that echoed back to Charlie's ears, the winged troublemaker disappeared into the distance.

'Well, looks like young Nibbler got off OK,' said Jensen, giving Charlie a quick, reassuring pat on her back. 'So, then, ya have been in Sylvaris for, wot, five days? And from wot I've heard ya've hardly seen any of it, so how about a proper tour? Ya know, get ta see the real Flower of Deepforest?'

Charlie's eyes lit up.

'Or wot about a decent game of K'Changa? *I* heard ya haven't been getting enough practice lately,' offered Kelko.

'Great!' said Charlie. 'I wanted to practise my landings so I could stop falling on my –'

'Gentlemen,' said Azariah, interrupting. 'I'm afraid that the young Keeper will not be able to take up these generous offers. At least not until this evening.'

'And why's that, then?' asked Jensen. 'We haven't seen her properly in days, Azariah.'

Charlie looked expectantly at the councillor. She was desperate to do both things.

'Because it is time for the young lady to begin her education as a Keeper,' he explained. 'It is time for her to learn – properly this time – the Ways of the Path, the Portal and the Will.'

45

An Education

'If you do not learn to concentrate, you will never succeed. Pick yourself up and try again.'

Charlie did as she was told. Pushing herself into a kneeling position, she gritted her teeth and heaved her weary body upright. She wanted to groan as her muscles protested. She felt torn and bruised and she had a harsh headache, the kind that felt as though hot needles were being stabbed repeatedly through her skull.

'Good. Now focus your Will. Control it. Use it! Show me what you can do!'

Azariah was no easy teacher.

All morning and for most of the afternoon the two of them had been hard at work in Azariah's garden. First Charlie had learned all about the theory of the Will, the Way and the Paths. Theory had been easy but the practical aspect of it was taking a little longer to master. Once again all she had managed to do was set her hands glowing and when Azariah had instructed her to open a Portal the best that she could do was make the air shimmer and wobble. Charlie was beginning to lose her patience.

'It's not fair! I'm doing exactly what you tell me to do

but I still can't get the Portal to open. What's wrong? Why isn't it working?'

'Not fair? Not fair?' mimicked Azariah. 'Nothing in life is ever fair, Charlie Keeper! But that has nothing to do with our lessons for today. The reason why it is not working is because you are not concentrating hard enough. I want to see you focus like you mean it. Now try harder!'

'Harder?' muttered Charlie to herself. 'I'll show him harder!'

Angry with herself for constantly failing and furious with Azariah for nagging her, Charlie sucked all her temper into a small, compact ball of rage and focused. Really focused.

The light from her hands intensified. Blossoming, it spread across the width of Azariah's beautiful garden. Creasing her forehead into a frown, Charlie concentrated like crazy.

'So he wants a Portal?' murmured Charlie. 'To Jensen's house? No problem!'

Straining her Will into an even tighter knot, she grunted as sweat began to bead across her face. She focused intensely on where she wanted to go . . . and suddenly something inside her seemed to go click.

The air above Azariah's prized T'ellis-T'ellis bush rippled and shimmered, then tore itself open. The light from Charlie's hands flared into brilliance, washing the garden, herself and Azariah in a warm golden glow. The fissure in the air quivered as though uncertain, then steadied and grew firm.

She'd done it, she'd opened a Portal!

'Wot in Leaf and Shade is dis? Wotcha think ya doing?' squawked a startled voice.

Jensen went white with shock and tried to dive deeper

beneath the soapy suds of his bathtub. Waves of water went splashing over the side. Orchid leaves, bath salts, bubbles and a little rubber duck went slipping and sliding across the floor.

'Have ya no decency! Can ya not let a hard-working Treman enjoy his bath in peace?' squealed Jensen as he frantically pulled more bubbles about his waist. 'Shut that blooming Portal before anyone else sees! Shut it dis distant!'

Charlie was so shocked by the sight that she released her hold on the Portal. It sprang shut like the jaws on a bear trap and the force sent Charlie reeling backwards to slam quite heavily against a small sapling.

'Oof!'

Delicate copper- and bronze-coloured leaves fell to the ground, Charlie plucked some loose debris from her hair and sighed.

'You must not simply let go of a Portal!' scolded Azariah. 'You must Will it to go, which is what I have been repeatedly telling you.' He stared disdainfully down as his young student. 'Now then, if you would be so good as to get out of my Idryllis bush. Carefully! Good. Very well . . . where were we?'

'Ooh! Why is this lesson going so badly?' moaned Charlie in dismay. 'I never seem to get anything right! This . . . this power, it seems to randomly switch on and off whenever it wants. I just can't seem to control it.'

Azariah pulled a stern face and placed his hands on his hips. His beard bristled and his forehead wrinkled into a deep scowl. Suddenly he threw back his head and roared out a deep, chuckling laugh.

'Oh, Charlie. You have done well. So very, very well! To be honest, I was shocked by how quickly you picked up the basics, and so I have pushed you much further than any other novice. For you to be able to open a Portal this early, even for a few brief seconds, is astonishing! Frankly, young Keeper, I am very, very impressed.'

'You are?'

'Yes, Charlie Keeper, I am. Of course your technique is sloppy and the application of your Will is totally inadequate. Not to mention that your self-doubt leads you to stumble and cause foolish mistakes, but all of these errors are elementary and will improve with time.'

'But how come I can only use it some of the time? Why is it that it never seems to work when I really, really need it?'

'When you really need it? Young lady, I don't think you quite realize just how often you have already used your Will since arriving in Bellania.'

'I have?'

'Yes, you have.'

'When?'

'When? Just think back to your house. There was a door, was there not? A door that led you from Earth to Bellania? That, Charlie Keeper, was a Gateway. Only by focusing your Will could you have opened such a door.'

'No, no. That's not what happened at all! I'm sure it was Jensen or someone else who opened the door. I screamed and shouted at it, but it only opened when I said "please".'

'Hhmm. Well, of course "please" is the magic word and if you say it often enough and in the right circumstances it'll get you far in the world.'

'Are you serious? If I say "please" I can open Gateways?' gasped Charlie with wide eyes. 'Wow!'

'Er . . . no, young Keeper.' Azariah coughed and tried to hide his smile behind his hand. 'I was only joking about it being the magic word.'

'So it's not magic?'

'Young Keeper! No, it is not magic! I have told you before, what we do is the practical application of a science. There is no mumbo-jumbo involved. There is no waving of hands and mumbling of incantations! The word "magic" is for idiots who do not accept powers that their feeble intellect cannot comprehend,' scoffed Azariah. 'The Way of the Will is an art, a science. Cast your mind back. You were in the Hall of Doorways and you were faced with a Door that would not open. You desperately wanted it to open. In fact, you needed it to open in order to save your life, correct?'

'Yes,' said Charlie in a small voice.

'And did you feel anything at the time?'

'Anger, frustration. Fear . . . rage.'

'Hhmm. All very powerful emotions. And emotions such as those will focus the Will like nothing else. Which, Charlie, is exactly what happened. Your fear of Bane, mixed with your anger and rage, caused your mind to really focus on the matter at hand. Which was to escape. It was your Will that first opened the Door, allowing you to escape, and it was your Will that shut the Door to bar Bane's way.'

'It was?'

'Yes, young lady, and that impossible jump you made on to the Torn Bridge . . . Remember when you were fleeing from the Shades in Willow Tower? That too was fuelled by your Will. And, of course, let us not forget when you were trapped on the same bridge, with no chance of escape, what was it that you really needed?'

'Help?'

'Exactly! It was your need that caused the pendant to awaken Nibbler and it was your Will that alerted me to your predicament. Will, young lady, is the key to your survival, and don't you ever forget it. Now then, before I release you to spend the rest of the day with Jensen and Kelko, I believe a reward is due for all your hard work.'

Charlie looked surprised. 'A reward?'

'Yes, young Keeper. I believe it is time for us to go shopping.'

46

Dark Schemes

'Mother, surely not all of the Jade Circle were fooled?' said Stix. 'Some of them must have realized we have joined with Bane. We must do something and we must do it fast.'

'I am well aware of the risks involved,' snapped Narcissa. 'But all is not lost. We have access to Bane's wealth, remember. We can use it to begin bribing councillors and buying votes. Flint will assist us in this.' She smiled as a thought came to mind. 'If we are lucky we might even be able to buy enough councillors that we can strip Lady Dridif of her title and have me as First Speaker. Imagine! It would be me, not her, ruling Sylvaris.'

'What about the council members who can't be bribed?' asked Stones.

'If they won't see reason we can blackmail them. Whatever it takes to win over the Jade Circle. But the councillors are not our main adversaries, the Keepers are. We must get the pendant! Everything else is secondary.'

'Do you want us to go around to Azariah's house and slit their throats?' asked Stix, straight-faced.

'Or burn his house down with them still in it?' added Stones.

'No! Are you stupid?' Narcissa took a deep breath and

continued calmly. 'Killing a Keeper as powerful as Azariah will be no easy task. As strong and as skilled as the two of you are, you are no match for such an experienced master. Which is why we will wait for Bane's mysterious servant to arrive. Once the servant is here we will be powerful enough to confront the Keepers directly. Until then we will follow Bane's instructions. I will use Constantina to humiliate Charlie and ensure that she fails to endear herself to the people of Sylvaris. At the same time I will continue to use Sylvaris's outdated laws to our advantage.'

Stix and Stones shared a look. 'Do you think Constantina is capable of the task?' Stones asked his mother.

'Yes, I do. With Constantina's K'Changa skills, Charlie Keeper won't stand a chance.'

'And wot would sir like done with the lady's old clothes?' asked the wizened old shopkeeper.

'Burn them,' replied Azariah.

'A most wise decision, sir,' agreed the wrinkled Treman. Stooping down, he picked up Charlie's discarded, torn and smelly clothes before hobbling off to the rear of the shop to dispose of them.

Charlie was too busy admiring herself in the polished bronze mirror to be bothered by the loss. Azariah had bought her the most amazing set of new clothes. Not even in her dreams did she ever think she would wear anything as luxurious as this. According to the shopkeeper, her midnight-blue shirt was made from orchid-flower silk, her soot-black trousers from eastern Bellanian wire wool and the snug-fitting boots from a leather-like fabric that seemed to suck at the light. A single ribbon of tempered silver tidied her hair into a topknot and around her wrist was a bracelet of woven lionbark. But that was not all. In a large parcel that sat on the chair next to her was a second and third set of clothes, each as impressive as the one she was now wearing. Azariah had refused to say how much everything had cost but Charlie got the impression that it had been a lot.

'Wow, Azariah! No one has ever bought me stuff like this before . . . I just don't know what to say.'

'Well, how about thank you?' suggested Azariah.

Charlie smiled apologetically. 'Azariah Keeper, thank you so much for your gifts,' she said with a very sincere expression. 'I . . . I think these are the best clothes anyone has ever given me. Thank you.'

Azariah beamed with delight at her words. 'I'm glad you like them, young Keeper. The style suits you and it is a pleasure to see you out of those old clothes. They were practically falling apart! Now then, if you would be so good as to follow me, it is time for us to go to the Willow Tower.'

With a farewell nod to the shopkeeper, the two departed the luxurious shop and headed across the sweeping bridges of Sylvaris.

'While you are not by my side I have arranged for Sic Boy to act as your bodyguard until Nibbler returns from Alavis and Alacorn. You will be quite safe.'

'When will I see you again?' she asked.

'Oh, not to worry – you will see me every day. I will expect you at my house no later than eight o' the clock each morning. You have much to learn about your heritage, young Keeper, so your mornings will be spent with me for tuition, and the afternoons are yours to enjoy with those two rascals Jensen and Kelko. Then you will spend your nights in Willow Tower with Salixia, Jensen and Sic Boy.'

'What will you be doing in the afternoons?'

'I shall be playing the political game. I must warn as many of the councillors about Narcissa's treachery as possible. It is vital that I prevent the rot from spreading across the Jade Circle. If I can stop Narcissa from turning too many of the councillors towards Bane, then perhaps Sylvaris can survive. If not . . .'

'What? Do you think that Narcissa could really damage Sylvaris?'

'Yes, I do,' Azariah admitted as they crossed a narrow walkway. 'She is a most formidable opponent and if she is left unchecked she could cause real harm to this city. And with Bane involved, who knows how far or how quickly that could spread. I simply cannot allow it.'

Charlie fell quiet as she mused over Azariah's words. The two of them continued in a thoughtful silence as they proceeded through Sylvaris. Reaching the Willow Tower, Azariah lifted the heavy knocker and pounded on the door.

'Bless me Sap!' exclaimed Jensen when he opened the door. A wide grin spread across his face. 'Charlie, ya look great. Cor! Just look at yer new clothes. Now ya really look like a Keeper.'

Charlie blushed shyly at his words. 'Thanks, Jensen. Azariah bought them for me. As a reward for all my hard work.'

'Well, he's got a great eye when it comes ta buying clothes!' said Jensen. Throwing an arm over Charlie's shoulder, he pulled her aside. 'Er . . . ya haven't told anyone else about the incident in the bathroom, have ya?'

'What bathroom incident would that be?' asked Charlie teasingly.

'Ya know!' groaned Jensen. He threw a hasty look over his shoulder to make sure no one else was listening. 'The one with the Portal . . .'

Charlie chuckled loudly, she couldn't help it. 'Don't worry, Jensen, I promise not to tell anyone else that you like to relax with bath salts, girlie bubbles, orchid leaves or . . . that you own a little rubber duckie!'

Azariah snorted in the background, but when Jensen spun around to confront him the old Keeper appeared to be examining one of the cherry trees that grew along the side of the small entrance bridge. Frowning, Jensen turned back to Charlie.

'Well, ya know, I find it relaxing. Helps me focus me mind, so I can really concentrate on important matters. Running me company, especially in these troubled times, is no easy matter.'

'Oh, sure.'

'And the bath salts, they're really for me aching back, soothe me muscles something wonderful.'

'Hhmm. Sure.'

'And the orchids clear me sinuses out.'

'Oh, of course,' sniggered Charlie. 'And the rubber duck?'

Azariah snorted much louder, but when Jensen furiously snapped his head round the bearded Keeper had his nose pressed firmly into the cherry blossom and was obviously enjoying the scent. Jensen threw him a suspicious look before slowly turning his attention back to Charlie.

'The duck?' said Jensen with a perfectly innocent look. 'I never saw a duck. Perhaps it was yer imagination?'

'Oh no,' insisted Charlie. 'I'm quite sure I saw a little yellow duck.'

'Nah, surely it must have been yer fancy that saw it. I reckon Azariah must have been overworking ya too much.' Jensen blushed. 'I'd never keep a rubber duck in m—'

'I hate to interrupt,' said Azariah, appearing beside them, 'but I don't have time to hang around all day and listen to you two squabble about whether or not there was a duck in your bath. Jensen of the Willow, I must be off about my business. I leave Charlie Keeper in your care and I shall expect her at my door no later than eight o'clock tomorrow. Furthermore, I look forward to seeing her safe and well.'

'You can count on that,' said Jensen.

With a final nod for Charlie, Azariah strode off.

Before Jensen could close the door, a familiar voice shouted out, 'Hey, Charlie!'

Charlie and Jensen turned to find Kelko strolling up the bridge towards them. Sic Boy ambled along by his side with a huge bone in his mouth.

'Hi, blossom, how ya doing?' Kelko smiled and gave Charlie a big hug. 'Methinks the time has come for me ta show ya around.'

Sic Boy nuzzled his head beneath Charlie's armpit and rumbled a low growl as a way of greeting. Charlie absent-mindedly scratched him behind his huge ears.

'That'll leave Jensen some time ta sort out his business and then in the evening we'll both take ya for some K'Changa practice. Wotcha say?'

'What do I say?' Charlie grinned in delight. 'Sounds like a deal to me!' After the morning's hard work with Azariah, she was looking forward to a fun afternoon. 'Lead on!'

47

A Conversation
with Constantina

'Yes, Mother, what do you want?' asked Constantina sulkily. 'I hope it's important, because you know how much I dislike stopping in the middle of K'Changa practice. And did you have to bring Stones?' she complained, staring at the Stoman. 'Couldn't you have sent a footman to get me? It's just so embarrassing to see that clumsy oaf stomp all over the playing field.'

Lady Narcissa sighed. She was very proud of her daughter, but sometimes she wondered if she overindulged her. Perhaps she should cut back on her allowance for a bit. Maybe if she went without clothes-shopping for a week or two she might develop some proper manners.

'Do I really need to remind you that Stones is your brother? Don't you think you should show him some more respect?'

'He's not my *real* brother,' replied Constantina with a grimace.

'That may be true, but nevertheless he is still family and I expect you to treat him accordingly.'

'I'll think about it,' said Constantina, and stuck her nose

up in the air to show she had no real intention of following her mother's suggestion.

Narcissa rubbed at her forehead. How could it possibly be that plotting to overthrow the Jade Circle was far easier than managing her own family? 'We shall talk about you and your brothers later.' Narcissa frowned. 'Now tell me, have you heard about a young girl called Charlie Keeper?'

'Wasn't she the one who stayed at our tower while I was visiting Alavis? The one who drugged Stix and painted his face like a clown?'

The corner of Narcissa's mouth twitched in irritation at the memory. 'That's right.'

'Well, there have been some rumours floating around at school. I've heard she's half royalty and is engaged to marry a Winged One. Oh, and she's supposed to be working with the Jade Circle to destroy Bane. Is this true, Mother?'

Narcissa rolled her eyes. How was it that simple facts always got twisted into such wild tales?

'Well, is it, Mother? Is it true?'

'Not quite, Constantina. Close but not quite. Charlie Keeper is a wilful brat who is not even slightly royal. Although she has the acquaintance of a young Hatchling, she isn't, I believe, engaged to a Winged One.'

Constanina shrugged. 'How disappointing.'

Narcissa continued. 'However, you are right about her working with the Jade Circle. She carries a pendant from the Winged Ones that supposedly holds the key to stopping Bane's attack on Bellania. The necklace is what makes her so special.'

'But she's the same Charlie who burned our roof and drugged Stix?'

'Yes, one and the same.'

'Well, if she's supposed to be the one who's going to save us from the Western Menace, how come she caused so much trouble here?'

'How? Because she's a dangerous, evil-minded brat! She's a manipulative, scheming little spider and she has somehow managed to trick the Jade Circle into thinking that she is the most suitable candidate to use the pendant against Bane. I, however, think that there's someone closer to home who could do a better job. Someone who could rise high enough to become the hero that Sylvaris so desperately needs.'

'Who?' asked Constantina breathlessly.

'Why, my dear, I would have thought that *you* would prove to be a perfect candidate,' suggested Narcissa.

'Me? Really, do you think so?' gushed Constantina. 'Do you think I could be . . . Well, hang on, of course I could! Now that I think about it, I can see that you're absolutely right, Mother! I should be the one who holds the pendant. It should definitely be someone from our family who leads Sylvaris forward. After all, we are the most prestigious Human family in this city, not the Keepers.'

'That's my girl!' Narcissa smiled. Her face shone with beauty, yet deep within her eyes something nasty glittered as she watched her plans begin to unfold.

'But how are we going to get the pendant?'

'How? Well, my dear, that is a very good question. Now, let me tell you . . .'

48

The Challenge

'All right, then, lass, enough of the touristy stuff,' said Kelko
as the evening approached. 'Methinks it's time ta see something that's a bit more special.'

'Kelko, *everything* I've seen so far has been special. All
these sights that you've shown me . . . Well, I've never seen
anything like it before, ever!'

Charlie's head was still spinning. Kelko, with Sic Boy at
his side, had been taking great delight in showing her around
the city. It felt like she'd explored every last inch of Sylvaris.
She'd seen the Great Bazaar, where almost every imaginable
item was for sale or trade. Even some unimaginable items
were there too, like the Lacquer Tea Step, a tool for making
tea that doubled as a footstool, or the Spiral Telescope Picker,
which allowed star-gazers to watch the night skies and
discreetly pick their nose at the same time.

She'd been to the Whispering Heights – Sylvaris's tallest
buildings, which made mournful sounds when the strong
southern wind blew – and she'd walked through the Vanilla
Orchid Fields. She'd applauded the daring acts of the street
acrobats and trapeze artists who busked for money along
the Crooked Silver Bridge and she'd even admired the great

piles of teeth that were on display in the shop windows down Dentist Street.

In fact, every corner that she turned seemed to hold some new surprise. Every building or street or square or bridge that she visited promised something strange or exotic. Charlie had to admit that she was falling in love with the Treman city.

'Yeah, well, if ya thought everything else was special, then dis is really gonna blow yer mind,' said Kelko with a wide grin. 'Blossom, hold on ta yer little cotton socks as I now present ta ya . . . Hold on, shut yer eyes while I lead ya around dis corner, ready? OK, open yer eyes and behold! The Colosseum – home of K'Changa!'

Charlie's eyes boggled as she took in the view. The Colosseum was a huge open-air affair similar to the ancient Roman arenas on Earth. With the last glimpse of the sun setting behind it, it appeared magnificent.

The Colosseum was heaving with people and the noise was almost deafening. Bubbling cheers, catcalls and raucous shouts washed over Charlie as the trio entered. Blazing torches lit both the stadium and the darkening sky. Thick smells and spicy scents from Tremen snack food wafted across the air. She could hear the hawking cries of vendors selling their food, yelling and calling at the tops of their voices so that they could be heard above the mass of cheering spectators.

'Here,' said Kelko as he paid one of the enthusiastic vendors. 'Try these Gingered Snugglegruffs, and these little beauties are Candied Thistleloves. Ya'll love 'em!'

Charlie took the sweets with a grin. She couldn't help but be caught up in the excitement of the place.

'Now then, let's see about getting us some seats.' Kelko turned to Sic Boy. 'All right, boy, seats! Seats!'

Sic Boy got the message. Using his raw muscle as a battering ram, the dog forced his way down through the stands right to the very front of the Colosseum. Kelko and Charlie simply followed after. Some of the fans wanted to protest, but when they saw the sheer size and brutal appearance of the dog they swiftly changed their minds.

'Righto, we'll sit here. These seats are reserved especially for the Jade Circle, but I reckon they won't mind if we take advantage of 'em!'

A huge cheer swept the crowd as the action within the arena intensified. The pounding drums and the rhythm from the band swelled as the K'Changa players battled for the Zephyr and then, with a final, intense flurry of limbs, the game was over. The crowd went wild and the winner was waving his hands in jubilation, a thick grin plastered over his face.

Charlie loved every minute. The sheer spectacle of it all, the crowd, the music and the exhilaration of the game. It was, without a shred of doubt, the most awesome thing she had ever seen, and it made her want to practise her own K'Changa moves even more.

'Ha! Wot a match, but don't ya worry, blossom, there's more ta come yet. There's a team game, an honour match and let's not forget the Fleet-Foot Title match. Oh yeah, we picked the right night ta see the games!'

Charlie sat on the edge of her seat for the rest of the evening as excitement gripped her and held her fast. Match after match passed before her eyes, each more spectacular than the previous. The crowd around her became wilder as time went by until the stadium was awash in a non-stop wave of noise. And then quite suddenly a hush settled across the crowd. A lone contestant had entered the arena and was impatiently awaiting the arrival of her opponent. The teenage Treman girl, standing in the centre of the Colosseum, put her hands on her hips and tapped her foot in agitation. For several minutes she stood there while the crowd waited in expectant silence.

'What's happening?' asked Charlie. 'Why hasn't the other player turned up?'

'It's the champion,' whispered Kelko. 'She's something of a show-off. She always likes ta make a grand entrance.' He rolled his eyes. 'You should probably know that she's Lady Narcissa's daughter, Constantina.'

Charlie raised her eyebrows. 'Yeah? I never got to meet her. Is she as bad as the rest of her rotten family?'

'Ta be honest, I'm not too sure. I've never talked ta the lass so I couldn't form an honest opinion,' mused Kelko. 'She seems all right. And she's real popular with all the K'Changa fans, but I guess that doesn't mean anything. After all, Lady Narcissa is well loved, but we know she's a real nasty piece of work when ya get down ta it.'

'So how come Constantina's the champion?' asked Charlie, her brow wrinkling in puzzlement. 'I thought all you Tremen were supposed to be the best?'

'Yeah, well, we are. But that doesn't mean other races can't play and it doesn't mean that others can't become great as well. I mean, just look at ya, playing for a matter o' days and ya already stole the Zephyr from me and Jensen!'

A commotion from behind them had people turning in their seats and pointing. A low rumble from the crowd soon grew to a shouting crescendo. All of a sudden, there was their champion, descending through the stands. The mass of spectators broke like a wave to let her pass and down she swept, head held high and dressed in white silken finery. A purple cloak flowed from her shoulders and diamonds glittered in her ears. Down the long bank of seats she came, with all the grandeur and pomp of a princess.

Charlie groaned when she realized Constantina was headed straight for her and Kelko. 'Well, if it isn't the little Keeper who everyone has been talking about. My, my, you are small, aren't you?' Constantina leaned forward and hissed in her ear. 'And to think that the fate of Bellania could possibly lie in your hands . . .' She squinted at Charlie's pendant. 'Or even around your neck.' She smiled to the attentive crowd. 'Well, I'd love to hang around and talk,' she announced loudly, 'but my audience awaits and I can't keep my opponent waiting all day, now can I?' With a toss of her head and a final sneer, the champion turned her back on Charlie and strode into the arena. The fans cheered and chanted her name as she sauntered over to face her challenger.

Sic Boy growled deep and low in his throat. He obviously didn't like Narcissa's toffee-nosed daughter and if Charlie was honest, neither did she. She couldn't believe how rude the girl was and she couldn't have been that much older than her – sixteen or seventeen at the most. All of Charlie's previous excitement and great expectations for the night evaporated. Meeting Narcissa's daughter had left her with a sour taste in her mouth. She wriggled uncomfortably in her seat while she waited for the outcome of the match.

As it turned out, she didn't have long to wait. Constantina quickly trounced her opponent and once again the crowd went wild. Narcissa's daughter, victorious and overjoyed by her easy win, raised her arms in a bid for silence. The crowd was only too willing to please their beautiful champion.

'Tremen, Humans, Stomen, my fellow lovers of K'Changa,' she called out, her voice swollen with pride. 'Once again I have bested those who you send to me. Have I not proved time and time again my skill, my prowess? Am I not rightfully your champion?'

The crowd roared its agreement.

'Is there any better than me?'

This time the crowd howled out a throaty, 'No!'

'And in this time of trouble and uncertainty, when the Western Menace grows near, do we not need all the champions we can get?'

'Yes!' cheered the crowd.

Charlie turned to Kelko. She didn't like the way Constantina was leading the crowd along. 'Kelko, what's going on?'

'I'm not sure, blossom,' said Kelko, worry causing his brow to furrow. 'Trouble by the looks of things.'

'Very well, then,' cried Constantina. 'As I'm sure you all know, there is a new Keeper in town. *Charlie* Keeper,' she added, pointing directly to her.

Charlie felt thousands of eyes drawn to her.

'My fellow Sylvarisians, you need to know that she holds the fate of Bellania around her neck. The pendant she wears is a gift from the Winged Ones. They say it is a secret weapon that might stop the Western Menace in his tracks! But Charlie Keeper herself is under threat from Bane and draws his unwanted attention towards our fair city.' She paused to let the information sink in.

Kelko instinctively stood closer to his friend. Charlie took the opportunity to discreetly tuck the pendant out of sight.

Constantina's green eyes glinted. 'But is this Keeper not too young for the task? Is she not too inexperienced for the rocky road that lies ahead?' The crowd was totally silent now, listening to what their champion was saying. 'May I suggest that another take up the task of keeping Sylvaris safe from the Western Menace? May I suggest that another take up the pendant? Someone with more experience. Someone more capable of defending our way of life. My friends, my people, my fellow citizens of Sylvaris, I humbly offer myself up for the task. What say you? Am I worthy?'

Kelko turned to Charlie in shock.

As one, the crowd roared out its reply, the gigantic cry of consent shaking the stands. 'Yes! Yes! Constantina! Constantina for Sylvaris! Constantina for Sylvaris!'

49

Confrontations

The flock of crows beat their way through the air. Growing hungry, they angled down towards the Great Plains that lay below. Flying lower, they spotted a small herd of deer led by a proud stag with heavy antlers.

Descending in a wall of black feathers, the crows dropped upon the terrified stag. Sinking their talons into its soft fur, the mass of birds hauled their wriggling catch into the sky. Then, feeding piranha-like upon the bleating and still-struggling stag, they continued their hurried pace eastward. Towards Sylvaris.

'What's her problem?' snapped Charlie furiously. 'Is she mad? This pendant is mine! My parents gave it to me. She's got to be crazy if she thinks I'm gonna give it up!'

'Er . . .' said Kelko as he nervously patted his stomach. Constantina was strutting across the arena towards the two of them. 'Er, this doesn't look good, blossom, not good at all.'

Striding up the steps into the stand, Constantina shouted

out to the crowd, 'Sylvaris! People of Sylvaris! Will you bear witness to my request?'

'Yes!' roared out a thousand delighted voices. 'Yes!'

Leaning over towards Charlie, Constantina whispered, 'Sweeten up, buttercup! Time to make way for someone who knows what they're doing!'

Charlie quite firmly resisted the urge to push the arrogant girl back down the steps of the stand.

Aloud, and for the benefit of the crowd, Constantina called out, 'Charlie Keeper, do you relinquish your pendant to me, Sylvaris's K'Changa champion, in this, our greatest hour of need, to be used for the saving of our way of life?'

Charlie stared at her in amazement. Surely this couldn't be happening? Aware that thousands of eyes were staring at her, awaiting her response, she blushed a deep, deep crimson. 'Kelko!' she whispered. 'What should I say?'

'Tell her, "Blight me Leaf, but you can jabber off home!"'

Charlie rolled her eyes. That wasn't the most ladylike response. Taking a deep breath, she forced herself to stand up in front of the crowd and voice her reply. 'No! You can't have it. Didn't anyone teach you it's not right to ask for what isn't yours?'

Like some giant beast, the crowd groaned and muttered its disapproval. Charlie could practically feel their displeasure pressing down on her like an oppressive burden. She blushed an even deeper shade of red, but an angry spark began to burn within her heart. Who were these people to judge her? They didn't know what she'd been through. What she'd already sacrificed to help Bellania. Straightening her back, Charlie stood even taller and addressed the crowd.

'Sylvaris, I'm sorry but no, you may not have this pendant! It is mine, given to me by my parents, and it is all that I have to remember them by. This is the very last shred of contact between me and them so, Constantina –' Charlie took a very big breath before continuing – 'you can Blight me Leaf and jabber off home!'

There was a shocked moment of silence before the Colosseum erupted into a cascading wall of noise as half the crowd roared in laughter while the other half booed out its anger. Kelko laughed so hard he actually fell off his seat. With one shaking finger, he pointed at Constantina's disbelieving face. She looked like she'd been slapped by a wet fish.

'What?' whispered Charlie. 'That was the right thing to say, wasn't it?'

Kelko's stomach was wobbling so hard it threatened to break the buttons on his leather shirt.

'*What?* Why's half the crowd laughing? That's what you suggested I should say, isn't it?'

'Yup, yer right, I did suggest it. I just didn't think ya would actually say it, at least not in public! Oh, Charlie, lass, ya were excellent . . . Just look at her face! It's the best thing I've seen all year. No one's ever dared talk ta her like that – even her own mother – and ta say that in front of the Colosseum crowd . . . ha!'

Constantina, having got a firm grip upon her dignity, raised her arms for silence. The crowd grew quiet.

'Charlie Keeper, for your rudeness and failure to support Sylvaris in its hour of need I formally challenge you to a Silent Duel!'

'Burn me Sap!' muttered Kelko.

'I don't care what you challenge me to, you chump!' retorted Charlie. 'Feel free to challenge me until your face turns blue for all I care. I'm not here to play games with spoilt brats and I'm certainly not planning on being here long enough to get into any fights. Blow your big mouth off all you want, but the answer's still gonna be no!'

'Er, Charlie,' said Kelko, leaning in. 'Constantina's the K'Changa champion and she's just challenged ya ta a Silent Duel. Ya've got no choice but ta accept. If ya don't ya will forfeit all yer rights . . . Even the right ta be called "Keeper"!'

'What? But that's rubbish. I'm not even from here . . . I don't have to follow any of your rules!'

'Blossom, yer a Keeper. Yer family is just as bound by these rules as is anyone who steps inta Sylvaris.'

Charlie pulled a face. 'What is a Silent Duel anyway?'

'It's a game of K'Changa, but with a more drastic outcome. The challengers traditionally play at the full moon.' He thought for a moment. 'The next one coincides with the Three Winds Festival. The loser either submits ta the winner's demands or spends a year banished ta the Halls of Eternal Echoes.'

'Halls of Eternal Echoes?'

'It's a blooming big cave beneath Sylvaris with no light, no heat and they don't serve breakfast in bed.'

'A whole year stuck in a cave! Isn't that a bit drastic?'

'Yup, but it's traditional!'

'So I've got the choice of either giving her my pendant or going crazy in a damp cave?'

'Er, yeah,' said Kelko uncomfortably. 'Well, there is one other option,' he added.

Charlie gave a bleak smile as she stared over at Constantina. 'Yeah, I know . . . beat her at K'Changa.'

Constantina spoke to the crowd. 'Sylvarisians, not only is she rude, she's a coward. As she has denied her right to accept the challenge, I formally lay claim to the pendant that will save Bellania, as is my right.' The raven-haired girl made to approach Charlie.

'Wait!' shouted Charlie. Giving Kelko a strangled look, she continued, her voice hoarse with anger and determination. 'If you want to play it like that, fine. I might not be from around here and your laws might be strange to me, but if that's what you want you've got it. And even though I didn't ask for this, I'm going to wipe that smug look from your dumb face if it's the last thing I do!'

The crowd roared out its delight. There hadn't been a Silent Duel for years; this year's Three Winds Festival would certainly be something to remember.

50

Words of Encouragement

'She what?' growled Azariah with a furious frown. 'Kelko, by the Seven Heavens and the Seven Hells, how could you let this happen? You were supposed to be looking after her, not getting her into more trouble!'

'How was I supposed ta know Constantina was going ta do a daft thing like that?' protested Kelko. 'Do ya think I would have taken Charlie ta the Colosseum if I did? Seeing as I can't tell the future, I can't see how it can be me fault!'

'You should have improvised!' snapped Azariah. 'You should have –'

'It's not his fault,' said Charlie, coming to her friend's rescue. 'Neither of us had any idea what she was planning. I've never even met her before! I tried to refuse but she kept throwing that daft Sylvarisian Law in my face, and because she did it in front of the whole crowd there was no way we could wriggle out of her trap.'

Azariah sighed when he saw Charlie's honest expression staring back at him. 'Hhmm. OK, I concede that it might not have been entirely Kelko's fault.'

Charlie grinned triumphantly and slapped Kelko enthusiastically on his shoulder.

'But,' continued Azariah, 'are you aware of what this means? You have no choice other than to accept this challenge. A Silent Duel is not a normal game – it means the best of three. This means that you must best the champion of Sylvaris not once but *twice* in order to keep the pendant and, much as I hate to say this, as things stand I am certain that you shall lose.'

Charlie blanched at Azariah's forthright analysis. But after witnessing Constantina's amazing display of skills, Charlie grudgingly admitted to herself he was right. She couldn't hope to match Narcissa's daughter. She would lose the pendant.

'Is there really no way to back out of this match?' she asked.

'From a Silent Duel?' said Azariah. 'I'm afraid not, young Keeper. Once the challenge has been issued, the defendant must either accept or bow to the challenger's will. It is one of Sylvaris's most ancient laws.'

'OK, so what happens if I run away? What happens if I leave Sylvaris?'

Azariah shook his head, the beads in his beard gently clicking together. 'You lose your right to the name "Keeper", a price will be put on your head and you will become a fugitive, even if you return to London. Not to mention the fact that you will not be here to receive Nibbler's message from Edge Darkmount, which means we shall be no closer to our ultimate goal of defeating Bane. Nor will we have any hope of freeing your parents without the pendant here in Bellania.'

'So that's it, then? We get trapped once again by your silly Sylvarisian Law? Narcissa and her spiteful family get their hands on the pendant and laugh in our faces? Come on, guys, there's got to be a way out of this mess!'

Azariah smiled. 'Of course there is. Have you so quickly forgotten your heritage and all that it means?'

'Wot are ya getting at?' asked Kelko with a frown.

'The girl is a Keeper,' said Azariah, his lion-like voice laced with pride. 'Narcissa and Constantina, in their haste to lay claim to the pendant, have underestimated this fact and that shall be their downfall.'

Charlie stared at Azariah with a puzzled look. 'What do you mean?'

'What I am saying, young Keeper, is that if there is a "Will", then there is a "Way". Which is especially true if you happen to be a Keeper! Just think, Charlie, if you apply your Will to your K'Changa-playing, you could become unstoppable. All of Constantina's years of experience and her formidable skill with the Zephyr will amount to nothing. You could win this.'

A jaunty knocking came from Azariah's front door. Sic Boy, rising up from where he had been dozing by Charlie's feet, padded over and, using his enormous teeth to grasp and tug at the many latches and locks, pulled open the leaf-shaped door.

'Ho-ho! How're ya all doing?' smirked Jensen by way of greeting, his topknot bouncing from side to side as he sauntered into the room. His smile faltered as he saw everyone's long expressions. 'Wot? Have I missed something?'

Azariah, Kelko and Charlie took it in turn to fill him in.

'Blight Narcissa and her cursed family!' swore Jensen upon hearing all the facts. 'So how long do we have ta put dis plan inta effect? Let's see now, the next full moon is at the Three Winds Festival, which is in –'

'Five days' time,' said Kelko, finishing Jensen's sentence for him.

'Yeah, five days,' agreed Jensen. 'Is that enough time, Azariah?'

'It will have to be,' said the old Keeper in a gruff voice. 'So what I suggest is that tomorrow the three of us combine our knowledge to turn Charlie into the kind of K'Changa player who legends are made from.'

Charlie suddenly felt the weight of responsibility crash down on her young shoulders. *Were they mad to think she could beat Constantina?*

'Don't ya worry about a thing,' said Jensen when he saw Charlie's face fall. Leaning over, he gave her a friendly nudge. 'Charlie, I have absolute faith in ya. If anyone can teach Constantina and her family a well-deserved lesson it's ya.'

She sighed. 'Er . . . if you don't mind me asking, what is the Three Winds Festival?'

Both Kelko and Jensen's faces split into huge child-like grins. Even Azariah's frowning face momentarily brightened.

'The Three Winds Festival, blossom, is the most amazing of festivals,' said Kelko. 'It's the best . . .'

'The most amazing . . .' continued Jensen with a glimmer in his eye.

'The most phenomenal . . .' offered Kelko with a look of enchanted wonder.

'The most spectacular . . .'

'The most stupendous . . .'

'The most awe-inspiring . . .'

'The most breath-stealing . . .'

'The most heart-quenching –'

'OK, boys, I think she gets the message,' interrupted Azariah before they could continue. He'd seen the two of them like this before and knew they could go on for hours. 'Young Keeper, the Three Winds Festival marks the end of spring and the beginning of the summer and, as legend would have it, it also marks the last day of the Cataclysm. It's a festival that is celebrated all over Bellania but Sylvaris, in particular, is renowned for the enthusiasm of its festivities.'

'Yeah, that's cos nowhere celebrates it like we do!' bellowed Kelko with a big, dopey grin.

Azariah merely raised an eyebrow at the interruption before continuing. 'There will be parades, fireworks, feasts, acrobatics, treesinging, fireworks, sword-swallowing, orchid competitions, floating lanterns, fireworks and just about everything else that you could possibly expect to create a sense of wonder and delight.'

'Er . . . you said "fireworks" three times,' pointed out Charlie.

'I know, that's because I enjoy them so much.' Azariah chuckled with a boyish grin. 'They remind me of my child-hood.'

'But why is it called the Three Winds Festival?'

'Hhmm?' asked Azariah, who had been lost in childhood memories. 'Oh yes, well, with the change of season the three western winds get stronger, bringing with them the scent of the summer. I believe that Kelko has shown you the Whispering Heights, has he not?'

Charlie nodded. 'The tall towers that make all those strange sounds when the wind blows through them?'

'Yes, that is the place. Well, as the southern wind loses its power and the three western winds begin to blow, you will hear the towers play a delightful new melody. The sound that echoes from the Whispering Heights indicates that summer is truly upon us.'

Charlie's eyes gleamed. The Three Winds Festival sounded like a very special event. Under other circumstances she would be excited, but not with the Silent Duel hanging over her. Instead of enjoying it, she was going to be the reluctant star attraction.

51

Family Squabbles

'Well?' asked Lady Narcissa.

'Well what?' Constantina replied rudely.

'How did it go with Charlie Keeper? Did you lay down the challenge like I told you to?'

'Oh, that,' huffed Constantina, looking uninterested.

'Yes, that,' snapped Narcissa as she finally lost her temper with her spoilt daughter. 'Did you or did you not challenge the Keeper? Answer me this instant, young lady, or I shall punish you like you've never been punished before!'

'Yes, of course I challenged her!' screamed Constantina. 'I did what you asked me to do and I even won the Fleet-Foot title match, but what do you care? I always do what you ask and I always win, but you never seem to notice! All the other kids at school don't do half as well as me but they get more affection from their parents! Why can't you, just for once, say, "Well done, Constantina. I'm proud of you"? What kind of mother are you?'

'What kind of mother am I?' hissed Narcissa as she rubbed at the bridge of her nose in disgust. 'Well, not only am I one of the most powerful women in the land of Bellania, but have you forgotten that I'm the one who buys you all those designer clothes from Alavis and Alacorn? I'm the one who keeps you supplied with all those sapphires from the Western Mountains. I'm the one who gets you the best K'Changa tutors in Deepforest. I'm the one who sends you and your other petulant little friends off on exclusive holidays to the Dream Isles and the Scented Mountains. Having me for a mother ensures that you enjoy the life of a celebrity!' She glared at her daughter, who was cowering from her rage. 'Now, would you like me to stop lavishing all these luxuries on you or are you going to be quiet and do what I demand like a good little girl?'

Constantina's lip began to quiver and her eyes grew teary. Leaning over so that her hair covered her face, she answered her mother. 'Y-y-yes.'

'Good. Now then, let me get this straight. You issued the challenge and she agreed, yes?'

'Yes.'

'Excellent. And there is no way she can beat you, correct?'

'What? Beat me?' squawked Constantina, regaining her confidence. 'An inexperienced little creature like that? Fresh from the Other Realm? She won't last a minute in the K'Changa circle against me!'

Lady Narcissa smiled coldly. 'That is good news, my dear, good news indeed. And seeing what a good girl you are, I shall see what can be done about arranging you a celebratory banquet.'

'Excuse me, ma'am,' announced a footman, 'but Councillor Flint is here. He requests an immediate conference with your ladyship.'

'Very well. Please inform him that I shall meet him in the audience chamber on the fifteenth floor.'

The footman nodded. 'Certainly, ma'am.' Bowing low, he departed.

'How big will my banquet be?' asked Constantina with a petulant toss of her hair.

'Constantina, now is not the time to be bothering me with such minor details. I have said that you may have one and a banquet you shall have,' Narcissa promised. 'You and I shall discuss this later.'

'Later! It's always later with you,' stormed Constantina with a bitter tone. 'You're always busy, aren't you?'

'Yes! Yes, I am, and that is the price that you must pay for having a member of the Jade Circle for a mother.'

'It's a price that I never asked for!' screamed Constantina as she once again lost her temper.

'And you think that I care?' replied Lady Narcissa with an arched eyebrow.

Straightening her skirts, she swept from the room, pretending not to see her daughter furiously stick her tongue out at her departing back, and headed off to her rendezvous with Flint.

Striding along passageways lined with ancient, self-important portraits of the Narcissa family, Lady Narcissa made her way through the Ivory Tower. Pushing open a wide door carved from pale maplewood, she entered the audience chamber.

'Flint.'

'Lady Narcissa.'

'What can I do for you?'

The large Stoman councillor with his many, many necklaces and bracelets sighed and grimaced horribly. 'It is Azariah Keeper. It appears that every time I approach one of the councillors with our *proposal*, he has got there first. Blackmail or bribe, Azariah is countering our every move with one of his own! We are losing the battle.'

'That poisonous old man!' barked Narcissa. Her eyes blazed furiously and her hands tensed into clawed fists. 'How dare he! How dare he try and undermine me. I will not have it!'

'That is all very well for you to say, but dealing with a Keeper is no easy task,' Flint reminded Narcissa.

'I do not care what you think. Deal with him I shall!' retorted Narcissa.

'Oh yes, and how do you plan to do that?' replied Flint, his tone mildly mocking.

'Lord Bane has arranged to send me a servant of power to aid me specifically for events such as this. Heed my words well, Councillor Flint – Azariah Keeper's time has come.'

52

An Ill-fated Zephyr

Charlie tensed her jaw, rolled her hands into fists and concentrated as the Zephyr came spinning towards her. Summoning her Will, she burst into motion and leaped towards it.

PHFOOM!

Kelko and Jensen stared with wide, disbelieving eyes as the Zephyr exploded in a cloud of smoking feathers and Charlie, off balance, landed in a heap of tangled limbs.

'Wufa-whargh?' mumbled Charlie as she sat up. Her hair, previously so tidy and neat for once, was now a mess, she had dirt on her cheeks and, after flying through the remnants of the burst Zephyr, her mouth was full of blue and slightly singed feathers. She used her fingers to pull what she could from her mouth. 'Why does that keep happening?'

It took Kelko and Jensen a second or two to regain their composure. They weren't used to seeing such wild displays of the Will and the Way, and certainly weren't used to seeing how powerfully destructive they could be when applied incorrectly.

'Uh . . .' began Jensen. 'Perhaps a little too much of the old Will and the Way there, me little Hippotomi.'

'Ah . . . yes,' agreed Kelko. He stared around at Azariah's back garden. It was covered in feathers, not only from the latest Zephyr but from twelve others they had used previously. Charlie had managed to burn, mangle, crisp and exterminate all of them. So far her training to mix her Will with K'Changa-playing wasn't proving a success. 'Um, methinks think we'd better tidy up dis mess before Azariah gets back.'

'We can do that later,' disagreed Jensen. 'We need ta keep practising. We have ta get dis right and get it right soon. We're running outta time. There are only three more days until the match and we ain't got it right yet. We've got ta work harder. Get another Zephyr and we'll try a different method.'

Kelko rummaged inside his training sack. 'That was the last one. We're outta Zephyrs.'

Jensen sighed. 'Want ta wait around until Azariah gets back or shall we go and get some more now?'

'No, let's get some more. We can get ta the shop and be back here in no time. We'll take Sic Boy with us so we don't have ta worry about any trouble.' Kelko heaved Charlie to her feet. 'C'mon, lass. Let's roll ta the shop.'

Walking along the crowded boulevards, they headed towards one of Sylvaris's shopping districts. Kelko and Jensen led Charlie into a shop called Fah Sweet Vibrations, which was full of K'Changa-related merchandise. There was a selection of snug-fitting boots, sleek-looking trousers, streamlined gloves and, of course, a huge selection of Zephyrs. They lined two of the shop's walls and were in every colour imaginable. There were the traditional blue-feathered variety, but also a range of vibrant greens, shimmering golds and others that were a mishmash of loud colours. When Charlie leaned closer to look at one of the labels she realized that some of the novelty Zephyrs also came in different flavours (for those who got the munchies during practice).

'Yes, gentlemen and, er, lady. Can I help ya?' asked the shopkeeper.

Jensen brightened at the idea of spending some of his money. 'Yes, ya can. We're in need of several Zephyrs for our young protégée here.'

The shopkeeper eyed Charlie and her dishevelled appearance warily. 'And what type of Zephyr would the, um, young "lady" be requiring?'

'All of them,' answered Jensen, his eyes shining.

The shopkeeper goggled. 'All?'

Jensen grinned and reached for his moneybag. 'Yes, all of them.'

'Do you really need all of them?' asked a sneering voice. 'Sounds like someone must be having trouble mastering the finer skills of K'Changa.'

Charlie groaned. It was Constantina and she was surrounded by a small crowd of pretty and very well-dressed Human and Treman teenage girls.

'Of course,' continued Constantina, 'only a skank from the Other Realm would be rude enough to buy out a whole shop of Zephyrs so no one else in Sylvaris can play K'Changa.'

The girls surrounding Constantina giggled.

'What?' squawked Charlie, suddenly embarrassed. 'Look, I don't need all of them. If you want some that's not a problem.'

'Me?' said Constantina in mock surprise. 'I don't need them, buttercup, but it looks like you really do, so please take them. After all, I wouldn't want to go up against a player who didn't know what she was doing. My, imagine how humiliating it would be if you only lasted a couple of seconds against me. Take the Zephyrs and go home and practise some more. Believe me, you're going to need it.'

'What? Why, you . . .' began Charlie, feeling her anger rise. 'Listen, you empty-headed chump –'

'No, *you* listen!' warned Constantina. She stepped forward so she was almost nose to nose with Charlie, ignoring the warning growl from Sic Boy. 'Do you really think you can waltz on over from the Other Realm, come here to Sylvaris and suddenly become a big shot? You think that you can come to my mother's house, burn down the roof and get away with it? And on top of that you think that you can become some kind of hero who's going to save Sylvaris and win the war? Do you really think you're worthy, let alone capable?'

Already tired and worked up from the day's training, Charlie could feel her calm completely unravelling. The hatred and anger that had festered since her stay in the Ivory Tower began to simmer and boil inside her chest. 'You've got everything twisted! If you think that's what –'

'Wot methinks,' interrupted Jensen, before Charlie and Constantina started a fight, 'is that dis is no way for a champion of Sylvaris ta behave. Constantina, if yer a real K'Changa champion and really believe in everything that ya just said, then I suggest ya clamp yer mouth shut and save it for the Colosseum. Now then, we're here ta do some shopping so . . . shopkeeper, here's a little something for ya.' Jensen threw his moneybag into the surprised shopkeeper's hands. 'Kelko, grab the Zephyrs. Charlie, Sic Boy, we're outta here.'

Kelko went along the walls of the shop and stuffed the Zephyrs into his sack as the shopkeeper greedily began to count the coins. Jensen, putting a firm hand on Charlie's shoulder, began to guide her out of the shop.

As they pushed past the group of girls, Constantina leaned close to whisper in Charlie's ear. 'I like the look of the pendant but the chain seems cheap. I'll have to have my jewellers reset it on something more befitting a real champion.'

Charlie stiffened and opened her mouth to reply, but Jensen forced her out of the shop. Kelko swiftly hurried after with his bulging sack. Sic Boy, however, took his time. He walked straight through the pack of girls, forcing them to squeal and jump out of the way, and even knocking a couple of them backwards with his muscular, furry bulk.

Once outside, Charlie spun around. 'Why did you have to go and stop me?'

'Blossom,' began Kelko, 'we can see that Constantina is a blight ta anyone's tree, but ya can't afford ta get in a fight with her before the match.'

'He's right, me little Hippotomi,' added Jensen. 'Ya've got ta keep calm, at least for the moment. Anger's a good thing in certain situations, but yer using it wrong. If ya use yer anger right here and now on Constantina, ya will have wasted it. Ya've got ta use yer anger wisely.'

'Use it?' asked Charlie, suddenly puzzled.

'Sure. Use it ta focus on yer training. Use it ta give yerself purpose and then, when ya face Constantina in the arena, use yer anger ta make yerself a better K'Changa player. If ya use it the right way ya can use it ta win.'

Charlie chewed on her lip while she thought about it. 'Constantina is a brat and there's nothing I'd like more than to use my Will on her, but . . .' Charlie sighed. 'You're right, this isn't the best way to go about this. I want to get back at Lady Narcissa and the Delightful Brothers and I have to defeat Bane. So . . . if I beat Constantina at K'Changa it'll not only wipe the smile off her face but it'll be a real kick to Lady Narcissa and, most importantly, it means that I get to keep the pendant, so Bane had better look out too.'

As Charlie talked her way through it and imagined how angry both Narcissa and Constantina would be if she won, a grin began to spread over her face. Seeing it, Kelko and Jensen smiled too.

'That's me Hippotomi!' said Jensen. 'Now, let's get back ta Azariah's and tidy up his garden before he turns us all inta donkeys or something!'

The long black ribbon of crows dropped the stag's carcass, allowing the clutter of bones to fall to the distant earth. Cawing excitedly, the marauding pack flung themselves onward. Soaring over the crest of a large hill, they caught sight of their final destination: Deepforest.

And just there, twinkling like some jewel against a magnificent green background, was Sylvaris.

Mr Crow would soon be making his presence known.

53

Tough Training

Charlie squeaked in terror as her concentration faltered, then suddenly failed her. With a wild cry she toppled from the narrow beam and fell with a splash into the murky water of Azariah's ornamental fishpond.

'Gah!' snorted Azariah. Even Kelko and Jensen, standing on either side of the garden, looked on in dismay. 'You must do much better than that, Charlie. Much better! The Three Winds Festival is tomorrow and this is the best that you can offer? We might as well just hand over the pendant now and save ourselves any more trouble.'

Charlie's training wasn't going anywhere near as smoothly as it should have and although she had stopped burning the Zephyrs to a crisp she hadn't progressed as much as she needed to. Even now, on her fourth day of training, she had still failed to combine her K'Changa skills with those of a Keeper. She was glad, really glad, that they had continued training in the garden at the back of Azariah's house. At least this way no one else could see what a mess she was making of things.

'I just can't stay focused,' she complained, dragging herself from the water to stand dripping wet and covered with weed on the beautifully trimmed grass. 'Every time I try to hold my Will and spin the shuttlecock –'

'It's called a Zephyr!' snapped Jensen.

'Sorry,' apologized Charlie. 'Every time I try to hold my Will and spin the *Zephyr* things just seem to . . . well, just fall apart. I can't do it! I can't do both at the same time.'

'Bah!' snapped Azariah. 'Stop complaining. You're amazingly talented at K'Changa for a virtual beginner and have quickly mastered some of the skills to become a Keeper. So stop moaning, stop griping and put the two together!'

'But it's not that easy,' insisted Charlie as she plucked a wriggling tadpole from her shirt.

'Hhmpf, nothing in this world is ever easy,' grumped the old Keeper. 'If it was then surely everyone would be rich and happy. But that is not the point. You are a Keeper and you will do this . . . Now, get up there, concentrate and do it again!'

Shaking her head from side to side in misery, Charlie did as she was told. Climbing up the steep ladder, she eased herself out on to the narrow beam that hung high above the garden. Maintaining her balance, she edged outward to stand in the middle of the plank.

'OK, Charlie,' cried Kelko. 'Are you ready?'

'Er.' Charlie frowned as she stared at the garden below. It was a long drop. 'I guess so.'

'That's me girl!' said Kelko with an encouraging smile. Reaching down for the brightly coloured shuttlecock, he flung it upward. Kelko, Jensen and Azariah held their breath as they waited to see how Charlie would react.

Charlie saw the Zephyr coming. Bunching her fingers together into tight fists and pulling her eyebrows down into a tight squint, she summoned her Will. She felt the blossoming of power as her Will began to focus and she could see the deep glow of golden light bursting forth from her blazing hands. She was ready.

Watching the arc of the shuttlecock flying towards her, Charlie bent her legs and, with an intense shout of determination, ran across the narrow beam. Leaping into an intricate somersault, she prepared to snatch the Zephyr as it flew towards her.

Suddenly her eyesight began to blur. The shuttlecock appeared to double, then triple, until it seemed as though a multitude of Zephyrs approached her. Her stomach began to cramp and waves of dizziness washed through her body.

'Aaaaaaaaaahhhhhhhhhhh!' screamed Charlie as once again she tumbled through the air to land with a gigantic splash. Water lilies went flying and one of Azariah's prized koi carp was flung aside to bounce indignantly among the clipped plants until Jensen scrambled over to tip it gently back into the water.

Coughing up lungfuls of muddy water, Charlie spluttered and snuffled as she pulled herself to the side of the pond. Azariah didn't look amused.

'What was that?' he growled. 'Was *that* the best you had to offer?'

'I don't understand why it's not happening,' protested

Charlie. 'I do exactly what you guys tell me to do, but when I put it into practice my head goes all dizzy and my body just doesn't seem to want to do what I tell it to do.'

Azariah sighed in disappointment. Letting his frustration flow away, he leaned down and offered Charlie a hand. Pulling her from the pond, he stared at her in dismay.

'Young lady, the reason why you continue to fail at this task is because you lack the Will! If you cannot focus on what needs to be done you will fail miserably.'

Azariah sighed yet again as he stared at his dripping-wet apprentice. Lifting up one glowing hand, he casually waved it in Charlie's direction. With a faint wumphing noise, the water from Charlie's clothes fell away to splatter and tinkle at her feet. Charlie was suddenly very dry, but unfortunately her hair had ballooned into a tangled, frizzy mess.

Ignoring Charlie's outrageous hair, Azariah continued. 'Enough. That is enough for today. I must be off to meet with Dridif and certain members of the Jade Circle so I am afraid that I must leave you to it. What I would suggest is that you use the remainder of the day to practise and do your best to get this right.'

'Do you have to leave?'

'I must, for this battle against Narcissa is being fought on more fronts than one. However, I have some news that might cheer you up. With a bit of luck, today should see the majority of the Jade Circle united to stand as one against Lady Narcissa and her treasonous ways. Lady Dridif and I have managed to prevent many of the councillors from being tempted to join her forces. And if our luck stays strong, we could even eject Narcissa from the council in as little as two days' time!'

'That's excellent news,' said Charlie.

'Yes, it is. However, I must be off, whereas you shall remain here with Jensen and Kelko to practise while there still remains enough daylight to see by.'

Charlie's face fell. Groaning, she turned back to the high beam.

'Bring me a pot of Witchflower Tea and a selection of Krete Delights.'

'Yes, mistress,' grovelled the servant, bowing low.

He departed to fetch the refreshments, scurrying past the watchful eyes of Stix and Stones, who were standing guard.

Narcissa sat reclining on a magnificent chair upholstered with silk and decorated with her heron and rose motif. Flint was on a similar chair beside her. The two of them had been discussing strategies on one of the large, sweeping balconies that adorned the Ivory Tower. Huge waves of orchids, lilies and lotus flowers grew from the side of the tower to form a canopy of brightly coloured petals that shielded them from the strong rays of the setting sun.

'So tell me, Lady Narcissa, where is this servant of Bane's? Should he not have arrived by now?'

'Patience, Flint, patience. The Stoman Lord himself assured me that the servant would be here in time.'

'Yes, well, if that was so he should have arrived long ago.

We cannot afford to wait much longer. The First Speaker and that idiotic old Keeper are growing far, far too strong for my liking.'

'Be that as it may, I still expect . . .' Narcissa fell silent. Shielding her eyes from the last of the sun's rays, she gazed at a shadow that hung on the horizon. 'What is that?'

Squinting his eyes into narrow slits, the large Stoman councillor leaned forward to get a better view. 'I . . . I am not sure. It looks like a large flock of birds, does it not? They appear to be ravens . . . or crows. Most unusual to see even one this far east of the Western Mountains, but to see a whole flock? Most unusual indeed.'

The birds, now clearly identifiable as crows, quickly drew nearer, seeming to head straight for the two councillors. Their harsh, haunting cries crashed against the side of the Ivory Tower and with a loud flapping of wings they spiralled down towards the balcony. Stix and Stones stepped forward from the shadows to stand protectively on either side of their mother. The Delightful Brothers eyed the approaching flurry of birds with mistrust.

With a last bursting shriek, the birds kaleidoscoped together, melting into one large mass, and with a sharp sound, similar to that of breaking glass, Mr Crow lightly stepped forth.

'Good evening,' he whispered. 'My name is Crow, Mr Crow.' The skinny lawyer smiled nastily. Sunlight gleamed and reflected off his frighteningly sharp teeth. 'Now, where is that little filly, Charlie?'

54

The Arrival

'So where is she?'

'There is no need for you to express an interest in that little brat just yet, Mr Crow,' snapped Lady Narcissa, recovering from the man's unusual arrival. 'I have a plan that will allow us to get our hands on the pendant without having to involve ourselves in open bloodshed with either Charlie Keeper or the Jade Circle.'

'That is not what I have been led to believe. The Great Lord instructed me to bring him both the girl and the pendant to the Western Mountains with all due haste.'

Narcissa's mouth twitched. 'Maybe so, but did he not also instruct you to do as I requested?'

'Yessss,' Mr Crow whispered grudgingly.

'And did he not arrange for you to act as my tool and servant in this task?'

'Yes,' agreed the lawyer with an angry glint in his eye.

'Good.' Lady Narcissa smiled with a lazy wave of her hand. 'Do not trouble yourself with thoughts of Charlie. By the end of tomorrow night my daughter will have claimed the pendant for herself, so what I need from you is help with another headache. Charlie's mentor, Azariah Keeper, has proved to be very bothersome. Given more time he could quite possibly ruin my plans. I want you to remove him.'

'By saying "remove", I do assume that you mean "kill"?' asked Crow with a sharp, bird-like twitter of his head.

'Yes, I do mean that,' acknowledged Narcissa with a cold smile. 'Tonight.'

'That is something I can do,' replied the lawyer, an odd shadow flickering across his beady eyes. 'Will his death cause Charlie Keeper much pain?'

'Oh, I expect so. The two have grown quite close. They are almost like family.'

'Excellent. I shall enjoy plucking this Azariah Keeper's soul that much more.'

With a sickening grin, Mr Crow jumped and bounded his way over to the balustrade and, with a final glance at Narcissa, leaped over.

Councillor Flint and the Delightful Brothers rushed to the balcony's side. Gasping in horror, they quickly stepped back as a black wave of feral birds swept upward and away into the darkening sky.

'So you have still failed to bend your Will to the task at hand,' stated Azariah with regret. 'I am truly sorry to hear that. And you shall get no more done tonight, young Keeper, for the hour is late and you above all need your rest.'

'But –'

'Charlie, no arguments. Just remember that you are a Keeper and so long as you remember to focus your Will you will find a Way. I have faith in you and, what is more, I am proud of you,' said Azariah with a fond glance.

Charlie blushed, she couldn't help it. Those were some of the kindest words that anyone had said to her in a long, long time. If she'd had any sort of existing family other than her grandma, she supposed that those were the sorts of words they would have used. Perhaps someone like a wise uncle. Once again Charlie blushed.

'Well then, it is too late for you to be going home at this hour, so I suggest that you spend the night here. That goes for you two as well,' said Azariah with a nod to Kelko and Jensen. 'I have spare rooms a-plenty, so if the three of you settle down here for the night it will be that much easier to commence training upon the morrow.'

'Sounds fine ta me,' said Jensen.

'Me too,' grinned Kelko, slapping at his stomach in satisfaction. 'Saves me a long walk back ta me house it does. Splendid.'

'Excellent. If you would be so good as to follow me, I shall show you each to your rooms.'

'Azariah?' asked Charlie. 'What about Nibbler? Shouldn't he be back by now?'

'Tomorrow, Charlie. If things have gone well I would expect him by tomorrow morning, or by midday at the very latest. Now then, if you please, this way.'

It was some time after midnight when Charlie awoke from her dreams. For a second she lay still, confused

as to where she was. But as her sleep-befuddled mind
slowly kicked back into gear she realized that she was
not in her bedroom at the Willow Tower but lying in
one of Azariah's spare rooms. A faint cawing startled her
from her doze. Charlie grumped, pulled up the bedcov-
ers and was just about to roll over when the sound came
again.

Closer this time.

Slipping from beneath the warm sheets, Charlie wriggled
her feet into her shoes and silently tiptoed out into the hallway to investigate.

'Aah!' shrieked Jensen as Charlie bumped into him. 'Oh,
Bless me Roots! But it's ya! I thought ya were a ghost!'

'Hhmpf,' muttered Charlie. 'What are you trying to say?
That I look like a ghost?'

'Well, with hair like that . . .' admitted Jensen. 'Yeah, I do
think ya look like a ghost, especially when ya bound outta
yer room like that.'

'I did not bound out of my –'

'Blight me Leaf,' protested Kelko, coming out of a nearby
room. 'Wot's all dis noise about? Don't you two ever sleep?
Ya heard wot Azariah said, Charlie – ya need yer sleep.'

'I, uh, I heard an odd noise,' said Charlie. 'It woke me up.'

'Me too!' said Jensen. 'T'was sort of like a "ca-CAW,
ca-CAW" noise, wasn't it?'

'Yeah, that's right,' said Charlie. 'I wonder what made it?'

'So I see I'm not the only one who has been hearing odd
noises in the night,' rumbled Azariah as he stepped around
the corner. Once again his cheeky red slippers peeked out
from beneath his robe.

'What was it?' asked Charlie.

'I'm not sure –'

The shrieking and cawing erupted once again. Strident and loud, it came from just beyond the windowpane in the dimly lit hallway. Again and again the sound burned through the night, growing louder and louder, more intense and high-pitched, until the very sound tore at everyone's ears. Inky wings, blacker and darker than the night, began to flash past, and long feathers rubbed noisily against the glass. Whatever was outside was trying to find a way in.

'Wot is that?' asked Kelko with a faint catch of fear in his voice.

'I'm not too sure,' admitted Azariah. 'They appear to be birds of some sort but I have never come across any that acted in such a way. Whatever they are I can feel their hatred.' Frowning, the old Keeper swept downstairs towards the leaf-shaped doorway.

'Wot are ya doing?' protested Jensen, as the three of them hastily followed him. 'Don't open the door! Yer'll let 'em in!'

'Do not worry yourself, Jensen. The day that I fear a pack of birds is the day I tie little pink ribbons into my beard.'

'Wot are ya, nuts? Can ya not see that they are not normal crows? They're obviously evil! Even me old auntie could've told ya that and she was deaf as a drunk walrus and blind as a bat!'

'Jensen of the Willow, have you forgotten who you speak to?' retorted Azariah. 'I am Azariah Keeper and I have survived many great perils in my lifetime. I have survived two years of wrongful imprisonment in the Soul Mines of Zhartoum, I have fought tooth and nail against the Patchwork

Daemons and even battled against the unquenchable Tides of Despair! Do you honestly think that I will stand back from a lowly pack of feathered birds attacking my house, evil or otherwise?'

'Er . . .'

'No, of course not!' concluded Azariah. 'And do you think that I would quail like a baby, terrified to step out of my own home?'

'Er . . .'

'Of course not! Whatever mischief those birds are up to, they are about to find out that Azariah Keeper's home is not the place to do it!'

And having had his say, Azariah flung the door open and stepped outside.

Kelko, Jensen and Charlie couldn't believe it. Quickly shutting their mouths, they rushed forward for a better view. Poking their heads through the leaf-shaped doorway, they peered out.

Azariah strode into the middle of his well-kept lawn, thrusting his head from side to side as he stared around for the birds. But there was nothing to be seen. The garden had fallen mysteriously still and silent. Nothing could be heard, not the twitter of an owl, nor the burp of a mollylizard, nor the rustling of a bramblehog on the prowl.

Azariah frowned. Raising his hands above his head, he slowly focused his Will. Warm, golden light blossomed from his fists to spread across the garden, illuminating it as though it were caught in the afternoon sun.

'Burn me Leaf!' gasped Kelko in surprise, as his eyes grew accustomed to the light.

'Blight me Root!' said Jensen in horror as he took in the sight.

Hundreds of large black crows with evil glinting eyes sat perched on every available surface. They formed a wide, menacing ring that circled the garden and, disturbingly, Azariah appeared to be the focus of their attention.

55

Crow's Revenge

Still and silent the birds sat, neither moving nor twitching. They simply stared and stared with their beady eyes, glaring with such an intense hatred that even Charlie could feel it from where she stood in the doorway.

A vibrating blackness slowly pulsed and thrummed its way from the flock to ooze outward, pushing back at Azariah's Will. The circle of glowing light that marked Azariah's line of safety began to dwindle and diminish until he was almost completely enveloped by the dark.

Sweat began to drip from the old Keeper's head, tendons tightened around his neck and his powerful shoulder muscles tensed as he fought to maintain the small wave of light emerging from his fists.

'We've gotta help him,' said Jensen. 'Grab those torches. Quick, quick! Get them lit.'

Picking up one of the candles, Charlie hurriedly lit the torches and swiftly passed them to the two Tremen. The three of them ran to Azariah's side and their light, combined with Azariah's Will, slowly pushed back the thick, oily darkness.

'What do you think you're doing out here?' growled the old Keeper through clenched teeth.

'Wot does it look like we're doing, ya old rascal?' Jensen grinned with a wild look in his eye. 'We're giving ya a hand.'

'Yeah,' said Kelko. 'Looks like ya needed some back-up.'

'Can't you two fools see how ugly it's getting out here?' barked Azariah.

'Oh, don't worry. That's just Kelko.' Jensen chuckled. 'Place a paper bag over his head and everything will seem right as rain!'

'Ugly? Who ya calling ugly, ya pompous, big-nosed twit?'

'Idiots! Be quiet!' snapped Azariah as he stared at the surrounding dark. 'You should be guarding the child, not helping me!'

A horrible chuckle spun out from the darkness. 'It is not Charlie Keeper who you should be worrying about . . . at least not yet. It is your life that I want, old man. I need your soul.'

Charlie shuddered in dread. The voice was awful. It sounded like nails being scraped across tombstones and yet . . . there was something familiar about it. Something that she thought she recognized.

Suddenly the thick, unquenchable darkness receded to be replaced by the more familiar dark of night. Azariah's fists glowed brighter and, aided by the torchlight, illuminated the garden so that once again it shone as though beneath soft sunlight.

The birds sat calmly upon their perches, waiting and preening themselves until they were quite sure that they held everyone's attention. Then, cawing and screeching, they leaped into the air. Rushing together, they flowed into one large, wriggling, feathery mass and, with that odd sound of breaking glass, Mr Crow the lawyer sprang forth and on to the grass.

'Surprise, surprise!' he screamed with a nasty glare, as Charlie jumped back in horror. 'Did you miss me, little filly? Did you? Did you? Well, not to worry, Mr Crow is here!' Roaring with high-pitched insane laughter, he began to stride back and forth along the edge of the light, cracking his knuckles and picking at his nose.

'He knows you?' said Azariah with a startled look. 'You know this . . . this man?'

'Oh my gosh . . . Oh my gosh . . .' stuttered Charlie with sheer disbelief. 'What's he doing here? What's he doing in Bellania?'

'Charlie, how comes he knows ya?' gaped Kelko.

'He's, uh, he's my lawyer. Well, my parents' lawyer,' muttered Charlie. She still couldn't believe her eyes. 'But what's happened to him? How did he manage to do that?'

Mr Crow twitched and twittered his head from side to side, then, grinning mirthlessly, he strutted forward. 'Well, I can see that you're surprised, my pretty little mischief-maker. And you must be wondering how I came to be here and how I can do all of these wonderful, wonderful things.'

'What do you want, you horrible, skinny chump?' snapped Charlie as she finally mustered her courage. 'Run out of people to steal from?'

'Oh no, nothing of the sort, my dear.' He grinned. Leaning down, he casually picked up one of Azariah's heavy garden statues and flung it furiously at the old Keeper. Azariah only just managed to claw it to one side with a titanic wrenching of his Will. 'I no longer need to worry about such small pickings, for my master has promised me such rewards that everything that I could possibly take from you or this city pales in comparison.'

'So what do you want?' shrieked Charlie, as she and the others dodged yet another flung statue.

'Isn't that obvious? I've come to cause you pain and sorrow!' snarled Mr Crow with a terrible grimace. Reaching out with a long, pale finger, he pointed nastily at Azariah. 'I've come to kill this old man and let me tell you, my pretty little filly, my day's work won't be done until he lies dead at my feet!'

Screeching loudly, the lawyer flung back his head and cawed maniacally up into the night sky. A thick grey tongue snaked its way out from between his sharp teeth to writhe and paw at the cold night air before Mr Crow began his attack in earnest. Flinging trees and stones, statues and whole lengths of fencing, the lawyer began to dance his way towards them. Kelko and Jensen ducked and weaved from side to side in an effort to avoid the furiously flung objects, but they couldn't withstand the onslaught and soon they fell unconscious, grazed and bloody, to the floor.

Which left just Azariah and Charlie.

'What are we going to do?' said Charlie as she hurriedly dodged a spinning length of wood that whickered and strummed as it whisked past her ear.

'We must combine our Wills,' growled Azariah. 'If we weave them together we can defeat this capering idiot.' His eyes glared furiously at the skinny lawyer. Punching his hand forward, he deflected yet another thrown missile. 'And whatever happens, we need to do it soon, before he totally ruins my garden! Now then, Charlie, focus! Focus like never before. Show me how strong your Will can be!'

Mr Crow's insane laughter cut Charlie to the very core, chilling her soul and driving fear deep into her heart. Her Will fluttered and wallowed – no matter how hard she strove to grasp it, it remained just out of reach. Gritting her teeth, she tried to focus, to do as Azariah had taught her, but it was useless.

'Do not fail me,' grunted Azariah. 'I have faith in you. You can do it. Do it for me! Do it for your family! Do it!'

And suddenly Charlie knew that she could. But as she reached down for her Will, Crow shrieked with a wild, cackling cry.

'Too late, filly! Too late!' Sprinting forward on his gangly legs, he punched Azariah so hard on the underside of his jaw that the old Keeper flew backwards to land like a sack of potatoes on the hard ground. Crow smiled nastily at Charlie. Reaching out, he casually slapped her, once, twice, three times around the face, and because he was enjoying himself so much he kicked her in the stomach. Charlie groaned in pain and toppled to the floor.

'Oh my, will you just look at that! All four of you lying helpless . . . Whatever should I do?' chuckled Crow. 'Oh, I know, how about I kill this one?'

Leaning over, he lifted up Jensen's head.

'Or this one?'

Reaching over, he rolled Kelko on to his front. Gripping

the poor Treman's topknot, he raised his head so that Charlie could see the glazed look on his face.

'Hhmm, no, no. I think that perhaps these two can wait for another day. I think that perhaps I'll just have to kill . . . this one!' he snarled. Reaching down, he yanked Azariah to his feet.

Charlie couldn't believe what she was seeing. Wearily she tried to get to her feet, but her head wouldn't stop spinning and she felt like throwing up. *Get up! Get up!* she told herself. But her legs refused to move. Her whole body was exhausted from Crow's attack and her attempts to summon her Will.

'Aah, does your head still hurt, my little filly? Does it? Well, tough luck, you little brat! Just lie back and watch this. It'll be a memory that I'm sure you'll want to treasure!'

Leaning Azariah into his embrace, Mr Crow bent his mouth to the old Keeper's neck. The lawyer's head bobbed up and down as he sucked at his throat like a vampire.

Charlie tried desperately to scramble to her feet. '*Stop!*' she begged. Tears streamed down her face as her numb fingers tried to tug at the unconscious figures beside her. 'Jensen, Kelko, wake up!'

With a last hungry suck, Mr Crow pushed Azariah's life-less body to the ground. Turning back to Charlie, his beady eyes blazed with a sick, sated appetite. Blood, thick and crimson, caked his lips. 'How do you feel, Charlie? Does it cut and gnaw at your soul to know that I killed him while you lay helpless at my feet? I'm sure it does.' Rolling back on to his heels, he smiled up at the almost-full moon. 'Today is just the beginning. Tomorrow Narcissa's daughter will rid you of your pendant and the day after that I shall come for your two friends. And the day after that? Well, who knows, I might just have to come for you.'

Leaning down, he bestowed a bloody kiss upon Charlie's forehead, then with a hop and a skip he leaped up into the air to disappear into the night sky with a flurry of wings.

56

Farewells

The midday sun that shone through the stained-glass windows in the Jade Council Chamber seemed pale and thin. It did little to soften Charlie's emotions of rage, bitter sorrow and guilt. How could he be dead? Strong, powerful and wise Azariah . . . dead? It didn't seem possible.

Azariah's body lay upon the turquoise surface of the Jade Table. The blood had been carefully washed from his neck, he had been dressed in clean robes of state and his thick, luxuriant beard had been combed until it shone. If Charlie didn't know better she might have been fooled into thinking that he was merely sleeping. The sombre-looking councillors still loyal to Dridif wore long black robes of mourning. They talked and whispered to one another in shock and disbelief, and Charlie could see some wiping tears from their eyes.

Dridif, standing at the head of the enormous table, raised her hands for silence. When she spoke, her warm voice echoed and resounded across the vaulted room, filling it with rosy warmth. 'Councillors, guests, friends, I am sorry ta say that a great man has been taken from us. A man of honour, a man of silent, steadfast strengths.' Dridif paused to stare at Azariah's body. 'Old friend, the Jade Circle will sorely miss ya and we shall surely notice the emptiness in our souls left by yer passing. We shall mourn ya like a brother stolen from our side. Yet yer wisdom and pride shall live on as the gentle breeze that meanders through the magnificent trees of Deepforest. Yer courage and loyalty will be remembered as we tend our fields of orchids. And yer unquenchable heart will beat forever more so long as dis city stands free from the Shadow that arises from the West. Azariah Keeper, we bless ya and shall honour yer memory for now and evermore.'

Falling silent, Dridif placed her hands on the Jade Table, and the other council members followed her lead. Lifting back her head, the First Speaker began to sing. One by one the others joined in, their voices intermingling with hers. The soft, sorrowful melody swirled throughout the cavernous chamber, filling Charlie's heart and causing the torches, large candles and incense to wildly blaze, spit and spark. A soft breath of air flickered around, gently tugging at the councillors' robes, ruffling Charlie's hair and tickling at her nose. The Jade Table began to writhe and move as its amazing dew-drop green hue changed bit by bit to a deep, deep blue. Slowly yet surely, Azariah's body began to sink into the table's surface.

'What's happening to him?' exclaimed Charlie in shock.

'Relax, blossom,' said Kelko, stepping up to stand by her side. 'They're entombing his body ta preserve it until it can be handed over ta a Triad of Keepers.'

'A Triad of Keepers?' asked Charlie.

'Aye, that's right. They need three Keepers ta send him through the Portal.'

'Portal to where? Where are they sending him?'

'Ta the Nether Realm,' replied Kelko.

'The Nether Realm?'

'Sorry, I guess I should have explained a little better. I'm just not thinking straight at the moment.' He sighed. 'Azariah is a Keeper, right?'

'Right.'

'Well, when a Keeper dies his body is sent ta the Nether Realm. It is a realm of dreams and whispering memories. It is said that all those who pass inta that realm will live with us forever and visit us through our sleeping moments. Because of dis the Nether Realm is a resting place reserved only for those of great honour. Majestic leaders, fearless heroes and Keepers are always granted the right for their mortal bodies ta be entombed there. But it takes a great deal of power ta open such a Portal. Only three Keepers combining their Will can hope ta achieve it. And that is why Azariah's body is being entombed. With all the unrest and war crossing Bellania, it is most unlikely that three Keepers will be found together any time soon. So only when peace reigns once more across Bellania will he find his true resting ground.'

'Oh,' said Charlie. She knew it sounded weak, but at that moment she didn't know what else to say. Emotions, bitter and raw, still tugged at the back of her throat.

Turning to look at the table again, she noticed that Azariah's body was now completely enveloped beneath the jade surface. Only by squinting could she make out the old Keeper's outline. With his arms crossed over his chest, she couldn't help but think that he looked like a medieval knight laid to rest on his tomb. Somehow that seemed fitting.

Dridif and the other councillors finally grew silent, allowing their flowing melody to cease. Bowing their heads once more in respect to Azariah Keeper, they stood back and slowly filed from the room. When they were alone and had some privacy, Lady Dridif approached Charlie, Jensen and Kelko with sorrowful eyes.

'We have lost a great friend today and we shall have ta carry dis bitter tragedy in our hearts for evermore . . . But I have not come ta talk of such heavy matters, Charlie. Rather I have come ta wish ya all the best of luck for yer duel tonight.'

'You won't be there?'

The First Speaker shook her head. 'I cannot. I must now work twice as hard ta prevent the treason and treachery in the Jade Circle. Without Azariah working so boldly by me side, I could still lose the council ta Lady Narcissa. I cannot afford ta rest.'

'Oh.'

'I'm sorry that I cannot be there ta support ya, but I share the same confidence in ya that Azariah had. Charlie, ya are a Keeper and ya will do us proud.' Dridif gazed deep into Charlie's eyes, as if searching for something. Then, with a final nod, she turned and walked off. Before she reached the huge jade doors she turned back. 'Whatever happens, ya cannot afford ta lose. Ya must not hand that pendant over ta Constantina. If it falls inta Lady Narcissa's hands, then Sylvaris will surely be lost ta Bane. As too will Bellania be.' With that, she strode from the Jade Chamber.

Charlie turned to Kelko and Jensen. 'Beat Constantina, the K'Changa champion, in a Silent Duel even though I can't hold my Will? Oh, sure,' she remarked sarcastically. 'No problem. Save Sylvaris from Lady Narcissa and her spiteful children? Oh, of course. Easy. And save Bellania from an unstoppable giant? All in a day's work for your average thirteen-year-old, right?' With a face like thunder, Charlie stomped her way from the room.

Kelko and Jensen eyed each other in shock.

'Blight me Leaf!' whispered Jensen.

'Methinks we're gonna have ta work on that girl's confidence . . . or we're doomed!' wheezed Kelko in dismay.

'Ya can say that again.' Jensen sighed, rolling his eyes up to the ceiling. 'Wot a wonderful Three Winds Festival dis is turning out ta be!'

57

Final Preparations

Sylvaris blazed with a flowering explosion of multicoloured fireworks that whizzed, banged and whooped into the night sky. Bright orange, yellow and red paper lanterns hung from the sides of the floating bridges and myriad scented candles flickered on almost every surface across the city. With all the extra light, the soaring towers were washed in a warm and inviting glow, so that they shone like great beacons above the treetops. And everywhere, absolutely everywhere that Charlie looked, the people of Sylvaris were celebrating.

There were Tremen dancing and fooling around in flamboyant masks of mythical creatures. Stomen men and women laughed merrily as they applied metallic body paint and glitter to their muscles, and exotically dressed Humans joined in the festivities with broad smiles. Acrobats and tightrope-walkers, fire-eaters and sword-swallowers, strongmen and jugglers darted in and out of the crowds, showing off their skills to the delight of their audience. Trees and flowers wriggled and shook as Tree Singers persuaded the wood and stems to grow into new and unusual shapes with their lilting song.

Restaurants had moved their kitchens outside for the night so that their customers could watch from the boulevards as their favourite dishes were created and cooked right in front of their eyes. Delicious flavours and scents wafted through the air as whole brigades of chefs prepared great batches of Veryvaverry Tart, Idlefinger Puffs and Billabellar Steak with Jumping Bean Sauce.

But Charlie was neither hungry nor in the mood to party. Tucking her head down and swinging her arms from side to side, she marched towards the Colosseum like a girl possessed, Sic Boy pacing along beside her.

'But, blossom, why d'ya wanna go ta the stadium now?' asked Kelko as he and Jensen struggled to keep up. 'Yer match ain't for another two hours yet.'

'I've got to do something, Kelko. If I sit still I'm sure I'll go mad. Watching the K'Changa matches will keep my mind occupied. It'll stop me thinking too much about . . . well, you know, Azariah.'

Jensen and Kelko shared a look between them but dutifully followed their young friend. When they arrived, the Colosseum was packed tighter than a can of sardines. Boisterous Tremen, joyful Stomen and overexcited Humans had squeezed into every available space. Almost all of the seats had been taken, but with Kelko's giant stomach and the muscled weight of Sic Boy the four of them managed to push their way to the front of the busy stadium. As before, Kelko, Charlie and Jensen casually stole some of the vacant seats reserved solely for the Jade Circle. Sic Boy bared his teeth in a horrible growl as one of the ushers hurried over to complain. But after a close-up of Sic Boy's teeth, and realizing that it was Charlie Keeper in the stand, the usher wisely turned around.

Unlike Charlie's first visit, several of the Jade Circle seats were occupied. Many of the councillors had come to attend the Three Winds Festival celebrations and unfortunately Flint and Nazareth were part of a group sitting nearby. Seeing the small party arrive, Nazareth tugged at his beard and glared at them, harrumphing loudly. Charlie furiously glared right back. Oddly enough, it was Nazareth that turned away first. There was something he didn't like staring back at him from Charlie's eyes, something that scared him. Wriggling uncomfortably in his chair like a child with an itchy bottom, the irate councillor did his best to pretend that Charlie and her friends weren't there.

'Excuse me, but I believe that these seats aren't taken,' lilted a beautiful voice. 'I do hope you won't mind if my sons and I joined you.'

Charlie stiffened. It was Lady Narcissa.

Smiling wickedly at Charlie and her companions, Narcissa and the Delightful Brothers sat down in the last few remaining seats.

'What do you want?' snapped Charlie.

'What do I want? Why, nothing more than a chance to enjoy the show. I believe that Sylvaris's most prestigious celebrities will be here, so of course my sons and I simply had to attend.' Narcissa smiled. 'Hhmm, how odd . . .'

'What is it, Mother?' enquired Stix with a slightly knowing look.

'Well, it could just be my imagination, but it appears as though Azariah Keeper is not attending.'

'You're right, Mother, that is odd. I wonder where he could –'

'Don't push it!' snapped Charlie. The venom in her voice startled both Jensen and Kelko, who turned to stare in astonishment. 'I won't put up with any more of your mockery! If you have anything of importance to say, say it now or otherwise jabber off!'

'My, my,' said Narcissa, grinning nastily. 'It would appear as though the little girl has grown a backbone. How very surprising.'

Stix and Stones chuckled dutifully.

'Tell me, my little Keeper,' continued Lady Narcissa, 'did you enjoy meeting my new servant, the Crowman? He asked me to assure you that it was a great pleasure to meet both you and Azariah Keeper.'

'What do you know about . . .?' cried Charlie. 'Wait a minute! Your *servant*? You sent Mr Crow to Azariah's home? It was *you* who ordered his death?'

'Of course, you silly little girl!' hissed Narcissa, her eyes suddenly narrowing into fierce slits. Abruptly she leaned forward and pushed her face close to Charlie's. 'And if you have any foolish ideas about attempting to best my daughter, I shall make very, very sure that the delightful Mr Crow crushes your two foolish friends here into bags of blood and bones!'

Charlie tried to stand, but her emotions were so overpowering that she staggered and nearly fell. Her blood began to boil and ice stabbed at her soul. With a raging shout, she lunged towards Narcissa. She almost succeeded in grabbing the smug councillor by the throat, but Kelko and Jensen managed to pull her back and hold her fast. Together they hauled Charlie's wriggling form away from the busy stands, Narcissa's taunting laugh echoing after them.

'Charlie!' shouted Jensen as one of her flailing fists smacked him in the eye. 'Will ya hold it in! Ya can't just get inta a fight with Narcissa like that!'

'Why not?' snapped Charlie. Her chest heaved up and down as though she'd just run a marathon.

'Because the Delightful Brothers are there with her. They're just too dangerous, even with us and Sic Boy watching yer back.'

'I don't care! I don't care!' snapped Charlie with sheer frustration. 'Can't you see she's a murdering witch? She's the one who ordered Azariah's death. You heard her! And you guys wouldn't let me do anything about it.'

'Of course we couldn't let ya do anything!' said Jensen. 'Someone would have got hurt – hurt real bad. And with the Delightful Brothers thrown inta the mix, more than likely it would have been one of us! Now then, I want ya ta relax and just concentrate on the Silent Duel. Remember, blossom, the best way ta hurt Narcissa right now – and hurt her good – is ta win dis K'Changa game. Win it and laugh in Constantina's face. Let's see how much Narcissa and her cursed family like that!'

Charlie grudgingly nodded. She calmed down slightly and Kelko and Jensen carefully released her from their grip. As much as she didn't like to admit it, Jensen was absolutely right. First things first.

58

The Silent Duel

'It is time,' said the match official as he watched the last two K'Changa contestants leave the arena. 'Ya must enter.'

'What about Constantina?' asked Charlie.

'As the challenger she has the right ta enter last,' said the official with an imperious look.

Charlie snorted. 'Hhmpf. No doubt so that she can make another one of her spectacular entrances.'

'Wotever the case, ya must enter first,' he insisted.

Charlie stared out at the vast tide of faces that swamped the Colosseum. There were thousands and thousands of people out there. All of them were waiting to see her, Charlie Keeper. She gulped as she felt the first little tremor of stage fright.

A firm hand gripped her by the shoulder. 'Good luck, me little Hippotomi,' said Jensen.

'Aye, good luck,' said Kelko. 'We believe in ya.'

Charlie wanted to smile, but with all the butterflies rampaging around her stomach she found it hard to control herself, so instead of getting a confident smile her two friends received a sickly grin. 'Thanks, boys,' she said in a small voice that quivered and shook.

She tried to draw strength from the outfit that she wore, one of her treasured gifts from Azariah. First she touched the jade hairpin that secured her top knot, then trailed her fingers down across the dark weave of her shirt, past her spider-silk belt to finally wrap her trembling hands in the fabric of her black baggy trousers. But although she took comfort from Azariah's gift, it did little to quench her fear.

'Will ya please hurry up?' urged the official. 'We haven't got all day!' He sneered at her. 'Why don't ya simply give the pendant over ta Constantina anyway? Save us all a lotta hassle.'

'Watch yer mouth!' growled Jensen. Stepping close to the arrogant official, he waved his fist beneath the man's nose. 'She'll go out as and when she's ready, so stand there and be quiet before I thump ya!'

Sic Boy growled too and took a couple of menacing steps forward.

The official quickly clamped his mouth shut.

'Good,' snorted Jensen. 'OK, Charlie, lass. Just remember ta do everything that we've done in practice. Move fast, stay light on yer feet and, for the Seven Heavens' sake, keep a firm grip on yer Will. Now get out there and show us wot ya've got!'

Leaning down, he slapped Charlie hard on the back to propel her out into the arena. Unfortunately Charlie squawked, staggered forward a couple of paces, then promptly tripped to fall flat on her face.

The crowd roared with laughter.

Blushing furiously, Charlie leaped to her feet. Quickly

dusting herself down, she threw her chin out, straightened her back and then stomped the rest of the way into the middle of the arena. Unfortunately, some joker in the Treman band decided it would be funny to tootle a horrible, shrieking squeak from his flute every time that Charlie took a step. For all those thousands of spectators looking on, it appeared as though the young Keeper was so uptight that she squeaked when she walked.

Again, the crowd wept with laughter.

Shame began to ripple through Charlie's stomach. Embarrassment coloured her cheeks and dismay sent sweat coursing down her neck to puddle uncomfortably in the small of her back. Thankfully, when she reached the centre of the arena the idiot playing the flute grew bored and fell silent. So too did the rest of the Colosseum. Everyone was waiting for the champion to arrive.

They didn't have long to wait, as one of the large gates that lined the arena was flung open and a long line of Alavisian Watchmen, pounding and rattling their swords against their shields, marched into the arena. Constantina followed in their wake, accompanied by a dozen maids scattering lilies in her path. The crowd roared out their approval.

Constantina sauntered over to stand in front of Charlie. 'Hello, buttercup. Ready for your humiliation? Well, I certainly hope so, because I promised all my fans a real show,' she purred.

Charlie, still frantically embarrassed by her own entrance into the arena, struggled to come up with a suitable reply. All she could manage was, 'Let's get on with this.'

Constantina sneered. Turning her back on Charlie, she

faced her audience. 'Sylvaris! Sylvaris! Hear me now! When I defeat this impudent outsider I promise to show you just how great I can be. With me holding the pendant I will lead this city to a great future, free from Bane's threat. A future of wealth and fame, so that throughout all of Bellania, Sylvaris will be known as the one great city . . . the city that saved our realm. Will you stand by me? Will you support me as your champion? What do you say?'

The crowd surged to its feet and bellowed out its approval: 'Constantina! Constantina for the pendant! Constantina for the pendant!'

Delighted with the response, Constantina turned to Charlie and smirked. 'Well, buttercup, it looks like your time has come,' she hissed. 'I hope losing to me hurts so much that you tremble in shame for the rest of your miserable life! Prepare to say goodbye to that precious pendant of yours . . .'

Staring into Constantina's confident face, Charlie's doubts grew more intense. How on earth was she going to win? Not once during practice had she succeeded in blending her Will with K'Changa, so what chance did she have now? But as nervous as Charlie was, there was no way she was going to show Constantina how she felt.

'Yeah, well don't expect it to be too easy,' she blustered. 'I might surprise you yet.'

'With what? You're a thirteen-year-old loser from the Other Realm and you've only just learned to play K'Changa. The only surprise that's going to happen tonight will be if I allow you to touch the Zephyr.'

Charlie opened her mouth to say something witty, but fear for the future struck her dumb. Cold fingers of doubt churned through her stomach. Her head pounded with the need to do something, anything, to ensure that the pendant remained hers and hers alone. But she could not move.

Seeing Charlie's hesitation, Constantina grinned. But before she could say anything the arena doors opened and out stepped the referee. She was dressed in robes of gold and black and as she strode towards the contestants they could see the bright blue Zephyr by her side.

'Ya've both been briefed on wot ta expect with tonight's Silent Duel,' said the referee. 'The first ta win two rounds will win the right ta hold the pendant. Right, are ya ready?'

'I'm always ready,' smirked Constantina.

'And ya, Charlie Keeper, are ya ready?'

Charlie gazed around the stadium. Realizing what was at stake and that now was her moment to stand up for herself, she straightened her back and did her best to push her doubts aside. She wanted to make Azariah proud, even if he wasn't here to see her. 'I'm ready,' she said.

'Good. Sylvaris!' the referee shouted out. 'Let the Silent Duel begin!' She nodded at one of the officials, who in turn nodded at the Treman band.

They began to pound on their drums, filling the arena with a rolling, thumping rhythm. The beat echoed around the Colosseum, bouncing off the walls, and crashed into the night sky. The torches and illuminating fires seemed to burn brighter as the crowd, anticipating a match of legendary proportions, leaned forward in expectation.

The referee threw the Zephyr into the air.

59

Unleashing
the Will

Charlie breathed in and time seemed to slow.

The moan of the crowd sounded long and drawn out, the drumbeat seemed slow and thick. She could feel the brush of the wind on her cheek and the grate of sand beneath her feet. Torchlight glittered off the Zephyr's incandescent feathers and the referee's robes flapped slowly around her as though she were wading under water. Beneath all of this Charlie felt a sense of impending doom settle around her heart like a fist.

Breathing out, time returned to normal.

Charlie leaped desperately for the shuttlecock, but Constantina beat her to it. Landing lightly, the champion began to duck and weave from side to side, the Zephyr moving like a blue flash around her body. Horrified at just how quickly Constantina could move, Charlie started to pursue her. Somersaulting and cartwheeling, kicking and sweeping, the two opponents streaked across the arena. The shout of the referee beginning her countdown urged them to even greater speeds.

'One! Two! Three!'

It soon became apparent that Charlie was outclassed. Constantina moved with the speed of a snake. Elusive and slippery, she constantly evaded Charlie's efforts to take the Zephyr, moving even faster until she left Charlie groping helplessly in the dust of her passage.

Already disheartened, Charlie grew even more miserable as it finally dawned on her just how skilled her opponent was. Constantina was on a whole different level. Hearing the count drawing perilously close to the end, Charlie gritted her teeth and did her best to block out the sound of the crowd as she drew upon her Will. Azariah had been right – it was her only hope.

Focusing, she breathed deeply and summoned her Keeper power. It seemed to come easily this time, surging through her and racing down her arms until her fists started to glow. Grinning with new confidence, Charlie raced forward. Bounding and leaping effortlessly into the air, she swiftly caught up with her opponent. Eyes intent upon the Zephyr, she flung out a hand . . . But, just as it had during training, everything started to go wrong. Her head pounded, her heart jittered and her vision blurred.

KRA-KHUMPF!

The blast from the backfire sent Charlie tumbling across the sandy floor to land in a heap of sprawling limbs. Pain racked her body; it tore at her flesh with cruel fingers and caused her to arch her back. The crowd jumped to their feet in shock, the drums lost their rhythm and in the sudden silence came the shout of the referee.

'TEN! Round one to Constantina.'

There was a long moment of silence. Of stillness. Charlie

stared up at the night sky and wondered where everything had taken a turn for the worse. Then Constantina's unwelcome face appeared in her line of vision.

'Ha! I knew you'd be no threat.'

Misery swept through Charlie's soul. She clenched her teeth and bunched her hands into fists so that her nails dug into her palms. She wouldn't cry. She wouldn't show any weakness. She would –

'Charlie Keeper, this is no time for sleeping!' said the referee. Reaching down, she heaved her upright. 'Are ya all right?' She peered at her face for signs of sickness. 'Do ya want ta quit and forfeit the pendant?'

'No. No! I'm, uh, I'm all right. Really.' But she wasn't. Her Will had failed her and now she had no idea how to prevent Constantina from robbing her of her pendant. Her hopes of overcoming Bane and being reunited with her parents lay in tatters at her feet.

'Well, if yer sure. Here,' she said, holding out a towel. 'Clean yerself up, then please return ta the centre of the arena and we will commence with round two.'

Constantina grinned as she saw Charlie stagger towards her on unsteady feet. 'What's the matter, Charlie Keeper? Has your Will got the better of you or have you just lost your Way?'

Full of bleak despair, Charlie finally snapped. 'Shut your trap! You're stealing my parents from me and all you want to do is laugh about it? I've had enough. Enough, you hear me? I might lose this stupid Silent Duel, but that doesn't mean that I have to put up with you smirking while my parents hang in Bane's Tapestry. If I hear any more taunts coming out of your mouth I promise you that I'll see you after this match and we can settle this with a different type of duel!'

'Oh-ho! So you do have a backbone after all? Well, Charlie Keeper, guess what? I'm not done with you yet. This is a Silent Duel, best of three makes a winner, but if I win this round the duel will be over too quickly. No, this is a match of a lifetime. This is the K'Changa game that is going to make me a legend. After tonight I'll be more than a K'Changa champion, I'll be champion of Sylvaris! So, Charlie . . . I'm going to let you win this next round.'

'Say what?'

'Yeah, you heard me.' Constantina grinned. She turned to address the crowd. 'Sylvaris! I have already proved that this interloper is no match for me. But now this game passes too quickly for your entertainment and surely that should be a crime. Tonight is the Three Winds Festival, so why don't I make this Silent Duel last a little longer?' She turned to the referee. 'I, Constantina, give this second round to Charlie Keeper!'

Charlie's mouth dropped open. Could Constantina really do that? The crowd sighed first in delight, then cheered ecstatically. Charlie turned her gaze across the stadium to where Kelko and Jensen waited.

Seeing Charlie's look of awkward confusion, Kelko shouted over the sound of the crowd, 'Take it, blossom, take it!'

'He's right, lass!' hollered Jensen, holding his hand up in a thumbs-up gesture. 'If she's dumb enough ta throw it away ya should take the opportunity!'

Charlie bit her lip and nodded to show she'd heard.

'So, Charlie Keeper,' said the referee, 'will ya take Constantina's gift of a free round?'

'I will.'

'Very well, then. Begin.' The referee threw the Zephyr.

'What?' said Charlie. Unprepared, she allowed the shuttlecock to fall to the ground.

'This is a Silent Duel,' admonished the referee as she bent down to retrieve the Zephyr. 'Even if yer opponent doesn't want ta face ya, ya still have ta play.'

'What, by myself?'

'Well, of course,' snorted the referee. 'Who else would ya play with?'

'Well, uh . . . um,' stuttered Charlie. 'So I just have to keep the Zephyr in the air for a count of ten?'

'Obviously.' Once again the referee threw in the shuttlecock.

Charlie, uncertain with how to proceed but aware that she had no choice, jumped forward and, catching the Zephyr in the crook of her foot, began tapping it from foot to knee and back again. The referee began her count.

Charlie, very much aware of how ridiculous the moment was, felt like a fool. Someone in the audience began to snigger. Other spectators joined in and soon the sound of laughter swept across the stadium as everyone began to point and joke as Charlie was made to play K'Changa by herself.

Great torrents of shame, like nothing she had ever felt before, began to wash through Charlie's soul. The humiliation and disgrace of the moment was so real, so vivid, that it carved a wound in Charlie's being. And through this rift, *this tear* in Charlie's spirit, the hatred and darkness that she had buried within her heart began to wriggle its way free from the cage that she had constructed around it.

'And . . . ten!' The referee finished her count and, after a final round of laughter, the crowd settled down to see how the rest of the duel would go.

Constantina, confident and cocky, strutted across the sand. 'Think you'll be able to survive being a joke for another round?'

Charlie stared at the spoilt brat in front of her. She could feel her anger growing like a blossoming black flower. It made her bold. 'You want a show, you pampered fool? Fine, I'll give you one. So stop bragging, stop all your talking and let's get on with it!'

Charlie's words were so strong that Constantina took a step backwards in shock. She quickly covered her surprise. 'You'd better show me some respect. Don't forget that when I hold the pendant I'll stand higher than you, a broken and useless Keeper!'

Charlie groaned and almost doubled over as the sheer rage and volcanic anger seeping from her heart threatened to overwhelm her. But she held it all in. For now. 'Stop stalling and let's get this over with,' she growled through clenched teeth.

'Fine,' snapped Constantina. 'If you want to play it that way so be it. Third and final round. Let's do it.' She retreated and settled into a loose K'Changa stance.

Focusing on the turbulent emotions racing through her soul, Charlie merely stood still.

Again, at the referee's prompt, the Treman band began to pound out a fiery rhythm on their drums. The beat filled Charlie's blood with a desire to move and sway to the music. Suddenly she felt alive with the urge to twist and turn, to leap and bound across the arena.

Seeing that both players were ready, the referee threw in the Zephyr. Constantina gave a great shout and confidently sprang towards it.

Charlie just grinned and released the darkness that had been festering inside her heart.

60

Round Three

Once released, all the hatred and anger boiled free from Charlie's heart like a tidal wave. It burned in her veins like molten lava and shivered through her muscles like wild lightning. It filled her to the point where she thought she would burst. No longer did she feel as though she had to constrain her true feelings. No longer did she feel the need to behave like a good little girl with a mind for manners. For the first time in her life she felt free.

Charlie stared across the arena and smiled. She'd found her Will, or perhaps rather her Will had found her.

The beat from the drums flickered around her, the shouts from the crowd slithered through her hair and the wild breeze arising from the west thrummed across her skin. Charlie breathed it all in. Standing still, she watched as Constantina leaped confidently into the air to claim the Zephyr. She watched and listened as the crowd began to roar out a chanted count.

'One!'

Constantina landed lightly on her feet, the shuttlecock weaving from left to right.

'Two!'

The champion back-flipped and sent the Zephyr floating into the sky.

'Three!'

Somersaulting sideways, Constantina threw a triumphant grin at her fans, then caught the shuttlecock with a casual flick of her foot as it returned to earth.

'Four!'

Charlie stood still, not even bothering to move, the odd smile still fixed firmly on her face.

'Five!'

Ending a complex series of handsprings, Constantina noticed that Charlie hadn't even attempted to challenge her.

'Six!'

A worried frown crossed the champion's face.

'Seven!'

'What are you doing, you little scab?' hissed Constantina. 'Aren't you even going to attempt to make this round interesting?'

'Eight!'

Charlie's smile widened into a big grin as the darkness coursing through her body met with her Will . . . and exploded.

'Nine!'

Charlie's hands burst into flame, her hair stood on end and her eyes blazed. Springing forward, she snatched the Zephyr from Constantina and, moving so fast that she actually blurred, she began to twist and turn.

Like a tornado.

Like a Human hurricane, awesome and unstoppable.

Constantina, realizing that the tables had turned, began

to panic. Her face turned white, sweat appeared on her forehead and her K'Changa, so perfect before, began to unravel. Her stances grew sloppy, her acrobatics seemed hurried and her poise slumped.

The crowd fell silent as people pointed in disbelief. Even the band lost momentum. Shifting and bucking, leaping and bounding, slipping and diving, Charlie spun the Zephyr in intricate patterns. Taunting and teasing, she flicked the shuttlecock past Constantina's face, then snatched it away before the champion could attempt to swipe at it. Charlie was dizzy with power and overawed by her new-found might. With a wild cackle of delight, she flung the Zephyr skyward and watched it disappear into the night sky.

Over in the stands, Jensen nudged Kelko in the ribs. 'Well, I believe that must have been a count of ten.'

'Uh, er . . . yeah. Yeah, I guess so!' said Kelko, blinking away his shock. 'Although I have a sneaky feeling that even the ref forgot ta count.'

'Ha! Wot does that matter? Ten count or a hundred count, ain't no one gonna beat that in a million years! Wot a way ta go! That's me little stompin' Hippotomi!'

'Yeah, yer right! She won! She won! Go, girl!' hollered Kelko, waving his hands wildly above his head. 'Charlie Keeper, champion of Sylvaris! Champion! Champion!'

Jensen joined in the shout. It was quickly picked up by the audience and soon the whole Colosseum rang with the shout of 'Charlie Keeper, champion of Sylvaris!' The stands shook with noise as people began to stamp and cheer.

Constantina stared at Charlie, horror clearly painted across her petulant face. Her lips quivered and her hand trembled as she pointed at her adversary. 'B-b-b-but . . . how?' she stammered. 'No one is supposed to beat me. I'm the best. *I'm* the champion! Me!'

Charlie knew that she should rise above any tit-for-tat, but somehow she couldn't quite help herself. Sauntering over to Constantina, she bent close. 'Well, hey there, "buttercup". Is it just me or is there a new champion in town?'

Constantina squawked, blushed a bright red and fled. Lady Narcissa, sitting in the stands, grabbed the rail running round the arena with white-knuckled hands. Her face twisted into a bitter grimace of frustration.

Charlie laughed aloud. It felt good to win. The pendant was hers!

She raised her blazing hands for silence and the crowd, so sneering towards her before, was now only too willing to oblige their new champion.

'Sylvaris! Sylvaris! Who's your champion now?'

'Charlie! Charlie Keeper!' roared the adoring crowd.

'And do you accept that the pendant is mine?'

'Yes!' shouted the jubilant spectators.

'Good! Then hear this: I will use it to the best of my ability for the good of this land. I intend to defeat Bane, the Western Menace. Do you support me in this action?'

'Yes!'

'Well, know this,' cried Charlie, and pointed across the stands to Lady Narcissa. 'That woman is an agent of Bane's. She hides behind a false face and weaves a web of lies across this city. She has sneaked Shades into Sylvaris and it was at her command that Azariah Keeper was killed. Will you allow her to continue her wicked ways?'

'No!' growled the angered crowd, as people began to murmur about the accusations.

Lady Narcissa stood up and attempted to protest her innocence, but the crowd wasn't in the mood to listen. People rose from their seats. Reaching forward, they lunged for the councillor. Stix and Stones hastily knocked back the hands that grabbed for their mother, but the sheer weight of numbers was overwhelming and soon there were simply too many to fend off at once. The Delightful Brothers drew their weapons and growled menacingly, but the crowd answered back by throwing half-eaten buns, sticky bags of sweets, items of clothing and bottles of iced Chocolate Fuzz. Stix and Stones cowered to avoid getting bombarded as the situation rapidly spiralled out of control.

A sudden fluttering of wings caused people to look up in wonder as a vast wave of crows flocked into the arena. They swooped down into the stands and clutched Lady Narcissa in their talons. Twittering and cawing, the birds retreated into the night sky, heading towards the Ivory Tower with Narcissa safely in their grasp.

Stix and Stones gaped in astonishment as their mother dwindled in the distance. They stared at one another, then looked back to all the angry faces glaring down at them.

'Hey, Delightful Sisters!' Jensen yelled out. 'It looks like ya've been left behind. Wot's the matter, doesn't yer momma love ya?'

The Delightful Brothers fixed Jensen with their mean yellow eyes.

'Ooh! Wot a scary look! Why, I'm quivering in me boots!' Jensen chuckled sarcastically. 'Now then, if I were ya I'd scram before the people of Sylvaris decide ta ask wot yer part was in all dis.'

Stix and Stones hesitated as they stared at the angry, shouting mob and nervously licked their lips. Then they turned tail and scampered, a barrage of missiles landing in their wake.

'Ha!' roared Kelko with a joyful grin, slapping his belly.

Jensen turned towards the arena. 'Did ya see that, lass?' he asked, searching for Charlie. 'Did ya – Hey, where'd she go?'

Kelko turned too, to see that the place where Charlie had been standing just moments before was now empty.

61

The Face-off

Charlie sprinted through the partying streets of Sylvaris. Dodging joyful Tremen, skipping past dancing Stomen and sidestepping merry and laughing Humans, she leaped from bridge to bridge, determined to confront both Lady Narcissa and Mr Crow. She wasn't exactly sure why she was doing this, or even what she was going to say when she reached the black-hearted pair. All she knew was that she had a burning need to make certain that the two of them didn't get away scot-free with murdering Azariah. She would bring them to justice. She would.

The Ivory Tower, so bright and wonderful in the daytime, was completely different by night. With the full moon shining behind it, it looked dark and menacing, like a sword carving up into the heavens. Charlie could just about make out the fluttering ribbon of birds streaming through the sky ahead of her. Spiralling downward, the crows passed through a large open window and into the tower. And just before the birds were swallowed by the shadows, she caught a glimpse of Narcissa's lily-white dress fluttering in the wind as she was carried to safety.

Charlie put her head down and ran faster, tearing along

the boulevards and walkways. She finally slowed to a halt
as she approached the Ivory Tower's drawbridge. It was
ram-packed with bloodthirsty and ferocious-looking Alavisian Watchmen. They all wore their cruel, spiked armour
and all of them had their swords drawn.

'You may not pass, little girl,' snarled the captain. His
large moustache quivered with arrogance. 'And if you know
what's good for you I'd strongly suggest that you turn
around, go back to the home and get on with your home-
work.'

Charlie threw them her infamous smile and calmly walked
forward.

'I'm warning you, girlie. Don't come any closer or I'll
have my men cut off your arms and turn the rest of you into
mincemeat.'

Charlie stepped on to the drawbridge and slowly raised
her flaming hands.

'Right, you horrible little girl, you had your warning!
Lads, rip her apart!'

The Alavisian Watchmen bellowed ferocious war cries
and sprang forward. Sprinting down the drawbridge, they
raised their swords over their heads and screamed out their
defiance. Charlie boldly stepped up to meet them. Thrusting
her clenched fists forward in a violent motion, she knocked
all the approaching guards off their feet with a gushing
torrent of liquid light. With her Will rampaging through her
body, she pushed her way forward, slapping, beating and
kicking the guards aside like a gardener brushing past weeds
and nettles. She saved the preening, self-important captain
for last. Knocking him from his feet with a flurry of blows,

she stepped up to him. 'I'm sorry, what was that line about mincemeat?'

'Uh-uh-uh . . .' stuttered the captain.

'I didn't catch that last bit. Could you say it again?'

'Uh-uh-uh . . .' he repeated.

'Aah, I thought that was what you said,' said Charlie with a somewhat naughty and impish smile. 'Well, if you don't object I'd like to go on in. I really do need the chance to have a quiet word with Lady Narcissa. You know, catch up on old news and gossip. I hope you don't mind.'

'Uh-uh-uh . . . p-p-please be my guest,' stammered the captain. His eyes rolled wildly in his head.

'Thank you.'

With a casual flick of her wrist, Charlie sent the captain flying to join the large pile of groaning and unconscious Watchmen stacked high across the drawbridge.

Once inside the tower, she trotted from room to room, calling out as she did so, 'Oh, Narcissa! Lady Narcissa! Where are you? Come out, come out, wherever you are!'

Jogging up and down marble staircases, along deserted corridors and through still and silent rooms, she passed deeper into the tower.

'Aren't you getting bored with hiding, Narcissa?' Charlie sang out as she passed into the Great Dining Hall. 'Don't you want to come out and play?'

'I'm over here, brat!' spat a hissing voice.

Charlie spun around to see Lady Narcissa standing at the far end of the room surrounded by a horde of very angry-looking guardsmen. Charlie throbbed with righteous anger. Her mind simmered and smouldered with the need to see justice done. With the powerful, rolling force of her Will tumbling around inside her soul, she ignored the guards as nothing more than pesky distractions and focused purely on Lady Narcissa.

'I want you to give yourself up and come with me to the Jade Circle,' said Charlie in a voice that rumbled with the promise of lightning and thunder. 'Justice must be done.'

The Great Dining Hall fell silent as Lady Narcissa and her guards considered her words . . . then fell about laughing.

'What!' cried Charlie, stamping her foot to illustrate her determination. 'I mean it! I want you to give yourself up and come with me. You can't get away with all that you've done.'

The guardsmen held on to each other and wiped tears of laughter from their eyes. Narcissa chuckled for a bit longer, then focused her cold eyes on the young Keeper.

'Foolish girl, did you think that I would come with you that easily? And if I was stupid enough to follow your request, do you honestly think that the Jade Circle would be able to hold me? With Azariah Keeper out of the way, I *own* half the Jade Circle. They won't punish me, they will welcome me with open arms! This city is all but mine for the taking. I promise you this, Charlie Keeper, Sylvaris shall fall beneath Bane's fist.'

'Oh yeah? Well, you've got to get past me first!' hollered Charlie, and held up a blazing fist to show just how powerful she had become.

'Oh, has the little brat found her Will?' said Narcissa with a leering grin. 'You impudent, silly little child, how could you be so stupid as to think that I wouldn't have taken your

powers into consideration? I have planned for every even-
tuality! My servants will make short work of you and when
they are done I will send you broken and helpless to Bane,
who will take your pendant and reward me so very, very
well for my labours.'

Charlie crossed her arms and sneered dismissively at the
ring of armoured guardsmen that circled Lady Narcissa.
'What? You think that those weasels dressed in tinfoil can
defeat me? I don't think so.'

'Not enough for you? Well, how about these?' Narcissa
waved lazily at a dark corner of the Great Dining Hall. A
sibilant hissing oozed its way across the room to reach
Charlie's ears. Rustling and mewling, the darkness uncoiled
itself to reveal a living carpet of Shades. 'And, of course, if
those aren't enough to satisfy you, I have the latest addition
to my household guards. I'm sure I don't need to introduce
him to you.'

Crow stepped out from behind a column to stand by
Narcissa's side. He rubbed his quivering nose and grinned
nastily at Charlie. 'Hello, my little filly, my pretty, pretty filly.
Are you ready to play?'

62

Battle Royal

'So where'd she go?' said Jensen.

'Bless me Leaf, I don't know!'

'Well, we've gotta do something! We can't just let her wander off like that. She'll get in trouble, I just know she will,' said Jensen with a look of anguish fluttering across his face. 'Wot are we gonna do?'

'Sic Boy!'

'Wot?'

'Yeah, Sic Boy'll do it for us! Won't ya, lad?' Kelko scratched at Sic Boy's huge head. 'Who's a good boy, then?'

'Wot are ya going on about?'

'Her scent! He can pick up her scent and track her down!'

Jensen nodded, his green skin glowing in the light from the Colosseum's torches. 'Yer right!'

Moving quickly, the two Tremen led Sic Boy down into the arena, where the discarded Zephyr lay abandoned on the ground. Charlie's towel was on a hook at the side of the playing area. 'Sic Boy, now listen ta me,' said Kelko, taking the towel and holding it to the big dog's nose. 'Ya know Charlie, don't ya, boy? Charlie?' The giant dog's ears pricked up at the sound of her name. 'We got ta find her. Find Charlie, boy. C'mon, find Charlie.'

Sic Boy sniffed at the towel, then at the ground where the Silent Duel had taken place. With his nose to the ground, his hulking body took off in the direction of one of the gates. Smiling to each other, Kelko and Jensen raced after him.

Charlie dodged a dagger, evaded a snarling bite from a frenzied Shade and only just managed to duck beneath a large table that Crow had venomously thrown from across the room. Her predicament was getting dangerously out of hand.

Skipping over an upturned chair, Charlie vaulted over the back of a guardsman who had bent to retrieve his sword, leaped on to the mantelpiece and from there somersaulted on to a large dining table.

'Get her, you scabs!' shrieked Lady Narcissa. 'A thousand gold pieces to the man who catches that little minx!'

Mr Crow stood beside her as they both watched on, observing the guards attempt to grab the young Keeper.

Charlie groaned. She couldn't believe what an impossible mess she'd made of things. How could she have been so stupid? She needed to get out of here. She needed to get somewhere where the Shades and guardsmen couldn't overwhelm her with their sheer weight of numbers. Focusing her Will, she bowled over three guardsmen with her gleaming fists, leaped over a spitting and hissing Shade and sprinted for the doorway. Scrambling through the massive double doors, she scuttled around a corner, then dashed up the nearest flight of stairs. The Shades and the guards swiftly gave chase as she raced, helter-skelter, for the rooftop. Reaching the tower's summit, she spun around to face the oncoming tide as her attackers howled up the last flight of stairs.

Charlie grinned and released her Will. A thick wall of golden light blossomed across the stairs. It crackled and hummed, and even though the guards struck at it with their swords and the Shades lashed at it with their shadowy claws, it refused to break. Their way was barred. Charlie smiled in relief. Finally she'd created a moment's respite in which she could plan her next move.

So deeply was she concentrating that she failed to notice the long line of birds appearing over the side of the rooftop in a flutter of black wings. Mr Crow silently tiptoed out of the sudden merging of feathers and sneaked forward.

'Hello, my pretty!' he screamed into her ear.

Lashing out with a hand, he knocked her to the ground. Immediately Charlie's barrier of golden light collapsed into nothing, allowing the Shades and guards to rush, hollering and screaming, on to the roof.

'Well, my filly,' continued Mr Crow as he cruelly stamped on Charlie's fingers. 'I believe that the time has finally come for you to pay the piper.'

Dazed and slightly concussed, Charlie crawled away on shaky hands and knees until she reached the very edge of the roof. Flopping on to her back, exhausted and terrified, she faced her doom.

'Well, I don't know about you,' said a new but familiar voice right by her ear, 'but I'm getting a real sense of déjà vu!'

'Cor!' said Kelko. 'Will ya look at all dis mess. How d'ya think that happened?'

'What d'ya think, ya silly excuse for a Treman,' said Jensen as they slipped past the mountain of groaning Alavisian Watchmen lying upon the drawbridge. 'Charlie must have happened, ya flea-brained numbskull! I'd say she's really come ta grips with her Will.'

'Burn me Sap! Ya think she did all of dis?' muttered Kelko as he tried to wedge his stomach between two piles of unconscious bodies. 'Hhmpf, we might as well turn around and go on home. Someone who can cause dis much damage clearly ain't gonna need any help from us.'

'Wot, are ya mad? That weird Ravenman or wotever ya call him . . . er, Crowman is in there! Not ta mention the fact there's probably a whole legion of Shades and other nasties hidden inside with Lady Narcissa. We've gotta go in and help her. If she ain't managed ta get herself inta trouble by now, I can almost guarantee that she'll be in trouble before the night's end. So suck in that big tummy of yers and let's get going!'

Wheezing and puffing, Kelko squeezed his way forward to follow Sic Boy and Jensen into the Ivory Tower.

'Nibbler!'

'Well, who else did you think it would be?'

'What . . . I didn't think it would . . . oh, never mind!' said Charlie. 'Just keep them off me, OK!'

'No problem,' replied the small dragon. Opening his mouth wide, he released a rippling jet of flame. The Shades and guards jumped for cover. 'Wow, I never thought I'd go through all this again, but y'know what? It's still fun!'

Charlie rolled her eyes. Here she was almost half beaten to death, chased by just about every single bad guy in Sylvaris, and Nibbler thought it was 'fun'? She wanted to scream in frustration.

'So tell me,' continued Nibbler, 'how come you're back up here anyway?'

'They killed Azariah!'

Nibbler's wave of flames disappeared in a puff of black smoke. 'They what?'

'Yes, you heard me. Him,' said Charlie, and pointed at Mr Crow. 'And her.' She pointed at Lady Narcissa, who had just that second appeared on the roof. 'They killed Azariah. They're murderers!'

Nibbler growled deep and low, then, roaring out his defiance, he sent a massive explosion of fiery waves bursting across the rooftop. 'Let's get them.'

'That's what I was trying to do,' explained Charlie. 'But with all of them together, they're too strong.'

'Well, let's even the numbers up a little, shall we?' snarled Nibbler.

Leaping into the air, he flew towards Crow. The lawyer squeaked in surprise. Jumping up to meet the young dragon, he burst apart into a hundred black crows. Nibbler and the birds came together like a clap of thunder. Snarling and hooting, clawing and snapping, the two mighty adversaries tumbled out of sight.

Which left just Charlie with everyone else.

She clambered to her feet and, slipping into a K'Changa stance, danced from foe to foe, kicking and punching, pushing and pulling. Golden flaming hands glowing with power knocked back guard after guard and Shade after Shade. But the odds were still too high: she wasn't going to win this. More and more reinforcements flowed up the stairs to join Narcissa's troops and no matter how many Charlie defeated another two would spring up in their place.

Suddenly the reinforcements stopped coming and seconds later screams and shrieks of surprise began to echo out from the stairwell. It was Kelko and Jensen! They burst on to the rooftop, each brandishing a stolen sword. Rushing forward, they attacked Charlie's assailants. Moments later they were joined by Sic Boy. Howling and barking, the massive dog tore through the ranks of Shades like a hot knife through butter.

Narcissa screamed with pure malice as she saw the balance beginning to turn against her. '*Ten thousand* gold pieces to the first person to catch her! Gut her! Slice her! Slash her! Don't let her get away!'

But it was no use. Narcissa's guards were rapidly losing the battle. Holding their shields over their heads, they turned tail and ran for the exit.

'You whimpering cowards!' shrieked Lady Narcissa. 'Here, I'll show you how a real woman does things!'

Reaching for a dropped sword, she brandished it wildly. Raising the blade above her head, she brought it down with all her might, aiming straight for Jensen's unprotected back.

The birds were too fast, too agile and simply too determined. Fluttering in and out, they cut and tore at Nibbler's scales with their sharp talons and needle-like beaks. Long gashes and bloody tears appeared along his majestic wings and across his broad, muscular chest. Roaring in anger and confused pain, Nibbler lashed out around him. Too close to unleash his fiery breath, he had to do his best to beat back the flock of crows with tooth, claw and whipping tail.

But this was a fight he was going to lose. He couldn't overcome the sheer agility and ferocious close-ranged attack of the numerous birds . . . unless he changed his tactics.

With a titanic effort, Nibbler broke free from the fluttering pack of venomous birds. Stretching his long neck forward, he strained his mighty muscles and put everything he could into creating some space between him and his opponent. Flying low over pathways and ducking beneath bridges, weaving between rapid explosions of fireworks, Nibbler twisted and turned and with each passing second managed to create a tiny bit of distance between himself and the cawing crows.

With a ferocious shout, the young dragon skimmed past the Jade Tower, dived through a narrow gap between two busy boulevards and, looping around the Torn Bridge, suddenly reversed his position so that he was flying directly towards the large pack of birds.

With a big grin spread across his face, Nibbler opened his mouth wide and exhaled a huge, spouting gust of flame.

The birds squeaked in terror. Battling to stop their head-long rush, they attempted to flutter sideways. About half the flock made it to safety, but the other half were engulfed in the roaring, flickering flames. Crispy lumps of feathered carbon dropped from the sky and shattered into piles of ash when they hit the towers and bridges below. The remaining crows fled shrieking into the night.

Nibbler smirked triumphantly. Beating his mighty wings in victory, he made his way back to the Ivory Tower.

63

The Long Scream

'No!' screamed Charlie.

Lunging forward, she sprinted across the rooftop. Leaping with her arms outstretched, she rugby-tackled Lady Narcissa as hard as she could. Narcissa bounced off Charlie, staggered backwards and teetered for a brief second on the edge of the roof before slowly toppling over. Screaming with fear and a terrible determined malice, she reached out, grabbed Jensen by the arm and pulled him down with her.

'No,' whispered Charlie, as she stared in shock at the vacant patch of rooftop. 'No!'

Kelko knocked aside the last of his opponents, then rushed to the edge of the roof to join Charlie. Together they stared in horror as Jensen and Narcissa rapidly fell from sight.

'OK, OK. Gotta save him,' rambled Charlie, a look of dread spread across her face. 'Gotta concentrate . . . I've got to concentrate.'

Raising her glowing hands, she focused at a spot a couple of metres in front of her. Frowning with an intense, driven look, she made a slight opening gesture with her hands. Warm light rippled outward, the air quivered and then pulled back to form a circular Portal, from within which a wild, high-pitched, almost girl-like screaming echoed out. It rapidly grew in volume until the scream sounded like it was being made by a distressed elephant. Whooshing into view, a very white-faced Jensen zoomed through the Portal . . . only to continue falling back down the side of the Ivory Tower with a horrible cry.

'Heeeeeeeeeeeeeeeelp meeeeeeeeeeeeeeeeeeee!' he screamed.

Several seconds later he reappeared back through the Portal and once again continued to fall. Of Lady Narcissa there was no sign.

'Er,' said Kelko with an astonished look, as he stared at his friend, who rushed by screaming and falling for the third time. 'Well, that's, er . . . very good. I'm glad ya've saved him, blossom. But if ya don't mind me asking, why haven't you opened the Portal on to the roof? I mean, does he really have to continue falling like that?'

'I didn't know what else to do. He was falling too fast by the time I opened the Portal.'

'So?'

'Well, if I opened the Portal on the roof he . . . Well, let's just say that he probably would have splattered.'

'Huh?'

'Well, it's physics, isn't it? I mean, he's dropping really, really fast, right?'

'Well, by that expression of fear on his face, I'd have said so.'

'Well, if he's travelling that fast when I open the Portal and he hits the roof . . .'

'Aah!' said Kelko, and made an 'O' with his lips as he worked out the logic. 'I sees wot ya mean.'

Together the two of them watched Jensen continue his headlong flight, to repeat it over and over every four seconds. Sic Boy, fed up with growling at the unconscious guardsmen lying haphazardly across the rooftop, padded over to join Kelko and Charlie. He watched the hollering and yelping Treman with some interest. Surprisingly enough, Jensen hadn't grown bored with screaming.

'So, uh, wot are we going ta do?' asked Kelko.

Charlie shrugged. 'I think we're just going to have to wait for Nibbler to get back. He's the only one that can snatch him from the skies and bring him back safely.'

'And wot are we going ta do until then?'

'Erm, I'm not too sure. I guess we could just sit back for the time being and enjoy the view.'

All five of them walked wearily down the staircase in the Ivory Tower. Jensen still had a wild look in his eyes and was having more than a little trouble combing his dishevelled windswept hair back into a neat topknot. Every once in a while he would stop to pat the ground reassuringly, just to make sure it was really there. Kelko was hobbling a little due to a slight gash on his leg but was otherwise getting along fine by using Sic Boy for support. Nibbler, with his big, brash grin, wouldn't shut up about his wild airborne struggle with Mr Crow and his amazing rescue flight to save Jensen.

Charlie, however, remained unusually quiet. She had a lot on her mind. Lady Narcissa, one of her greatest foes, was dead and Charlie wasn't sure how she felt about it. She had no doubt that Narcissa was an evil woman with a terrible, greedy hunger for power, but did she deserve to die? And the fact that she had died at Charlie's hands raised some sticky questions. Questions that she wasn't sure her conscience could handle. Did Narcissa's death – even though it was accidental and done in the heat of the moment to save her friend – make her a killer? Could a thirteen-year-old girl, she wondered, really be a murderer? Charlie sighed and thrust the questions to the back of her mind. She realized sadly that if the situation ever arose again she would repeat her actions in exactly the same way. Loyalty to her friend had taken over and, for Charlie, that always came first. She'd had to save him . . . no matter what.

'So you got rid of him, then?' Kelko asked the young dragon swaggering along by his side.

'Mr Crow?' said Nibbler. 'Well, I'm not too sure, you know. I mean, I got about half of the birds, but the others flew away when I started breathing fire. So . . . er, you know what? I have absolutely no idea what that will do to him! I mean, what happens to a man made from birds when half of them are killed?'

'Now that's interesting,' mused Kelko, stroking at his chin thoughtfully. 'Do ya think that he'll be able ta change back inta a Human? And if he can, then would there only be half of him? Like, er . . . would, say, his legs be missing from the waist down, or . . . wow. That's really too weird ta think about.'

'Yeah, well half man or half crow, you should have seen our fight! It was amazing! Stupendous! We had to weave in and out of all the firework displays. Why, I bet that half of Sylvaris must have seen it all –'

'Nibbler,' said Charlie, interrupting the young dragon's wild boasts. 'Please tell me you got a message back from that Stoman bishop.'

'Oh, sure, Charlie. It's right here,' said Nibbler.

Reaching up with his forepaws, he pulled loose a cylindrical container that had been tied to his back. (It was a bit battered, dented and scratched from his adventures.) Unscrewing the top, he shook loose two pieces of parchment and passed them to Charlie.

'"Yes"? That's all he said on the first letter, "yes"!' exclaimed Charlie in disbelief. 'What on earth is "yes" supposed to mean?'

'It means that he agrees to see you and that he will examine your pendant,' Nibbler explained patiently. How was it that Charlie always failed to grasp the obvious?

'Oh,' said Charlie, who thought it was a little odd to waste a whole piece of parchment for just one word. Maybe this Edge Darkmount character was slightly eccentric. Frowning, she unrolled the second letter. 'It's a map! It . . . er, let's see now. It shows the University of Dust and there's a big red cross right in the middle of one of the courtyards. Now, what's all that about? There's no other writing or instructions.'

'It's where you're supposed to open the Portal,' muttered Nibbler. 'The bishop said it was the only place left in Alavis that was safe and private enough to use.'

'OK. Well, I guess that makes sense. You're sure he guarantees that it's safe?'

'Sure. He said that it would be perfectly safe for at least another four days.'

'Four days?' asked Charlie with a disbelieving look.

'That's what he said.'

'But Lady Dridif thought that Alavis and Alacorn were due to fall to the Stoman armies tomorrow!' insisted Charlie. 'Are you absolutely sure that's what he said?'

'Yes, I'm absolutely, positively sure I'm sure!' huffed Nibbler, and gave Charlie a quick glower for not taking his word at face value. 'And he said the only reason we've got four days' grace was because the Stoman army was having a whole world of trouble getting their heavy siege engines and battering rams across the river.'

'Wot's he like?' asked Kelko, overcome with curiosity.

'Edge Darkmount?'

'Nah, the little drunk lady that lives down Brewers Lane.'

'Who's she?'

'Gah! I was being sarcastic. Of course I meant Edge Darkmount! Are ya sure ya didn't get hit on the noggin during that fight of yers?'

'Do you want to hear about the Stoman bishop or do you want to trade insults?' asked Nibbler.

'I want ta hear about the Stoman bishop.'

'So are you going to let me talk or are you going to carry on pushing your luck?'

'I'm sorry. Please tell me about Edge Darkmount.'

'OK. Well, he's big, really big, even by Stoman standards, and he likes to wear black, lots of it. His boots are big and black, his trousers are really black and his robe is really, really big and –'

'And let me guess . . . black, right?' sniggered Kelko.

'Are you going to let me finish?'

'Sorry.' Kelko shrugged, hiding his cheeky grin behind a hand.

'Well, he likes black and when he talks he booms.'

'Booms?'

'Yeah, he sounds like rumbling thunder. Y'know, really big and loud?'

'Uh-huh.'

'And he glowers a lot even when he's not talking, and when he's not glowering he's frowning all the time. And he only ever, ever seems to be in two sorts of temper.'

'Wot sorts of tempers are those?'

'Grumpy and moody.'

'That's it?' asked Kelko in disbelief. 'Surely no one can be like that all the time?'

'Well, he does do grumpier and then, of course, there's always bad-tempered,' chuckled the young dragon. 'But don't forget I was only there for a couple of hours, so I couldn't tell you if he's like that all the time.'

'Hhmpf,' harrumphed Kelko, obviously not impressed by anyone who could be grumpy all of the time.

They carried on downward in companionable silence, a silence that was broken as Charlie realized she owed some-one a big debt of gratitude.

'Nibbler?'

'Yes, Charlie?'

'Thank you.'

'Uh, what for?'

'For flying there and back, for getting the message to Edge

Darkmount and, well . . . thanks for everything. You're amazing.' She reached over, wrapped her hands around his long neck and gave him a big hug.

Nibbler grinned, his blue eyes blazing. 'You're my girl, Charlie. I'll always be there for you.'

'Family,' said Charlie.

'Family,' echoed Nibbler with another grin.

The two shared another hug then hastened after Kelko and Jensen.

64

A Break Well Earned

Reaching the bottom of the staircase, they walked along the hallway, beneath the fearsome portcullis and out on to the drawbridge. Fireworks still whizzed and boomed overhead and in the distance Charlie could make out Sylvarisians partying wildly across the bridges and boulevards. She could hear joyful laughter and drunken, good-natured shouts. Obviously the Three Winds Festival was still in full swing.

'Wot time is it?' asked Jensen as he finally broke free from his terror-induced trance. Extended free-fall and repetitive screaming due to vertigo hadn't agreed with him, but now that his feet were firmly back on familiar territory the jaunty, wise-cracking Treman was beginning to revert to his old self.

'It must be about, wot, eleven? Say half past eleven,' said Kelko as he stared thoughtfully at the angle of the moon and the stars.

'Really?' said Jensen. Perking up, he looked around with renewed interest. 'That means there must be hours and hours left of the festival.'

'I like the way ya think, me good friend!' chuckled Kelko, giving Jensen a knowing look.

'What?' asked Nibbler. 'What's he thinking?'

'Well, me fine young Winged One,' said Kelko with a cheerful smile. 'Wot Jensen is suggesting in his round-about way is that we go and have us a party! Paaaaaaarty!'

Kelko startled Charlie and Nibbler by breaking into an outrageous dance. Waving his hands in the air, he pulled the silliest of smiles and let his fat stomach jiggle from side to side to help keep the beat of his bouncing, rhythmic feet. Sic Boy ignored all the tomfoolery and turned his attention to scratching the sweet spot just behind his big ears.

'Paaarrty!' shouted Kelko, and waved to an enthusiastic group of Sylvarisians frolicking on a nearby bridge. With a good-natured roaring laugh, they all waved back. Kelko grinned and turned to the Hatchling.

'So, wotcha say, me flying mischief-maker, wanna go party?'

'Yeah! That's a wild idea! Paaaaaaarty!' hollered Nibbler, copying Kelko's shout. 'What do you say, Charlie? Oh, come on, let's go out and party for a bit!'

Charlie thought about all that had befallen her since she had arrived in Bellania. All the hardship, the sorrow, the pain, the humiliation and not forgetting the tragic loss of her good friends Stotch and Azariah. It had been a long, painful and sometimes bloody uphill trek to get to where she now stood. But she had the bishop's message, did she not? She could take the next step towards defeating Bane and any move in that direction would bring her that much closer to freeing her parents. Things were on the up and up, so surely she could afford to relax for a little bit? A small smile tugged at the corners of her mouth, the twinkle in her eyes began to glitter and then, before she could help it, her face creased into a cheeky, impish grin.

'Yeah, why not? What was that saying, Kelko? How did it go again?'

'Er, let's see now . . . methinks it went something like dis: "Paaaaaaarty!"'

'Whoop-whoop!' shouted Charlie, and waved her hands in the air. 'Paaaaaaarty!'

'Paaaaaaarty!' shouted Nibbler. Standing on his back two paws, he blew massive jets of flame into the night sky.

'Paaaaaaarty!' hollered Jensen, finally letting Kelko's party spirit get the better of him.

With big grins on their faces, they all turned to see what Sic Boy would do.

The large, brutal-looking dog stared back at them as though they were all a bunch of fools. He firmly turned his back on the lot of them.

'Spoilsport,' snorted Kelko.

'So where do we start?' asked Charlie, a look of wonder in her eyes. 'Where's the best place to go to enjoy the Three Winds Festival?'

'I know just the street ta start on!' Kelko laughed with childish delight. Reaching down, he slapped his stomach with wild enthusiasm. 'It has the best Calice-Goldenberry Cakes and they give a discount on Threebird and Lazzery Pies if ya buy five of 'em at once!'

'Bless me Leaf, Kelko! I've known ya since we were both little boys. Do ya think ya could maybe make it through one day without thinking about yer stomach?'

'Hey, when ya've got something dis big walking around

with ya all day ya've got no choice but ta give it a lotta thought.' Kelko grinned, grabbing great handfuls of his stomach.

Charlie smiled as her friends carried on with their good-natured joking. Shielding her eyes from a particularly bright display of fireworks, she gazed across to one of the nearby bridges. She could see jugglers walking on stilts, acrobats somersaulting through rings, fire-eaters spitting out great gusts of coloured flames, contortionists doing eye-watering tricks and strongmen bending lengths of steel into rude shapes. She could smell the delicious scents of lemon-roasted meat, vanilla, wild cherry, candyfloss and the strange aroma of aniseed intertwined with the bright smell of freshly cut grass. And rising above all the haphazard whoops, bangs and crackles of fireworks, she could hear the unusual dolphin-like whistle and hoot of the western winds joyfully rushing through the Whispering Heights. Summer had finally come and Charlie couldn't wait to join all the partygoers and take part in the wild celebrations.

In the morning Charlie would have to resume the burdens of being a Keeper but for now . . . it was time to party.

65

The Next Step

The silence of the stony plain was broken by the harsh sound of broken glass. Cursing and whimpering in pain, Mr Crow stepped down on to the rocky floor. Holding his hand up to the light, he was shocked to discover that he could see through his flesh. He could see the horizon through the palm of his hand and, looking down, he could see the craggy and dust-strewn ground through his feet. He had become shadowy, almost transparent, like a ghost. Mr Crow held back a sob of fear as he realized that he was no longer complete, no longer 'real'.

Whimpering with terror, he bent down to grasp a rock. He half expected his hand to pass through the stone, but to his surprise he managed to pick it up. A puzzled look flashed across his face: what did this mean? Was he still alive? Did he still possess his amazing strength? There was only one way to find out. Clenching his hand into a fist, he attempted to crush the rock. He tensed his muscles and focused everything he had on the stone.

CRACK!

With a tooth-rattling crunch, the rock burst apart in a cloud of dust. Shards of stone stuck to his clothes and the rest fell with a tinkle around his feet. Mr Crow let loose a long, juddering sigh of relief. Shadowy and indistinct he might be, but he was still alive, still strong and powerful, and not the ghost that he'd feared he had become. He grinned and with a slight twitter and shake of his head he stared up into the sky.

He still had purpose.

Charlie Keeper hadn't heard the last of him, not by a long shot.

'Oh no, my filly,' he whispered, 'you don't get off the hook that easily! I shall punish you for all the wrong that you have done. You and yours shall pay, my filly. You and your friends shall pay with blood and life and pain.'

Crouching down, he tensed his skinny thighs and sprang, leaping up into the air. With a wild caw, he burst apart into a shrieking pack of crows. Smaller than before, it was still a terrifying sight to behold. Fluttering their wings, the birds flew westward.

'Are ya quite sure yer up ta dis?' asked Lady Dridif.

Charlie resisted the temptation to roll her eyes. She'd already said yes a hundred times, but the old Treman lady seemed determined to mother her.

'Yes, Lady Dridif, I'm sure. Don't worry. I won't be gone for long. Like you said, all I have to do is open the Portal, show Mr Darkmount the pendant, listen to his advice and then come back. Simple.'

The First Speaker looked pensive. 'Young Keeper, surely

ya should know after all yer experience that nothing is ever simple, especially in Bellania.'

'I know that, but what can really go wrong? Nibbler will be with me, as will Jensen and Kelko, and I'll have all those guards that you promised to send with me. So even if there is trouble, we'll be ready for it.'

Dridif sighed. 'Charlie, yer confidence is a great thing ta see, but nevertheless I wish that ya would display a little more caution.'

'I promise to be careful.'

'I know, Charlie, I know,' said Dridif, rubbing wearily at her forehead. 'Are ya sure that ya don't want me ta go over dis one more time? Ya feel confident about opening a Portal all the way ta Alavis?'

'Yes.'

'And I must warn ya that opening a Portal over such a long distance will be a great strain. It will greatly wear ya out.'

'I know, Dridif, you've already told me about twenty times!'

'I'm sorry. I do not mean ta nag, but I feel terrible sending ya all the way out there on yer own.'

'I'm not on my own! Look at everyone else that's coming. Besides, I'm the only one in Sylvaris at the moment that can open a Portal and we both know it needs to be done if we are going to defeat Bane, right?'

Dridif's large, wise brown eyes stared into Charlie's. 'Just be careful.'

'I will.'

Dridif nodded. 'OK, then.' Standing up, she led Charlie from her study and together the two of them went to meet the others.

'Are you sure that this is such a good idea?' rumbled Stones.

'What other choice do we have?' rasped Stix. 'This is the only way we can be sure of claiming our revenge.'

Stones was silent for a while. He stared moodily off into the distance while his fingers absently stroked at the tattered remains of his mother's dress. Finally he laid the shred of cloth on the ground before standing up. 'Very well, then, let's do this.'

Stix's yellow eyes blazed with a terrible anger. 'Yes, let us do this. For Mother.'

'For Mother,' repeated Stones as the light in his eyes blossomed just like his brother's.

The two of them turned their backs on Deepforest. With a fearsome rage flickering between them like a small thundercloud, they began to march towards the Western Mountains to offer their services to Bane, the Stoman Lord.

66

The Portal

The room that Dridif led them to was near the very top of the Jade Tower. Although the wide, circular space was magnificent, with hundreds of roaring dragons carved across every available surface, it was also very dusty and clearly hadn't been used in some time. The Treman guards who were to accompany Charlie to Alavis illuminated the windowless room with flaming torches that they then slotted into holders around the walls.

'Dis is the Keepers' Room of Travel,' explained Lady Dridif. 'It is the place traditionally reserved for Keepers ta use for the safe opening of Portals on behalf of the Jade Circle. Unfortunately, in these times of unrest, Keepers in Sylvaris have become something of a rarity. Still, that is no excuse for the apparent lack of cleaning. I shall be having a very firm word with the First Maid dis afternoon.'

'You clearly haven't seen my bedroom!' joked Charlie before Lady Dridif could work herself into a temper over the chamber's untidy state. She heard Kelko and Nibbler snort with amusement behind her.

'Hhmm?' said Dridif, and then realized that Charlie was trying to lighten the mood. 'Ha, well, yes. There are more important matters to worry about.' She led Charlie into the centre of the room. 'So, let us recap. The twin Human cities, Alavis and Alacorn, are in the west, halfway between here and the Western Mountains. West is that direction,' said Dridif, pointing with her outstretched arm. 'The University of Dust is in Alavis and the courtyard is in the university. Can ya picture it based on what Nibbler described ta ya? Can ya see the Chancellor's Courtyard in yer mind?'

'Yes,' said Charlie, who was startled to realize that she could indeed picture it and picture it very well.

'Good. Now focus on it. Breathe it in. Imagine the smell of the courtyard, the feel of the flagstones beneath yer feet. Feel the weight of the university around ya. Have ya got it? Can ya see it?'

'Yes.' Charlie grinned with sudden enthusiasm. 'Yes, I can!'

'Now open yer Will. Use it, focus it and –'

Dridif's words stuck in her throat as Charlie's hands exploded into flares. Warm golden light illuminated the chamber, much brighter than daylight, and with a shimmering, rippling motion the Portal opened.

'Er, yes, well done, Charlie,' murmured Lady Dridif, surprised by just how easily Charlie had managed her Will.

'That's it, then?' asked Kelko, as he looked through the Portal to the rain-spattered courtyard beyond.

The square was of a very different design from Treman architecture. It appeared almost Roman in style. Tall, graceful columns soared upward to meet the sloping rooftop of the university building. Mighty statues of scholars and warriors stood at intervals throughout the main square.

Charlie peered through. It was just how she'd pictured it. She could imagine students and teachers wandering across its flagstones in quiet contemplation. Now, however, the square was silent and empty.

'Er, why is it so quiet?' asked Jensen. 'Shouldn't there be more people there?'

'Seems perfectly reasonable ta me,' said Kelko. 'It's raining and there's a siege going on. If I was an intelligent student ya wouldn't catch me outside on a day like that!'

'Captain!' snapped Dridif, and beckoned over the fully armoured Treman guard.

'Yes, ma'am?'

'Take yer men through the Portal and secure the square. Make sure there's nothing sneaky lying in wait.'

'Ma'am,' saluted the captain.

Motioning his squad forward, they stepped into the shimmering space. Once through, the men spread rapidly across the courtyard, bows drawn and swords at the ready. After a minute the captain stepped back into the Keepers' Room of Travel.

'All clear, ma'am. Not a soul in sight.'

Dridif nodded. 'Very well, then. I'd just like ta say –'

'Urgh,' groaned Charlie through clenched teeth. 'If we can maybe speed things up? I can't keep this open all day. It, uh, it feels really heavy.'

Dridif flashed an apologetic smile. 'I'm sorry. I just wanted ta ensure yer safety first,' she said. She gave Jensen and the captain a go-ahead gesture. 'Charlie Keeper?'

'Yes?' grunted Charlie, sweat beginning to break out across her brow.

'Good luck.'

'Thanks,' said Charlie.

Then, motioning Jensen, Kelko and Nibbler forward, Charlie threw Lady Dridif a hasty wave and jumped towards the courtyard's flagstones. The Portal shivered shut behind her.

For a long minute Dridif stared silently into the space where the Portal had been, thoughts tumbling through her head. Then with a grunt she turned and walked from the round chamber. She had matters to attend to, a city to run and a council to uphold.

As she strode down the spiralling flight of stairs a footman rushed to her side.

'Lady Dridif?'

'Yes, wot is it?'

'The guards, as instructed, have arrested Councillor Flint. Would ya like ta speak ta him now or later?'

'Later. He has caused more than enough trouble and his treachery needs ta be punished. Throw him inta gaol. Let's give him time ta think about all the wrong that he has done. Tell him that if he behaves we'll see about giving him a trial by the end of the month.'

'Very good, ma'am. And wot should we feed him?'

Dridif thought for a moment, a smile creeping across her face. A touch of Charlie's cheekiness came to mind. 'Oh, methinks a good helping of stale, mouldy bread and pond water should do him fine.'

'Excellent,' said the footman. He hesitated before going on his way.

'Yes?' asked Lady Dridif.

'Well, ma'am, I'm not too sure wot ta do about another matter . . .'

'Spit it out, man.'

'Well, it's Constantina of the Narcissa family. She's been screaming and shouting outside the Council Chamber for hours and hours. Reckons she's innocent. She's been begging for an audience with yer ladyship but the clerks refuse to announce her until she goes through the proper channels. But . . .'

Lady Dridif sighed. She could see where this was going. 'There are always loose ends ta tidy up, aren't there?'

'Er, yes, ma'am.' The footman coughed and gave her a rueful look.

'Very well, then. I will see her, but not today, nor do methinks dis week. She can learn the meaning of patience. However, I do not think the child is really guilty of treason or of evil intent –'

The footman threw her a startled glance.

'I sees that me opinion surprises ya. Why, may I ask, is that?'

'Er, well, ma'am, surely if she's Lady Narcissa's daughter she must have been somewot involved with all the treasonous plots ta sell our city ta the Western Menace? Surely ya can't believe that such a spoilt, malicious brat could be innocent of such crimes?'

'Being malicious or being the daughter of an evil woman does not necessarily mean that she is evil herself,' said Lady Dridif with a frown. 'I believe that she has simply been misled by her mother and therefore I am prepared ta give her another chance ta redeem herself. Ensure that she is returned ta school and that she has a suitable guardian in the Jade Tower. Tell her she may expect a meeting with me some time soon. However, I'd like ya ta warn her that I expect her ta earn her keep from now on and that the Jade Council has frozen her mother's assets. No longer will she have such a lavish and opulent upbringing, so please instruct the First Maid that she has a new chambermaid.'

'Very good, ma'am.' Bowing to Lady Dridif, the footman made to depart.

'Wait.'

'Yes, ma'am?'

'Today is not a schoolday, is it?'

'No, ma'am.'

'Excellent, in that case ya can show Constantina ta the Keepers' Room of Travel. Ask the First Maid ta meet her there with a bucket and mop. Our new chambermaid can start earning her keep. Immediately.'

The footman grinned. 'Very good, ma'am!'

Turning, he scampered down the stairs.

'Oh, and if she gives ya any trouble,' Dridif called after the footman, 'please remind Constantina that I have only suspended the traditional penalty for losing the Silent Duel due ta the turbulent events clouding the games. But if she causes grief I can still see ta it that she spends the full year repeating her sins in the Halls of Echoes. I'm sure the threat of a year in a cold cave should curb her tongue.'

The footman's laugh of delight echoed back up the staircase and resounded pleasingly in Dridif's ears.

It was an end, no doubt, to Constantina's spoilt and petulant upbringing.

The Chancellor's Courtyard was devastatingly quiet.

'Bah!' snorted Kelko as he sheltered from the rain beneath the outspread arms of a large statue. 'Ya would have thought that dis moody old Bishop Darkmount could have kept an eye out for us. I mean, where exactly are we supposed ta go from here?'

Charlie stared at the Treman soldiers taking up positions around the edge of the square. Something just didn't feel right to her.

'Hey, Nibbler, what did Edge Darkmount say exactly? That we should open a Portal here and then what?'

Nibbler shuffled over to where Charlie was huddled with Jensen and Kelko, his waterproof scales protecting him from the drizzle.

'He didn't say anything else. All he said was that we should come here, he'd meet us and then examine the pendant.'

'So why isn't he here?' asked Charlie. 'We've been here for a while now. Surely someone must have noticed we've arrived?' A sense of alarm was beginning to tug at the back of her brain, demanding attention. 'There's something a little too odd about –'

Charlie's words were cut short by the sudden clatter of feet as hundreds of Stoman warriors burst into the court-yard. The horrid sound of twanging bowstrings cut across the flagstones, shortly accompanied by soft groans as the Treman guards fell to the floor with dozens of arrows sprouting from their sides. Fierce-looking Stoman soldiers with gruesome axes swiftly circled Charlie, Kelko, Jensen and Nibbler, fencing them in with a ring of steel. The soldiers chuckled nastily as they eyed their catch.

A Stoman colonel, looking proud and fierce in polished, blood-red armour and bearing a baton of command under his arm, strolled into the rain-splattered square. Grinning with silent mirth, he stared at the companions.

'Charlie Keeper, I arrest you in the name of our Great Lord, may history carry his name on winds of thunder from now until eternity!'

Smiling cruelly, the soldiers began to beat their swords and axes against their armour, chanting a single word over and over until the sound became deafening.

'BANE!'

'BANE!'

'BANE!'

'BANE!'

'Blight me Leaf! He's gone and betrayed us!' cursed Jensen, his green face turning pale with shock. 'Edge Darkmount has sold us out!'

NOW ENTER

THE REALM OF BELLANIA,

A PLACE OF MYTH,

MAGIC

AND EVIL LORDS WITH VERY BAD ATTITUDES ...

www.keeperoftherealms.com

- Follow K'Changa tutorials
- Watch action-packed trailers
  - Download awesome character artwork
- Find fan reviews, photos and more!

The future of Bellania relies on
Charlie's special powers. Even if she
escapes it may take more than she can
summon to overthrow the evil lord –
it may take an entire army . . .

www.keeperoftherealms.com

 # Listen

Do you love listening to stories?

Want to know what happens behind the scenes in a recording studio?

Hear funny sound effects, exclusive author interviews and the best books read by famous authors and actors on the **Puffin Podcast** at www.puffinbooks.com

#ListenWithPuffin

Your story starts here . . .

Do you **love books** and
discovering new stories?
Then **www.puffinbooks.com**
is the place for you . . .

- Thrilling adventures, fantastic fiction
  and laugh-out-loud fun

- Brilliant videos featuring your favourite authors
  and characters

- Exciting competitions, news, activities,
  the Puffin blog and SO MUCH more . . .

www.puffinbooks.com

It all started with a Scarecrow.

Puffin is seventy years old.
Sounds ancient, doesn't it? But Puffin has never been
so lively. We're always on the lookout for the next big
idea, which is how it began all those years ago.

Penguin Books was a big idea from the mind of
a man called Allen Lane, who in 1935 invented
the quality paperback and changed the world.
**And from great Penguins, great Puffins grew,
changing the face of children's books forever.**

The first four Puffin Picture Books were hatched in 1940 and the
first Puffin story book featured a man with broomstick arms called
Worzel Gummidge. In 1967 Kaye Webb, Puffin Editor, started the
Puffin Club, promising to **'make children into readers'**.
She kept that promise and over 200,000 children became
devoted Puffineers through their quarterly instalments of
Puffin Post, which is now back for a new generation.

Many years from now, we hope you'll look back and
remember Puffin with a smile. **No matter what your age
or what you're into, there's a Puffin for everyone.**
The possibilities are endless, but one thing is for sure:
whether it's a picture book or a paperback, a sticker book
or a hardback, **if it's got that little Puffin
on it – it's bound to be good.**